ANTIQUITY'S GATE

BOOK FIVE

WHISPER OF ECHOES

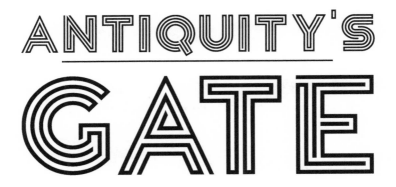

ANTIQUITY'S GATE

BOOK FIVE
WHISPER OF ECHOES

A NOVEL BY
R.F. HURTEAU

ISBN
978-1-951027-14-8 (paperback)
978-1-951027-15-5 (ebook)
978-1-951027-12-4 (hardcover)

Get In Touch
Twitter: @rfhurteau
Email: r.hurteau@outlook.com
Website: www.rfhurteau.com

Cover Illustration by Nushie
Twitter: @nushdraws
Website: www.nushie.com

For Asher.

Every word you speak is declared loudly and enthusiastically. You have a lot to say. I hope you never change.

The past will not stay buried
  though so many, they have tried.
It seeps through as a whisper and
  it cannot be denied.

It echoes through the corridors
  through time and space and then
It manifests itself so that
  the past comes back again.

Learn quickly, child, do not ignore
  the fates of those long gone.
And when the past comes calling, please,
  don't let it linger long.

For we cannot escape it, though
  in deepest dark we hide.
The light is just a ploy, my child…
  Don't let it seep inside.

A Pravacordian Nursery Rhyme

Contents

PROLOGUE

"I'VE LOST THE starboard engine. Attempting to re-route auxiliary power."

"We've got incoming! Two more, from the west."

"I see 'em." Penelope went into a roll that made Felix glad of his seat restraint as one of the Theran ships zipped past their nose, white hull glinting in the sun. "Tobias, take the controls."

"But—"

Penelope was already unsnapping her restraints. "Just do it!"

The *Wilks* broke through the clouds, stray wisps clinging to the windshield as the ground appeared beneath them.

Even now, with weeks of recon and evac missions under his belt, Felix's heart thundered in his chest, palms slick with sweat as he scanned the sky over Toby's shoulder.

"This is not a good idea," Toby muttered into his headset, eyes locked straight ahead. "This is the farthest possible thing from a good idea. We're not going to help anyone if we're dead."

Penelope ignored him, slamming something closed beneath her steering column and pulling herself back up into her seat. "That should do it. Bring us about, I'll put her down in that alley."

Felix was moving before the landing gear hit the ground. Popping the hatch, he skipped the steps, leaping down and looking around for signs of movement. He pointed. "Over there!"

Huddled under a ratty awning a small figure trembled, wide eyes peering toward Felix from beneath soot-covered brows.

"It's okay," he called. "We're here to help."

The little girl shrunk back, eyes darting around for an escape. He knelt before her and reached out an open hand. "Come on, we'll take you somewhere safe."

"I can't find my mommy." Tears whispered over smudged cheeks, leaving trails in their wake.

"She can't be far," said Penelope, already moving away.

Felix scooped the little girl up and she wrapped her arms around his neck. "No, Penny. We need to get out of here."

"If her family is nearby—"

A deafening boom rocked the alley, chunks of brick

and mortar raining down on him from the buildings to either side. He hunched over the girl, shielding her face from the onslaught. Struggling to find his balance as the street beneath him seemed to rock unsteadily, Felix cringed against the high-pitched ringing that muffled Tobias' next words.

"We've lost the tower! They're calling for a full retreat."

"Take the girl." Penelope shoved him toward the *Wilks*. "I'm right behind you."

He didn't argue, closing the distance between them and the ship at a jog. He handed the child up to Tobias, who was staring past him.

"She isn't listening, Felix! She's—"

Felix turned just in time to see the tail of Penelope's long red braid disappearing around the corner. He cursed. "Toby, be ready to high-tail it out of here!"

A flash of white overhead. Bullets sprayed the narrow street, hitting the walls and shattering windows as Nero's ships razed a path across the city.

Then a cry, cut short, somewhere just out of sight.

"Penelope!"

Bits of glass crunched beneath his boots, embedding themselves in his soles. He ignored the cloud of dust that had risen up, clogging the alleyway, choking him. Bolting toward the place where she'd disappeared, Felix skidded around the corner to find Penny's prone figure splayed on the ground.

She groaned as he dropped to his knees beside her. The

heavy shroud of terror cloaking the city weighed down on him as his fingernails raked across the cold gravel beneath Penelope, drawing her up as easily as he had the little girl. "You're going to be okay," he assured her. Her left side was a mess, fiery hair matted to her cheek by a mixture of blood and sand.

"But the others, her family—"

More ships screamed overhead. No more time. He wouldn't lose another friend—not here, not like this.

"I'm sorry." She didn't fight him as he carried her, retreating to the ship. "Get us in the air, Toby!"

Tobias was already on it, pulling up on the throttle as soon as the hatch closed. The acceleration tugged at Felix, stray bullets pinging against the hull as the propeller bit into the cloud cover.

Nobody spoke as Toby pointed their nose to the sea, the sounds of combat fading away as they made for the coast, leaving the city of Ithaca burning in their wake. Once again, Nero had won the battle.

They could not let him win the war.

CHAPTER ONE

"WHERE'S LAEVUS?"

LAEVUS prodded his brother's body with a toe, gazing at Felix with pity. The fortuitous explosions that forced them aground had also rendered his captors unconscious. He neither knew nor cared who it was that nearly killed them; he focused only on the opportunity this turn of events represented.

He alone had had the good sense not to get himself knocked out. Though his wrists ached and bled from the effort of escaping his restraints, they'd saved him from suffering the same fate as the others.

Sprawled around the interior of the amphibious craft, Felix's comrades were still breathing. He *could* ensure none of them ever woke up. He certainly wouldn't lose sleep over it. But his main concern was getting back to the Gate, and these fools posed no threat in that regard. He'd been looking for an excuse to take his leave—now he had one. That was the important thing.

He shoved the tubby one unceremoniously from the pilot's chair, the body making a dull thud as it hit the deck, and gave the control panel a critical once-over. It sparked in places, lights flashing in others. Given time, he could repair the damage. But was it worth it?

Unlikely. He'd find a more creative way to get home.

He glanced around for anything that might be useful. Perhaps the map? No. Laevus didn't know where they were, let alone where he was going.

Cracking the hatch revealed a dreary scene. The air was thick with smoke and angry storm clouds hovered in the distance.

Leaping nimbly from the top of the drill, Laevus sank knee deep in the frigid water, wet sand sucking at his boots.

He set off along the beach at a jog. Laevus did not wish to be anywhere near this place when his brother's ragtag team of would-be adventurers awoke. Though the shelter of the nearby trees made a tempting hiding place, it was also an obvious one. The waves lapped at his heels, swallowing up his footprints as he widened the distance between himself and his captors.

The stiffness of his muscles began to melt away. Laevus revelled in the freedom of his movement, breaking into a sprint. Adrenaline coursed through his veins; not born of fear, but rather the byproduct of elation.

It had been a long time since he had felt so free.

Salty air, heavy with the smells of the sea, formed a thin residue in his hair. Bits of seashells glinted under the faint light of an overcast sun, shimmering in his path as they disappeared and reappeared beneath the ebb and flow of seafoam caught in the receding tide.

The smoldering husk of the village was far behind him before he sensed the presence of humans.

Laevus slowed, exhilaration waning. He scanned the horizon. Curving off toward the east, the coast disappeared behind a rocky outcropping that jutted out into the sea; a pathetic peninsula for a pathetic beach. What foul miscreants lurked beyond?

Drawing closer, he could make out faint voices. He slowed, approaching the rocks with casual strides. He might not be a full blooded Theran, but he could easily outmatch whoever awaited him on the other side. Scaling the ten-foot, boulder-strewn barrier was almost effortless. He felt invigorated, ready for anything.

From atop his perch he gazed down, reveling in the awestruck faces of the men below. Uniforms like the one that idiotic ambassador wore suggested that these were Culeian military men.

That suited Laevus just fine.

"Hello." He spoke in a calm, even tone, descending from the rocks in a series of short, non-threatening hops, hands raised in submission. Humans were nothing if not skittish. He could not afford to have his best chance at escape scatter like roaches caught in a sudden burst of light. The lies came easily, gliding off his tongue as quickly as they formed, a skill honed over long years under Pike's tutelage. "I am Lord Laevus, emissary of the Theran Elder Council, sent to represent my people in the Theran-Culeian alliance."

One of the humans eyed him skeptically, approaching with cautious steps. "We have not received any communications from Ambassador Takahashi."

Laevus felt his face melt into a convincing expression of despair. "I bear sad tidings from our journey. The Ambassador has been lost."

This garnered an immediate reaction among the Culeians. They exchanged glances of shock and confusion. The one that Laevus took for their leader, judging by the number of gaudy embellishments upon his uniform, spoke up. "How?"

"Our vessel was damaged by an enemy missile. Rendered unconscious, I awoke to find water rising in the cabin. Most of the crew had already perished. Though I made every effort, pulling his lifeless body to the surface with me, he could not be revived. I left his body to the sea, knowing that was what he would have wanted, and swam until I reached these shores."

This, Laevus knew, was a risky play. He tugged at his sleeves, obscuring the injuries sustained escaping captivity. He did not wish to give them any reason to doubt his story. Especially when it would be easy for them to find the prototype drill if they bothered to put in a bit of effort. He hadn't travelled more than a half dozen kilometers from where it lay stranded.

But he had never been averse to taking risks. A flutter of excitement overtook him as he thought back to his well-laid plans to get his unstable mother into a room with the Elder Council. *That* had been a risk, and it had worked out better than he could have dreamed. If only Nero had not survived the encounter, it would have been perfect.

The humans consulted amongst themselves, unaware that their hushed tones were not enough to mask their words from Laevus' keen ears. He listened intently, wondering if he would be forced to kill them all. He would prefer that they made the right choice. He needed whatever mode of transportation they were using. Gaining their co-operation would be best.

"We will escort you to the capital," the leader declared after several long minutes of debate. Laevus noted the lingering hesitancy in his words. "If Her Majesty deems to grant you an audience, you may state your case."

The hint of a smile tugged at the corner of Laevus' mouth. "I live to serve," he purred. "I look forward to meeting Her Majesty."

He considered the future with relish as he accompanied the band of soldiers back to their vessel. True, he was not yet headed back to the Evenmire, but he was in no rush. It gave him more time to refine his plans. He hadn't been lying about wanting to meet the Queen; he wanted to see how she lived and imagine how much more glorious his own rule would be, when the Halfsie son of a traitor sat upon the throne as Thera's leader.

Nero was all that stood in the way of that dream. He was an obstacle, to be sure, but not an insurmountable one. Laevus could almost *taste* the sweet reality of proving, once and for all, that his parentage could not dictate his fate. He was not only equal to the Therans—he was *superior.* A lifetime of being told otherwise had not been enough to make him doubt this.

He would repay Nero, repay *all* of Thera, for what he had been forced to endure. He need only be patient.

And patience was something Laevus excelled at.

* * *

CAPTAIN SONOMA, of the Culeian attack vessel *Ningen*, was poor company on the long journey to the capital. His crew scurried about like ants, vapid and dull, while Laevus was forced to endure the stench of humanity in confined quarters, something he'd already had quite enough of for one lifetime. The submarine was massive, but Laevus was not permitted to wander unescorted.

Fortunately, the captain seemed to have little to do by way of commanding, and instead spent a good deal of time showing Laevus around—attempting, no doubt, to impress this would-be ally. If Sonoma was otherwise indisposed, Laevus had to content himself with the aft compartments, which offered little more than tasteless food and uncomfortable bunks. When the captain summoned him to the forward command center, he was eager to escape the monotony of the living quarters.

"Lord Laevus." Sonoma's head dipped in a subtle bow. "We are coming up on our destination. As our honored guest, I thought you might be interested in observing."

Laevus nodded as he stared out a porthole, waiting for the fabled underwater city to come into view. So far, all he could see was an endless stretch of inky blackness.

"What's that?" Laevus pointed, and Captain Sonoma moved closer to the thick glass, squinting toward the barely visible blip in the distance.

"Whale, if we're lucky."

This curious answer elicited a thrill on the part of Laevus, who delighted in a good mystery. He wondered what might constitute an *un*lucky encounter. Were there creatures down here that could wrap the vessel in monstrous tentacles, squeezing it until it burst and casting its hapless crew into the icy depths? The idea was intriguing, enticing him to inquire further, but the sub suddenly banked beneath his feet, and the dark seascape outside the porthole gave way to a dozen glowing dots in the distance.

"Behold!" Sonoma beamed with pride. "Paru, the city beneath the waves, crown jewel of our great nation."

Laevus did not reply, watching the dots grow larger. The domes bore a striking resemblance to the brief glimpse of Sanctuary he'd had after coming through the Evenmire. Wider and less opaque than their Antarctic counterparts, they were nestled in concentric rings on the seafloor, little lines of light that might have been tunnels connecting each to its neighbors. As the *Ningen* drew nearer, Laevus could see shadows moving around outside the city, though it was impossible to tell at this distance whether they were vessels or some form of ocean life.

Laevus had underestimated the humans. Despite their ineptitudes, Paru seemed a feat of marvelous ingenuity, especially considering the chaotic era in which it had been constructed.

The *Ningen* dove deeper as they came to one of the domes on the outer ring, light from the structure pouring in through the porthole and causing Laevus to squint and turn away. The now-familiar sensation of the submarine rising accompanied an echoing *boom* as they made contact.

One of the crew twisted in his seat to face Sonoma. "Docking complete, Captain."

Uncertain what to expect, Laevus emerged from the *Ningen* to find himself in a modest, circular, thoroughly disappointing room. The metallic walls were scarred and dull, and a nearby pool of water rose and fell mournfully, perhaps in response to the *Ningen's* disturbance.

Nothing in that sad little room prepared him for the spectacle that awaited. They proceeded through a small airlock and, when the door opened onto the city, Laevus could only stare.

The docking facility was at the edge of a vast, wide open space surrounded by bizarre architecture. Bubble-like structures stacked in tall formations stretched out of sight in front of him. It took a few moments before Laevus understood that the spherical oddities were buildings, each topped with its own complement of smaller spheres that glowed with a warm, golden light.

He turned to his left and found himself mere steps from the outer wall of the dome. Inexplicably drawn to it, he moved forward, reaching out to press his hand against it. *So cold.* Outside, the darkness of the sea was broken only by the glow of the next dome, which lay just barely in the periphery of his vision.

The Captain cleared his throat. "Paru is home to the vast majority of Culei's most respected citizenry. Over seventy thousand people call this their home, myself included."

"And yet Sanctuary could hold only ten thousand with half as many domes," Laevus noted.

Sonoma raised an eyebrow. "The domes of Paru are not only larger than those in Antarctica, they are also more advanced. We have no need to waste precious space growing food or raising herds. Our water purification systems tap the endless reserves of the ocean, the very oxygen we breathe is provided in like manner. The sea provides, and our terrestrial colonies fill in the gaps. We do not survive as a closed society, as was necessary for Sanctuary to do."

Laevus walked alongside the Captain. "And, these are...?" He gestured toward the stacked spheres, some of which rose nearly to the peak of the dome. While most were white or pale grey, more than a few of them sported gaudy shades of gold.

"Housing, mostly. The outer rings are almost entirely residential. Much of our commerce is located in the central ring."

"And the innermost dome? I presume that is where I am to meet Her Majesty?"

Nodding, Sonoma pivoted on his heel, marching down a winding path between two long rows of bulbous buildings. "I've sent someone on ahead to inform the royal staff of your arrival. They'll be expecting us."

Laevus noted how the humans seemed to swarm, their presence thickening in a semi-circle around the Theran interloper. He enjoyed the attention he commanded, the way they gazed at him with awe and uncertainty. Although most were on foot, several odd vehicles made their way slowly along the meandering paths, pedal-powered carts that held one or two passengers in their woven carriages.

The Captain led them to the mouth of a tunnel. It was impressive, boasting an arched ceiling twenty feet above their heads that appeared to be made of glass. One of the strange carts stood waiting for them. Resting atop three large wheels, a pair of woven seats faced each other. At the front, a small metal contraption held a man in a neat uniform embellished with ivory brocade. His shiny shoes rested atop the pedals and his head was topped with a flattened cap. He'd been leaning forward, resting his elbows across the handlebars, but now hopped lightly to the ground and bowed.

"Her Majesty bids you welcome," he said, "and has sent me to collect you."

Sonoma began to offer instructions as soon as they had boarded the carriage. "When you meet with Her Majesty, you must never turn your back on her. You are to exit as you enter—facing the Queen. You should bow when you reach the foot of the throne, and you should not rise unless she bids you stand. And, finally, you are not to make eye contact with Her Majesty at any time."

This was a familiar practice for Laevus, whose Theran upbringing had taught him that eye contact with a superior was considered the height of disrespect. To defer in such a powerful way to a human was distasteful, but unavoidable. This was their territory, and he would need to play by their rules in order to achieve his goals.

They had entered a new dome now, and many of the buildings were much wider, but not stacked as tall. The crowds were larger here than in the previous dome, the various wheeled vehicles and carts more numerous.

"This is one of several markets." Sonoma seemed to have a fond smile for every citizen they passed. "Our largest Nouritas brewery is just over there, Squid's Bane. The finest in all of Culei."

"Indeed." Laevus was not interested in the grand tour.

As they swept through another tunnel and into the center dome, Laevus noted a marked decrease in buildings.

There were only a few, and all of them were two or three stories tall at most. Sentries were posted at intervals along their path, waving them on with pompous, self-important stares.

The center of the dome featured what Laevus assumed to be the royal palace, an enormous version of the bulbous buildings, dotted all over with smaller auxiliary spheres. He sighed inwardly, depressed that Humans could turn such an incredible architectural feat into a mockery. The decor, the structures, everything within Paru was odd and gaudy, a show of how far Post-Sequencing Humanity had fallen.

Such a travesty.

The cart pulled to a stop in front of the palace and Laevus stepped down lightly. He waited for the Captain to lead the way, but Sonoma shook his head.

"No one can enter the royal palace except by express permission. You have been invited, Lord Laevus, but I'm afraid my escort ends here."

"I thank you for your assistance in bringing me this far, Captain Sonoma," Laevus' tone was somber as he bowed his head. "Your name will not be forgotten in the era to come, when peace between Thera and Culei allows both of our peoples to flourish."

He whirled toward the palace without a second glance and approached the tall entryway. The Council chambers of Thera had always been where he was most at ease. He thrived in any atmosphere where superiority was celebrated. Even if it was only superiority amongst humans.

Although servants and guards flanked the hall and indicated his path, he would have easily found his way to the throne room without their assistance—all he need do was walk straight. Plush carpeting lined the grandiose hallways, large canvases covering the walls and depicting the various leaders and stages of Culei's short history in painstaking detail. One exceptionally lavish work showed a broad-shouldered man with a rolled-up paper in his hand. He was pointing with regal dignity toward an unfinished dome while an adoring woman wearing a crown, no doubt the first queen, looked on with approval. Laevus thought the painting made very little sense. Although he assumed it portrayed the construction of Paru, where was the man standing? On the bottom of the ocean? Would he and the queen not have drowned? Where was all the light coming from? Shouldn't it be black, like the depths outside? These inconsistencies confirmed for Laevus the clearly unstable minds these humans possessed. It seemed obvious to him that they had only a tenuous grasp on reality.

This suspicion was solidified as he entered the throne room. In the brief moment that he used to take it in before dropping his gaze to the floor, he saw that the Queen had taken her outlandish eccentricities to the extreme in this, the epicenter of her domain.

An oversized golden throne in the center of the room was eclipsed in grandeur by the enormous aquarium that stood behind it. Spanning the entirety of the chamber and stretching to the curved ceiling, it showcased brightly colored corals and schools of fish in an array of shimmering hues. In his peripheral vision he thought he could make out a shark, but he would not know for sure until he had the chance for a second look. He strode confidently but humbly toward the throne until two guards stepped before the Queen, their ornamental pole-arms crossed in warning. He took a knee and smiled down at the thick pile of the carpet, willing himself not to laugh at the pathetic show of power. If it had suited him, Her Majesty and her guards would already be dead. He could snap their puny spears in half like twigs, and their bodies likewise.

He waited for long seconds for the monarch to speak. The aquarium had stolen his focus upon entry, and he had not had the opportunity to get a good look at her. He'd only seen the outline of a petite woman in crimson robes, dwarfed by the throne upon which she sat.

The voice that addressed him was that of a male. It rose and fell with a flowery cadence that suggested its bearer was a product of courtly life.

"Her Majesty the Queen, ruler of the seas and tamer of the shores, bids you welcome to Paru, the Pearl of the Ocean."

Laevus did not speak, acknowledging the welcome with a nod, continuing to study the floor.

"Her Majesty the Queen has satisfied her desire to look upon the Theran emissary. You will be shown to your quarters and shall enjoy the hospitality of our city."

Disappointing. "You honor me, Your Majesty."

"You are dismissed." The attendant's words carried a tone of finality. Laevus stood and backed slowly out of the throne room, only turning away once the doors had been closed.

"How did you fair?" Sonoma inquired as Laevus exited the palace, his charm during their voyage together had given the Captain a sense of ease around his new Theran friend.

A dangerous sense of ease.

"Well, I believe." The words came easily, not a trace of the frustration he'd felt escaping alongside them. "Although Her Majesty did not speak."

"She rarely does," Sonoma admitted. "Though I expect she has things she wishes to discuss with you. All in good time."

"Of course."

The night was spent in one of the oddly shaped buildings these Culeians called home. The floor was flat, but the walls and ceilings curved to form their peculiar bubble shape, giving Laevus the sense that he had never left the *Ningen*. The decor was tacky and overdone, but at least it was private.

The next morning he was summoned once more to the palace.

Yet again, the Queen did not speak.

By the third day of this treatment, Laevus had begun to view this quirky dance as some sort of a mental test. A battle of wills. If the goal was to infuriate him, she was certainly giving it her all. But, as always, Laevus was patient. He would endure. Each day he caught a fleeting glance of the monarch before casting his eyes to the floor. A small build, and a face—hideous, no doubt—cloaked beneath an ivory veil that trailed to her lap and pooled over delicately clasped hands.

"Rise."

This was not the attendant's voice. It was cool and commanding, but that did not surprise Laevus. What surprised him was that it belonged to a child. He rose smoothly to his feet, keeping his eyes focused on the floor.

"You are Lord Laevus, of Thera." The haughty statement issued from behind the veil with a tone of something akin to boredom.

"I am, Your Majesty."

"I will forego customs. I wish for you to look upon my face, so that I may look upon yours more clearly. Long have I studied the top of your head, when it is the eyes which are the windows to one's soul."

Laevus did not need further encouragement, though he doubted his windows would be as revealing as the little monarch would like. He locked eyes with the Queen, careful not to express emotion.

Lifting her veil, she gazed at him with a passive expression of mild curiosity, tilting her head delicately to the left. "So you are a Theran." He watched her eyes as they roamed from his face to his ears.

"I am, Your Majesty."

"And you are alone?"

"I came as an emissary of my people. But the Culeians who bore me across the sea were lost to a despicable attack." The Queen looked no older than ten, perhaps eleven years of age. Although her royal attire was tailored with precision, the elaborate headdress and stiff ruff around her neck served only to accentuate her youth in an almost comical manner. She sat stock-straight upon the throne, hands placed on arm rests much too high for her small frame.

"Despicable, indeed." She frowned. "The cowardly act of a cowardly people. Pravacordia will be punished for the loss of my Ambassador and his team."

Laevus found the audacity of her statement surprising. Did she truly believe those words? Her youth and her delusion made her a tempting pawn. It would not be much of a challenge to manipulate her to his will. She was an easy target.

The Queen spoke again, her voice exuding an authority that seemed far too strong for one so small. "I presume from your presence that our alliance with your people was a success, and that we can expect amnesty if and when they decide to return to our world?"

Laevus didn't miss a beat. "Of course, Your Majesty. A peace between our two peoples is assured."

"And the terms? What price will we pay for this peace?"

"Only that which you have already agreed to, Your Grace," Laevus said with a reassuring gesture. He could not risk upsetting his chances of returning to the Evenmire.

The Queen needed to be certain that her people were safe. If she believed otherwise, he would likely become a prisoner rather than a guest.

She eyed him for a long time without speaking.

"Your Majesty, if I may…" One of the guards shot him a warning glare, and Laevus quieted. Apparently addressing the Queen unsolicited was also a no-no.

"You will accompany my fleet to Sanctuary." The queen's declaration was sudden and resolute. "Your expertise in regards to Theran technology will be invaluable in preparing our newest assets."

The idea of being taken precisely where he wanted to go was appealing, but he was not yet sure how such an arrangement might be of use to the monarch.

"The people of Sanctuary have requested our aid, and we intend to answer their call. They are, after all, the city on which our own great capital was modeled. In return, they are offering something we desperately need…soldiers."

"The people of Sanctuary have agreed to fight for your cause?"

"No, Lord Laevus." The Queen gave a delicate shake of her royal head. "They have Theran clones. These can take the place of my own people on the ground, assuring our victory and preserving precious lives. I believe your assistance in handling and training them would prove a boon to our people."

Laevus' smile was genuine this time. Someone, somehow, had managed to get the Sanctuary CEDAR program up and running. They could have hundreds, perhaps thousands of clones.

And this child, foolish and naive, had just placed them into Laevus' hands. The basis of his very own army. The travelling, the human stench, the awful food, the wait…it had all been worth it. Things were working out more beautifully than he could have hoped, with surprisingly little effort on his part.

"Your Majesty," Laevus prostrated himself before her, "it would be my greatest pleasure to serve you in this manner."

*   *   *

HIGH AND SHEER, the ice shelf rose up before them. As the captain of the *Kraken* went about instructing those under his command on how to proceed, Laevus pondered his own plans. A last-minute communication that he had not been supposed to hear had suggested that something had gone wrong with the clones. They were uncontrollable, volatile. He knew what this meant, even if the humans did not. They had not produced the fine Theran clones of his home world. No. Sanctuary had the Forlorn on their hands. Unsurprising, really. CEDAR was much too complicated for mere humans to adequately control. And if they were not careful, they would soon be facing their own version of the Great War.

This was a setback for Laevus. He could no more control the Forlorn than the humans could. Should he make a break for the Evenmire, return home, bide his time as he continued his slow trek to supremacy? Or should he take the greater risk, returning the abominations to Culei in hopes of conquering the issues the Sanctuary team had run into? If he was able to do so, he could come out on the other side with a powerful army behind him. He had followed the CEDAR project quite closely under Pike. He understood the necessary components of producing and controlling an ideal soldier. But would it work on the Forlorn, or only on fresh specimens?

He was still mulling over the options as he donned his Culeain gear, the thick parka distasteful but necessary in the unforgiving weather. He boarded one of the transports and remained quiet as they made their way behind the drills that bored through the shelf before them. He disembarked with the others who would accompany him into Sanctuary, sparing only a brief glance toward the beautiful, cold light of the Evenmire. The Culeian entourage had barely made it inside the city before they were met by a pair of solemn-faced Sanctuarians.

"The clones are gone," a rosy-cheeked young man declared between quick, shallow breaths. "Dead. But that doesn't mean...I'm certain we can make it right. We just need a little time to get everything up and running again."

His ponytailed companion nudged the speaker. "We've got company, Nelson."

Flushing deeper still as his eyes narrowed, the smaller

of the two looked back and forth between the Culeian contingent and a second pair of men that had appeared further down the hallway, approaching quickly. "I'll take care of this. Please, just…give me a moment."

Two arguments ensued then, one amongst the Culeians and one amongst the Sanctuarians. Laevus paid neither of them any heed. No clones. The dream was lost. There was nothing for it; he would have to return through the Evenmire and pick up where he had left off.

The flustered man returned, quivering with anger. "We need to leave."

The Culeian captain looked shocked. "But you promised us—"

"I know what I promised. And you promised us aid. So, we won't take your aid and everything's back to square one, fair enough?"

The tall, heavyset man with the ponytail appeared hesitant. "Are you quite certain you've given this decision adequate consideration, Peacock? Anger can taint sound judgement. You can't put the ink back in the squid."

"I've had enough of this place. We're going, and we're going *now*. There's no way to be sure when the Elves will arrive. Their fleet could arrive anytime now."

This piqued Laevus' interest. *A fleet?* What a curious twist of fate. One thing was certain, however. If Therans were coming to Earth, Nero would be leading them. He would want to witness his enemies' demise firsthand.

Laevus took one more look at the Evenmire as the con-

tingent and its new tag-alongs filed out. The rows of transports waited patiently to unload supplies.

If Nero was coming to Earth, Laevus could not return
to Thera. He had to stay. This was where their destinies
would be decided.

As the troops shuffled about, preparing to depart,
the newcomers muttered amongst themselves. The words
"dead" and "Elf" caught his attention. He shot a glare toward the one called Peacock. "What's this about a dead
Theran?"

The ponytailed man looked at Laevus for the first time,
a sickly pallor falling over his face as his eyes widened.
"You're...you're an Elf!"

"The proper term," Laevus corrected with a hint of bit-
terness, "is *Theran*. And yes, I am."

Nelson was staring at him, having gone pale as well. *So
very frail, these humans.* "Felix?"

A stocky man with a thick beard whose name Laevus
had not bothered to remember approached, interrupting.
"Lord Laevus, Mr. Boggs, Terrance...you three head for
that supply transport at the end of the line, there. The pilot
is waiting for you. The rest of you lot, come with me."

Once inside, Laevus settled into one of several cold
metal chairs. Peacock, or Boggs, or whatever his name was,
did likewise, still staring at him.

"We'll be heading out in just a few," the pilot informed
them. "Just waiting for all the others to go. First in, last out,
unfortunately."

Ponytail shrugged. "I'm certainly in no great rush. There is a reckoning in our future once Her Majesty finds out that we have failed to procure her most precious cargo."

"What happened?"

"I'd rather not discuss it," Boggs snapped irritably, his attention at last drifting from Laevus. "I'm sure I'll be explaining it plenty of times in the near future, and I don't like having to repeat myself." His clipped, superior tone amused Laevus, who had thus far not seen any evidence that this particular human had any right to act superior to anyone. He was scrawny and short, hardly more than a child. Still, the Culeians had seen fit to elect a mere babe as their queen. Perhaps the same poor judgement plagued the Sanctuary humans as well. Could this Peacock be their leader? He wouldn't put it past them.

The transport lurched beneath them as the pilot initiated a wide turn, bringing them about to face the tunnels. "And here we go!"

The tell-tale dip of the vehicle indicated the point at which they reached the tunnel's entrance. They had not gotten too far when they stopped once again.

Ponytail sidled up beside the pilot's chair. "What seems to be the dilemma?"

"Well, most of the transports have hit open sea by now, but one of them has stalled out up ahead. Isn't that just the way…I always pick the slowest line." He chuckled. "I'm sure we'll be moving again in short order."

They had resumed their slow pace and had almost

reached the edge of the shelf when a voice came over the radio. "Be advised. Unknown activity near Antiquity's Gate."

"Unknown activity…" the pilot mumbled. "What the heck does that mean?"

"I'd think it was self-explanatory, don't you concur?" Ponytail retorted. "It's unknown."

The radio crackled to life again. "A new presence has appeared. Please stand by."

Laevus felt his skin prickle as he glanced at the others. Peacock had gone even paler than before, his skin so milky white that he might have been frozen.

"Stop the transport." Laevus wasn't asking. The time for supplication was over.

But the pilot only studied him with a queer expression. "I'm sorry, but you don't have the authority to make that call."

"No, he's right," Peacock insisted, unexpectedly coming to Laevus' defense. "Tell the others to stop, too, if they can. We're safer in the tunnels. It's happening. The Elves—I mean," he glanced at Laevus, "the Therans. They're coming through."

A look of relief spread over the pilot's face. "Oh, no need to worry. The treaty will protect us, we're in no danger."

"Stop the transport." Laevus stood as he repeated his order, his words icy. The pilot stared at him with a mixture of fear and indignance. He stood, too, drawing himself up to his full, unimpressive height. Then he raised an accusing finger.

"Now you listen here. I'm in command, and I'll decide what actions we take based on orders from my commanding officer."

Ponytail was still beside the pilot's chair, monitoring the situation outside. "The tunnel is clear. The others have undoubtedly reached the water already."

Biting his lip thoughtfully, Laevus continued to study the pilot for a moment until the man spun and lunged toward the controls, pressing a few buttons and pushing the throttle forward. *Always so troublesome, these humans.* The transport began to move forward on its own.

"Ponytail," Laevus positioned himself closer to the pilot as he spoke, "can you steer this thing?"

There was a moment of uncomprehending silence before he lifted his hand and snapped his fingers rapidly to get the idiot's attention.

Ponytail nodded. "I haven't availed myself of any formal training, being waylaid in this frozen wasteland—no offense intended, Nelson—for a fair bit of time, but I did oversee the design for the drills, and this transport appears to have quite a bit in common with my prototype..."

"How nice for you," Laevus cut in dryly. He grasped the pilot by the collar and lifted him up in one effortless, smooth motion. The crown of his head made contact with the low ceiling with a dull thunk, and his eyes rolled back. Laevus tossed his limp form to one side, where it lay slumped against the hull. Then he turned to Ponytail. "Congratulations, the vessel is yours. Make it stop."

"If we turn back, we might be able to help," Peacock was saying. Laevus let out a derisive laugh as he opened the hatch, the door scraping the icy wall of the tunnel as they continued their slow trek toward the sea. Then he grabbed the pilot and shoved him unceremoniously out of the craft. Peacock gawked at him. "Felix, you can't just—"

"He was not a good listener. And apparently, neither are you. My name is Laevus, not Felix, and you'd do well to remember that, Peacock."

The scrawny man bristled. "And *my* name is Nelson. Nelson Boggs. And furthermore—"

"I don't like people who don't listen." Laevus pulled the door shut and latched it. "If he makes it back to the city, he lives. Which is more than I can say for us right now. Ponytail, what's going on out there? Why are we still moving?"

"Regrettably, it appears he had time to transition it to autopilot before...hmm. I'm attempting to override it, however—damn!"

The vessel dropped abruptly and Laevus felt the familiar, unpleasant bob of the water as it swallowed them. He frowned. This was not going as well as he could have hoped.

"Get us back up there."

Ponytail scowled. "Contrary to how it may appear, this is not as effortless as it may seem. The control system might seem unassuming to the unskilled eye, but it's considerably more complex than—"

A low static issued from the speakers. Then it roared to

life with sounds of terror and panic. Through screams and explosions, Laevus was able to discern enough to learn that Nero had aircraft of some sort. Ponytail looked ill, his face pallid and glistening with sweat. His hand twitched over the controls.

"Don't get any ideas, Ponytail. There's nothing you can do for them, but you might still be able to save *us*."

Ponytail reached over and lowered the volume. "As I've already stated, I am attempting to do so!"

Too slow. Laevus knew it a moment before Ponytail confirmed it. The eerie sound of cracking ice penetrated the thin hull of the transport, and it rocked dangerously as huge chunks of the glacier crashed into the sea around them.

"Get back!" Laevus commanded. "Away from the shelf, and as deep as you can get us!"

"But—"

Laevus fixed him with an icy stare. "Do it now, or we all die."

Shoulders slumped in defeat, Ponytail complied. The transport sank beneath the depths. The portholes on either side were swallowed by water, showing muted flashes of light from the battle raging nearby. "Now get us away from here. If we're lucky, they didn't see us."

It was over quickly. Quiet once again blanketed the craft.

Nelson's hesitant query was little more than a whisper. "What now?"

"We wait," Laevus replied. "We need to be sure they are gone before we resurface."

"But what about survivors?" Nelson pressed. "We need to get up there. Assess the situation. See if—"

"I'm afraid it no longer matters what we 'need' to do." Ponytail cast a despondent glance over his shoulder. "I don't expect we'd even make it back to the ice shelf. By the looks of it, we're losing fuel at a disturbing rate. I can't be certain whether it's a fault in the system or if one of those great ice cubes tore through our fuel lines. That's the problem with leaving important work to second rate engineers, isn't it? If I'd have been in charge of this project, I'd've made good and sure the integrity of the vital systems was protected."

"Spit it out, Terrance, what does that mean?" Nelson blurted out. "Can we fix it? Can we make it back to Sanctuary?"

Ponytail shook his head. "We aren't going anywhere, 'least not of our own accord. In a few moments we'll be no more than flotsam, subject to the whim of the currents."

Nelson's mouth worked silently for a while before he was able to choke out a feeble question. "Can...can we swim for it?"

Idiot. "You'll be frozen solid before you manage to climb back into the tunnel," Laevus snapped. "Is that how you want to die, mounted on the side of that ice shelf like a trophy?"

Nelson cringed. "Not particularly."

Scowling, Laevus stared through the porthole, gritting

his teeth. There had to be a way out of this. He just needed time to think.

The engine stuttered. Then, only silence.

At least he'd have plenty of time to think now.

They were dead in the water.

Chapter Two

A City on the Mend

B EN'S COMM WAS on the fritz again. He'd dropped it one too many times and as a result it rarely wanted to cooperate when he needed it to. "Killian?" He waited a moment for a reply, then pulled the comm out of his ear, giving it a little jiggle before popping it back in. "Killian, this is Ben, can you hear me? Just looking for a quick update."

There was no response beyond a low-grade static. He would need to requisition a new one. He grimaced at the thought. Ben tried to avoid the new administration whenever possible. He made a mental note to take better care of the next one.

If they even agreed to issue him another. When Ben had been on the Council, it had been important for him

to be in constant contact with the others. Now, though…
well, very few of the old Council members had retained
their seats when the Citizens for Truth Committee took
over.

Ben had not been one of them.

The CTC's defacto leader, one Doris Fincher, was
something akin to a natural disaster. She'd devastated most
every aspect of daily life for Ben and everyone else who
still worked for Sigil. She'd wasted no time implementing a
number of rapid changes to the way things were done, and
because Ben was no longer in the loop, he only knew the
half of it. The best he'd been able to do was to keep his head
down and try to stay out of the path of her relentless efforts
to drive everyone there to the brink of insanity.

Something about the CTC, and Fincher herself, rubbed
him the wrong way. It wasn't her demeanor, which at least
on the surface seemed approachable and understanding.
Nor was it her non-threatening appearance. Barely cresting five feet tall and a hundred pounds soaking wet, she
did not appear a force to be reckoned with. Perhaps it was
the way she had weaseled her way into a position of power, overthrowing Edwin's team in a quiet, bloodless coup.
Underneath an ever-present smile, she struck Ben as rather
slimy and devious.

Just now he was sitting in Sylvia's lab. Or, at least, what
had been Sylvia's lab. The CTC had deemed it a 'misallo-
cation of valuable resources.' Its usefulness had dwindled
steadily since the Reclamation Day riots, and so they'd

had the medical pod facility absorbed into the hospital wing. Sylvia had been returned to her old position at the Information Desk. She hadn't been thrilled to give up her work in the lab, but between the darkness of the domes, the Theran invasion, and the changes in the hierarchy, people had a lot of questions. Sylvia was once again the comforting voice of reason representing Sigil. She spent her days placating the masses and in her free time kept her promise to assure that the Geo restoration was running smoothly.

Ben glanced around at the empty space, scuff marks where the pods had once rested the only evidence of the time and energy his sister had invested in this place.

The door slid open behind him, and Ben turned to find Sylvia silhouetted in the doorway. She seemed surprised to see him there.

"Oh! Ben. What are you doing here?"

He shrugged, stuffing his hands in his pockets and taking one more look around. "Nothing. Just wandering around."

Sylvia's eyes flitted about the room, and Ben felt like he could see inside her mind. She was seeing the events of the past unfolding all over again. The lives saved in here, the lives lost, the lives forever changed. "I just wanted to make sure everything was taken care of," she admitted in a quiet voice.

"Yeah." Ben nodded. "Everything's been situated in the hospital wing. You want to walk with me?"

"Where are you going?"

Ben thrust his lip out in a pout as he pulled out his comm again. "To see Killian. I haven't been able to contact him. This thing isn't working."

Sylvia reached out, taking the earpiece as her brows knitted in disapproval. "You ought to take better care of your things. You know I'm not in a position to just replace whatever you want because you can't keep from goofing around with it. All of our requisition forms go through the CTC now. I'm under a lot of pressure to account for every last item in distribution."

Ben snatched the device back with a scowl. "I didn't ask you to get me a new one. I'll fix it myself."

Sylvia had always been like that. Always chastising him like he was just some silly kid. He loved her, but she could get on his nerves, too. "Just haven't had a chance yet, that's all."

Sylvia's expression softened. "Sorry. I'm just a little on edge lately. All these changes…"

"Yeah, I get it. No worries. So, you wanna walk me to the lift or not?"

"Sure."

The halls were busy, people streaming in both directions, their chatter echoing off the walls in a cacophony of incomprehensible conversations. Ben walked beside his sister, pondering the strange dichotomy of the lively atmosphere in the Sigil building and the quiet darkness outside. People went about their days as normal, but the dimming of the domes had fallen like a blanket over the city. Transactions were made in hushed tones, conversations held just above a whisper. It was as if everyone feared that somehow their voices on the darkened streets would slip through the dome, alerting the Elves to their continued presence here.

When they reached the lobby the crowd thinned, and Sylvia hesitated as they came to the lift.

"Hey." Ben flashed a smile. "I wasn't expecting you to come down with me."

She bit her lip, glancing over her shoulder toward the Information Desk. "I would, it's just…"

Ben took his sister by the shoulders, giving the tiniest shake to get her to look him in the eye. "There is nothing down there that you need to worry about. We're handling it. There's no need for you to be involved."

Relief flashed across her face. "I really should get back. I was just on my lunch and thought I'd…" She blinked twice. "I really should get back."

"Yeah. I'll see you at home later."

"Okay."

They parted ways, and Ben found himself alone in the lift, headed down to the basement level. The prospect of visiting the Nursery did not appeal to him, but he felt responsible for the mess that others were busy cleaning up down there. He'd helped to create it, though precious few people knew of his entanglement in Ripley's plot. If nothing else, he should at least make himself useful in the efforts to erase this ugly blip in their history.

The door to Ben's old office in Pods was open. He peeked in and found Killian Jones hunched over a control panel with his back to the door. "Hey, Killian."

Killian straightened up with a start, coughing. As he turned, Ben could see that he hadn't been working, but rather eating. As his cough subsided, Killian nodded in acknowledgement, beating lightly at his chest to dislodge whatever he'd inhaled. "Hey. Wasn't expecting you."

"Couldn't get through on the comm." Ben strode into the office, trailing his hand along the familiar workstations. "Thought I'd come down and see how things are going."

Killian frowned at him. "You aren't in charge of the project anymore, Ben. Fincher says I shouldn't—"

"What Fincher doesn't know won't hurt us." Ben pointed to the crumb-covered plate that sat balanced atop a sensitive set of controls. "Like the fact that you're eating at your station, for instance."

Killian's chair squeaked as he stood up, brushing the front of his uniform self-consciously. "I know, I know. I get it. We just, we don't get a lot of breaks. And I'd rather not eat down there where…you know. All that stuff happened. I was just trying to enjoy a few minutes of quiet before I get back to work."

"Your secret is safe with me," Ben assured him. "Now come on, quit stuffing your face and show me what's happening."

The Rat took them down to the Nursery, the lingering scent of burnt flesh wafting in as the door opened into the cavernous underground room. Everywhere he looked people flitted about like ants, carting disassembled pod components and shouting instructions to one another across the room.

"All of the, uh, organic material has been taken care of," Killian said as they skirted around two men waiting to get into the lift with a heavy sheet of metal. Ben shuddered. *The organic material.* A very innocuous way to refer to the thousands of fried clones that had been left behind when Ripley overloaded the pods. In the harried days after the Elven fleet came through the Gate, as the CTC was busy taking over, the bodies had been left untouched for almost a week. Though Ben had not been involved, he could only imagine how arduous the grisly undertaking must have been. All non-vital department business had been temporarily suspended so that their workers could assist. Ben had volunteered to join the effort, but the CTC had shot down his request. They seemed to think he was somehow unfit for the new government, but still too vital to be reduced to hauling bodies. They had him working on a number of simultaneous projects, none of which seemed, in Ben's opinion, particularly vital. "We put the Elf's body into the last working pod on Fincher's orders. She said it could come in handy in the future."

Ben scowled reflexively. "She was a *person* and she had a name, Killian. It was Onyx. And she helped save our lives. We shouldn't be holding onto her body like it's some kind of gruesome untapped resource. She deserves a decent end."

Killian eyed him with a tight-lipped frown. "You didn't mind using the Elves' bodies in the cloning experiments back when this whole mess started."

"That was different!" Ben's tone and posture had both turned defensive. "*I* was different." Desperate to steer the conversation in another direction, he cast around for a new talking point. "What have you done with all the rest?"

"I've had it all incinerated. That was the biggest obstacle. Everything else is really just a matter of sorting and moving, not as time-sensitive. Pod components don't start to smell if you leave them hanging around for a while. It's slow going, but we'll get there."

"Has the CTC given you guys any further instruction on what's heading where?"

Killian pointed toward the glass enclosure where Ben and his team first discovered that the clones they'd created were actually monsters. It was piled high with neatly arranged stacks of parts, all metal panels and buckets of bolts and panes of glass. Though it was almost unrecognizable, it still made the hairs on the back of his neck stand up to remember what had taken place there. "Everything is being sorted. We've got the model numbers you gave us, anything salvageable from those is heading upstairs for the hospital. Guess they're going to attempt reconstructing a few for medical experiments. That'll probably land on me as well. Pretty much everything does these days, now that you're gone." Killian's face showed the slightest signs of irritation as he sighed. "I never wanted to be in charge, you know. I liked following instructions a whole lot better than I like giving them. Anyway, over there," he pointed again, drawing Ben's attention to a different pile. "That's all headed straight for Reclamation. They can sort out what to do with it. Just about everything is going to head that way, to be honest. Most of this is useless beyond recycling the components and starting from scratch."

"What about—"

"Yeah, yeah." Killian waved a hand to stop Ben, already knowing what he was going to ask. Ben had repeated the request more often than any other. "Don't worry, Fincher's already signed off on ten percent of everything we scrap being earmarked for Geo. I knew you'd never let me hear the end of it if I didn't make it happen."

Ben gave a wry smile. "Thanks, man."

"Don't thank me, thank Fincher. She's the boss, now."

"Ugh. Don't remind me."

Unlike Edwin, Doris Fincher had not stuck her head in the sand where Geo was concerned. She understood that it was a crucial part of their continued survival, and whatever feelings she had toward the Halfsies, she was a strong advocate for prioritizing its repair despite any other threats the city was facing. Ironically, now that Ripley had been incarcerated and could no longer spearhead the project, Edwin had been assigned to do so. Molly, having lost her status when the Tapestry-heavy Council had been replaced, was forced to continue in an unofficial capacity beneath Edwin. He wasn't particularly good at this sort of thing, but he was available, and he was doing his best.

"Listen, Ben. You're a good kid. But there's a new order now. Why don't you stop worrying so much about everything and try to relax? We've got this place under control. Go home. Take a nap. Or do something you're actually being paid to do. I don't care, but quit being such a glutton for punishment. Anyways, I'd better get back to work. And you'd better get out of here. It'll be my head if they find you poking your nose where you aren't supposed to be."

"Right. I've got to get back anyway. I'm supposed to meet Molly."

Killian seemed surprised. "Oh yeah? A little old for you, don't you think?"

"Don't be daft, it's not a date. It's work stuff."

Killian grinned. "If you say so. Go on, get lost. You're in the way."

He'd meant it literally. Ben glanced behind him and saw a handful of bitter-looking laborers trying to squeeze past him in the narrow row between the stacks. "Oops! Sorry."

Ben waited for Molly by the lobby entrance. He'd considered meeting her at the Tube Station, but didn't like walking around in the dark. He found it unsettling. He shifted impatiently from one foot to the other as he awaited her arrival. When he spotted her approaching, he held open the heavy door. She had a child by each hand, and her face was exuberant. "Sorry we took so long! Traveling on the Tube with kids is a lot harder than I realized."

"More trouble than it's worth," grumbled a sour voice behind her. Ben held the door wider to admit Denton and his charges. He had one kid by the collar as if the child had been trying to make a break for it, and a toddler tucked under the other arm like a wriggling package. "How many more times you gonna make me do this?"

Molly rolled her eyes. "Until everyone's had a chance to visit. And then we'll do it *again*. So get used to it. I'm required to have a Security escort and they assigned you."

"It's bad enough I can't get no peace and quiet in my own home, now I gotta deal with 'em during my work hours, too."

Denton had fallen from grace along with the rest of the Council. Fincher wanted a head of Security that she had control over, and Denton had proven on multiple occasions that he was not a good fit. He'd been reassigned to oversee the defense team—his nerds, as he liked to call them. But because they were better off left to their own devices for the most part, he often ended up taking on smaller assignments to keep busy.

"You don't have a choice," Molly reminded him, eyes sparkling. "Besides, it's a great opportunity to work on your people skills."

"They aren't *people*," Denton retorted.

Ben cringed, fearing that Denton was about to go on one of his old hate-filled rants about Halfsies.

"They're *children*. They're supposed to be seen and not heard. And they're definitely not supposed to be this much–" he grunted as he shifted the child squirming under his arm, "*work*." He set the toddler down and she scurried behind him, clutching a fistful of his pant leg and peering around to stare at Ben.

"I don't know where you got your child-rearing education," Ben said, chuckling, "but if I were you I'd ask for my money back."

He knelt down so that he was level with the children, smiling. "Hey kids. My name's Ben."

"I'm Eloise," one of the children replied in a whisper, still clinging to Molly.

"It's nice to meet you, Eloise." Ben held out his hand. After a glance up at Molly for reassurance, Eloise reciprocated, giving his hand a gentle shake of greeting. "Are you excited to go see your..." he looked up at Molly, too, who mouthed the answer soundlessly. "Mommy?"

Eloise's eyes went wide and she nodded.

"All right, then." Ben stood back up. "Let's get going!"

Despite having no real say over what was happening in Geo, Molly had earned herself a modicum of respect with the new administration because of the initiative she'd shown in getting the restoration project off the ground. She'd used this leverage to convince the CTC that familial visits for the Halfsies in Geo would go a long way toward encouraging good morale. And good morale would make for better workers. Ben spent most of his free time in Geo, one of the only things the CTC hadn't attempted to stop him from doing. The general public still clung to their dis-

trust of the Halfsies, and volunteers to help with the restoration were few and far between. But as long as Ben kept
on top of everything Fincher required of him, she did not
seem to mind how he spent his own time. With the uncertainty surrounding the Theran fleet's whereabouts and the
possibility of more on the way, the CTC's leader seemed
eager to get a victory under her belt. This project was a
relatively attainable means to that end.

The halls were less crowded and the swarm of people
during shift change had dispersed, leaving the long passag-
es empty. The children ran circles around them, darting off
ahead and then back again in fits of excited giggles.

"Can't you stop them doing that?" Denton grumbled
half-heartedly.

"No, and I wouldn't even if I could." Molly's matter-
of-fact tone indicated that the subject was closed, and Ben
was surprised when Denton didn't argue. Somehow this
petite, soft-spoken woman had learned the secret of boss-
ing around the likes of Denton Murphy, the mighty security guard. Ben wasn't sure how such a thing was possible,
but he certainly respected her for it.

They came to the secret lift at the end of the hall, spark-
ing shouts of delight from the children as the solid wall slid
away. When it shuddered and began to move there were
more exclamations, this time of alarm. The toddler darted
in front of Ben, smacking the control panel to express his
disapproval.

The children wrinkled their noses as the party drew

closer to the plant's entrance. The ventilation system had been restored to near completion, but the smell still lingered. Ben didn't notice it much anymore, but he imagined that the Halfsies, with their keener senses, found it more disagreeable than he did. Still, once they were inside the little noses unwrinkled, replaced by expressions of exquisite joy. Their parents were waiting for them just inside, scooping up their respective offspring into eager, loving arms. He lingered back from the group with Denton, who looked as uncomfortable as Ben felt. Trespassing on a private moment like this made Ben wish he were just about anywhere else instead. He distracted himself by moving further into the plant, taking in all the progress they'd made so far.

It was a long way from finished, but the ventilation alone had made a world of difference. He could see clear to the floor of the main room, while before it had been shrouded in a thick, steamy haze. All around him, teams of Halfsies were hard at work replacing pipes, scrubbing ducts, and taking notes. The general atmosphere of the place had improved as well; when they'd first begun, the Halfsies had seemed defeated and broken. They went through the motions without any actual motivation. Now they looked as though they'd rekindled a sense of purpose. A few of them were even smiling or laughing with a companion. This dark hole beneath the city had gone from a torturous prison to just another work assignment—so long as you ignored the fact that they were not allowed to leave.

There was a blur of motion to his right as Ripley

dropped from a catwalk above, landing neatly beside him. "Hey Ben!" his friend greeted him. His mismatched eyes sparkled. "Denton."

Denton was glaring at him with apparent disgust. "Quit acting like such a freak. Jumping around and climbing like a monkey. You're as bad as them kids." He hooked a thumb back toward the entrance, and Ben glanced that way too. Molly had stopped her conversation long enough to wave, and Ripley waved back.

"You're in an awfully good mood." Ben couldn't help but notice the way Ripley's wave was accompanied by an almost shy smile.

"Well, it's not so bad down here." Ripley's gaze lingered on Molly a moment more. "Things are predictable, the people are nice, and I get to spend all day fixing stuff." He shrugged, a cringe flashing across his face but passing quickly.. "It could be worse."

Denton scoffed. "Yeah, sounds like a real great time."

Ripley responded with a grin. "At least I don't have to stare at your ugly mug all day anymore."

"I could say the same." Denton seemed ready to continue arguing but Ben interjected, raising a hand to stop them.

"As much as I'm sure you'd both like to catch up, there are a couple of things I wanted to talk to Ripley about while we're here." Ben tried to lean casually against the railing, but it groaned at the weight and he straightened back up, heart racing. He brushed at his sleeve, trying to remember what he'd been about to say before the thought of falling off the walkway had stolen his train of thought.

Ripley's grin faded, his expression going serious. "Sure," he said. "What's up?"

"Well, it's like this," Ben began, trying to order the thoughts that had been bouncing around his head in between everything else he needed to do. "I keep thinking about what…what Onyx told us. How the ships that came through are only the first wave."

"Yeah." Ripley leaned against the railing, raising his face skyward. "I've been thinking about that too."

"We've got some measures in place," Ben said. "Your idea about setting up a microphone system on either side of the Gate went over really well with the CTC. I was able to program it to alert us if it picks up any of the frequencies we recorded when the first ships came through. So we'll have at least a tiny bit of warning. The range isn't fantastic, but it's a lot better than nothing."

"What about the domes? Is everyone still walking around in the dark up there?"

Ben nodded. "Most of the time. We kept them completely off as long as it took to find a way to connect the early warning system to the lights. Definitely could have used your help with that part, buddy. Tricky business. But the CTC didn't trust you not to put up a fight if they let you out to assist. Anyway, I figured it out eventually. Now if we detect incoming ships, the alarm should trigger the domes to dim automatically. The only problem is, we aren't really able to test it until it's the real deal, and that's a big risk. So for now we've shortened the daylight hours to six as an extra precaution." He sighed. "No one is happy about it, but most people understand."

The three of them moved aside to allow the reunited parents and children to pass. The kids seemed eager to see the place in which their parents had been imprisoned, and to say hello to the others. The Halfsies had always been a tightly-knit community, united by the disdain shown them by the rest of society. Ben felt sure that everyone in here had known everyone else long before they'd been forced down to Geo. It was more like one giant family than a group of neighbors. The parents seemed almost as eager as the children; perhaps hoping to give the kids some comfort by showing them that this life wasn't so horrible. He wondered what they were telling the poor kids and hoped that the visit wouldn't do more harm than good.

Ben worried, not for the first time, that if nothing changed these families may never be reunited on a permanent basis. Fincher seemed all for improving conditions but had made no move to discuss plans to release the Halfsies from imprisonment. Maybe Reclamation Day was just too recent, the wounds inflicted by the Elves too fresh. Ben could only hope that the discussion would eventually take place.

Ripley continued once they'd passed. "What happens if the system *is* tripped? Is there a plan in place to prevent panic?"

"Yeah, Sylvia's got that covered. She's got a whole team of people who've been out canvasing the domes, handing out flyers and giving demonstrations on how to deal with a sudden blackout. I mean, as long as people are close enough to get to a light switch it shouldn't be a big deal. Just disconcerting for anyone caught out in the streets at the time, I imagine. School-aged children have all been assigned a buddy, so that none of them will be caught alone in the dark. Overall, people are taking it really well." He shrugged. "I mean, what choice do they have, really?"

Ripley was nodding thoughtfully. "Seems like you've got things pretty well in hand." Ben thought he sounded rather impressed. "I just wish I could be more help to you."

"Actually, I think you can." He shot Ripley a mischievous grin. "See, here's the thing. The Agridome requires a certain amount of light to grow the food, right? Six hours a day won't cut it. They can manage for a while, but not for long, and certainly not indefinitely. If we don't figure something out, we'll be facing a food crisis worse than any we've faced in the past."

Ripley was shaking his head with regret. "I'm sorry, Ben, but I don't know anything about growing food. Maybe someone who actually works *in* the Agridome could—"

"No, you misunderstand. I don't want your help finding a way for Agriculture to deal with less light." He cast a conspiratorial glance around before leaning in close to Ripley. "I want your help finding a way to make it so that we don't have to worry about turning off the lights *at all.*"

Ripley's raised eyebrows showed Ben that he wasn't quite following. "I don't get it. Do you want help testing the early warning system? Someone to go through and trigger the alarm from the other side, see if it's working?"

"No." Ben shook his head. "I want to get rid of it."

"The warning system?"

"No! Are you daft?" Ben gave Ripley a frustrated look, wondering how his meaning could be anything less than obvious. "The *Gate*, Ripley."

There it was. Ripley's expression transformed to one of understanding and Denton, who had leaned in to hear what was happening, whistled.

"You want to…" Ripley's voice trailed off.

"Yeah," Ben replied, drawing himself up to his full height as excitement overtook him. "I want to cut off Nero's forces once and for all. I think it's time we found a way to destroy Antiquity's Gate."

Chapter Three

Across the Sea

TOBIAS GROANED. "I think every muscle in my body has forsaken me." He reached up to massage his shoulder. "I never realized how exhausting flying a ship could be."

"It's actually quite relaxing, when no one is trying to kill you." Penelope made a move to sit, but Felix rested a firm hand on her uninjured arm. "Oh, come on Felix, just let me take her in. Toby isn't great at docking, you know that."

"You just took a face full of shrapnel. You're lucky you didn't lose an eye. Not to mention your side...you're not piloting anything until we have you looked at by someone who knows what they're doing."

Penelope squinted up at him, her lips forming a tight line beneath narrowed eyes. "Is it really that bad?"

Felix looked her over before nodding smartly. His heart was still pounding, but the fear of the experience was beginning to fade. She would be okay.

Still, it had been a close call. Too close. "Seriously. You're a mess. Just lay down. I'm sure Toby can handle it this once. Besides, he needs the practice."

Toby snorted, but didn't turn. "I can hear you, you know."

The little girl hadn't spoken a word since boarding the ship. She came up alongside Felix and stared at Penelope with hollow eyes. Felix felt a lump rising in his throat as he took in her appearance. Physically, she was dirty but otherwise unharmed. Emotionally…he could not begin to fathom what she was going through. It was a struggle to look at her and see anything but his own children, imagine any scenario where things were going to be all right, for any of them.

"Hey." He forced his mouth into a warm smile. "Would you mind keeping an eye on Penny for me, while I go see if Toby needs a hand? Can you make sure she stays here?"

The girl did not acknowledge him, still staring at Penelope. After a long moment, she slipped her hand into Penny's, and Felix took that as acceptance.

He slid into the pilot's chair. It felt strange, being in the cockpit. "Should I…press anything?"

Tobias raised an eyebrow. "Probably best if you didn't."

He leaned in front of Felix to flip a small toggle from *on* to *off*, then spun a dial from orange to slightly less orange. "We're almost at the rendezvous point. I believe my training in docking protocol, while not mastery by any means, should be sufficient."

Felix let his eyes wander to the sky outside, scanning the horizon for some sign of the *Timeless*. "We crossed a line this time, Toby." He lowered his voice, glancing back into the hold. "We could have lost her."

"Technically, we could have *all* been lost," Tobias pointed out. "We've discussed the risk of what we're doing, and we all agreed it was acceptable. We're needed in this fight. Though, if you recall, I did say that this was a bad idea."

"No, you said it wasn't a good idea. There's a difference."

"I don't think—"

"The thing is," interrupted Felix, "General Hall was pretty explicit. We aren't supposed to *be* in any fights. We're to assist in humanitarian aid and evacuation. We've been toeing the line the whole time, but this…this was a mess. Plain and simple."

Tobias' eyes flickered in his direction before refocusing on the course ahead. Felix scowled.

"What?"

"Nothing." Tobias attempted what might have been a casual shrug. "It's just that the Felix I've grown accustomed to has never had much of a problem with bending a few rules now and again."

"Yeah, well," Felix retorted, tensing, "maybe the Felix

you know has grown up a little. Seen a few things." He glared out at the setting sun. "Learned one too many lessons the hard way."

The clouds parted and a massive dirigible came into view. Tobias opted to ignore Felix's reply, hailing the *Timeless* instead. The sight of it was almost serene, cloaked in the pinks and purples of sunset, nestled in the clouds. Little ships flitted around it like bees carrying supplies to the hive.

There were precious few Cumulous class vessels left, and the *Timeless* was packed to the brim with troops and attack ships. Though she herself carried an impressive armament, the warship was no match for Nero's smaller, faster fleet. Designed for combating ground troops in a world where the Pravacordians were the sole nation with airships, it was never meant to outmaneuver enemies in the air.

General Hall instead commanded the ship as a rallying point, keeping well away from the actual fighting. Felix knew that was hard on him. The general was the type to lead the charge...not to sit behind the scenes and wait for news from the front lines. This was a new type of war, something the fledgling nation had never dealt with before. The steep learning curve had left them at a clear disadvantage. What had begun as a hope for a swift victory had dissolved to little more than a desperate will to survive.

Meanwhile the Culeians were doing their best to atone for their own actions, many working to evacuate the same coastal towns that they themselves had threatened not long ago.

The tides of war had changed everything. Nero was systematically destroying the Pravacordian way of life, and there was very little that the Alliance could do to stop the growing body count.

Felix watched their approach, marvelling anew at the ingenuity behind creating such an incredible vessel. In terms of pure volume, the *Timeless* could easily hold a hundred ships the size of the *Wilks*. Something like two hundred crewmembers staffed its interior, once again boggling Felix's ability to understand how it managed to stay in the air. No matter how large the balloon-like structure that held it up, it still seemed to defy the laws of gravity. Such a hulking amalgamation of metal had no business being airworthy, all sleek and glinting in the sun and impossibly long.

He smiled. Perhaps this was the kind of reticence that Ambassador Bohai was always feeling when faced with the possibility of flight.

Felix cringed in anticipation as Tobias eased the *Wilks* into the already crowded aft docking bay. Everything on the *Timeless* was made for efficiency, and the bay was no different. The outer door retracted neatly into the hull below at their approach, and Felix ducked instinctively as they narrowly avoided scraping the top of the *Wilks* against the low ceiling. A row of slumbering Chronohawks parked impossibly close together were tucked in at the far end, facing the opposite wall where an identical bay door allowed them to exit without having to turn the ships around. Numerous older models flanked them to either side and in several neat rows behind. Tobias lacked Penelope or Ambrose's experience, but he managed all right in the end, squeezing in between two boxy popos.

"There!" Toby exclaimed. "That wasn't nearly as difficult as I'd expected it to be."

Felix clapped him on the shoulder before moving back into the hold and helping Penny to her feet. She put her chin to her chest to look down at herself, nose crinkling at the sight, or perhaps at the sharp pain that accompanied the movement.

"Let's get you cleaned up."

"Yeah." Her grimace deepened. "I'm glad Bastian isn't here to see me like this."

Felix's grip on her waist tightened, the statement bringing a pang of longing for his own family.

Medical personnel were standing by, moving from ship to ship throughout the hold, assessing injuries. Felix gave one of them a brief rundown of Penelope's escapades before turning to find crewman Bartholomew, stone-faced and silent, standing behind him.

"The General has asked me to escort you to his quarters."

"Sure." Felix chuckled nervously. "Am I in some kind of trouble?"

Barty didn't answer. He pivoted on his heel and marched stiffly toward the interior of the ship.

Despite their many interactions in the past, there was

something about the crewman that gave Felix pause. He wondered if Barty was so formal and aloof with everyone, just doing his job…or if he simply didn't like him. It was difficult to say.

Felix glanced over his shoulder at Toby, who raised an eyebrow and shrugged. Then he followed the crewman into the complicated series of tight passageways that made navigating the *Timeless* so tricky…at least for Felix. It was a bit like the old days, trying to make his way to Pod Manufacturing back in Sanctuary. At least those halls had been wide, with high ceilings. Ironic, really, that he would feel less claustrophobic under the ground than in the wide open sky. He did, at least, recognize the entrance to General Hall's quarters. It might have been that he recalled the distinctive three way intersection that converged just outside the hatchway…or it might have been the plaque secured to the wall that said "Captain's Quarters." He nodded his gratitude to an emotionless Barty as he stepped inside.

"Mr. Felix." The General greeted him brusquely without looking up from his desk. "Thank you for joining me. I'll be with you momentarily."

"No problem." Felix took a step toward the chair, hesitated, then opted to remain standing. The room had been different the last time he'd visited. Most of the knicknacks had disappeared from the desk, and the opulent bed replaced by a cot not unlike those found in the brig. Gone were the fancy tapestries that had adorned the wall, replaced by an enormous map speckled with colored pins.

Pravacordia was thick with red ones.

At last Hall set the pen down, leaning back in his chair with a heavy sigh. He gestured.

"Forgive me, just finishing up a report on our latest encounters. Please, have a seat my friend."

"Thanks." Felix slid into the second chair, more at ease now. "What was it you wanted to see me about?"

"We're being recalled. The heads of state wish to be apprised of the current situation, and what is being done to remedy it."

This took Felix by surprise. He leaned forward, squinting, uncertain if he'd actually understood. "They're recalling the *Timeless*? But the threat here hasn't been eliminated, how could they call us back now?"

Hall pushed his chair back from the desk and stood facing the map, hands clasped behind his back. "The threat will not ever be eliminated at this rate," he said grimly. "The Pravacordian military complex is faltering. This is an enemy we were not equipped to fight."

"So we're retreating? We can't just lay down and die," protested Felix, rising to join the general. His eyes roved over the map as if it might hold the key to victory somewhere between all those crimson dots. In his peripheral vision he saw the way Hall bristled at the suggestion.

"Of course not. Surrender is not an option. The reason we're being recalled, besides the debriefing, is that your team has come up with what they believe to be a viable strategy. I hope, for all our sakes, that this is true. You'll be presenting this new option at a formal meeting of the Alliance members."

My team. No matter how often Felix's friends had been referred to in this way, the words still seemed an awkward fit. "But I don't even know what my team is up to. They've been working on ideas and I've been here, with you. Wouldn't Ambrose be a better choice for this kind of thing?"

Hall said nothing for a moment, gazing at the map intently. Then he nodded back toward the desk, and Felix retook his seat. After a while Hall leaned forward, resting his elbows on the lacquered mahogany surface as he offered a weak smile. "When I am called away from the *Timeless* and then later return, am I no longer her commanding officer? Do those I trust in my stead still recognize my authority?"

"Of course, but—"

"You do yourself and your friends a disservice when you question your own ability to lead. Do not sell yourself short. In war, there isn't time for second guesses. You must own your decisions, take responsibility for every outcome. You are a leader, Felix. There's no weaseling your way out of it. So far, I believe you've been a good one. Don't make me change my mind."

It was Felix's turn to bristle. "I'm not trying to weasel out of anything!" He snatched up a compass from Hall's desk, turning it over and over in his hands. "I just thought that it seems like a bad idea to recall the *Timeless* just so I can go give a room full of bureaucrats a second-hand report on work Ambrose and Baba are leading. I feel like I could be of more use here."

Hall plucked the compass from his grasp and set it delicately back in its place. "Do you think the Culeian monarch spends much time in scientific labs, mixing chemicals and designing weaponry?"

"No," Felix admitted with a shrug. "But that's different. Isn't it?"

"She is a leader. She was chosen to direct and guide those she leads, not to do everything *for* them. They look to her as the unification of their efforts, the embodiment of everything they believe in. She is a symbol of hope and comfort and, despite her tender age, wisdom. She is not involved in every detail, nor would any of her people expect her to be. That is not the role of the leader."

"So…" Felix's nose crinkled as he tried to dissect the general's musings, "you're saying that I am…hope and comfort?"

Hall chuckled. "In a manner of speaking. Regardless, none of that matters. The *Timeless* is being recalled, our compliment intact, in order to hold it in reserve."

"In reserve for what?"

"To assist with *your* plan. If it pans out, that is. I look forward to your presentation. If Ambrose has truly had a breakthrough, it may be just what we need to turn the tide of this war. We are to be your support in any way necessary."

Felix shook his head. "All of that soul-searching rambling just to tell me you had to go either way. Unbelievable."

General Hall rose from his chair and moved around the desk to rest a hand on Felix's shoulder. "I'm going to be candid with you, leader to leader. Your friends chose you to lead them because they have faith in your abilities. I think that you sometimes lack that faith. And that's normal. What I want you to understand is that, even when you question yourself, it is crucial that you stay strong. For them. Because that is what gives *them* strength. Do you understand?"

Felix pondered it for a long moment, then gave a slow nod. "Yeah. I think I do." General Hall raised an eyebrow. "Fine. Fine. I do. Better?"

A wink. "You're learning." The general gestured to the door. "Would you accompany me to the bridge?"

Felix's heart fluttered. His mind drifted toward the warmth of being reunited with Willow and the twins. It was sooner than he'd dared to hope, but the excitement faded as quickly as it had sprung up. There was so much to do.

"I think I'd better go find Toby and Penny, let them know what's happening."

"Good. Now you're thinking like a leader."

Felix hesitated on the threshold. "Speaking of which…"

Hall offered an exaggerated sigh. "You need someone to show you to the infirmary?"

"Hey," Felix raised his hands defensively. "I'm a leader, not a field guide. This ship is convoluted."

"There you go insulting my ship again." Hall opened

the door and gestured to Barty, who was lingering just outside. "You know, if you can make yourself half the pain in the backside for the Therans as you have been to me, I'd say we've got a fighting chance."

*   *   *

FELIX HAD ONLY JUST begun to consider Pravacordia his home before they had been forced to flee. Now Babaneau Ganoush's estate was the closest thing he could lay claim to, the feeling of being a stranger in a foreign land as fresh as the day he'd left Sanctuary. But, stranger or not, General Hall's words echoed in his mind over and over again. His team was composed of Therans, Pravacordians, and former citizens of Sanctuary. They were all strangers here, and they were all looking to him. He would do his best not to disappoint them.

Penelope and Tobias had departed from the *Timeless* before reaching the city. The *Wilks* had taken some minor damage, and Penelope had said she'd wanted to get a head start on the repairs. Felix had stayed behind to continue his discussions with General Hall, but once the *Timeless* reached the port they'd parted ways. He'd offered to find his own way home, but Hall had insisted on an escort. Now Felix found himself in the gunner's seat of a Chronohawk behind a stalwart pilot who wasn't much for conversation.

He'd never actually been in a Chronohawk before, but secretly decided that they were best admired from the outside. With room for only two people, one pilot and one trained on the weapons, it was cramped and awkward. He missed the ability to move around the ship, and fidgeted in his chair as the minutes ticked slowly by. He didn't know where to put his hands; the entire console in front of him was covered in ominous controls, red buttons, and flashing lights. Which of these might he accidently trigger, firing who knows what at who knows where?

To distract himself he tilted his head back, gazing out through the curved glass enclosure that encased the two of them. He was a bit taller than the ship was designed for, it seemed. His breath condensed on the glass, causing a circle of fog that blurred his view of the sky. He wiped it away, but it kept returning. Sighing, Felix closed his eyes for a while.

When they'd first come to Oldetown after Atmos fell, he had not had high expectations. It did, after all, have 'old' right in the name.

But the capital city of Nequiem had surprised him. Felix must have dozed off, but woke as he felt the Chronohawk dip lower. He looked out over the landscape as the city came into view.

In the vacuum left by the Sequencing, the Nequienite people had not been as frantic to become a military power as Pravacordia and Culei had. Instead they'd placed their focus into the preservation of those things which had come before. This city, their pride and joy, consisted of many pre-Sequencing era buildings, painstakingly restored and interspersed with newer buildings. They were such good replicas that the differences were imperceptible at first glance. Towering high into the air, glass and steel reflected the sun in a blinding display. Several of them featured airship docks similar to those in Atmos, presumably for visitors from across the sea, but most were just sleek, unblemished behemoths.

One side of the city bordered a river, shorter buildings butting up against its shores for miles. He imagined that in times past it would have been dotted with trading ships and small sailing vessels. Now it was clogged with Culeian submarines and warships that seemed much too large and out of place. Part of their agreement in the Alliance was to bulk up the defenses of this peaceful nation, for whatever good that was worth.

All around the rest of the city, fields of crops stretched out as far as the eye could see. They were arranged into huge rectangles separated by strips of brown dirt road. The most plentiful seemed to be wheat, the golden heads swaying gently in unison, like quiet pools of amber liquid. Harvesting equipment dotted the landscape, tiny mechanical islands rising up from the sea of crops.

An involuntary shudder travelled up his spine at the thought of what it would look like if Nero was allowed to get this far. The fields would burn bright and fast, black smoke blotting out the neon lights that plastered the city in colors so vivid that they flickered beneath his eyelids in the night.

The streets below were just as cheerful as the lights. Well-tended, unlike their Pravacordian counterparts, they were alive with a constant stream of ground vehicles. Just now the morning traffic gleamed as they passed overhead, each glinting vehicle a blinding flash. At night they transformed into streams of glowing insects, speeding along and leaving trails of light in their wake. Where they were going, or where they had come from, he knew not.

He only knew that if they could not find a way to win this war, all of this would be gone.

"Almost there." The pilot's declaration in Felix's headset was loud, saturated by static. "I'll be setting down as near to your destination as possible, but it'll be a bit of a walk still. Oldetown wasn't built for aircraft, options are limited."

"That's fine." Felix attempted a stretch, but the cockpit was too confined. "I could use a little fresh air, anyway."

*　　*　　*

BABA'S ESTATE RESTED AT the edge of the city, bordering the fields. Eighteen stories above the ground, his expansive home in one of the skyscrapers boasted an impressive three-hundred-sixty-degree view of the surroundings, evidence that his "spare parts" business was much more lucrative than Ambrose had first let on.

Felix stood on the balcony of Baba 's home, arms wrapped around Willow's waist, the sound of the river barely audible over the din of the busy streets far below.

"What's the matter?" Her cheek rested lightly on his chest. "You're very quiet."

"Just thinking about the meeting with the Alliance, and how much I really don't want to go."

Willow looked up at him, the lights of a neighboring tower reflecting in her eyes as she offered one of her gentle smiles. "It's not really about what you want, my love. This meeting is more important than that."

"I know that." Felix squeezed her tighter. "And I'll do what needs to be done. But sometimes even a great leader needs a confidante to confess his fears to, right?"

Willow's laughter was soft, almost snatched away by the wind to be swallowed up in the cacophony of the city's voice. "And that falls to me?"

He nodded. "Do you accept the position, and all that it entails?"

"I suppose." Willow feigned an exasperated sigh. "Don't worry, my love. You can always come to me. I won't let you down." Her smile dimmed. "I wish you didn't have to leave again so soon, though. I wish you didn't ever have to leave at all."

She turned back to look out over the city, and Felix rested his chin gently on the crown of her head. "It won't be a long meeting. I'll be back in time for supper. A part of me is glad, you know. That you're here, with the children, safe. But the rest of me hates when we're apart. You know, it's funny, isn't it? You and Ripley...I was used to being the one following. You're smarter. Wiser, more patient...every good thing I lack. I guess the old adage about how opposites attract is true."

She turned within the circle of his arms to face him. "You never lacked the skills, Felix, you just...lacked motivation. Those traits might be harder for you to embrace, but they were always there. You just didn't feel the need to exercise them. But you're certainly getting it now. It shows, too. You've grown. And as far as our safety, Felix, don't cling to that. Safety here, it's an illusion."

She tilted her head, indicating the streets below. "The Alliance soldiers don't patrol the city because we're safe. They do so because we are not. My father's war will be here soon enough. He may not be seeking us out specifically, but still...it feels as though he's still chasing us. We ran from Sanctuary, we ran from Pravacordia. Where will we hide when there is nowhere left to run?"

Taking both of her hands in his, Felix gripped tightly, never wanting to let go. "I'm done running."

Willow's lip turned up at the corner, ever so slightly. "You see?"

"See what?"

She shook her head. "Never mind. You'll go to meet with the Alliance?"

Felix made an irritated sound in the back of his throat. "Fine."

Willow pressed. "Not exactly comforting."

He leaned in, kissing her softly as her hair whispered against his face. "How's that?"

"Better. Come on, Waldo's probably done with his bed-time story by now."

Felix groaned. "You *know* how I feel about Waldo. That thing weirds me out."

Fingers intertwined, they stepped back inside of Baba's home.

Penelope, half her face swathed in gauze that disappeared beneath her braid and wrapped back around like a gaudy headband, sat cross-legged in the midst of the expansive living area. Along the vaulted ceiling, warm lighting ran on tracks, flooding the room and casting long shadows across the plush carpet that dominated the floor. She was rummaging through a ragged-edged box for something while Sebastian worked with quiet persistence to unscrew two small metal disks. His tongue peeked out of the side of his mouth, indicating the high level of concentration he had devoted to the task at hand.

One side of the room was composed of a brick wall, a huge electric fireplace nestled in the center, and a doorway leading to the living quarters and exit tucked off to one side. But the other three walls all featured floor-to-ceiling glass. Despite their height and the lack of insulation, the room was always pleasantly warm. If Felix hadn't gotten so used to being constantly uprooted, he thought it might be easy to settle into a place like this. It was large, but not intimidating. Industrial, but not lacking in warmth. It felt homey. Comforting.

"Too late, that's that, no turning back! The sea rose up to

eat them."

The strange refrain, chanted in a sing-song, mechanical voice, caught his ear. He turned toward the sound, which came from just out of sight behind the makeshift playpen that had accompanied Felix's children on every grand adventure they'd been a part of in their short lives so far. He could make out tiny feet between the wooden slats, kicking softly against the quilt as the twins lay listening in rapt attention.

"Waldo, what on Earth are you reciting to my children?" Felix felt as though he should be outraged but lacked the energy to muster up much in the way of indignation. "You're going to give them nightmares!"

The mechanical marvel that was Waldo tilted its head to one side, gears clicking and whirring.

Three feet tall and comprised of what looked like parts scavenged from the wreckage of an airship battle, Waldo was Baba's pet project. Constructed with post-Sequencing materials but imbued with an AI interface from pre-Sequencing times, the quirky little bot seemed to have taken a shining to Sebastian and the twins. Sebastian, in turn, had taken a shining to tugging playfully on the long springs attached to Waldo's head in a sad approximation of hair. He liked the way they tinkled, like a wind chime in a soft breeze.

"It is a traditional Pravacordian nursery rhyme." Waldo's hollow voice was matter-of-fact. "In the current geopolitical climate, it is important for young citizens of

Pravacordia to have a firm understanding of their heritage."

"They aren't Pravacordian citizens," Felix retorted. "Pravacordia didn't want their kind."

Waldo's head wobbled dangerously as he regarded Felix, his optical sensors opening and closing in a simulated blink. "They were born in Pravacordia. By the law of the land, they are therefore Pravacordian citizens, with all the rights, privileges, and duties afforded thereto."

Felix opened his mouth just as a new figure appeared in the doorway.

Kestrel surveyed the situation as she entered and raised an eyebrow. "Arguing with the tools again, Felix?"

"I am not a tool!" For a machine, Waldo had mastered a fair approximation of indignation. "I am an artificially intelligent being, programmed to—"

"Yeah, yeah, whatever," Kestrel replied, her shrug nonchalant. She focused on Felix again. "They sent me to get you. They aren't ready to call it a night just yet, they want to show you what we've been up to."

Felix cast a wary glance at Waldo and the twins, and Willow raised a knowing eyebrow. "I'll stay with the kids. Why don't you and Penelope both go?"

"Nah." Penelope didn't even look up. "I'll stay, too. I'm sure I'll get a thorough rundown over dinner. And I'm still pretty sore." She did not need to add that she had only just been reunited with her son and was not inclined to leave him again so soon, even if just for a couple of hours.

Felix glanced around, expecting to see someone else.

"Where'd Toby get off to?"

"Running errands in the city," replied Penelope. "He'll be back later, no sense waiting for him."

"Well then," Felix shrugged, "guess it's just you and me, Kestrel."

He followed the Theran out into the long hall, her long silvery hair a glimmering moonbeam beneath the track lighting. She led him past the series of doors that passed bedrooms and bathrooms and all sorts of other rooms that Felix had yet to explore, stopping only when she came to the very end of the hall. She pressed a small button that glowed yellow, summoning the elevator to their level. When it reached them, she stepped in without a second thought, but the elevator always made Felix a little nervous.

The lifts in Sanctuary hadn't had so much as a window, and it was easy to forget that they were suspended above a deep, dark shaft. But this...this was something different entirely. It was nothing more than a glass box with a metal frame, looking out over the cityscape from eighteen stories above the ground. The ride was smooth and quiet, the elevator whispering down the side of the building as his stomach made a concerted effort to climb into his throat.

"So, where are they working today?" Felix was doing his best to focus on Kestrel instead of the blurred streaks of light outside. They slowed, coming to a gentle stop, and Kestrel spoke over her shoulder as she strode out into the street.

"North warehouse."

"Is that the one with all the corn?"

"Wheat."

"Ah."

Felix stepped aside to let a pair of Culeian soldiers pass. They didn't spare him a second glance—Elves and Halfsies streaming to and fro from Baba's residence had become a common sight for most of the folks around here, though occasionally a new guard would give them a hard time.

Kestrel seemed unfazed by the people they passed, completely at ease. Out of the half-dozen Therans who had climbed out of Gavin's ship the night Atmos was destroyed, she was the only one who seemed able to take everything about Earth in stride. She always appeared relaxed, completely confident in who she was and where she was heading. Felix wished he had half of her composure. He was just the opposite most days—struggling to maintain the appearance of calm while every fiber of his being screamed that he didn't belong here. And he'd had more than six months to get used to this world, whereas she had only just arrived. Was that the difference between them? Was it not confidence, but ignorance, that let her walk so freely among a people who were threatened her very existence?

No, it was more than that. Kestrel had grown up on Thera, not in Sanctuary. She would have no reason to understand the deeply held prejudices that existed here.

Not like Felix did. Still, he could not let his insecurities get the best of him. There was a lot of work to be done, and a lot of people counting on him. It didn't matter how many times he had to remind himself of that—he wouldn't let them down. He couldn't.

The sidewalk led to a wide, busy street where a squat vehicle sat idling. It made no pretense, and had certainly never won any beauty contests. Boxy, like a popo, but all sharp edges and windows. The side doors were plagued by rust that was creeping up from the undercarriage, but the inside looked clean and cared for.

"I asked him to wait for us," she explained. "Flagging down a ride with these eyes isn't exactly easy, you know?"

Maybe she had been paying attention after all. Felix climbed into the back seat while she slipped into the front. "Not sure why you'd expect anything else."

"I guess I just figured they'd know we're working with the good guys by now." She shrugged as she turned to the driver. "Thanks for waiting. Back the way we came, please."

The engine roared to life, a gutteral sound akin to anguish. It remained loud, but not intolerably so, as they drove.

Now *this* was the way to travel. Felix had been in a dozen different types of automobiles since arriving in Nequiem, and none had been anything short of miraculous. No trekking for miles on foot, no crowded underground Tube, no flying, no crashing. They were even better than the Floaters on Thera, because their wheels were firmly planted to the ground. Felix especially enjoyed the *thrum* of the engine and the grinding of rubber over pavement and gravel. It felt solid, dependable. The bucket seats were comfortable, their pale gray fabric worn in places from years of use. He didn't mind the wear. It showed that the beast had been around a while. It was old and reliable and safe.

"Hey," Kestrel whispered, leaning close to him. "Have you…have you listened to their music?"

"What? No. Haven't really had the chance."

"Excuse me?" Kestrel grabbed the back of the driver's seat, bringing her head up next to his. "Would it be okay to turn on some music?"

"Sure." He reached over and depressed a round black button, and the melodious strains of some sort of stringed instrument flooded the vehicle, competing with the growling of the engine.

Kestrel appeared to be watching him for a reaction, but music had never been a passion of his. He tried to think of something to remark on, but came up empty. "It's nice, I guess."

She grinned. "I think it's fantastic. Wait until you hear jazz. Baba's got a whole shelf of pre-Sequencing data chips that are just full of all kinds of different music. Waldo knows how to play them."

Felix grimaced. "Great. Just what I was hoping for, the chance to spend more time with Waldo."

They made steady progress through the city traffic. Once they reached the fields, theirs was the only vehicle on the road. It wasn't as well-tended as those within the city limits, but Felix could not complain. It was a long walk to Baba's other properties. He was keenly aware of that, since they'd been unable to secure a ride on several previous occasions.

Set miles away from Oldetown, Baba's workshops and warehouses popped out of the colorful crops like giant boulders. A huge glowing sign was the first indication that they were closing in, Baba's attempt at bringing a little of the city life to his humbler workplace. It flickered weakly, several letters having gone out. It was supposed to read *Ganoush Antique & Sundry*, but now it said *Ga oush Anti undry*. Beneath the lit sign, a large banner declared, *No matter who found it where, we can fix it here!*

The driver drew to a stop, took the money from Kestrel's outstretched hand, and offered a wordless nod before pulling away, leaving them in front of the nearest building.

"Come on." She waved vaguely out across the field. "They're way out back."

They cut through the first warehouse. This place was not unlike Ambrose's workshop at home, except that instead of airships, it was filled with a wider variety of items, stacked on huge metal shelves that rose to the vaulted ceilings.

There were crates of bits and bobs like the one Sebastian and Penelope had been playing with sitting beside massive engine components that looked as though they might belong to the *Timeless*. There were propellers, wheels, gears, and all manner of tools.

It hadn't taken Felix long to see why Ambrose and Baba got along so well. They seemed to have quite a bit in common.

Felix followed as Kestrel exited through the back of the building, now walking along a path of trodden wheat. They hadn't spoken much on the trip. He felt like he should say something, so he just went with the first question that came to mind.

"How's Gavin holding up?"

"Hard to say," she replied, stretching her arm out to skim the tops of the plants with her fingertips, leaving the wheat swaying gently in her wake. "You know he's not much of a feelings guy."

"Yeah, I know. I just...I'm sure it's hard for him. Thrust into someone else's war and losing his mentor all at the same time."

"The Weaver was more than a mentor." Kestrel's voice was soft, barely audible. "He was like a father to Gavin. To all of us, really. When he vanished, we wanted to go back for him. It was so bizarre. One second we're on Thera and he's there...the next we're on Earth and he's just...gone. Like he jumped out of the ship without anyone noticing."

"You think that's what happened?"

Her nose wrinkled. "No. There wasn't time. He just disappeared." Kestrel shook her head in frustration, her silvery hair shifting back and forth like liquid. "But Gavin said we couldn't leave the fleet. It would give us away, take the only advantage we had. He said the Weaver would have wanted us to complete the mission. That humanity meant more to him than his own safety. And we all knew it was true. But that didn't make it any easier. It might have been what the Weaver would have wanted, but he would have never left one of *us* behind."

And yet here you are. "That must have been a hard call," he offered. "Continuing the mission with your leader gone."

Kestrel shrugged. "It wasn't my call to make."

"So it was Gavin's decision, right?"

"Yes."

"Why?"

"Why what?"

"Why was it Gavin's decision? What if everyone else had wanted to turn back, look for the Weaver?"

She stopped walking to look at him, appearing confused by the question. "Because Gavin's in charge when the Weaver's not around."

Felix didn't know what answer he was looking for, but this wasn't it. "But *why?*" he pressed. "Why is Gavin in charge? Who decided he would be the leader? What makes him qualified?" On his one and only trip to Thera, Felix and Gavin had gone to the Weaver for help. Gavin had made it very clear that he wanted no part in Tapestry, that he was done with that life. So what had changed?

Kestrel sighed. "Listen," she told him earnestly, "a lot has happened on Thera. It's complicated. But what I can tell you is this; Gavin's made some bad choices in his life, just like anyone else. But the fact remains that Tapestry was virtually useless after the Weaver disappeared and Gavin resigned himself to life in Solara. We tried to go on, but without a leader, it was difficult to rally the troops. We were scattered, disjointed, cut off from one another. But when the Weaver was captured, Gavin stepped up. He knew it was the right thing to do."

"Yes, but from what I've been told, his plan was a failure."

"That's not the point."

"Then what is?"

Kestrel glared suspiciously at him, stepping closer. "What is it you want to hear, exactly?"

Felix wasn't entirely sure himself. His words had tumbled out even as he struggled to understand why he was arguing about it in the first place. Gavin always seemed so stoic, unfazed. Maybe what Felix really wanted to know was if the older Theran struggled, as he did, with the position he'd been thrust into. Gavin seemed an unlikely leader in the same way that Felix felt like one. Maybe there was some correlation, something that could help him understand why people turned to him, rather than someone else. But all he said was, "I just want to know why you'd choose to follow someone who turned his back on the cause. And when he changed his mind, he still couldn't get things right."

"Don't say that. Don't talk about him that way." Kestrel's eyes flashed with an angry light. "Yeah, he screwed up. He rushed in when he should have waited. But the fact remains that when we needed a leader most, he was there. And that was a painful lesson for him, I'm sure. But he didn't slink off into the shadows to lick his wounds. He's loyal, and passionate. That passion got him into a mess, but it's also that quality that makes him qualified for the position. It's a big responsibility, being in charge. He's bound to make mistakes. But he's one of us, and we'll stand with him." She seemed to have calmed down a bit as she locked eyes with Felix. "Being a leader means different things to different people. Nero thinks it means being above everyone and everything and having fear and control. Gavin thinks it means leading the charge when there's danger, protecting each other. Tapestry is a family, Felix. We're there for each other when mistakes are made. I'd rather follow someone who learns from their past, like Gavin, than someone like Nero who uses the past to justify terrible actions in the present."

The remaining fire in her eyes died down as she cocked her head to one side, waiting for him to say something. It was a lot to digest, but also...comforting. "Well," he replied at length, "that's good. That you've got faith in him, I mean. In each other. And for what it's worth, I'm glad you came. We need all the help we can get."

Kestrel grinned. "I'm just glad we weren't killed the moment we stepped out of our ship in Atmos. Talk about a bad first impression."

"Yeah. It went a lot smoother than I expected it to, to be honest."

The Ministry of Pravacordia had been almost entirely

wiped out the night the Therans showed up. When he'd declared his intent to aid in whatever way he could, the surviving members of Pravacordia's government had clung to this small lifeline with a ferocious death grip. The irony of Felix having arrived during a time of peace and ending up caught in the political red tape that had caused him and Willow such grief, versus Gavin showing up with the very fleet that destroyed their city and being welcomed, was not lost on him.

Felix certainly didn't begrudge the man an easy transition, but it would be a lie to say it didn't sting, at least a little. The Ministry had set Felix up to fail, had planned to use him as a scapegoat in their schemes. But they'd welcomed Gavin into the innermost dealings of the new Alliance with open arms.

Felix's internal struggle was cut short as they came to the northernmost building at last. The door opened on a lively scene. Gavin caught his eye from where he stood, off to one side a bit, apparently not wishing to be dragged into whatever was going on.

"We used to fly among the stars!" lamented Baba, his plume of grey hair swaying and his false leg clacking ominously as he stomped in a circle around the Theran ship that dominated the space. Felix had never asked him how he came to need the prosthesis. Baba didn't seem the type to be open to sharing his private affairs. "And now look at us!"

"We just need to figure out—" Ambrose was saying,

hands raised in an attempt to calm his friend.

"I have some concerns," Ollie was trying to interject over the others. Gavin's face was an unreadable, stony mask as Felix sidled up beside him.

"What are they arguing about?"

"I'm not entirely sure," Gavin admitted. "Ambrose uncovered something useful, but then Babaneau went off on a tangent about the deplorable state of mankind. Ollie, well, mostly I tune him out. I've stopped listening. I'm just waiting for them to settle back down."

"Ah, *concerns*." Baba's chest puffed out as he scoffed. "Of course you've got concerns. We *all* have concerns. The fate of humanity may well be decided by what takes place in this very workshop, and it's *very concerning*."

He sat heavily in a nearby chair which squeaked in protest. Ambrose ran a hand down his beard, which seemed to have less red in it with every passing day.

The war was taking its toll on all of them.

Then, spotting Felix, a wide smile spread over Ambrose's face.

"There you are!"

He ambled over and encompassed Felix in a tight bear hug. "Thank you for bringing my Penny back safely once again. More or less."

"Technically Tobias—"

"Psh, I'll hear no more of that. It's good to see you. It's strange, isn't it? I'd grown so accustomed to having you around, that when you leave, I worry as if you were my own son." He released Felix and clapped him on the back. "I'm glad you're here. I think we've had a breakthrough. And about time, too. I'm getting too old for this sort of thing."

"Ironic, isn't it?" Baba gave a weary sigh. "We used to be too young to be considered wise, and now we're too old to be considered relevant."

"Baba," Ambrose made a disapproving sound as he fixed his friend with a frown. "Quit being such a dark little rain cloud. Everything is going to be fine, you'll see."

"Is anyone going to fill Felix in," interjected Kestrel impatiently, "or do I have to do it?"

"Oh! Of course!"

Ambrose gestured, and Felix followed him into the gleaming white ship. The others filed in behind him, dispersing through the roomy interior. Kestrel took a seat, leaning casually against the bulkhead. Ambrose squatted down, pointing to a little box bolted between the pilot and copilot's chairs. "Remember this?" He looked up at Felix, his eyes sparkling with excitement.

Felix hated to be a disappointment, but he scrutinized the box for only a moment before admitting defeat. "Should I?"

"Aye," declared Ambrose, standing up with a little grunt of effort. "That little box is the key to winning this war."

CHAPTER FOUR

A NEW PLAN

TELLING RIPLEY about his idea had been a lot easier for Ben than telling everyone else was. They had spent a week of late nights in Geo putting their heads together on the specifics, and Ben had left confident that they had a solid plan. Now, however, standing before the entirety of the CTC, feeling unwelcome in the old Council meeting room, Ben felt his thoughts and arguments slowly draining away. His mind went blank as Doris Fincher stared at him, awaiting his proposal. He only recognized a handful of the people in the room, and Fincher's was the only one whose name he could recall.

He felt a chill of foreboding run up his spine, tingling at the base of his neck. Would they shoot him down before he'd even finished, or would they allow him to stumble through his whole speech before mocking him for such a foolish idea?

At the moment, Ben thought it might not matter. He could not remember his speech, anyway.

Molly stood just behind him on his right. She'd offered to accompany him for moral support, but he'd almost forgotten she was there until she cleared her throat after several moments of uncomfortable silence.

"Mr. Parker," Fincher said at long last, "Do you or do you not have a proposal which you would like to present for the consideration of the people?" He noted the superior, bored tone of her voice.

"Yes," Ben managed. He swallowed hard. "Yes I do."

"Very well then. Please do so, so that we might get on with the myriad of other matters which require our urgent attention."

"Ah...right. Of course." Ben looked around at all the unfriendly faces. Three tables formed a u-shape which seemed just now to be bearing down on him. He felt the sudden urge to turn and bolt for the door. These people, their presence was stifling. He'd liked things so much better when Edwin had been in charge. Things had been less formal, not so harsh. At least, that's how he remembered it.

Ben's eyes flitted from Fincher to the man beside her. That had been where Nelson always sat. Edwin's right-hand man. The thought of his friend made him angry and sad, and fueled his resolve.

"I think I've come up with a way to neutralize Antiquity's Gate."

This did not elicit the response he had expected. In fact, it did not elicit a response at all. The CTC, one and all, continued to stare at him for what seemed like an exceedingly long time. He glanced back at Molly, who offered the tiniest of shrugs. She apparently didn't know what was happening here, either.

"I, uh, that is, Ripley Prior and I, we've been working on this idea." A lack of questions or protests encouraged him to continue. "What little we know of the Gate, we know from the scientists who first studied it, right? Back before the Sequencing. We know it's impossible to cut into it or break it. And we know that it has exhibited several signs which mimic life quite closely."

"We knew that?" The words were incredulous, the speaker unknown to him. Several others confirmed their ignorance of these facts with their skeptical expressions.

"Yes," Ben assured them. "We were taught all of that at school."

Doris Fincher leaned forward in her chair. "Just what do you mean when you say the Gate 'mimics life'?" Her eyes narrowed. "It doesn't move, or talk, or eat. It doesn't procreate. Are not these the signs which indicate that something is alive?"

There were a few quiet chuckles from around the table.

"Actually," Molly interjected, "it may very well eat, just not in the same sense that you or I do. It doesn't consume food, but it most certainly draws power from somewhere. The sun is our best guess. The throbbing light it emits is proof of that; things don't just glow unless they have some source of power."

"And it *did* grow." Emboldened by Molly's words, Ben felt it necessary to point this out. He was glad he'd brought her along. "It started out as a big hunk of crystal, didn't it? Just some crazy meteorite. Something caused it to take its current form."

"All crystals can grow." Fincher waved her hand dismissively, as if she had not just made a statement to the contrary. "That's common knowledge. Basic science."

"Yes, but how many of them transform into gateways to an alternate reality?" Ben countered.

Fincher considered this for a moment before nodding. "I admit that that particular fact does set it apart. However, although some may consider knowledge for knowledge's sake priceless, I do not. Let's get to the point here, please, Mr. Parker."

Ben felt his cheeks redden with embarrassment. It was one thing for his older sister to mother him, but to be chastised like a rambling child by Doris Fincher, in front of the entire CTC no less, felt somewhat degrading. Still, he was now determined to finish his proposal. "I'm getting to it, but please let me finish. The science aspect is important in order to fully understand my plan."

He took Fincher's solemn nod as approval. "Another thing we know is that Antiquity's Gate isn't still. It's vibrating. The electromagnetic fields of the Earth interact with the crystal on a molecular level, resulting in a unique resonance. The frequency is very specific, and it never changes. I believe that this frequency is what gives the Gate the ability to bridge the gap between Earth and Thera."

This raised some eyebrows, Fincher's among them. "What evidence do you have for this theory?"

Ben cringed. "Not a lot. It's just that...a theory."

"But it's one we can test," Molly was quick to add. "And it won't be all that difficult to do."

"How's that?" This came from one of the nameless members of the panel. That was encouraging. They were, at the very least, intrigued.

"We can build an array that transmits a targeted frequency. One that is the exact opposite of the Gate's." Ben wanted to keep this in layman's terms. He didn't want to lose his chance by making it hard to follow. "If we position this array close enough to the Gate, the two frequencies *should* cancel each other out. It's basically like noise cancellation technology. It needs to be precise, and it needs to be as close to the original source as possible in order to cancel it out completely—but the original source is right outside. The Gate itself. If this works, I believe we have the chance to neutralize the Gate once and for all. Break the bond between worlds."

"And stop any more Elves from coming through!" Fincher's declaration was accompanied by an expression of revelation. She clapped her hands together in excitement.

"Mr. Parker, that is a remarkable plan. *If* it works as you say it will."

"I'm not one hundred percent certain it will work. If I'm being honest, I'm not even ninety percent sure. But what other options do we have? We can't just sit around and wait for them to come, we have to do something. If any of you have any other ideas that could potentially stop the inevitable continuation of the Theran invasion, I'm all ears."

The eyes around the room shifted from Ben, to each other, and finally to Fincher. She seemed to be mulling it over. At last she asked, "What are the risks, and what are the requirements?"

A wave of relief washed over Ben. The worst was over. "There's no risk whatsoever. All that's required are materials we already possess. There won't be any overlap with the needs of the Defense department, and most of what we need can be salvaged and reclaimed from the Nur—the uh, Pod Manufacturing department."

"And if it doesn't work?"

"I feel confident that the odds are in our favor. But if it were to fail, there would be no harm done. All that you would lose is me and a small team for whatever length of time it takes to build the array. I'm more than willing to be in charge of arranging for the necessary components to be gathered and to head up the project." He narrowed his eyes at Fincher, trying to read her thoughts. Did she hesitate because she was afraid to take the fall if this failed? What would it take to push her over the edge and onto the side of reason? "If the plan doesn't work, you can use me as the fall guy. It was my idea, I'll take the heat. But if it succeeds... well, that will be an enormous victory for the CTC, right?"

Her eyes flashed. They both knew the CTC was hungry for a victory. "How long will this plan take to implement?"

Uncertain, Ben scrunched up his face and shrugged. Fincher sighed. "And if the Therans that are already on this side of the Gate were to return, and find this array of yours, then what? It would signal our continued survival as surely as a beacon, and not only would they destroy it, but us as well."

"I've thought of that, too. If we were to bore holes around the Gate, we could place the array below ground, disguising the holes when we're through. We still have the plans Terrance shared with us from the Culeian drill. Modifying a smaller version to bore simple holes, straight down, would be easy enough. Even if Nero's troops come back and discover the Gate no longer functions, the array would not be visible to the naked eye. They'd have no reason to think it was our doing. And, without access to the Gate, they'd have no reason to stick around. And..." He paused to take a deep breath. The words were tumbling out in a rush now, and he felt himself growing more confident. "If the ships that are already on Earth end up returning to see why reinforcements haven't arrived, we can turn off the array long enough to let them through, effectively trapping them back on Thera."

"It seems you've put a lot of thought into this, and for that I commend you. However, there is no doubt that this plan has a lot of moving parts involved. Things that will require maintenance, upkeep. In order to assure our safety, it would need to operate indefinitely. Can it?"

Ben and Ripley had considered this, and though he hadn't wanted to bring up the second part of his plan until he'd had more time to think it through, he had no choice. He needed to clinch the deal. "The thing is, there's more to it than just disabling the Gate. With enough time, I think we could destroy it all together."

Fincher cocked an eyebrow. "Why didn't you lead with that? Why would we bother to disable the Gate if you believe you can destroy it? Wouldn't that be the wisest course of action to pursue, rather than waste time and energy on a stop-gap measure?"

"Well, not really. Disabling the Gate, if our theory holds up, is relatively easy in comparison. It won't take long, won't require much. But destroying it will depend on our ability to find and sustain certain conditions. The power requirements would be massive, and the equipment a much more complex version of what I'm suggesting, capable of handling said power. The type of generators we have now aren't designed for that, as you're probably aware after the, er, incident with the overload. But if we can just stop more troops from coming through, that could buy us the time we need to research the second part of the plan."

Fincher looked around at the others.

"Very well. I would ask you to wait in the hall while the CTC considers. We will call you back in shortly with our decision."

Ben's insides were all in knots as he and Molly moved out into the hall. He was surprised to find Sylvia and Denton there, Sylvia wringing her hands in typical fashion, Denton doing his best to look uninterested. That he'd come at all spoke volumes.

"How did it go?" Sylvia's question was immediate, rife with worry.

"I think...I think it went really well," Ben told her. Relief flooded her face.

Denton grunted. "They say yes?"

"Not exactly," admitted Ben. "They're conferring."

"They'll say yes." Molly looked confident. More confident than Ben felt. He smiled gratefully.

The four of them stood around, Ben scuffing the toe of his boot back and forth across the floor. There wasn't anything else to be said. It was up to the CTC now. He'd done everything he could.

Sylvia broke the silence after several tense minutes.

"If you'd asked, I would have helped, you know. Come up with the plan. I'm not great at science, but maybe there was something I could have done."

"I wasn't trying to exclude you. I just know you're really busy. Ripley and I did all right on our own."

Sylvia smiled, but she looked hurt. "You always used to bounce your crazy ideas off me. I miss it."

"This isn't a crazy idea, Syl!" Ben said, his defensiveness rising. "It's a reasonable theory. We worked hard on this."

His sister looked taken aback. "Of course you did. I didn't mean anything by it, I just meant—"

"We both have jobs, you know. I don't just goof around all day. You're busy, I'm busy. I didn't have time to wait around for this to fit your schedule."

"Oh. That's okay, Ben. I understand."

Ben couldn't put his finger on what made him snap at Sylvia like that, but he immediately regretted it. He sighed. "I'm sorry, Syl. I just...I'm feeling a lot of pressure to succeed here. After what happened with the Forlorn..." His voice trailed off, and he tried again. "I just don't want to mess this up, alright? And I was afraid to get you involved, because I don't want you to take the fall with me if I screw up again."

Concern flashed across Sylvia's face. "Ben, what happened with those monsters wasn't your fault. You know it wasn't."

"Wasn't my fault?" Ben scoffed, glaring at her. "We've been over this a hundred times, you aren't going to change my mind. It was *my* idea. *My* project. But I blew it. And Ripley and Onyx and Nelson...they paid the price. It should have been me."

Sylvia shook her head. "Nelson made the choice to leave, Ben, you didn't force him to do it. That has nothing to do with—"

"It has everything to do with it." Ben's voice reverberated

in his own ears as he spoke through gritted teeth. "I don't want to talk about it anymore."

Nelson had died because of *him*. If Ben had never suggested the cloning project, it wouldn't have happened. If Ben hadn't screwed up the cloning project, it wouldn't have happened. His friend wouldn't have made a deal with Culei, and he wouldn't have had the opportunity to lose it when the deal was sabotaged. And if Ben had had the guts to do what Ripley had done, before the whole mess had time to fester, then maybe Onyx would still be alive, Nelson would still be alive, and Ripley wouldn't have been sentenced to Geo.

The door behind them opened. "Mr. Parker, Miss Watanabe, we have made a decision."

Ben glanced at Sylvia one last time, and she did her best to put on a brave, encouraging smile for him. Then he followed Molly back into the meeting room.

"Mr. Parker, upon consulting with my colleagues, we have decided that your plan holds promise and is worth pursuing in earnest."

Ben had to stop himself from shouting in victory. He clenched his fists by his side, forcing his face to remain neutral instead of breaking into a grin.

Fincher continued. "Our acceptance of this proposal is conditional on your ability to complete the disabling project in three weeks' time." *Three weeks? Where did that come from? She's just pulling random numbers out of thin air.* "After that you will be expected and required to resume all of your current duties in addition to continuing your research into the Gate's destruction. It is *also* conditional on your ability to find a suitable temporary replacement to assume your necessary duties during the duration of the project."

Ben thought about Killian Jones, and how he'd been so reticent to be in charge of things. He would not thank Ben for throwing him to the wolves, but he *had* said he wished he could follow orders instead of giving them. Well, Ben would give him some orders to follow. He knew Killian was capable of handling much more than he let on. He'd proven himself up to many a lofty task in the past. "I have the perfect candidate."

"Very well. All those in favor of the proposal and conditions as set before this assemblage?"

There was no hesitation. Every hand in the room rose into the air. Ben bit his lip. He'd saved the hardest part for last.

"Actually," he said meekly, his victorious feeling draining away, replaced by dread. "There is *one* other small condition I'd like to discuss."

*   *   *

BY THE TIME BEN reached the entrance to Geo, an official furlough form clutched tightly in his hand, he had regained a little bit of his previous excitement. He hadn't told Ripley his plan to request this. His idea of asking for a reprieve had seemed a long shot at best, and he hadn't wanted to get his friend's hopes up. Now, feeling like the CTC might appear at any moment and rescind the offer, Ben didn't want to waste a moment getting Ripley out of that hole in the ground.

"Here." He thrust the paper at the guard, who made no move to accept it. "It's a release request for Ripley Prior, effective immediately, signed by Doris Fincher."

The guard shrugged. "Okay."

Ben peered at him, confused. "You don't even want to look at it? Make sure it's not a fake?"

The guard shrugged again. "Is it a fake?"

"No."

"Okay, then."

Ben rolled his eyes and stepped into the Geothermal Plant, scanning the room for Ripley. Not seeing him, he made a beeline for the first familiar face he recognized.

"Hey, Daniel!"

The Halfsie paused from his work and offered Ben a tired smile.

"Benjamin Parker," Daniel said, wiping a grease-stained hand on his tunic before offering it to Ben. "Always a pleasure."

"Have you seen Ripley around?"

"He's not on duty right now," Daniel said, nodding toward the passage that led to the sleeping quarters. "You'll probably find him there. I'm just about finished here, I'll walk with you."

Daniel led the way through the convoluted catwalks

and ladders that crisscrossed the main cavern, parting ways with Ben when they reached the squat, dark corridor that led in one direction to the sleeping area and the other the mess hall. "I'm on my way to eat. It was good to see you."

Ripley was sitting up in bed, his back to the door, hunched over and scribbling something. He paused when Ben entered, shoving whatever he was writing under his pillow before turning to greet him.

"Whatcha working on?"

"Nothing," replied Ripley enigmatically. "How did it go? Did they accept your proposal?"

"*Our* proposal. And yeah!" Ben exclaimed. "They loved it!"

Ripley smiled. "That's great." Ben couldn't help but notice that the smile seemed a little sad, the enthusiasm a little forced. "I imagine you'll be getting started right away, then. No time to lose!"

"I think you mean *we'll* be getting started right away." Ben grinned, brushing aside Ripley's subpar response. "They're granting you furlough for the project! Three weeks of freedom, what do you say to that?"

Ripley gazed past Ben, his eyes focused somewhere in the far distance. His reaction seemed strangely delayed. It took a few long moments before the hint of a smile appeared on his face, and even then it looked somewhat forced. His reactions were not at all what Ben had been expecting. "Thank you," he said, and the words, at least, sounded sincere.

"I kind of thought you'd be more excited," Ben admitted, a little disappointed. Ripley gave an apologetic shrug.

"I'm sorry, Ben. I really am grateful. And I'm excited to help with the array." His eyes flitted past Ben again, just for an instant. "Please believe me. It's just that…well, leaving Geo doesn't really feel like freedom to me anymore. It feels like moving from a small cage to a bigger one. Does that make sense?"

Ben understood, even if he didn't feel the same. "Yeah, I guess," he replied. "Still, a bigger cage is the best offer I can give you. You want to take it or leave it?"

At this, Ripley laughed. "I'll take it."

Ripley didn't have much in the way of belongings beyond a few changes of clothing. He was ready to go in just a few minutes, but it took them significantly longer to get out of the plant. Ripley stopped every few feet to let some concerned Halfsie or another know what was going on. After he assured them that it was only temporary, they seemed relieved.

"You seem to be pretty well liked down here," Ben commented after the fifth or sixth encounter.

"Hmm?" Ripley said, "Oh. Well, like I said before, the people here are nice. And I think maybe a little confused as to why the only person who deserves to be down here is on his way out." He chuckled to himself, but Ben scowled.

"You don't 'deserve' to be down here," he muttered angrily. "You're a scapegoat."

Ripley shrugged. "No. I did what I thought was right,

even though it was against the rules. These people, *they're* the scapegoats. They're paying the price for something they were never a part of at all. All they ever did was have the audacity to exist."

The guards didn't even give them a second glance as they left. Once they were out of earshot Ben whispered, "If I'd known how lax security had become, I would have busted you out ages ago."

Ripley smiled. "I think they've just gotten complacent because the Halfsies have never tried anything. It used to be an actual penal colony, with actual criminals. Now it's just a bunch of unfortunate victims of circumstance."

Ben mulled this over as they exited the lift into the East wing. "Yeah, makes sense."

When they came to Sylvia's old lab, Ripley paused, confusion and alarm clear on his face. "What happened here?"

"Huh? Oh. They took Sylvia's pods and put them in the hospital. She's back to heading up Public Relations now. Didn't she tell you?"

Shaking his head, Ripley's reply was morose. "Sylvia hasn't been down to see me in a while."

"Oh," said Ben. "I didn't realize. Well, don't sweat it. She's just been really busy, that's all."

When they reached the Sigil entryway, Sylvia was sitting at her old spot behind the Information Desk. She offered a hesitant wave and then turned quickly away, trying to appear busy.

"She's avoiding me, I think," Ripley commented, and

Ben noted a hint of sadness in his tone.

"Nah, she's just got a lot going on right now." Ben frowned, pondering this as resentment gnawed at him. "But then, we *all* have a lot going on. She should make the time. I mean, she was involved—"

"Don't even say it," Ripley hissed, shutting him down. "I don't want to hear it. She doesn't owe me anything, especially not a visit based on guilt or pity. If she's busy, she's busy. That's fair."

Ripley stopped short when they reached the big double doors that led out of Sigil. "I didn't even think—where will I go? Back to the Edge?"

Ben nodded. "I mean, you don't have to. Your apartment is still there, but so is Denton. I think if you wanted to, my parents wouldn't mind you staying with us. It's small, but I prefer to think of it as cozy."

Ripley glanced back at Sylvia. "I don't want to impose," he replied after a long moment. "Boy, won't Denton be excited to see me." They both laughed.

Ripley was strangely quiet as they took the Tube to the Thurston Cross station. Ben watched him curiously, expecting him to breathe in the cleaner air with relish or to gaze around in renewed wonder. Pretty much expecting him to do anything but sit quietly and stare at the floor of the Tube. Once in a while he would grimace, but otherwise he just…stared.

The landscape had not changed much here in the Edge, despite Ripley's project to reclaim the garbage for use in the Geothermal Plant. The volunteers had cleared the area of anything useful, but the rest had been left behind. The heaps of rubbish were still there, even if they were a bit smaller than before. When they reached the apartment building that Ripley was assigned to, Ben watched him take a deep breath at the door before opening it, as if preparing himself.

When the door swung open, Ben and Ripley were bombarded by sounds. Laughing, arguing, and at least one child throwing an enthusiastic tantrum. The halls were no longer littered with crumpled paper and shards of plexiglass. Instead, they were littered with children.

Ranging in size from a crawling infant to a young teen, at least a dozen of them were streaming in and out of the apartments lining the first-floor hallway. All the doors were wide open, and there appeared to be a vigorous game of tag underway.

Ripley looked to Ben for an explanation, but Ben just shrugged. He had not been out here since Ripley's incarceration. Life had simply become too demanding to spare the time. The children seemed to take no notice of the two interlopers as they picked their way across the playing field, making for the stairwell.

"Well, this is new," Ben admitted. "It's absolute chaos. Hey! Who's in charge here?"

"Molly, I'd expect." Ripley gestured toward the nearest group of children. "Look around, Ben. They're all Halfsies."

It was true. Once Ben focused on the individuals instead of the flurry of movement, he spotted Eloise. As he panned the young faces he realized he recognized most of them from their visits to the Geothermal Plant. Did they live here?

Ben made his way through the running kids, trailing behind Ripley. The delighted screams and ongoing tantrum following them into the stairwell. Ripley's old apartment door was propped open and the smell of paint wafted into the hall. They let themselves in and found Denton and Molly in the sitting area having a heated discussion.

"I *told* you not to leave your supplies where the kids could get to them!" Molly was saying with an exasperated tone. The wall behind her was covered in tiny powder blue handprints that ran the length of the room and stopped at about waist-height.

"You *told* me to paint. How do you expect me to get anything done with all this noise and commotion?"

"Well, you'll just have to get more paint and start again."

"Damn it, woman, I am *not* starting over!"

"The entire building is covered in handprints!"

"You should keep them," Ripley cut in. Ben couldn't help but notice that his friend's tone was considerably warmer than it had been on the trip. "I think they're a nice touch."

"Ripley!" Molly's expression transformed from frustration to joy in an instant as she covered the distance between them. Her long plait of hair swung cheerfully as she threw her arms around Ripley's neck. "I didn't expect you to be here so soon! I wanted to have more done! We've been busy."

"I can see that." Ripley's smile was warm. "What's happened downstairs?"

"An explosion!" Denton yelled, snatching up a blue-stained towel and balling it up between his giant fists. "The little hellions are like a hurricane of sound and fury. And they won't leave!"

"Of course they won't leave," Molly chastised, turning back to Denton. "You knew that this was going to be a long-term commitment."

"What's this?" Ben asked. "The big guy's started an orphanage?"

"No," Molly said, a blush rising in her cheeks. "I have. The Human parents left behind, they were doing their best to take care of all the displaced children. But they are already cramped, shunned, and struggling. I thought, there's space here, so why not use it? I've moved in downstairs, too, of course," she added quickly. "For supervision."

"Wow," Ripley said, sounding impressed. "And then what, do you take them all to school during the day?"

"Nah," Denton growled, "she brought the bleeding school here. They've taken over the whole downstairs. Can't hardly get out to go to work without some grubby little hand grabbing me by the ankle and trying to drag me back into their lair."

Molly raised her hands apologetically and shrugged. "It

was the easiest solution and there's more room to spread out here." Her eyes searched Ripley's. "I hope you don't mind?"

"What? You care what *he* thinks? You didn't seem to care what *I* had to say about it!" Denton roared, storming into the bathroom and slamming the door behind him.

"Of course I don't mind." Ripley was gazing at Molly with the type of expression that made Ben feel like an intruder. He cleared his throat.

"Listen, Ripley, I'm, ah, gonna head home for the night. Been a long day. We've been assigned a workspace next to the Defense department, south wing. Meet me there first thing tomorrow, okay?"

"Sure." Ripley barely glanced up. "See you bright and early!"

CHAPTER FIVE

ADRIFT

PONYTAIL, IT TURNED OUT, had a weakness for the drink. They had been adrift for just over three weeks, unable to do anything but allow the currents to steer the vessel where they may. Ponytail spent most of that time buried in bottles of a foul black liquid he lovingly called *Nouritas*. Laevus had suggested more than once that their pilot should keep his wits about him. Ponytail had retorted every time that a dead ship did not have need of a pilot at all.

Perhaps he had a good point.

The vessel they'd commandeered had been a boon in keeping them alive this long. The heavy transport was not built for comfort, but the rear compartment was stocked to the brim with food and drink, all originally intended for Sanctuary's residents. Blankets and similar supplies would have been nice, but those types of things must have been aboard other transports. This made the journey all the more painful.

It was a nightmare. Hardly better than that filthy drill he'd been forced to share with his brother and the rest of those undesirables. Fifteen paces separated the cockpit from the rear compartment, and it had most certainly not been designed with long journeys in mind. Only Laevus' thick parka acted as a barrier between him and the cool metal decking which seemed to radiate the frigid temperature of the sea surrounding them. And the parka proved less than adequate at even *that* meager task.

Between Ponytail's snoring and Nelson's fidgeting, it was difficult to fall asleep. He spent hours staring out the porthole, watching the waves lapping against the side of the accursed transport, scanning the small sliver of horizon for land. Laevus had even attempted to separate himself from the others by making a space of his own in the rear, in the narrow passage between the stacked supplies. But this had proven impractical, as any sudden motion of the vessel would cause things to shift and sometimes fall, creating a hazardous sleeping environment.

Ponytail could be quiet when awake, content with his bottles, but Nelson was a constant source of irritation. He insisted on constantly busying himself with nonsense, imposing rationing and schedules. Laevus was not particularly concerned about such things. If the supplies became scarce, he would kill one of the others. Nelson, most likely. At least Ponytail could be easily managed.

But as much as they irritated him, he was hoping it would not come to that. He preferred to keep his options open, and they may yet prove useful. That was the biggest difference between himself and Nero. Nero was hotheaded, quick to exact vengeance. Laevus looked at his fellow passengers on this strange journey and saw only potential. Potential hostages, pawns, distractions. They were very little use to him dead.

"Terrance," snapped Nelson, stooping to pick up an empty bottle that had rolled across the floor toward him, "there are *crates* for these. You're going to trip someone. You need to keep the area clear."

"Why?" Ponytail was watching Nelson with a bemused half-smile. "Are we, perchance, expecting company? I'm the pilot of this ill-fated vessel, I shall enjoy all due remuneration when and how I see fit."

Laevus spent a good portion of his time meditating. It helped to block out the constant bickering from his two companions. Though the Culeian had assured him that they would eventually either be rescued or be carried within swimming distance of land, Laevus had expected their stay in the transport to be much shorter than this. His patience grew thinner by the hour.

Nelson shoved the bottle into a crate with its fellows, rattling the glass. "Why don't you just go check the systems?"

"All right, all right." Ponytail's face disappeared behind an upturned bottle as he took a defiant swallow. Then he stood, swaying gently as if to music the others couldn't hear. "Try to refrain from working yourself into such a lather. This environment is not conducive to the volume of your vocalizations. It really might behoove you to partake, you know. Calms the nerves."

"I told you already, that stuff looks like tar and smells like death. I don't want it!"

"It's an acquired taste," quipped Ponytail. "Only those with a sufficiently refined palette can truly appreciate it."

"I'll show *you* a refined palette!"

"Gentlemen," Laevus interjected, refraining from knocking one or both of them unconscious through the sheer power of his will, "please."

Nelson and Ponytail exchanged a somber glance. Neither of them seemed willing to test him. Not after he'd tossed that poor sap out into the Antarctic to fend for himself and, most likely, die. Ponytail moved to the pilot's chair and quietly began looking over his charts. They'd lost control of the engine when fuel had run out, but Ponytail had been able to maneuver them into a major current that he'd said would eventually push them past the horn of the southernmost Nequienite territories. Laevus did not care about the geography lesson, he just wanted to reach land. The sea was no place for a man on a mission. He needed to get somewhere, anywhere, where he was once again in control.

He glanced upward toward the hatch leading to the roof, thus far the only good thing about this trip. He no longer cared what the temperature outside was; he just needed some air.

Laevus ascended the short ladder and hefted himself out. The salty breeze peppered him with ocean spray as he shut the hatch door, muffling the argument that had resumed below. It felt good to breathe deeply, without the constant stench of the vessel's interior. He'd thought, by now, he'd have been used to it. But it persisted. The drill had been worse. Even the *Ningen* had been worse, with a full complement of humans aboard and nothing but recycled air to be found. At least the *Kraken* had not been as bad. The open deck had been much like this, allowing him to look up at the stars and enjoy the crisp air. The stars were so familiar to him. They were the same stars as back home on Thera, yet their cool, twinkling glow shone down on a world very different than his own.

He gazed up at the sky, the predawn light drowning out the stars one by one as the sun prepared to make itself known. He watched them go out, each striving to be seen until the last possible second. It reminded him of the way people so often acted. Each a weak light, indistinguishable from any other, each competing to be seen until a greater light washed them out.

Laevus would not be like that. He would be the suns.

It was only a matter of time.

A sound like a geyser erupting drew his attention back down. Not far off from the transport, the domed hump of a whale crested above the waves. He had seen depictions of these creatures in much of the artwork in Culei but had underestimated their size. The paintings had not done the majestic creatures justice. He watched as it rolled over, exposing its vast white underside. He wasn't sure if there were whales on Thera, but he didn't think so. The creature rolled again and dove, its massive tail fin crashing against the surface of the water in a final farewell.

Perhaps there were some high points to this reality, after all.

Laevus watched the place where the whale had disappeared for a long time, hoping to catch a second glimpse, but it did not reappear. Something new caught his eye, drawing his attention to the horizon. Another whale?

No, not a whale. Not a sea creature at all.

It was land.

For a moment he wasn't certain if he could trust his eyes. But then he heard a muffled, excited exclamation from within the transport. Nelson had seen it, too. There were the sounds of scrambling below, and suddenly the hatch door flew open, crashing against the outer hull with a thunderous *boom*.

Nelson's head popped out of the opening like a curious gopher. "Land, Laevus! I saw *land!*"

Laevus did not answer, watching the little man who eagerly dipped back out of sight. The words floated up through the forgotten hatch. "How do we get there?" Nelson was demanding.

"Ocean's tide, Peacock! Use that magnificently keen brain of yours. We'll swim, naturally."

"*Swim?*" Nelson's voice cracked and the word came out in a squeak. "But I thought you said we were going to come ashore! I don't know how to swim!"

"And how, in practice rather than in theory, did you expect us to bring this lifeless configuration of useless parts ashore?" countered Ponytail. "Relax. As fortune would have it, there are plenty of vests in the rear hold. It is then only a matter of how best to streamline the process of transporting our most vital supplies."

"I swear, if you're talking about that vile drink again—"

As the two below bickered, Laevus stood, stripping off his boots and tying the laces to his belt. "As much as I'd like to say, 'It's been a pleasure…'"

He dove headlong into the icy water.

The shock was invigorating. It felt good to work his muscles after such a long, cramped journey. He propelled himself forward with long strokes, enjoying the sensations of the waves licking at his face and the drag of his boots straining at his belt. He spared a brief thought for the whale, wondering what they ate. He could only hope that they preferred their aquatic diet to more exotic terrestrial fare such as himself.

The island was a long way off, each wave propelling him forward before receeding again, attempting to pull him back, too. Slowly the ocean floor rose up to meet him as he approached the beach, and he stood, wading into shore, his sodden clothes heavy as they clung to him. He took off his shirt, wringing it as he trudged through the ankle-deep water, tiny turquoise waves nipping at his heels, the white sand beneath his feet pulling at him, whispering an invitation to return to the depths.

Shaking the water from his hair, Laevus took a deep breath. The scent of the forest was intoxicating. At long last. Though the water had been cold, the air here was significantly warmer than he'd expected. The strange trees that lined the beach were squat at the base, jutting upward and bursting outward with a glorious array of thick, jagged green leaves that cast the sand below into shadow. The shifting sand was warm beneath his toes, a delight after the long journey. He reveled in the temporary reprieve as birdsong swept past him like a siren call.

Laevus did not look back at the ocean. He had had quite enough of the sea for one lifetime. He laid his shirt across a rock, placing his boots beside it to dry in the sun and set off on the start of his next great adventure.

The sounds of the jungle enveloped him as he moved further from the coast. The plants were foreign to him, the animal sounds unfamiliar. After a while, it became more difficult to keep his bearings, as everything began to blend together. The laughter of a gurgling spring caught his attention and he sought it out, stooping to take a long drink from the cool, clear stream. Though it slaked his thirst, it did little to assuage the empty feeling in his stomach. He felt a twinge of regret for not having thought to eat something before abandoning his traveling companions. Laevus was not usually so impulsive, but the idea of spending one moment more than necessary on that wretched craft with Nelson and Ponytail had repulsed him. He might be hungry, but at least he was alone. The peace was worth some mild discomfort. Still, it wouldn't hurt to assess the plants surrounding him with a more discerning eye from here on out. There was vegetation all around him; some of it was bound to be edible.

Feeling more like himself with each passing moment, Laevus began to formulate a course of action. He would return to where he had left his things by the beach and gather wood for a fire. The sun was warm where it peeked through the canopy of the trees, but it was no guarantee of what the nights would be like. So, first he would prepare for nightfall, and then in the morning, he would find something to eat. Having sorted out his priorities, Laevus doubled back the way he had come, wondering if his things would be dry yet.

"*Why you...!*"

The voice assailed him as he broke through the tree line. Stomping unsteadily toward him across the beach, Nelson wore an irate expression. A garish orange vest several sizes too large gave him an odd, puffy appearance like a bright and bloated corpse. He was waterlogged, liquid streaming from his vest and clothes and leaving a trail of wet sand in his wake. His hair was matted to his head, and water dripped down his brow as he blinked furiously, wiping at it with a sand-covered hand and cursing as the grit hit his eyes.

"Of all the dirty, rotten things to do! How could you just leave us behind like that? We could have used your help. We had nearly drifted out of sight of the shore before we were able to fashion a raft. Then we had to drag it with us, fighting the waves the whole time, what an absolute nightmare!"

"What's this incessant 'we' business?" Ponytail query reeked of indignance as he brought up the rear. Laevus looked past him and saw that they had indeed managed to bring several crates ashore. Perhaps he would not need to take his chances with the native vegetation, after all. "If I recall correctly—and the memory is impressively clear, as it occurred mere moments ago—*I* was the one doing all of the hauling. It's incredibly fortuitous for you that all Culeians are born strong swimmers. All you accomplished was to not drown, a low bar indeed. Unless you consider clinging to the raft, ranting and splashing like a lunatic, an accomplishment."

"*That is beside the point!*" Nelson retorted, crossing his arms and raising his chin, eyes haughty. His face had gone so red that Laevus was surprised the seawater wasn't evaporating off of him in curtains of steam. "Anyway, I'm just grateful we made it at all. No thanks to *you*." This last he directed at Laevus with a glare.

Laevus put on his most simpering smile. "Well, now that that's out of the way, why don't we see about getting a fire going. I've already collected some kindling." He pointed up at the sky. "You took quite a bit longer than I'd expected. The sun will be setting soon."

Nelson gaped, his mouth opening and closing wordlessly like a fish.

"A fine idea," agreed Ponytail, beginning to unbutton his shirt. "I don't think there's time to dry off before we lose the light, and I wouldn't thank you to make me sleep in the nude. Let's see about that fire, get ourselves dry, perhaps warm up with a spot of drink. We've certainly earned it after that harrowing escapade."

Picking his way through the underbrush and gathering suitable tinder, Laevus tried to block out the sound of Nelson's grumbling. Ponytail made short work of rummaging through the supplies and producing yet another bottle of his vile brew, and Laevus was forced to wonder just how many of the crates contained actual food.

For the time being, Laevus would be stuck with the pair. They could yet prove useful, though that would depend on what mysteries the island held. At least they'd brought sustenance. And he would not have to worry about keeping the fire roaring through the night all on his own. As long as they continued to serve a purpose, he would continue to tolerate them. Keeping him warm and fed would meet that requirement—for now.

Still, when the sun rose the next morning, the nagging

flame of irritation sprang back to life deep in his gut. If it were possible, he'd say they were somehow even more infuriating on land than they had been in the tight confines of the transport. He attempted to excuse himself to do a little exploring, but after his decision to abandon ship, Nelson was loath to let Laevus out of his sight. He and Ponytail trudged along behind Laevus through the brush, speaking loudly and often with little regard for the care with which he himself moved. Both of his companions seemed incapable of anything even remotely resembling stealth.

"Will you please be *quiet?*" he whispered, not for the first time. "I am *trying* to listen."

Nelson scoffed, his face a mask of indignation. "Listen for what?"

"People, animals, machines—whatever there is to hear. None of which will be discernible over your incessant stomping and constant blathering."

"We're shipwrecked on an island, it seems pretty clear that we're alone."

"Actually, shipwrecked would imply that we have, in fact, wrecked a ship. Stranded would be a more proper description of our current state," Ponytail pointed out, earning himself a glare from Nelson. "And I've been giving it a great deal of thought. It's quite possible that there are, in fact, others on this island. The Culeians have outposts everywhere…"

Typical. The moment one of them had something to say that Laevus was actually interested in hearing, they couldn't be bothered to form a complete thought. "You mean we might be in Culeian territory and you didn't think that that might be worth sharing?"

"Well, not precisely. What I mean to say is, we're most *definitely* in Culeian territory. There aren't many islands that Culei doesn't control. But I'm not one for overland adventures, as you may have gathered. I can't get my bearings without the proper equipment."

"Maybe if you'd thought of that when you were busy loading our raft with your putrid—"

But Ponytail waved off Nelson's accusation. "It would have made very little difference, since the transport lacked any portable equipment of mention. However, I have a strong hunch as to our whereabouts, and my feelings have rarely led me astray." Ponytail had one hand around the strap of his rucksack, the other stroking his chin. Laevus prided himself on the ability to be mysterious. It was *not* a quality that he tolerated in others.

And just now, Nelson looked exactly how Laevus felt.

"Would you care to elaborate?" Nelson's clothes were stiff, a film of salty white crust broken along the creases that had formed during their explorations. His hair was unkempt, full of twigs and sand, his eyebrows unruly. Wide-eyed and panting from the exertion of trying to keep up with Laevus, he resembled a wild rabbit who had only narrowly avoided being eaten.

"Well, herein lies the rub," Terrance said after a lengthy pause. "It's not outside the realm of possibility that this is the very isle Her Majesty was compelled to offer the Therans in the negotiations. Their base of operations, as it were."

Ponytail narrowed his eyes, peering around suspiciously as if Nero's army might appear out of nowhere now that he'd spoken this revelation aloud. "Strategically positioned, hospitable climate...sure it took us near on a month to happen upon it, dependent on the whims of the currents, but geographically speaking, it's not that considerable of a leap. If all had gone as planned, and I'm not one to say I told you so, mind, but I did tell them...it wouldn't have taken long to get them here under normal circumstances. Now, travelling by air as they seem to be? Well, it would have been little more than a short jaunt. There are other islands closer, to be sure, but this one's apt the closest that could support a force so grand."

He was still casting furtive glances into the jungle as he continued, so lost in his musings that he neither noticed nor cared that Nelson, at least, had long since lost interest in the minutia. "It's easy to extrapolate that we've landed ourselves well south of Nequiem. That would have been a strategically safer option than plopping the Theran army down on Pravacordia's doorstep, but not too close for comfort to our own major holdings." He stopped talking and nodded to himself. "Yes, I'd say there's a decent enough chance that we're not alone here, gentlemen."

Laevus felt a surge of renewed optimism. Had fate so favored his quest as to place him exactly where he needed to be? From where he stood, it certainly felt like destiny.

"Now, if we assume that I'm correct," Ponytail said, perking up a bit, "there ought to be a communications tower, and it would behoove us to locate it. We'll need to find our way to higher ground. Climb a tree, see if we can ascertain what direction we should be heading. If we can make it to the tower, theoretically we can radio for rescue."

"We can contact Culei!" Nelson's bedraggled face brightened.

"As much as I'd like to be able to applaud your gumption, Peacock, I doubt that my people will be much assistance in that regard. After the massacre in Antarctica, it's hardly worth mentioning that they'd not be too keen on getting anywhere near this place."

"All right, Pravacordia, then. You said it yourself that your two nations were on the outs, right? Pravacordia probably doesn't know anything about this place. If we could lead them directly to the base of the Theran forces… maybe they could take them by surprise. Nip this whole invasion in the bud."

"Now just hold on," Terrance said, shifting his rucksack to a more comfortable position on his wide shoulder. "We're talking about rescue, not revolution."

"But we'd be saving the world—we'd be rescued *and* we'd be heroes!"

Laevus' deep frown drew both of their attention.

"Oh," said Nelson, backpedaling, "I didn't mean, uh… that is, I'm sure you have reservations about betraying your own people…" His voice drifted off and he cast a nervous glance in Terrance's direction. Laevus knew what they were both thinking. Had he suddenly become their enemy? Would he deliver them straight to Nero rather than allow his own kind to be exposed? He could see the fear in their eyes as they contemplated their hasty words.

And they were right to be afraid. But not for the reasons they suspected.

"You needn't fear *my* wrath," he told them in a soothing, sing-song voice. "*I* have no love for Nero. No, rather, I was considering your plan. We *could* try to find this tower, and we *could* contact Pravacordia." He was tilting his head back and forth as if offering the idea a thorough vetting. He had spent more than enough time with these two to know how to pull their strings. Ponytail was motivated only by self-preservation…but Nelson, ah. Young, naive Nelson. *He* wanted much more out of life. He had dreams, goals, always unattainable.

Laevus fixed him with a knowing smile. "If you want to be *real* heroes, we could simply end this war ourselves, here and now."

This brought only puzzled looks from the pair, and Laevus sighed. "If we find Nero's base, we find Nero. And if we *kill* Nero, it's all over. We cut the head off the snake, and the army won't know what to do with themselves. They're only clones, after all. Without someone telling them what to do, they'll be as harmless as mice."

Unless they have a new leader.

Ponytail seemed hesitant, but Nelson slowly began to nod. "It might work," he said, his excitement evident and growing. "It really might work!"

"I hesitate to acquiesce," Ponytail replied. "I think a radical plan such as this—meaning no disrespect, mind—deserves due consideration. There are only three of us. There is a veritable army of spry young Theran warriors."

But Laevus could not be deterred. "We only need to worry about *one*. Nero."

He looked like he wanted to argue further, but finding himself outnumbered, Ponytail did precisely as Laevus had predicted: he submitted.

And just like that, Laevus was one step closer to attaining his goal. One step closer to his very own army and a ready made fleet of flight-worthy killing machines, courtesy of the soon-to-be-late Most High Elder Nero.

It was almost too perfect. Too easy.

Almost.

* * *

WITH A NEW SENSE OF purpose, or perhaps just the fear of being captured by Nero's troops hanging over them, the humans managed to find it within themselves to tread lightly. They marched behind Laevus in single file, like sheep being led unawares to the slaughter. Laevus wasn't certain how big the island might be, but at their current pace they would not cover nearly as much ground as he would have liked.

As far as size, the island proved with every passing minute to be larger than it had first appeared. The terrain was rough, the stout trees no great help in assisting them in locating Nero's forces. They were just tall enough to form an annoyingly thick canopy overhead that blocked the sky from view. Several times, Laevus recognized a unique landmark that suggested they'd travelled in a broad circle. He'd never had much use for skills like tracking before, but now he would have given anything to have learned a few more tricks from the Envicti.

"I thought we'd have reached clear across the island by now." Nelson's indignant declaration echoed Laevus' own thoughts. "This is ridiculous."

Ponytail, who'd been trailing some distance behind, piped up. "Well, if you stop to consider, even the largest continent is just an island."

"Under no circumstances are you to stop to consider anything," Laevus snapped.

But Nelson ignored him. "So? What's that got to do with anything?"

"I just want you to understand that the fact that we're on an island has very little bearing on the vastness or lack thereof of the terrain," Ponytail replied. "And Her Majesty is many things, but she's no imbecile. She'd've picked this place with the potential size of the Theran forces in the forefront of her mind."

If she wasn't an imbecile, she'd never have offered them a thing. Laevus allowed himself the simple pleasure of an eye roll, then pointed at a tree that seemed to have pushed its way up through the canopy. "Try that one."

"Why am *I* the one who has to climb them all?" Nelson grasped the lowest branch even as he grumbled. "You're a Theran. You could probably be up and back again before I even reach the top."

"Perhaps," said Laevus. "But climbing never was one of my passions."

"Oh, and you think I got a lot of experience climbing trees in Sanctuary, do you?" Nelson grunted as he pulled himself, with some effort, higher into the tree. "And just what *are* your passions, anyway?"

"Oh, this and that." *World domination, mostly.*

"Well, they certainly don't include things like being helpful, or preparing food, or..." The murmuring dissipated as he climbed.

"The Peacock has a valid point," Ponytail said, using the opportunity to catch up to them, his chest heaving from the simple act of walking. "Ah, we've stopped. Excellent. Bad knees, you know. Regardless, it occurs to me now that we lingered together, bobbing in the ocean, for rather a long time."

"And?"

"And we still know less about you or your intentions than we do about the thoughts of a starfish stranded in a tidepool."

"There isn't much to know," Laevus replied dismissively, watching Nelson's backside disappear into the canopy. Then he flashed Ponytail a smile. "I enjoy a certain level of mystique."

"I can see the tower!" Nelson shouted down to them, causing Laevus to cringe. Just because they hadn't run into anyone didn't mean they weren't near enough to be heard shouting. "It's, wow. It's a ways off. And…a valley, but it dips out of sight. That would be a good place for an army, I think. We need to head that way."

"You are aware that we can't see you?" Laevus asked.

"Oh. Right. I'm not good with directions. North, maybe?"

Laevus sighed. "Just come down and point."

Nelson reappeared moments later, dropping from the lowest branch with all the grace of a dead cow. He brushed himself off and straightened up, getting his bearings. After a moment he pointed. "That way."

They set off again, and Laevus kept the pace slow enough so that they would not lose sight of him, but quick enough to keep them out of breath. They were marginally more tolerable when they were incapable of speech.

Terrance's suspicions were confirmed a short time later. Had the patrol been the Envicti rather than untrained clones, Laevus might not have had the upper hand in the stealth department. But as it stood, he was able to spot them before they spotted him. Heart quickening, he backtracked, motioning for the others to get down. They weren't the brightest, offering only blank stares of incomprehension until he was close enough to physically shove them both behind a nearby embankment. He squeezed in beside them. Nelson made to speak, but Laevus' warning glare was enough to stop him.

He concentrated, straining to hear. The footfalls slowly died away. From now on he would need to scout further ahead. He wasn't certain how easily he himself could avoid detection, let alone these two bumbling oafs.

He nodded once he felt it was safe to speak.

"I'm tired," said Ponytail. "I think we ought to take a rest."

"What do you call this?" Laevus snapped.

Ponytail shrugged. "I believe I was pondering the likelihood of my imminent demise? Very similar to existential dread, with which I'm quite familiar. And if you weren't already aware, existential dread has never, and *will* never, qualify as anything even remotely resembling a leisurely respite."

The weak rays of sunlight that had managed to pierce through the canopy were growing dimmer by the minute. It stood to reason that the patrols would increase in number as they drew closer to the camp. It made the most sense to settle in here for the night, in relative safety.

"Very well," Laevus said. "But no fire. I'll take the first watch." Ponytail looked as though he would like to argue, but a withering glare from Laevus caused the complaint to die on his lips.

Despite the chill air, Laevus enjoyed the solitude of the

night here in this strange land. There were very few sounds, but all of them were alien. Not even the insects were the same as those in Imradia. The birds cried out in sporadic, mournful wails that sounded more like infants than animals. Laevus saw no signs of movement as he contemplated the tasks ahead, sitting apart from the humans on an outcropping of rock, eyes roving in the direction of the patrol he'd spotted earlier.

The sea air wafted over him on the cool breeze, weaker now that they'd moved farther inland. The smell soured as it triggered memories of all his dealings with the Culeians. He would be happy enough never to board another sea-faring vessel for as long as he lived. He relished the thought of his glorious return to the White City, of leaving behind this wretched place and all of its miserable inhabitants. Perhaps in a sign of how disconcerting this land was to him, he found even thoughts of the quiet village of Solara more tolerable than remaining here. At least it was far from the sea.

He stood and walked briskly around their little campsite, shaking off the intrusive thoughts. Now was not the time to concern himself with the life that was stolen from him.

Now was the time to avenge it.

*   *   *

"THERE!"

"What? Where?"

"Shh! Listen!"

Nelson did as he was told, drawing his lips into a tight line and squinting his eyes as though that might help him to hear more clearly. The droning that had caught Laevus' attention grew louder, and then there was a brilliant flash as the sun's glare hit one of Nero's ships.

Laevus smiled, tracking it with his eyes until it disappeared above the trees. He pointed. "We follow their trajectory," he commanded. "That will lead us to the encampment."

And, as usual, he was right. They did not have to travel long before they reached a rocky peak. Laevus crouched low and scooted to the edge.

There it was. A huge open area lay in a sheltered valley, thick-bladed grass swaying waist-high in the wind where it had not been trampled by troops or tents or ships. It was difficult to get an accurate count. Some of Nero's fleet were in the air, others blocked by scattered clumps of trees. The landscape was thick with uniformed clones, all going about their duties with the type of clockwork precision Laevus had found so desperately lacking amongst the humans he'd so far encountered.

"How many?"

He scooted backward and did not speak until they were well out of earshot of the Theran troops.

"There are at least forty ships down there," he informed them. "If the size is anything to go by, I'd estimate they fit perhaps a few dozen troops each."

"So," Nelson said, his eyes closing as he did the math quickly in his head, "We're looking at…wow. That's a lot of clones, isn't it?"

"Yes, Nelson, it's a lot of clones," Laevus replied, scowling. "I expect that there are many more than that. Some may be on attack missions, some outside our view. For all we know, there could be more than one encampment. All we can be certain of is that there are more than enough of them to make the rest of the plan rather tricky."

"But *how* will we find Nero among all of those soldiers?" Nelson asked, gawking at Laevus, who smirked in reply.

"They're clones, Nelson. He'll be the one who doesn't look like all the rest."

"They can't *all* be clones," Nelson protested. "What about the pilots? What about—"

Laevus heard a hint of his impatience shining through in his next words. "Surely in your time as a citizen of Sanctuary you laid eyes on Nero? He *was* on the Council, you know. Tall, brooding, always in a foul temper?"

"Sure, but—"

"Finding him will be simple. Getting caught is what frightens you. You're just looking for an excuse to succumb to your cowardice."

Nelson drew himself up, chest puffing outward with indignation. "I am *not* a coward!" he growled. "I would have done anything, *anything*, to save Sanctuary. I was willing to do unthinkable things. Things the others were too afraid to do. Release monsters into the world. I'm *no coward.*"

This triggered a memory, something that had slipped his mind during the long weeks alone with the two humans on that dreadful floating coffin. "Yes," he purred. "Yes. I remember that. And I remember you said something about...a dead Theran."

Nelson's face twisted into an ugly scowl, his balled fists whitening at the knuckles.

"She ruined everything," he said, disgust in his voice. "Her and that arrogant fool, Ripley. We could have had a chance. Culei would have given us everything we needed to defend ourselves, and they had to go and blow it all up." He swallowed hard, his glare piercing the forest floor with misdirected vehemence. "This is all *their* fault," he concluded in a cold whisper.

But Laevus had focused on only one thing in this tirade. Something that made him uneasy, which was not a feeling he was accustomed to. *"She?"*

"Yeah," Nelson said, still so angry as to be oblivious to Laevus' intense gaze on him. "She came to warn us about Nero's fleet, or so she said. If she'd *really* been on our side, she never would have destroyed our only chance of defending ourselves! She called herself...what was it again? Oh, yeah. Onyx."

Laevus stood, rooted to the spot. His insides churned with something he had never experienced before. Nelson seemed worried. "Are you all right?"

Laevus didn't answer. The forest seemed to spin around

him. *Her name was Onyx.* Nelson's words kept ringing in his mind, driving out all other thoughts. His quest for domination, his revenge on Nero, his desire to rule. Everything was momentarily quieted by a loss that he'd never expected to mourn.

His mother was dead.

She had died on an alien world, abandoned by one son and trying to save the incompetent friends of another. Laevus had never considered the ideas of familial connection to be very important. He'd been raised by the Elder Council. By Pike, in particular. He had endured things… things no child should have to endure. Had been molded into a tool for their pleasure. He had been an experiment, less than Theran, just a Halfsie to use as they saw fit. And his mother, she'd been the one who'd allowed it to happen.

How could he ever love someone who had abandoned him to such a fate?

And now she was gone.

Both of the humans were staring at him now. Laevus struggled to bring them back into focus. To keep his mind on his mission. If he could only remember what that mission was.

Terrance was chewing anxiously on his lip, eyes darting around the trees. "I believe I'm growing fonder of our original plan by the minute," he said slowly. "Perhaps it would be wisest just to contact the Pravacordian government and let them contend with this formidable foe. If we waltz into that camp, it will be no different in outcome than disturbing a kraken's lair. We'll most certainly be caught, and that will be the bitter end of it for us. But surely these interlopers are no match for the force that would be brought to bear on this island if we were to sound the alarm as to their whereabouts?"

A few hundred Theran troops are worth five thousand of your measly comrades. The thought flashed hot and fast across Laevus' mind, bringing his mission back into sharp clarity. He smiled placatingly. "You might recall the decimation of the ships Her Majesty sent to Antarctica," he reminded Terrance. "You would do well not to underestimate the Therans. "

"It's not to say I don't respect their strength..." said Terrance, still sounding uncertain. "The sea knows I am in no position to boast of superiority in any way. But you've only made my point more clearly. What chance do we stand, the three of us, on foot, unarmed, and dead center in the middle of their stronghold?"

"And what do you hope to accomplish by contacting Pravacordia, hmm? They're the enemy of your people."

"Well, you know what they say. The enemy of my enemy is my friend, and all that."

"The enemy of my enemy is *me,*" Laevus growled. "Come on. Let's backtrack a bit and find a quiet place to set up camp. By morning, I'll have a plan."

Laevus let the humans do the work, not that there was much to do. They ate cold cans of something Laevus did not make an effort to identify.

The sounds of night coalesced over Laevus as the humans snored quietly nearby. He had no intention, nor desire, to sleep. He was too busy processing emotions he didn't know he'd been capable of feeling.

He'd wanted to punish his mother, make her experience the same pain he had growing up under Pike's constant psychological torture. He'd wanted her to know what it was like to be in constant pain that chipped away at everything that made a person a person, until he was a hollow shell, an empty puppet.

Pike had tried to accomplish this, but he'd fostered one emotion. Just one. The one that he should have most strongly discouraged.

Because Laevus could still *hate*. He hated Pike, the Elder Council. His mother. Thera. Earth. Sanctuary. His brother, who had at least had some semblance of a family, who his mother had loved from afar. He'd hated them all. He *still* hated them all.

But he'd never wanted her dead. He'd only wanted her broken.

That way, he wouldn't have to be broken alone.

Laevus could not remember the last time he'd cried. But hot wetness gathered in the corners of his eyes and slipped silently down the sides of his face. Tears of loss. Tears of anger.

Someone would pay dearly for every last one of them.

Nero, he thought, staring up at the stars through blurry eyes. *You are the last vestige of the Council that sought to destroy me. You believed I was not good enough. Not Theran enough. Not worthy of concern. But you were wrong, and I will prove it. I'll accomplish those things of which you've only dreamed. And I will do it on my own.*

Laevus *did* fall asleep that night, rocked into the quiet oblivion by sweet visions of vengeance.

Chapter Six

The Array

I N GEO, THE DAYS had passed slowly. Out here on the surface, it seemed as though the clocks ran on a different schedule. Ripley had lost track of time as his work with Ben consumed him.

The first morning when he rose early to leave, he had wondered at the curious lack of oversight. It seemed that, unlike Edwin, this Fincher character had realized what Ripley had known all along. There was no reason to waste resources keeping track of him.

There was nowhere for Ripley Prior to run.

Ripley wished, if only for Ben's sake, that he could have done a better job faking excitement at his furlough. He was enjoying the opportunity to see Molly. She'd been a frequent visitor in Geo but being able to see her more often was nice. Despite her commitment to feeding, teaching and caring for a dozen children, she still made time for him each evening.

But other than that, he felt very little difference between being up here and being down there. New Sanctuary was his prison, and he'd accepted that fact a long time ago. He didn't let it bother him anymore. Nothing could change it. He'd made his choice on top of D6. He'd died on top of this city. Now he'd been buried here.

The array project was coming along at a remarkable pace. Between the unlimited access to materials and Ben's programming prowess, there was nothing to hold them back. This was good, since the CTC had put them on a tight deadline.

The concept itself was quite simple, and Ben had assembled a competent team to help design and construct it. Ripley secretly felt unnecessary, knowing that many of Ben's people could contribute any of the mechanical knowledge that he had to offer just as easily, but he was grateful to Ben for thinking of him all the same. It felt good knowing that Ben valued Ripley's friendship enough to stick his neck out like this. Ripley refused to let him down.

"Are you trying to stall or something?" Ben called from behind him. Ripley had been trailing his fingers along the curve of a long, smooth piece of aluminum. He was intimately acquainted with this particular design. It had been a part of one of the configurations in which he had spent most of his pod therapy sessions. It made him think of Sylvia, who still seemed to be avoiding him despite what her brother had said.

"No." Ripley hefted the long piece easily as he shook his head, a familiar stabbing pain resonating out from his right shoulder. He ignored it. "Sorry. Just reminiscing."

Ben chuckled as he approached, looking the part over with an appraising eye. "Yes, this will do nicely," he decided. "Good choice!"

"Thanks," Ripley murmured, glancing around at the other members of Ben's team. They had completed the design stage and were busy in Pod Manufacturing, scavenging through the disassembled pods for the proper alloys and components for their plans. Though the Forlorn were long gone, Ripley's keen sense of smell could not ignore the lingering scent that permeated the air. The scent of charred flesh. It brought him back to the night he'd destroyed the Nursery, and it wasn't a night he liked to remember. A flash of anger surged through him as he once again pictured Onyx's lifeless body. He hadn't been able to go back for her. She'd lain in the wreckage with the clones, forgotten, left to rot among monsters until some impartial worker got around to tossing her body in the incinerator.

"Whoa, Ripley. Take it easy."

Following Ben's gaze, Ripley looked down at his hands. He'd been grasping the edge of the metal so tightly that a little stream of blood was dripping from beneath his clenched fist. He let go of the scrap and flexed his hand curiously, looking at the imprint of his fingers on the metal. Sometimes he forgot how strong he was. One more reason he was grateful to be stuck down in Geo with the other Halfsies. A sudden burst of emotion like this wasn't much of a threat down there, surrounded by equals. Up here, around regular humans, he could hurt someone if he wasn't careful.

"We should get that looked at," Ben said, reaching out, but Ripley pulled his hand back.

"It's fine," he replied with a small, reassuring smile. "It doesn't even hurt."

"Are you sure?" Ben asked insistently. "It looks painful to me."

"I promise. Now let's get back to work. What have we got so far, and what do we still need?"

Ripley and Ben referred to their list, walking amongst the growing collection as the rest of the team worked around them. "The drilling is underway. And it looks like we've got most of the materials squared away," Ben said at last. "Except some components for the generators, of course. We have a disturbing lack of those. Capacitors in particular." Ben was not trying to make Ripley feel guilty— the young man didn't have a vengeful bone in his body— but the guilt rose up all the same. Ripley had made a mess of the pods when he overloaded their systems. This shortfall was his doing. Of course, Ben had helped; but Ripley would have done it with or without him.

"We can make what we need, though, right?" Ripley

asked, and Ben nodded quickly.

"Oh, sure. We manufactured them just like everything else back when Pods was still in operation. Just adds a bit of extra work, that's all. Everything in the department has been shut down for a while; it'll take a bit of doing to get things up and running again. The machines are in a state of disrepair after being neglected for so long."

"That sounds like something I'll be good at," Ripley said. "Just show me where to start."

After Reclamation Day, the manufacturing aspect of Pods had been shuttered. They'd had more pods than they'd known what to do with, after all, and no pressing need to construct more. The machinery was in good shape but needed some tuning and priming to restore it to peak functionality. This was the sort of thing Ripley excelled at, and it was certainly a hell of a lot less work than retrofitting the entire Geothermal Plant. Reconfiguring the necessary components to allow for small scale production was a bit tricky, but as evening faded to night, Ripley felt confident that it would be ready to go the next day. He and Ben were the last ones left in Pods, the other members of the team having gone home at a more reasonable hour.

"We did some good work today," Ripley observed as his stomach gave a less-than-gentle reminder of the time. "I think we should call it a night."

But Ben didn't look up, instead shaking his head. "You go ahead," he said. "I'm going to stay a bit longer."

Ripley watched quietly for another moment. Ben had a

conveyor belt dismantled, the pieces strewn in a wide circle around the place where he sat. He was fiddling with a broken strap, intent on completing his task. "You don't have to finish that tonight," Ripley insisted. "You don't have to finish it at all, in fact. Leave that kind of thing for someone else. You should focus on the more technical stuff."

"I just…want to finish…this one last thing," Ben replied between the cranking of his ratcheting tool against a stubborn bolt.

Ripley could tell there was more to it than that. "We're making great time," he said gently. "We're going to finish well within the allotted three weeks. You don't need to push yourself so hard."

Ben stopped his futile motions. "I would think you, of all people, would understand." He cast a tired glance up at Ripley. "This *has* to work. The sooner I can prove that it does, the sooner I can prove that I'm not just some massive screw up. That I have something of value to offer this city."

"You don't have to prove anything to anyone." Ripley knelt down and reached out. Ben placed the tool and the offending part into his outstretched hands. "Everyone already knows you're a valuable, contributing member of society, Ben. No one has ever doubted it." With a quick twist, Ripley freed the bolt and handed everything back. "There. Now you can be done."

Ben leaned in a bit as he took the bolt, eyeing it with disdain. "They don't know I helped you destroy the Nursery."

"And they never will," replied Ripley firmly. "You're

needed up here, Ben. The Therans won't stop with the ships that have already come through. There are bound to be more. And you're the only one who can stop that."

Ben let out a bitter laugh. "No pressure, huh?"

Ripley sighed. "The Council, the CTC, whatever they call themselves now—they got what they wanted. I went to Geo, justice was served. Coming forward to confess your involvement wouldn't help anyone. You're looking for a way to punish yourself for doing the right thing. But let me tell you something—I would have done it either way. I didn't do it because you helped me. I did it because it was the only way to stop them."

"But I *did* help you."

"That doesn't matter. You need to stop punishing yourself, Ben. As much as I'd enjoy having you as a bunk-mate down in Geo, it's the city that will suffer from your absence."

Ben nodded after a while, letting out a sigh. "Go on," he said at last. "I'm just going to stay a bit longer."

Ripley understood the desire to be alone, though he worried about how long the young man might sit ruminating on his faults and failings. Ripley knew exactly what Ben was going through, and he wanted to help. He just wasn't sure what he could do. Ben was going to have to work this out on his own.

He left the young man to his thoughts, making his way back through the labyrinthian underground passageways alone. All the lights were dim, the whole building taking on the air of a place forgotten. It would be dark outside Sigil, as well. Not a day had passed during his furlough when he'd made it outside during the brief window of light. Ripley wasn't bothered by it. He liked the way the domes almost disappeared at night.

In the dark, he could almost imagine he was free.

Emerging from Sigil, he was greeted by the still form of someone sitting on the steps. Ripley could tell who it was before she turned. She smelled the same as she had the first day he'd stepped out of his pod and into a new world. Citrus and honey.

"Sylvia?"

"Ripley!"

He'd startled her, but her exclamation seemed almost disappointed. It took a moment before Ripley worked out that he wasn't the one she'd been waiting for.

He glanced up, catching the faint curvature of the dome's peak high above. *Almost invisible. But not quite. Not anymore.* Then he made his decision and moved down the steps to sit beside Sylvia.

"Waiting for Ben?"

She nodded, a yawn escaping her lips as she did so, which she covered with a delicate hand. "I thought he'd be done ages ago," she admitted, not looking at Ripley. "I wanted to walk home with him. We…haven't really spoken much lately."

Ripley nodded. "He told me he snapped at you. Everything all right?"

Sylvia's heavy sigh was answer enough. She drew her knees into her chest, wrapping her arms around them and laying her cheek on top as she turned to look at him. She gave him a faint smile. "I don't really know anymore."

I don't really know anymore. Yes, that about summed up how Ripley felt himself. "Anything I can do to help?"

An exasperated chuckle escaped from Sylvia's lips. "Not unless you can put the world right again."

Ripley's shrug felt forced, but he was able to keep his voice nonchalant, at least. "It just so happens," he said, leaning in and speaking in a low whisper, "that I'm working on it."

At last, Sylvia's eyes caught the light spilling out from the Sigil lobby, and Ripley saw a sparkle of genuine laughter there. He felt warm inside, happy that they were talking after such a long silence. "Ben sent everyone home," he told her. "I tried to get him to leave, but…"

She lifted her head and gave it a little shake. "No one tells Ben what to do." The shadow of her old smile, the real one, returned. "He does what he wants. Especially now, when he thinks he has something to prove."

Ripley bit his lip, hesitating. "Do you want me to wait with you?"

Her quiet nod spoke volumes.

Side-by-side they waited, faint noises drifting through the streets from the comings and goings of other late-night denizens of D1. Ripley could hear more than that. The city thrummed like a living thing, reverberating through his body in a way that he had never noticed before his internment in Geo. He wondered if it was because he had become so used to it over a lifetime and then been transplanted to the loud underground plant, or because of what Ben's experiment had turned him into. Either way, the quiet night was pregnant with the low resonance of the dome's infrastructure. The city was dark, but it never slumbered.

"You know, I never did properly thank you."

Sylvia's voice was hesitant, and she fidgeted as she spoke, twisting a handful of her uniform shirt between her fingers. Ripley had the sinking feeling that she was on the same train of thought as her brother, and he did not know how to head it off. "No problem," he tried, keeping his tone light.

She looked sideways at him, frowning. "If you hadn't done what you did, I don't know what would have happened."

Now it was Ripley's turn to squirm. "Listen, I was just talking about this with Ben. I'm going to tell you the same thing I told him. It's not your fault how things turned out. I knew what I was doing. I knew what would happen. The CTC didn't blindside me when they tossed me in Geo. I wouldn't have expected anything less."

"But that's just it, isn't it?" Sylvia raised her eyes, and for a moment he wondered what she saw up there. Was she looking for the dome? Or was she seeking the veiled stars beyond? "Why were you the only one willing to not only do the right thing, but to be brave enough to own up to it?"

"I wouldn't call it being brave." Ripley was frustrated. "I was unconscious. Maybe I'd have run if not for that, tried to escape the fallout of my actions."

"No, you wouldn't have."

"You don't know that."

"I do."

"Well, it doesn't matter. What's done is done. And if you'd stayed, you'd have been caught, too. Or worse, killed. Those monsters…I'm not sure I could have protected you. I'm glad Ben convinced you to leave when you did."

Sylvia was quiet for a long moment. "But he didn't, Ripley. *I* convinced *him*."

Ripley didn't answer, just stared at her with a curious expression as he tried to process this.

"Ben wanted to stay. *I* convinced him to go. I was afraid. Afraid of what would happen if Edwin, or the CTC, found out what we'd done. That's the difference between us, Ripley. You were thinking about everyone but yourself. I was thinking about what was best for *me*." She sighed, turning away again. "And I'm sorry. I'm sorry I wasn't brave enough to stand up for you."

Ripley thought back on the fuzzy memory of that day in the Nursery. How Ben and Sylvia had argued in the hall. How he'd felt almost hurt that Sylvia hadn't put up more of a fight. Now she was telling him that she hadn't put up a fight at all. He wasn't sure what to make of his feelings. Betrayed? Angry? No. She'd made the right call. It was wrong to project blame onto her. He was being selfish.

They both lapsed into a long silence. Sylvia seemed to ponder the night while Ripley pushed his emotions aside to focus on other things. He made a mental checklist of everything he needed to finish the next day. The shift in focus helped, and soon he was lost in thought. The array was way ahead of schedule, and though he was keen to put it into action, he felt a twinge of regret. Once they were done with the array, he'd be sent back to Geo.

For the first time since Ben had come to find him, Ripley realized he didn't *want* to go back. It was not that he'd suddenly had some epiphany. The domes were still there, caging him in. But sitting here with Sylvia, even with everything she'd said, it felt nice. The simple fact that she felt she'd somehow wronged him proved that she cared about him. He missed Felix, but he'd found something in this new life that he had given up hope on ever having again. Friendship.

He wasn't sure how long they'd been sitting when the sound of the lift doors opening broke him free from his musings. He stood up, brushing absently at his backside and turning back to face the building. "Ben's coming," he informed Sylvia.

She looked surprised. "How do you know?"

He winked in reply. "Wait for it," he said, listening to the single set of footsteps as they moved slowly across the lobby. The large door swung slowly on its hinges and Ben's tired face appeared, his eyes registering slight confusion at the sight of them.

"Ripley? Sylvia? What are you guys—were you waiting for me?"

"Nah," Ripley said dismissively. "We were just enjoying the scenery." He waved a hand toward the darkness behind them and watched as his sarcasm went over Ben's head. *Poor kid is exhausted.* "Come on. Let's get you home."

Ben perked up on the way to the Tube station, filling Sylvia in on the project's progress as they waited for the train to arrive. It almost felt like old times again, though it struck him as odd that he would romanticize *old times* with these two, when his life since meeting them had been nothing but one crisis after another.

Still, it had drawn them closer, and he'd missed it. The way Ben spoke so animatedly when he was excited, or the way the corners of Sylvia's eyes crinkled ever so slightly when she smiled. Or how that single lock of curls slipped down over her brow when she dipped her head, and how she brushed it carelessly back into place with the back of her hand…

"Ripley?"

Ben was looking at him queerly, and Ripley struggled to recall the last moments of conversation as he felt heat rising in his cheeks. Ben cocked an eyebrow.

"Forget it," Ben said suddenly. His chatter stopped as suddenly as it had started, and this time, the silence felt awkward. The train lurched almost imperceptibly as it began to break, and Ripley knew they were coming up on the D5 station. He stood.

"Oh," Sylvia said as she followed suit, "you don't have to get off here, Thurston Cross is so much closer."

"I don't mind," Ripley assured her. "It's a nice walk."

"It's *dark*," Ben protested.

Ripley shrugged. "It's fine."

They made their way through the abandoned market and up the quiet street into the residential area. When they reached the Parkers' building, Ben hesitated by the entrance. "Hey, I just thought of something I wanted to ask Ripley about," he blurted. "Go on ahead. I'll be up in a minute."

Sylvia looked somehow unconvinced as her eyebrows knitted. "You just want me to take the brunt of mom's disapproval," she accused.

Ben gave a short, forced-sounding laugh. "Caught me," he said. "Go on, I'll be right behind you."

Sylvia bid Ripley goodnight before disappearing into the apartment building, and Ben rounded on him.

"Listen, Ripley," he said, his voice earnest and his expression serious. "I don't know what you're playing at, but it needs to stop."

When Ripley's only reply was a stunned silence, Ben plowed on. "I know it must be hard. I know you've been through a lot, okay? We all have. And you've taken the fall for more than your fair share, and I owe you. I get that. But you're walking a thin line, and you've got to choose before someone gets hurt."

"I'm...sorry," Ripley said slowly, drawing the words

out. "But I don't think I understand what you're getting at."

Ben's eyes widened with disbelief, and he shook his head. "My sister has feelings for you, Ripley. And so does Molly."

Ripley made a weak sound of protest, which Ben cut off with a raised hand.

"I'm not saying you did it on purpose but, well, it's a problem. So just...fix it, okay?" Ben let his hand drop to his side. "I love my sister. I'll help her get past this if she needs me. But if you draw this out, if you break her heart..." He shook his head.

"Ben, I—"

"Think about it," Ben said curtly. "See you in the morning."

He disappeared the way his sister had gone, leaving Ripley feeling lost and cold outside the sleeping building.

*   *   *

THE NEXT FEW DAYS passed in a blur. Ripley found himself avoiding Sylvia, which was easy since she was busy with her own work. But Molly seemed to be everywhere he went, whether it was at home in the Edge or during one of her visits to Geo, after which she would make the trek down to Pods to encourage Ripley and Ben's progress. Their exchanges felt strange now, tainted. On more than one occasion Ben had caught Ripley's eye with a meaningful glance as Molly cheerfully commented on the array's progression from idea to reality. She seemed unaware of Ripley's discomfort as he struggled with the internal battle that Ben's heartfelt plea had ignited within him. She stood too close, touched him too often, too casually. The gentle brush of her fingers across his shoulder, a quick excited squeeze of his hand. It had always just seemed like a part of who she was before. Now Ripley found himself ascribing meaning to every action, overthinking every look.

Someone is going to get hurt.

How could he have been so stupid? Had he really been so desperate for companionship that he had, as Ben had insinuated, been unwittingly leading both Molly and Sylvia on? *Had* it been unwitting? A constant stream of questions assailed his mind as he worked. The simple truth of the matter was that, with the fate of the city constantly hanging in the balance, love had been the last thing on his mind. Now, however, it seemed to be the *only* thing on his mind.

Ripley couldn't be certain, but he thought he might prefer dealing with New Sanctuary's never-ending state of impending doom over this. He was now almost wishing that the array would be completed quickly, just so he could escape back into Geo, where he wouldn't have to deal with the things he was feeling. Where he wouldn't have to worry about hurting anyone.

What was left of the project had to be completed outside. Ripley soon found himself helping Ben bring order to the chaotic work of their half-frozen team.

Ripley skirted around each of the twelve holes that had been dug out to accommodate the machinery, offering assistance wherever it was needed. Which, apparently, was everywhere. The resonators and conducting equipment were too large to carry out fully assembled, so the entire team was now working furiously to complete them, disappearing and reappearing from the holes like gophers popping out of the ground. Every man and woman was rushing to complete their assignments, eager to comply with each of Ben's hollered commands. They scrambled between the harsh illumination offered by a spread of floodlights, slipping on the thin coating of snow that shifted along the icy ground as if alive, a giant optical illusion that forced Ripley to battle against constant vertigo. Their shouts to one another were swept away by the heavy winds, and each one seemed keen to be back inside the safety and warmth of the domes. Ripley found that although he was cold, the temperature outside seemed much more tolerable to him than to the others. Their thick outerwear helped stave off the chill, but it was difficult to accomplish the more detailed work with heavy gloves on. Instead they would slip off the gloves, hastily attend to their task, and then replace them, rubbing their hands together vigorously as they tried to coax warmth back into their extremities. It made for slow progress.

As the wind began to pick up many of the workers were struggling to complete their objectives. Ripley moved from group to group, assisting others in holding some of the larger pieces that needed to be bolted into place. Several workers grew too weary in the unforgiving weather, heading back in and leaving more work for the rest of them. Everything seemed to be happening in slow motion.

And then, at long last, they'd finished. The array fit neatly into the underground burrows. Ripley walked beside Ben, checking the connections one final time and fastening down the coverings that would keep them out of sight. The others stood around, bouncing on their heels with hands tucked under their arms for warmth as they anxiously awaited their release.

"All set!" Ripley shouted, snapping a wire harness into place to complete the circle and climbing back up to the surface. Ben gave two thumbs up and the rest of the team scurried back toward the tunnel without a second glance. Ripley stayed behind, walking on the outside of the circle as Ben strode along the inside, each checking off a separate list of final details.

"I think we're ready," Ben said with a grimace.

Ripley nodded. "Just hurry up. I don't want to be out here all day."

"Got your comm?"

Tapping his finger to his ear to test the device, Ripley nodded as static filled his ear. "Good to go!"

Ben didn't bother to reply, spinning on his heel and jogging away. Ripley began to count the seconds, wondering how fast Ben could get up to Core Operations. Although he'd volunteered for this, he'd had about enough of the Antarctic for one lifetime. He was eager to confirm that the array was working and get back inside with the others. The thick scarf that covered his nose and mouth was doing very little, besides causing his breath to condense uncomfortably against his skin.

It was a long, cold wait before the comm filled his ear with Ben's voice. "Okay, Ripley. Can you hear me?"

"Yes, loud and clear."

"Everyone's watching. You can go ahead with the demonstration."

"Just turn it on," Ripley pleaded.

"No, first, show them what happens when you stick your hand through the Gate."

Ben wanted to make a show of this. The entire CTC was, at this very moment, crowded around the big view screen in Core Operations, waiting to see what they'd accomplished. They wanted to know if betting on Ben had been the right choice and Ben seemed desperate not to let them down. Ripley rolled his eyes emphatically as he drew closer to the Gate.

But all sarcasm drained away as he stepped up to it. The Gate seemed to throb with energy. The immense structure emanated a deep purple glow that washed over him, basking him in a light that offered no warmth. They'd been out here for hours and yet Ripley had kept so busy with the array that he hadn't taken the time to appreciate the Gate. He'd considered it part of the problem and, as such, paid it little heed. And yet now, standing so close, feeling the way it pulsed, he felt detached from New Sanctuary, from Antarctica, from everything and everyone. There was only a deep sense of foreboding, an emptiness. It brought memories of his time in the Emerald Hell flooding to the surface, and Ripley felt himself stumble backward, panting.

"Ripley? You okay?"

He'd forgotten that he was being watched. He'd forgotten everything.

"Yeah," he said at length. "Sorry." Not wanting to disappoint Ben with a poor performance, Ripley shook himself and stepped up to the structure. With his best attempt at a dramatic flourish, he thrust his arm beneath the great, throbbing arch.

Everything below his elbow vanished.

Disconcerted, he yanked it back, rubbing at his hand although it felt no different than before. "There, happy now?"

"Yeah. Yeah, that's great! And…maybe step back. Just in case."

Ripley didn't need to be told twice. He took several long strides away, stopped, then took a few more for good measure.

"Okay," Ben said in his ear. "That's plenty. Now just hold tight."

There was a pregnant pause, and then Ripley felt the skin on the back of his neck begin to prickle. A split-second later, the array hummed to life.

"Configuring the frequency now," Ben muttered nervously. "Okay. We're a go." His voice dropped low enough that Ripley got the feeling that he didn't want the CTC members to hear his next words. "Sweet Evenmire, this better work."

"Only one way to find out," Ripley replied with grim determination. The distance between himself and the Gate seemed infinitely longer now. Once again it felt like he was moving in slow motion, and a thousand questions tried to force their way to the forefront of his mind. It had to work. But had it? If it did, what did that mean? If it didn't…

Ripley was no longer in the mood to humor the CTC with a show. As he came into position just below the arch, he held his breath before thrusting out his arm once again. Once again, it disappeared. He stepped back. "It's okay," he said bracingly into the comm. "We knew we probably wouldn't get it on the first try. Go again."

As Ben tweaked the frequency, Ripley felt like a machine himself, futilely pressing his arm under the arch over and over on command, always expecting a different result, a little less hopeful each time. "Ready. Try again." Ben's voice sounded dismal, panicky. Ripley sighed, extending his arm once more.

It remained visible. Ripley, still wary, forced himself forward. He stepped beneath the great archway, looking up to where it peaked high above his head, the light pulsing in soft violet hues. He stepped again, and he was through. He was still in Antarctica, still freezing.

"It worked!"

Ben's victorious cry made him cringe, ruining the moment as it pierced through his ear like a knife. "Keep it down!" he shouted back.

He retraced his steps through the Gate and headed past the camouflaged array, making a beeline for the tunnel, no longer able to suppress a grin. The cold seemed unable to touch him. He was warm all over, flush with victory. They'd done it.

The Gate no longer posed a threat.

New Sanctuary was safe.

For now.

CHAPTER SEVEN

THE ARCA-TECH

I T TOOK SEVERAL vehicles to get them all back to Baba's
home, and Felix found himself in the middle of Gavin
and Violet, Baba's wife. She was the friendliest person Felix
had ever met, but on this ride her constant chatter was not
directed at him, but at her husband, who was driving. She
seemed to be alternating between the topic of how well
the shop had done that day and what was on the menu
for dinner. Neither of which could hold Felix's interest just
now, as he pondered everything that Ambrose had shared
about his plan.

"Do you think it will work?" Felix asked Gavin, keeping his voice low to avoid drawing the others into the
conversation.

"I don't know," Gavin replied. "But it's the only plan we've got."

This was true. And Gavin didn't offer any further insights. He hadn't spoken much to Felix since his arrival. Felix didn't take it personally—Gavin wasn't much of a talker. At least, not under normal circumstances.

He'd certainly had a lot to say the first night he'd been released from Pravacordian custody.

Felix had pulled him aside at the first opportunity. *Why isn't my mother with you?* It had been his first thought. He'd wondered if the tension that had remained between them at their parting had somehow been enough to keep her away. But Gavin had eased at least some of his worries. She'd gone to Sanctuary to warn them of Nero's plans. She wanted to make certain that they maintained the pretense that the city had fallen. *She wanted to do what you'd have done, Felix,* Gavin had told him. *She wanted to come here, to find you. But she knew you wouldn't want the city destroyed, not after the price you paid to save it.*

The little automobile hit another bump in the road, jostling its occupants and bringing Felix back to the present.

"Oh do be careful, dear!" chastised Violet.

"I'd thank you to let me drive, Vi," grumbled Baba, veering to the left, presumably to avoid another pothole. "Hard enough doing this with a false leg, without your backseat driving lessons."

"Perhaps if you would slow down just a bit."

"I'm going the same speed as the lads in front of us! It's

nothing to do with my speed, and everything to do with all the cowards fleeing for the hills are tearing the roads to shreds. Just look at the state of it! These lanes were meant for a couple of farming vehicles, not a whole bleedin' caravan every day."

"At least it's probably good for business, right?" inquired Felix as he slid up against Gavin when the vehicle veered again, this time to the right. "That's something, isn't it?"

"Oh, we've certainly kept busy," she was saying now, furrowed brows the only part of her shining face to hint at the gravity of the situation. "A lot of folks are worried, and rightly so. There's been an influx of people looking to fix up all manner of things, or trying to trade for coin enough to leave the city. They're all concerned that it's only a matter of time before the Elves—" her eyes flickered over to Gavin, "pardon me, Therans—come looking for a fight."

"What about you?" Felix asked. He was rewarded with one of her endless warm smiles.

"Oh, we could never leave. Oldetown is our home."

"Besides," Baba added, twisting around a bit to glance back at them from the driver's seat, "won't matter if it comes to that. All these people tryin' to run, but there isn't anywhere for them to go. Bloody Elves can find us wherever we're at, might as well stand our ground."

"You can't blame them for being afraid," chided Violet. "A healthy dose of fear can be the difference between life and death."

"Perhaps, but if we're to die, I plan on doing it in my own home. Preferably whilst asleep in my own bed. After a good meal."

"For the last time, Baba, we are *not* going to die."

"My therapist says I should be more open about my feelings."

"You don't *have* a therapist."

"Sure I do, I've got Waldo. And if you ask me, he's over-qualified. Regardless. When the dust settles and the war is over, one way or another, I don't want the victors to find my charred skeleton where I fell, fleeing. They'll think I was just another coward scurrying for the deepest hole like those slimy Culeians."

Baba's tone was bitter. Felix couldn't get a good read on the man. At times, he seemed very similar to Ambrose, but he also had a much shorter fuse. While Ambrose exuded patience and wisdom, Baba could often be irritable and even intimidating. But he had opened up his home without question for his friends, and that alone spoke volumes. And not just friends, either. His house was now a thoroughfare for Elves and Halfsies who had only Ambrose's good word backing up their honor. Humanity was fighting for its continued existence, and here was Baba, offering a safe haven for the kin of those who would destroy him. Felix thought he could overlook just about any character flaw Baba possessed on these grounds alone.

"I thought we had agreed," Ambrose said with a frown from his seat beside Baba, "to stop referring to the entirety of the Culeian nation as 'slimy.'"

"I agreed to no such thing. They are slimy, and you aren't going to convince me otherwise. Attacking from under the water like a bleeding sea monster, slithering back to the safety of their caves at the first sign of danger—"

"There are Culeian troops patrolling your city right now," Ambrose pointed out.

"And you think they're doin' it out of the kindness of their sea foam-slicked hearts? They're looking out for their best interests, that's what they're doing. Cozying up to the rest of us under the pretense of cooperation, on account of their whole damn plan to rule the world crumbled. They're just scrambling for cover, same as they always do. Only instead of the sea, this time they're looking to hide beneath the safety of the Alliance."

Beside Felix, Gavin let out a sigh. "So far, I have my doubts that the Alliance can protect anyone, Culeian or otherwise."

Ambrose looked back at them, offering a coy smile. "You'll see. This idea is going to work, I'm sure of it. Those Theran ships won't know what hit 'em!"

"I admire your confidence," replied Gavin, "But I'm not sure I share it."

"Don't you worry. You just don't understand some of the finer details, that's all. It'll work. I'll explain everything again once we're back at Baba's. I want Tobias and Penelope to hear, too. We just need to stop and get a few things first."

"Oh, Ambrose," Violet said, leaning forward. "It's getting late. Let's get home and get supper on the table, then we can talk. The errands can wait."

"But Vi, we need to test—"

She raised an eyebrow. "I've got a house full of hungry guests to feed. There's no use fighting a war on an empty stomach. Oldetown never sleeps. First, we eat. You can explain everything over supper, and then you can get whatever you need."

Ambrose sighed, but didn't argue. Felix looked from him to Violet, and then to Baba glowering in the front seat. If another debate broke out over dinner, it might be nice to have an out. "I could go get whatever it is you need," he offered. A raised eyebrow from Violet caused him to add, "after we eat, of course."

Ambrose seemed hesitant. "I'm not sure if you're familiar enough with—"

But Felix did not need to be told what he was unfamiliar with. He was painfully aware already. "I'll bring Toby with me."

This seemed to appease Ambrose, who nodded.

Baba spent the rest of the ride redirecting his anger at the traffic. The sun had almost set as they entered the dining room, the bright orange burst of its last light flooding in through the floor-to-ceiling windows that lined two of the walls. It took a bit of doing to get everyone situated at the table. How Violet managed to keep the polished wood surface pristine and gleaming was still a mystery, with everything else she did. They'd barely made it in the door before she was hustling Ollie and Tobias into the kitchen to help prepare dinner.

Ambrose and Kestrel were conversing quietly at one end of the long table and Penelope was attempting to herd Sebastian onto a chair. Felix watched Sebastian squeal and dart away from Penelope's outstretched arms as Ripley sat in his lap, grabbing at the silverware with uncoordinated hands. The toddler he had met in Pravacordia had become a little boy while nobody was looking. His antics brought a smile to Felix's face, but it faded quickly. Would his own children even get the chance to grow up, too? Did they really have any hope of defeating the Theran invasion?

He shoved the thoughts down into the recesses of his grumbling stomach, intent on burying them beneath his dinner. He couldn't allow himself to wallow in defeatist thoughts. He had to remain cautiously optimistic. That was about the best he could do.

Ripley gnawed on Felix's wrist, creating a soggy patch on his sleeve that was growing at an alarming rate.

"Your mother would love that." Gavin spoke from beside him, pulling up a chair and resting his elbows on the table as he gazed at the infant.

"Yeah," Felix replied, "who doesn't love soggy sleeves?"

Gavin offered a rare guffaw, and a smile tugged at the corner of Felix's mouth. "I'm not sure I've ever heard you laugh. Didn't realize you knew how."

Gavin's expression dimmed. "I just don't have many occasions to do so. Not for a long while."

Felix looked around the table, picking out the other Therans from the group. "Maybe it's not that you haven't had occasion to laugh, but that you haven't allowed yourself to."

When Gavin raised a questioning brow, Felix tried to better convey what he was feeling. "Life is hard. I get that, trust me, I do. You and I may not share the same experiences. But that's something we can agree on, right? For a long time I dealt with it by laughing. And then there came a day when that wasn't enough anymore. When the shadows refused to scatter when I turned on the light." He looked down at his son, who had turned his attention to the tablecloth, which he swatted at with an unwieldy fist. "So now, when the occasion arises, maybe I don't feel like laughing anymore. Maybe I'm punishing myself for all the things I've gotten wrong. Maybe I don't deserve to laugh. But I'm learning…I'm learning to accept the things I can't change, and to cling to those moments. The ones that make me smile. The ones that make everything else worth it. Because anything else feels like a waste. Like I'm dishonoring the people in my life who make it worth living by not embracing what I have."

He squeezed Ripley a little tighter.

Gavin didn't speak for a long moment. Then he said, "Your mother is very proud of you, of the person you've become. More than anything, she wanted to be here, with you and your family. The only thing that kept her away, I think, was wanting to make you proud of who she is, too.

And I think…" he shook his head, a bemused smirk on his face. "I think you're right. That makes twice now I've been schooled by the young when I least expected it. I'll do my best. I can't promise I'll be any good at it, but I can try."

This had been the most that Felix had ever heard Gavin say, and it took him a few seconds to digest it all. He was about to speak when Kestrel walked up behind them. "Gavin, can I talk to you for a sec?"

"Sure."

They moved off into the living area and Felix turned to the other side to find Willow smiling slyly at him.

"What?"

She shrugged. "And you say I'm the wise one."

He felt warmth rising to his cheeks as he realized that she'd been listening to the whole conversation. But he was saved from further discussion by the sight of Ollie, Tobias and Violet returning from the kitchen, arms laden with steaming dishes. Violet always seemed to have a feast prepared and waiting. Her and Baba had raised a half a dozen children in this home, all of whom had families of their own now. He suspected that cooking for a crowd was something she enjoyed, if the beaming smile on her face at each meal was any indication.

Soon the table was heavy with serving bowls and dishes, and the clanking of spoons and knives echoed against the high ceilings as everyone helped themselves. The Nequiem delicacies were far more enjoyable than the cooking had ever been at Ambrose's home, though Felix would never say so out loud. Ambrose and Penelope had always been so absorbed with their work, and none of their Sanctuary adoptees had been much use in the kitchen. Violet had a knack for transforming ingredients into a kind of edible art, and she made certain that no one ever left the table hungry.

Just now their hostess was seated between Baba and Sebastian, encouraging the toddler to try an unfamiliar dish. He seemed unwilling to acquiesce, eyeing it with suspicion. Felix ate slowly, looking around the table at the others. Therans, Halfsies, Humans, not only coexisting, but actually enjoying one another's company. If only the two worlds could just sit down to one of Violet's meals together. Maybe then, everything would be alright.

A chime from the hallway indicated someone had just arrived. Tobias leapt up from his chair and went to answer it, reappearing a few moments later with Bohai Takahashi in tow.

Though the Ambassador had been offered lodgings closer to the Alliance negotiation headquarters, he seemed to have developed something of a bond with the adventurous lifestyle Felix and the others led. He was always keen to be close by, lest he miss out any of the action. Felix wondered what would happen if Bohai were to hear Baba refer to his people as slimy cowards. He doubted the Ambassador would take kindly to the insinuation. But at the moment, he was content to sit with them at the table, loading his plate up and joining in on the conversation.

Willow gave Felix a little nudge, and he turned to

look at her. "That's everyone," she whispered. "Don't you think...?"

Felix nodded. "Right." He cleared his throat once, then a little louder. Everyone turned in his direction, the various conversations dying down until all eyes were focused on him. At least the adult ones. Sebastian was prodding something on his plate with one finger, face awash in indignation.

Felix felt suddenly self-conscious as the only remaining sound in the room became that of Ripley banging his spoon repeatedly on the lip of the table. "So, now that we're all here, maybe it would be a good idea to unveil your master plan, Ambrose."

The attention turned away from Felix, who breathed a sigh of relief. Ambrose finished chewing and swallowed slowly, looking ponderous. "It's only a plan if the Alliance sees fit to approve it. I planned to send the proposal back with you, Bohai, if you don't mind setting up a meeting for us. And even if they agree, we'll have to do at least a test run first."

Bohai opened his mouth to reply, but Baba cut him off.

"If they agree?" Baba's angry voice caused Waldo, who tended to hover wherever there were people to be found, to take a few jerky steps back from the table. "What choice have they got? We're dying out there!"

"Yes, well," Bohai said gravely, "we all know how slow governments move on these things. No one wants to be bitten by the failure of a hasty decision."

"General Hall will be there," Felix pointed out. "Along with the other heads of the joint military. I know maybe better than anyone how slow the wheels of bureaucracy turn. But this is a war, Ambassador. Surely that is cause enough for them to come to a decision quickly."

"I don't understand the problem," Kestrel said, her gaze roving over the table as she frowned. "The government on Thera is corrupt. So Tapestry formed to put it right. If your governments can't figure out what's good for them, what's stopping us from carrying out the plan on our own?"

Many of the group looked around at each other, sharing looks of surprise and consideration. "Nothing, really," said Felix, flashing a grin in Toby's direction. "I've never been much of a rule-follower, myself. So, Ambrose. Tell us the plan. We'll make it happen, one way or another."

Ambrose gave a heavy sigh, but nodded. "The Therans used poor Pluto to create these ships. They're more advanced, sure, but they're essentially my design. They've incorporated everything from the original into the new models. Everything, including things that were broken on Pluto."

"They fixed the Arca!" Penelope guessed, delight and understanding brightening her face. "That's it, isn't it?"

Ambrose nodded.

"What is an 'Arca'?" asked Bohai.

"It's, uh, not something we'd normally share with another nation," Ambrose said hesitantly. "But these aren't normal circumstances, I suppose. The Arca is a piece of technology required in every Pravacordian ship. Residential, commercial, even military grade. They allow a ship, should the pilot be combative, unresponsive, even a thief…to be controlled remotely."

"And yours was broken?" Bohai asked, his expression innocent as his fork hovered several inches from his mouth.

Penelope let out a laugh. "Disabled, more like. Looks like we have more rule-breakers at this table than we thought." She looked down at Sebastian, who was ignoring the conversation as he stared stubbornly at his untouched plate. "Please, Bastian, just try it. You might like it."

Ambrose had gone a delicate shade of pink. "I didn't like the idea of them taking control of my ship without my permission!"

"But they do need your permission, don't they?" Felix was thinking back on the time they'd been captured in the Wilks. "You had to give them some kind of a code, don't you?"

"Under most circumstances, yes," Ambrose admitted. "But there are circumstances in which they can receive a warrant to force compliance, code or not. Generally speaking, that's pretty rare. Usually only invoked when dealing with a dangerous criminal or a stolen vessel. But during times of war, the government reserves the authority to seize any ship for any reason."

Penelope was still muttering to Sebastian as the others were focused on Ambrose. "At least a bite. Look, it's got your favorite vegetable."

"I can see why that would be something the Pravacordians would want to keep to themselves," Bohai said, nodding sagely. "This information in the hands of the enemy could lead to chaos."

Sebastian stood in his chair, folding his arms across his chest and glaring down at his plate. "Chaos is my favorite vegetable!" he declared before hopping down and scurrying away.

"Well," said Felix, grinning as he gestured to the running boy, "it seems that rebellion runs in your family, Ambrose. So, what you're telling us is that it doesn't matter that you disabled your Arca, what matters is that Nero's people saw a broken feature and fixed it all on their own. They probably aren't even aware of what they did. I bet he's had them working around the clock to get the ships in the air, not worrying about unnecessary details."

Gavin seemed to agree. "Air combat isn't something Therans have ever tried before. He wasn't focused on making them better, he just wanted something capable of getting them past Antarctica and carrying ground troops, which they manage just fine. The fact that they're outmaneuvering the Pravacordians at every turn is a testament to Ambrose's fine workmanship, not any superior flight training."

Ambrose cringed. "Not exactly something I'd like to take credit for right about now."

"That explains quite a bit, though, doesn't it?" mused Toby. "Even Pravacordian civilians have more flight training than Nero's troops. Their ships are faster, but our pilots have more experience."

"And here's the part you've probably all figured out for yourselves," Ambrose said, clutching his fork excitedly while a bit of pork sagged, forgotten, on its prongs. "We can use the Arcas to take control of Nero's fleet. In one fell swoop, they'll all be ours, with nary another drop of blood spilled."

He beamed at them, glowing like a dewdrop in the morning sun.

"That's assuming we can get close enough," Baba pointed out over the excited buzz that had erupted around the table. "The Arca activation system was designed for short range use, at least from what Ambrose tells me."

"Well, the Pravacordian government didn't want a ready-made kill switch that could be used from just anywhere," Ambrose explained. "That's a good way to end up donating your entire fleet to an enemy force."

"Which is exactly what we need to do with Nero," Felix interjected. "So how do we go about it?"

"We have my ship," Gavin said in his gruff, quiet voice. "We fly in under the pretense of being one of his own and take control before they can figure out what happened."

Felix nodded, his lips pursed.

"But we'll only have one shot," Tobias added. "If we don't succeed, it's likely we'll lose Gavin's ship, not to mention the lives of those on board. And we aren't going to have a second chance to sneak that close to the base in one of our own craft."

"No," Felix agreed. "We get one shot, and we need to get them all at once. Kind of a tall order."

"It gets taller." Ambrose's face had gone grave as he pushed away his plate. "Gavin's ship doesn't have the capacity to grab the whole fleet at once, the power requirements are too great. We need something with more range. The *Timeless* could do it, but she could never get close enough before being blasted out of the sky."

"Nero's base is situated near a Culeian communication relay station," Bohai offered. "What about the tower? Might that be of use?"

Baba snorted. "You're assuming the tower is still in one piece. They decimated the sea towers near Antarctica on their first pass. No reason to believe they didn't do the same with that one."

"I haven't heard any better suggestions," Felix countered, looking around the table. "Would it be enough, Ambrose?"

"If it's intact and functional, yes. I think so."

Baba scowled. "And if it's not?"

"It is indeed intact," Bohai informed them. "Reconnaissance teams have confirmed as much."

"Ah, but that's only half an answer," countered Baba, wagging a finger at the Ambassador. "Suppose it's not functional? Suppose they messed with it to stop us spying, eh?"

"Then we fix it." Felix nodded, more to himself than anyone else. "We'll make sure our team is familiar with

Culeian technology...Ambassador, I assume you could make the arrangements?"

"I'll have the schematics brought from Paru at once. One of our engineers would be happy to convey any necessary information."

"We'll still need a way to test it." Penelope had returned to the table, plopping Sebastian back into his chair and smoothing back her bangs as she slumped, exhausted, into her own. "We can't just hope. We need evidence that this will work before we get to that island. The Alliance will never authorize a mission like this, not with so much riding on it, unless they can be sure it's got a chance of success."

"What about a small-scale trial?" Ollie suggested, digging a serving spoon into the remains of a casserole and enthusiastically scraping it across the bottom of the dish. "The crispy bits are my favorite," he whispered to Kestrel as he finished.

Felix nodded thoughtfully. "Yes. We can use the Wilks. Take it into a skirmish and try to take down the two or three ships involved. We'll have to act fast after that, though. We can't give Nero a chance to figure out what's happened. Given that he's only lost a handful of ships so far, he's going to be suspicious if he loses that many at once."

"Fast we can do," Ambrose said firmly. "All we'll need is provisional consent from the Alliance. And the master codes, of course. We can test our theory and, when it works, we'll waste no time making our way to the Therans' base." He grinned. "This is going to work. I know it will."

The conversation devolved back into pockets of chatter around the table, and Felix felt a sense of hope gurgling up inside him. Not just at the prospect of defeating Nero once and for all. But at the beautiful feeling of community around that long oak table.

Maybe, just maybe, things would be okay.

Ambrose broke through his hopeful reverie. "Felix, you still up for a jaunt into town? Baba doesn't have what I need at the shop. And there are a few components I'll need to rig something up to the tower, as well."

"I could have gotten the parts you need." Felix detected a hint of indignation in Baba's tone. "I can't have one of everything just lying around the shop waiting on your pleasure. But I could have gotten them."

"No worries," replied Felix. He caught Tobias' eye. "You feel up for coming with me? Ambrose doesn't think I can handle it on my own."

Tobias smiled. "Certainly."

*   *   *

TOBIAS SQUINTED AT THE list beneath the streetlamp, Felix glancing at it over his shoulder.

"Do you know where to get all this stuff?"

"Indubitably. Judging from the varied assortment, we may have to patronize several locations. Ambrose has a very strange concept of what entails 'a few components.'"

Felix chuckled. "We'd better get moving, then."

Their first stop wasn't far, so Tobias suggested going on foot. They walked side-by-side down the street, Felix taking in the sights. The city sparkled around them, all neon signs and holographic billboards. He wasn't as awed by it now that he'd grown used to it. Frankly, the bright lights assaulting him from every direction hurt his eyes. The whole city was an attack on his senses. Even now, when the streets had only a sprinkling of foot traffic, the hum of electronics and engines and machinery enveloped him. The cool evening did nothing to deter the local businesses from propping open their doors, and the rowdy voices of those enjoying their evenings funneled out into the open air.

He focused his eyes downward, concentrating on his steps as Tobias led the way. Loose gravel crunched beneath Felix's shoes as the sounds around him coalesced, drowning one another out.

Tobias had stopped, and Felix followed his gaze over the heads of a small gathering of people. They were all watching one man speaking passionately at the front of the group.

"The Alliance is just another way they're seeking to destroy our autonomy." The man was waving a clenched fist, his brow furrowed as his eyes moved around the people before him. "They want to take our homes from us, they want to take our nation, our heritage!"

"Rubbish," shouted someone from the crowd. "That's what the Elves are trying to do. *They're* the real enemy!"

"Yeah," agreed another. "We're stronger together."

"No one can be a master of all things," insisted the speaker. "We are stronger when we stick to what we know best. Trade, comradery, that is all well and good. But we need to keep our nations separate. When the Elves are vanquished, what guarantee do we have that things will return to how they were? Who will protect our sovereignty, our heritage? Who will preserve the cultures that we have fought so hard to foster and grow? This Alliance sets a dangerous precedent for all of us."

"Go on," jeered someone else. "You're nuts. We're trying to survive, and you need to get your priorities straight."

There was a murmur of assent and Tobias caught Felix's eye. "Perhaps we should move on. I don't think it wise to linger in this place."

Felix did not need to be told twice. He gave the group a wide berth as the two of them passed, fixing his eyes on the ground and pulling his hood tighter. He doubted any of these people would be interested in the difference between an Elf and a Halfsie, not all riled up like this. But a familiar face loitering near the back of the group caught his eye.

"Crewman Bartholomew?"

Barty started, glancing up and looking for who had called his name. "Ah," he said, catching sight of them. "Mr. Felix."

"What are you doing here?"

"The Timeless will be in Oldetown for several more days. I am well within my rights to spend my time as I see fit." He separated himself from the crowd and approached

Felix, nodding back in the direction of the speaker. "I was on my way back to my lodging after dinner when I happened upon this blowhard and stopped to listen." His face darkened. "The cost of peace, I suppose. Everyone suddenly feels entitled to rant about their dangerous ideologies."

"Yeah," Felix said, shifting uncomfortably, more anxious than ever to get farther away from this place. "I guess so."

Barty looked from Felix to Tobias and back again. His eyes narrowed. "You aren't…interested in what they're saying, are you?"

Felix snorted. "I'm not sure if you're aware, but I don't think their message applies to people like me."

His face softening, Barty nodded. "Indeed. Well, I'd best be off. Mr. Everston, Mr. Felix." He turned and strode away at a brisk pace.

"Not much of a conversationalist," noted Tobias as they continued on their way.

"Actually, I was just thinking that that's the longest conversation I've ever had with old Barty. Maybe he's finally warming up to me."

Felix looked sideways at Toby and they shared a chuckle.

Their destination was sandwiched between two tall buildings like the one where Baba lived. Its narrow brick face rose five stories high, but it only looked about ten feet wide. Felix followed Toby inside, expecting a ramshackle collection of odds and ends and instead finding himself disoriented by the sudden change of atmosphere.

Cool blue lights illuminated the shop, with long glass shelves lining either side and stretching all the way to the back of the building where a narrow metal staircase disappeared into the level above. Everything gleamed, each item carefully tagged and arranged on little trays lined with colored velvets as if they were displays of fine jewelry. Two clerks minded either side of the store, standing as Tobias and Felix entered and greeting them with eager smiles. They appeared to be the only customers.

"May we help you find anything in particular, sirs?"

"Yes, actually," Tobias said, procuring the list from where he'd tucked it into his breast pocket. "We're looking for..."

As he began to prattle on about capacitors and inhibitors and other such technospeak, Felix drifted farther into the shop. One of the clerks trailed alongside him on the opposite side of the glass, mirroring Felix's curious expression. Trying to ignore the attention, Felix avoided eye contact, stooping down to peer through the case at a fascinatingly intricate part comprised of tiny gears in bronze and silver. The clerk stooped, too, following his gaze.

"Would you like to take a closer look?"

Felix shook his head. "I don't even know what it is." The clerk's attention was making him uncomfortable. He stood up and nodded toward the staircase. "Is there more up there?"

"Indeed. Please, feel free to browse while you wait for your companion."

Felix took the stairs two at a time, arriving on a floor identical in structure to the one below. This one was not attended, which surprised him. Weren't they worried about theft? But as he walked along the narrow room, trailing his fingers across the top of the glass case as he perused its contents, the answer came in the form of an echoing voice. "Kindly refrain from touching the glass, please."

His hand dropped to his side and he looked for the source of the request. His eyes scanned the area, stopping to rest on a little black half-dome in the center of the ceiling. It must hold a camera or something.

Wondering how long Tobias would be, he moved up to the third floor. More of the same. The shop had seemed impressive upon entry, but the trinkets held no meaning for Felix. He made his way back downstairs.

Tobias was exchanging money for a small brown bag. From the looks of it, quite a lot of money. Especially for the size of the bag. No wonder Baba did so well for himself. The contents of his inventory were, on average, much larger parts.

"We're all set here, Felix," Toby said, handing him the parcel.

"Great. Where's our next stop?"

Tobias scrutinized the list again. "We've got a couple of options. If you want to finish in the shortest amount of stops, we should head to Minkie's. But that's clear across the city."

"I'm fine with that," Felix replied, feeling the uncomfortable gaze of the clerk on the back of his head. "We can grab a cab."

Tobias' eyes lit up. "Or…we could take the SkyCab! It's just down the road!"

Felix groaned. "Don't we spend enough time in the air? I'm beginning to get why Bohai hates it so much."

"Come on, Felix. Who knows? It could prove to be an enjoyable experience."

Felix clutched the parcel under one arm and followed Tobias down the deserted street to the entrance of the cross-town gondola known as the SkyCab.

When they reached the front of the line at last, Tobias exclaimed with delight as the next bulbous carriage settled into the opening between the platforms. Several riders disembarked on the opposite side before Felix and Toby were allowed to enter.

The spherical ride was just as bad, if not worse, than the glass elevator that led to Baba's home. The metal frame and seats were padded in tired vinyl and encased in curving glass—even the floor had a large window so that you could look down while riding and wonder at the world below.

Or, in Felix's case, contemplate how long it would take to fall from that height.

The carriage rocked gently as they settled in and the attendant clicked the latch shut behind them. With a shudder, it looped around the carriage return and began to make its way toward the building's exit.

"I don't like this," Felix admitted almost at once. "Are

you sure it can hold us?"

"Sorry?" Tobias was already distracted by his excitement.

"The cable." He waved a hand, without looking, at the thick wire that snaked across the city, clinging to spindly towers gracing the peaks of the highest skyscrapers. How confident are you that this is safe?"

"Oh, goodness, it's perfectly safe! This gondola has been in operation for over fifty years."

Felix grimaced. "Great. Nothing more comforting than an old cable."

"Don't worry. We aren't actually attached to the cable at all. It's all magnetic."

Cringe deepening, Felix closed his eyes. "Could have done without that bit of information, in hindsight."

Once out of the loading station the gondola came alive, projecting holographic information that appeared to float over the landmarks below. Whenever Felix turned his head, the carriage tracked his movement, displaying relevant tidbits about whatever part of the city he was looking at. Names of buildings, historical sites, dining recommendations. The interactive technology might appeal to some, but he found himself nauseated by the onslaught of such an information overload.

Felix focused instead on Toby, who gazed out at the city with wonder as if he hadn't already seen it from above a dozen times over. His eyes tracked over scrolling paragraphs that Felix couldn't see, but his friend seemed enthralled.

"It really is incredible here." Toby pointed down and

Felix unwittingly looked that way, his gut wrenching as he watched a skyscraper pass below them. *Norwalk Tower,* the gondola informed him in bright pink letters scrawled across the building. *Pre-Sequencing construction. Restoration completed year ninety-eight. Home to the Historical Society and Agricultural Council, as well as several private businesses including...* Felix felt his eyes begin to blur. Tobias continued his enthusiastic musings. "The level of Pre-Sequencing technology that they've been able to appropriate is quite astonishing. Whereas Pravacordia built themselves a whole new way of life, Nequiem refused to give up on the past. Fascinating."

"Yeah," Felix agreed, "Fascinating."

"I was thinking of taking Penny and Bastian here." Tobias' blush was visible even in the dim glow from the city below. "I wonder if she's ever ridden it at night. It's like being in space, don't you agree?" He raised his hands in a flourish toward the sky. "Surrounded by stars." Felix followed his gaze and found the stars partially obscured by the words, *Ursa Minor.* He shifted his gaze and the words followed suit, transforming to read *Polaris, also known as the North Star.*

Felix felt a knowing smile tugging at the corner of his mouth. "You really like her, don't you?"

"Of course! She has a brilliant mind. She's strong, funny, tenacious..."

"Pretty?"

"Beautiful," Tobias agreed without thinking. Then his

eyes widened and his cheeks went even redder. "What I meant to say—"

"I know what you meant to say, Toby." Felix did his best to lean back against the rigid metal seat, finding it shockingly uncomfortable for something so technologically advanced. "And I think you should bring them. Do it soon. Don't let fear get the best of you. Sometimes...sometimes tomorrow is too late."

They lapsed into silence. Looking down at the lights softened by distance, little pools of color dotting the cityscape, he could see how Tobias might find it romantic. If you could ignore all the words, at least.

This did not, however, stop him from exhaling a long-held breath of relief as they stepped out onto solid ground at the other end.

"If you don't mind, I'd prefer if we took a normal cab home."

A flash of disappointment on Tobias' face vanished beneath a sheepish grin. "Oh, of course! Certainly!"

Minkie's was not a single store, but rather a large conglomeration of shops all sharing one massive building. It spanned an entire city block, the facade decorated with inset fountains and pillars with detailed sculpting that encompassed their massive bases. Huge windows allowed passersby to see into the shops, and many had stopped to admire the available wares. From what he could see, it was like an upscale version of the markets back in Sanctuary. The displays boasted everything from kitchen products to clothing.

Once inside, a wide hall wended between huge open doorways where shop vendors called out, and advertisements sought to outdo each other with flashing lights and enticing songs. A store devoted completely to toys was particularly full of patrons, leaving Felix to wonder what time the average Nequienite child might go to bed. He himself felt like he'd been up for days. But as they passed the wide opening leading into the bright and loud interior of the toy shop, Felix's steps slowed. A mobile was displayed close to the entrance, its soft lullaby almost lost beneath the sea of voices. Beneath a copper canopy meant to be hung from the ceiling, four tiny airships moved in a slow, entrancing circuit. There were no strings, and Felix guessed the device operated using magnets or some such technology. He looked around and found a box nearby. Picking it up, he scanned the text for clues as to how it functioned. One-one-hundredth-scale authentic models. Cumulous, Nimbus, Stratus, and Cirrus class! Made in Pravacordia.

"Delightful!" Tobias remarked. He had gone several paces past the store before he apparently noticed that his companion was no longer beside him. Felix saw him double back out of the corner of his eye, and Tobias bent to examine the mobile for himself, and his face was full of childlike joy. "I'm sure your children would love it. I imagine Sebastian would, too, though I expect it's intended for a younger demographic...good gracious! Is that the price?"

Felix's eyes fell on the sticker, and he grimaced. "I'm

afraid the kids will have to make do without," he said, moving to put the box back down beside the display.

"Hey! Just what do you think you're doing?"

Felix didn't realize the angry voice was addressing him until Tobias answered. "We were just looking at—"

"I wasn't talking to you, I was talking to him."

It still didn't register as Felix looked up, catching the eye of a disgruntled-looking man in a bright red vest. "Get out of here," the man said. "We don't want your kind hanging around. You're scaring the kids."

It wasn't until that moment that Felix realized the whole store, filled with sound and laughter just seconds before, had gone deathly quiet. Parents held their children close, eyes darting beyond Felix to the exit as if looking for an escape.

He placed the box down with a slow, deliberate motion. "I'm sorry," he said. "We were only looking."

"Yeah, right. Get out of here before I call the guards."

"Excuse me." Tobias' features were aghast. "This man has done nothing to warrant such rude behavior. You should apologize at once. How dare you treat a patron of your establishment in such a manner!"

"It's not what he's done, it's what he is." The man's eyes travelled over Felix's face like a laser, lingering on his ears and leaving Felix's cheeks flushed in the wake of his stare. "They can say what they like about some of you being on our side, don't matter to me. I don't believe a word of it. Go back where you came from and leave us alone."

Tobias looked back and forth between Felix and the shopkeeper, his indignance fading away, replaced by fear. "Felix, perhaps we should go."

Felix nodded. "Sorry to trouble you," he muttered. He turned slowly, and as he and Tobias walked away, a nervous chatter rose up behind them.

"They'll come around."

"Just get what you need." He pulled up his hood. "I'll wait by the street."

"I'm sure not everyone in here—"

"I said, I'll wait outside, Toby. And hurry, would you?"

Tobias swallowed hard, searching Felix's face, and nodded. "Won't take but a few minutes."

Long strides took Felix to the main entrance. He pushed open the tall glass door, welcoming the rush of cool air on his hot face. *So that's how it is, huh?* He wasn't angry with the shopkeeper. He was angry with himself. All it had taken for him to turn tail and run had been the misguided words of a scared little man. *Some leader.*

He sought out a decorative enclave that he'd noticed on their way in and stepped inside, pressing his back against the wall, making himself as inconspicuous as he could. Then he waited, counting the long minutes until Tobias' return.

Chapter Eight

Well Enough Alone

THERE WAS NO NEED to arrange a city-wide meeting. D1 was full to overflowing already. News of the array had spread like wildfire, and when the day came, no one was prepared to sit quietly in their homes and wait to hear whether or not their salvation was at hand. They took to the streets, pouring into the city square and waiting with bated breath for someone, *anyone*, to give them news.

They did not have to wait long.

Ripley had been standing just inside the main Sigil entrance, staring through the glass door panes at the burgeoning crowd. Some of the Security force had spread out in a line across the wide stone steps, but this proved unnecessary. No one seemed to want to try and force their way in. It was almost as if they wanted to know what was happening, but were too afraid of the possibilities to seek the answers. This was as far as they were willing to go.

Edwin came up beside him, looking bedraggled. His fall from grace had not done him any favors. He looked old and tired, but he offered Ripley a weak smile.

"Where's your guard dog?"

Ripley inclined his head toward the crowd. "He's not my guard dog anymore. Just my roommate."

"Huh," said Edwin thoughtfully. "That's worse, somehow."

Ripley snickered. "Here he comes."

Denton was shoving his way through the throng, and even at a distance Ripley could tell he was griping about it. His face was twisted in a scowl, his mouth forming unintelligible words.

Ripley waited for Edwin to say more, but the silence stretched out for long moments as he shifted his weight uncomfortably from one leg to the other. He searched the multitude of faces, looking for one in particular, but Molly was nowhere to be seen.

"They aren't going to give you the credit you deserve, you know."

Edwin's statement caught Ripley by surprise, and he tore his gaze from the throng of people to look at the man beside him with a questioning gaze. Edwin's weak smile returned, almost apologetic.

"The CTC, I mean. They aren't going to thank you for

saving the city. Again."

Ripley looked away. "Oh." He wasn't sure what to say to that. He didn't really feel deserving of thanks. "That's okay. It was Ben's idea."

Edwin gave an exasperated sigh. "I don't know if you're humble or just stupid. But the fact remains that once again, no matter what you say, or what Fincher *doesn't* say, you've done the city a great service, Prior. And if no one else will thank you, then I will." He thrust his open palm in Ripley's direction and, feeling a bit taken aback, Ripley shook it. "Thank you, Mr. Prior."

A smile tugged at the corner of Ripley's mouth. "Always a pleasure, Mr. Smalls."

There was a loud commotion from behind them as a large group approached from the direction of Core Operations. Doris Fincher was leading the way, her beady eyes glinting greedily, a hungry grin stretching her thin lips so wide that it looked like it must hurt. Ben was jogging to keep up, surrounded by the rest of the CTC members and a handful of the team from the array project. Ripley and Edwin stepped aside as they passed, Ben flashing him a double thumbs-up and Fincher ignoring him all together. Edwin cast a meaningful look in Ripley's direction as if to say, *you see?*

But Ripley wasn't looking for Doris Fincher's approval. He was trying to atone for the opportunities he'd stolen by destroying the Nursery. He hadn't made the decision to take matters into his own hands lightly, but he would do it again in a heartbeat. He'd stolen their hope for security that day.

But today…today he had helped make it right. It was over. Nero wouldn't be sending any more troops through Antiquity's Gate. All that was left was the relatively small fleet now somewhere here on Earth, and even if they returned there was the hope that they, too, could be trapped back on Thera. Not for the first time, Ripley felt his stomach clench. *Would* Nero return? Or would he meet his match against the outside world?

Denton had made it to the steps just before the CTC group assembled there, and he'd made his way inside to stand with Ripley and Edwin. "The mob is out in force," he growled. "I swear, Prior, whenever you're involved in something, there's a ruckus." He eyed Edwin. "Not that you're any better."

Ripley shrugged. "Well, at least we're consistent."

Denton scowled as, outside the door, Fincher addressed the crowd.

"My dear citizens," she said, her voice sickly sweet, "today we celebrate what we, as a city, can accomplish when we work *together*. With the right leadership, with the right team, we have managed to do in a few weeks what the old Council could not accomplish in the long months of their tenure." Ripley snuck a glance at Edwin, whose blank expression offered no hint of how he felt about the slight. "We have achieved…peace."

The applause was nearly drowned out by the cheering.

New Sanctuary had been living under the shadow of death for so long that the very idea of safety and security was little more than a distant memory. Ripley had tuned out Fincher's voice as the speech continued, focusing on Ben, who was grinning broadly and waving exuberantly to the crowd. It was nice to see the kid get a little positive attention for once.

Fincher nodded to a man on her right, who pressed a finger to his ear. Light flooded Sigil square as the dome sprang to life.

"Let there be light in New Sanctuary once more!" The crowd went wild.

"I don't know if that's a great idea," Ripley muttered, more to himself than to anyone else.

Denton raised an eyebrow. "Why not? You like it dark eighteen hours a day? Get so used to living underground you're turning into a rat?"

"No," said Ripley firmly. "I just don't think it's wise to light up the city like a beacon. If Nero's fleet comes back—"

Edwin rolled his eyes. "Sweet Evenmire, Prior, let them have this one. We've done our part for the world. Let the other nations worry about Nero. There are plenty of people out there to fight him. Without backup, he has no chance of winning. Not if they combine their forces."

"Maybe not," Ripley reasoned, "but if Nero returns to see what the problem is and we're lit up like a beacon, the array won't do us much good, will it?"

It was obvious that this thought had not crossed

Edwin's mind until this moment. Ripley watched concern and comprehension wash over the older man's face. "Has anyone spoken to the CTC about that possibility?"

Ripley scowled. "Ben tried. I tried. And, as usual, no one listened. All they care about is looking good for the citizens. Long-term problems be damned."

A huff of mixed indignant and amusement escaped Edwin's lips. "So this is what it feels like to be on the other side of the table."

"Yeah." Ripley didn't return his smile. "Not great, huh?"

Edwin looked sideways at him. For perhaps the first time ever, they were on the same page. Just as Denton and Ripley had united in opposition of Edwin, Edwin and Ripley had somehow bonded over their mutual distaste for the new regime.

"...and that is why we aren't stopping with this array," came the booming voice of Fincher from outside. "We will continue our tireless work until Antiquity's Gate no longer darkens the doorstep of this beautiful city. Very soon, we will destroy it—once and for all!"

The thunderous crowd must have obscured the words. Ripley couldn't believe he'd heard what he thought he'd heard. But Edwin and Denton's identical, stunned expressions confirmed it.

"Did she just promise to..." Edwin asked.

"Yeah, she said it, all right," Denton confirmed, shaking his head. "What'd I tell you? You politicians are all the same. Nothin' but trouble."

*   *   *

RIPLEY, SHELL-SHOCKED, stepped aside to let the CTC group pass. They made their way across the Sigil lobby, surrounding Fincher like a human shield. Ben trailed in behind them, his already fair complexion almost translucent.

Ripley grabbed his arm and pulled him over. "What just happened?"

Ben blinked several times as if groggy.

"Parker, you done lost your damn mind, letting that woman think—" Denton began.

"I swear, I never...well, I mean...I might have said there was a *chance*!" Ben said, finding his voice again.

"You told her we could destroy it?" Ripley asked, hearing the incredulity in his own voice.

"I might have implied..." Ben swallowed hard. "It looked like she wasn't going to agree with the plan. I had to sweeten the deal. But I also said that it would take time, and might not even be possible at all. She just...ah, man." He took a deep breath, exhaling slowly. "I'll talk to her. But she just promised the entire city...if I stand up to her now..."

He locked eyes with Ripley, a knowing look passing between them. Fincher would throw Ben to the wolves if he didn't do what she asked.

"We need to head this off," Ripley urged. Ben was like a frightened animal, eyes wide and shifting his weight nervously, perhaps about to bolt. "Ben? Listen. You need to take a breath, calm down, and then go talk to Fincher. Focus on the early warning system. Tell her the Gate has to be intact if Nero returns."

"So we can let them through and lock it up again."

"Right. Really stress how important that is. Tell her if we were able to destroy the Gate, and Nero returned, he'd most likely investigate. And that would be very bad for all of us."

Ben stopped fidgeting and stared at Ripley with plaintive eyes. "But why me? Why do *I* have to go?"

Ripley sighed. "Ben…"

"I know, I know. She's not going to listen to anyone else. I get it." He drew in a long breath, puffing out his chest and closing his eyes. After several seconds he released it, then gave a single, defeated nod. "All right. I'm ready. I'm going." He turned to leave, but threw a glance back over his shoulder. "Wish me luck."

"Good luck," said Ripley.

"You're going to need it," muttered Denton.

As Ben strode away, Denton looked sideways at Ripley. "Why are you still here? Go with him."

"They aren't going to let me into a meeting, they'll barely even look at me."

"Why's it seem like I'm the only one around here with half a brain anymore?" Denton's expression was incredulous. "Use some of your damn super powers. Ya got ears, don't ya?"

He was right. Ripley's hearing was probably good

enough to hear whatever was going on in the meeting whether they let him in or not. "You're right!"

"'Course I'm right. Hurry up."

Ripley caught up with Ben just outside the lift and walked with him to the old Council chambers. There were several conversations going on inside. Ben hesitated just outside the double doors. "I wish Syl were here," he said softly.

Ripley gave him an encouraging smile. "Well, I'll have to do. I'll be right here. I know you can do this, Ben. You've just handed them a major win. She's going to be in a good mood, and it's because of you. Remember that. It's all we've got."

The young man returned a faltering smile. Then he nodded once and stepped up to the doors. He paused only a moment before pushing one open and slipping inside.

"Ah, there he is, the star of the hour!" Fincher's voice was the most cheerful Ripley had ever heard. No, not cheerful. Exuberant. She'd gotten exactly the reaction she'd been looking for from that crowd, and she was loving every minute of it."

"Madam Fincher, with all due respect," Ben said, and Ripley was proud of the way his friend's tone was calm and steady, "you shouldn't have said that. You should have let the people enjoy the success we've had with the array and let me and my team work on viable options for the next logical step. It could take weeks, months…heck, it could take years to find a way to destroy the Gate, and you've given the city the impression that it's a done deal."

"I gave the people the truth. You just said it yourself. This is the logical next step. This is what you promised us during your impassioned proposal."

"It wasn't a promise," Ben muttered. "It was...I don't know. A theory. Something to work toward."

"As your ability to disable the Gate at all was only a theory, isn't that correct, Mr. Parker? And yet, here we are. Victorious."

"I'm only saying that you're putting a lot of pressure on me and my team. Expectations we may not be able to live up to."

"I know you are capable of delivering on your promises—"

Ben's reply was defensive, his voice cracking. "It wasn't a—"

"Mr. Parker, let me make something quite clear. This is not my doing. *You* came to *us,* remember? *You* sought permission for this project and *you* said that the ultimate goal was to destroy the Gate entirely. Are you trying to tell me that was a lie? Think long and hard before you answer that."

"But I—"

"Long and hard, Mr. Parker."

Ben sighed. Waited. Relented. "It wasn't a lie. That was what I intended."

"So what's changed?"

"I just didn't expect to be thrust into anything so quick-

ly. You told them soon. But what we have to work with…
it's not enough. Not yet. We need time, preferably lots of
it."

"What you need is the proper motivation," came
Fincher's swift reply. Her arrogance was no longer masked
by the sweetness she'd employed on the steps of Sigil. "I'm
confident that with the full resources of this facility backing you, you'll have no problems whatsoever."

"*Proper motivation?* You don't think that keeping the
Elves from destroying the city is enough *motivation* for
me?"

"Calm down, Mr. Parker."

"I am *perfectly calm!*" intoned Ben with deadly seriousness. "I just don't think you are hearing me. We can't destroy
the Gate, not yet. The whole reason we built the array was
to disable it. And we've succeeded. If we mess with it now,
we're just asking for trouble. We could destroy the array
and have to start over. You know what happens if we have
to start over? We're defenseless from attack for weeks. We're
back to dimming the domes and hoping against hope that
Nero's troops don't show up. Just how long do you think
they're going to wait? With the Gate disabled, we can use
the early warning system to turn it on and off at will, but
with it destroyed, we might as well paint a target on top
of the dome and blast the lights twenty-four hours a day!
Now, I'm happy to do the research, work toward that end,
but that's not something that's going to happen overnight.
If we rush this, we're the ones who will suffer. Trust me, I

know a thing or two…about rushing into things before you have enough information." Ben was silent for a moment, letting his meaning sink in. "You'll be sorry. If you screw this up by rushing it, they'll vote you out of office faster than Edwin. People are fickle, Madam Fincher."

"I would advise you not to threaten me, Ben." Fincher's voice was icy now. "I have taken the opportunity to brush up on the theory behind the array during its construction. I believe that you've underestimated what you have here. With the proper frequency and power, you should be able to shatter that portal to hell once and for all."

Another pause. Then Ben, more subdued this time. "It would require a tremendous amount of power. The array wasn't built for that. It can't handle the load."

"You'll have access to whatever you need. The entire city is at your disposal. We are running on borrowed time, as you yourself have reminded us on *several* prior occasions. The array is not a long-term solution. What I'm proposing here is."

"You'll have to give me time. A few months, at minimum."

Someone came up behind Ripley, startling him. He'd been so focused on the proceedings he hadn't heard her approach.

"What's going on?" Sylvia asked breathlessly. "Is Ben in there?"

"Yes." Ripley held up a hand for quiet. "I'm trying to listen. Just wait."

"You are the most qualified person for the project, because it was your brainchild. I do not wish to pass this off on someone else and waste precious time getting them up to speed. We cannot be sure when or if the fleet will return. This needs to be dealt with quickly. You have your array, you have the ability to modulate its frequency. You have two weeks to find whatever else you need."

"Even if I were willing to try with what we've got, we'd have one shot at best before we overloaded the whole system. You were there, you saw how many times I had to adjust it to find the right frequency."

Fincher sighed, and Ripley heard what sounded like fingertips rapping gently on the table. "I understand you are reticent, Mr. Parker. For that reason, I am prepared to offer your friend a full pardon in exchange for your *enthusiastic* cooperation."

Ripley's hands balled into fists and he had to work hard not to burst into the room. *Don't do it, Ben,* he willed. *Not for me. This is foolish.*

The pause was excruciating.

"No," Ben said with cold firmness. "Ripley wouldn't want to risk what we've accomplished for his own gain. I won't do it. I will take as long as I need. You'll get what you want, it just won't be as quick as you'd like."

"Very well. If you are going to force my hand, so be it." There were faint sounds. Paper rustling, footsteps. A long, quiet pause.

"You can't do that," Ben whispered. "You can't."

"I can, and I will, Mr. Parker. You'll see that it's already been signed and ratified. A two-thirds vote from the CTC board is more than enough to—"

"This is blackmail!"

"No," Fincher replied coolly. "This is politics."

There was an excruciatingly long pause. Sylvia fidgeted beside Ripley. When Ben spoke next, his defeated words were accompanied by the sound of the tearing of paper.

"All right," he said softly. "You win. I'll do it."

* * *

RIPLEY WAS DESPERATE to know what had just transpired. What could they possibly hold over Ben's head that would make him concede to their demands? The double doors swung wide and Ben came out, his expression bleak. Sylvia opened her mouth to speak, but Ben shook his head. "Not here. Go to Ripley's. I'll be there as soon as I can. There are some…some things I still have to talk to Fincher about."

"Ben," began Ripley.

"I said go."

The CTC filed out around Ben, Fincher in the rear. She was beaming with triumph.

"Mr. Parker," she said, ignoring the others. "Would you accompany me to my office so we can discuss the finer details, please."

"Yeah, sure." Ben's face was glum as he glanced at Sylvia one more time before following Fincher down the hall toward the lift.

Sylvia and Ripley made their way out of Sigil. The crowds had dispersed, but the limited capacity of the Tube meant the cars were still packed. Ripley stood quietly, pressed up against others. Inside, he was screaming. Ripley knew what the CTC's plan entailed—a miracle. The sheer scope of configuring the array, the amount of power required…the most likely scenario was that the array would be ruined, leaving them vulnerable for whatever span of time it took to repair. They should be focusing on restoring communications with the outside world, figuring out a way to contact Pravacordia or Culei to find out what had become of the seventy-five ships already on Earth, and if they were still a threat. And, though he knew the CTC would never *dream* of it, they should be trying to find a way to help. This wasn't New Sanctuary verses Thera. It was Thera verses Earth. Humanity needed to stand together.

When Ripley and Sylvia reached the Edge they found the building abandoned. Molly might have taken the kids to the gathering, or perhaps she was visiting Geo with them. A pang of regret replaced his worry. He'd been so preoccupied that he hadn't even done her the simple kindness of finding out where she'd be during the whole announcement debacle.

He didn't know what to do with himself while he waited, so he rummaged through Denton's pile of gear and started painting. He didn't much care for the color selection, many of which were mostly empty cans, but settled on the darkest he could find. Sylvia picked up a brush to help, and they worked side-by-side in silence. The paint turned out to be a deep blue-green. Not exactly what he'd call relaxing for a sleeping area, but it would cover up the sneering Elf on his wall, and that was the important thing. They had actually finished rolling three of the walls and were busy pulling the iron-framed bunk away from the fourth when there was a knock at the door. He dropped the bed with a loud *thunk* and rushed to answer it.

Ben wrinkled his nose as he entered. "Open a window, Ripley, you two are going to pass out in here."

Ripley left the door open and gestured to the sitting area. "Sure," he said, moving back into his blue-green bedroom and pulling open the window. "Sorry. Now that that's out of the way, you mind telling me what the heck happened back there?"

Ben shook his head. "It doesn't matter. What matters is, we need to figure out how to do what Fincher wants, and fast. So give me your best ideas. Hopefully the fumes in here haven't melted that beautiful brain of yours."

Ripley crossed his arms, looking back and forth between the Parker siblings. "It's a bad idea to push forward before we're ready," he pressed. "And you know that. I heard everything. So why did you agree to it?"

"She didn't give me a choice!" Ben spat, standing up and pacing back and forth across the small room.

"I don't understand!" Ripley said, feeling frustrated. "What could possibly be worth risking how far we've come?"

"If I don't do it, she's going to shut down the array just long enough to send all the Halfsies through," Ben said coldly, whirling on Ripley. "How do you think that'll go over?"

Ripley's mouth was hanging open as he struggled to process Ben's words. "But...that would be..."

"Yeah," said Ben, sneering at the carpet as if it had done him some great personal wrong. "A death sentence. If Sanctuary's Elves were any predictor, those families wouldn't stand a chance on Thera. Not when all pretense is gone. Not when we're at war."

"But she can't," Ripley said, feeling suddenly weak in the knees. "She must be bluffing. No one's that cruel. And even if she was, who would run Geo?"

"That's just it, isn't it?" Ben said bitterly. "We've made Geo safer, haven't we? More tolerable. It doesn't *have* to be a penal colony. It could just be a mildly unpleasant work assignment, just like anything else in the city. Not to mention two hundred less mouths to feed."

"We can't let that happen." Sylvia's face was determined, but her voice wavered. "We can't let them...all those people..."

"No, of course not," Ripley agreed. "So we have to find a way to give the CTC what they want." Mind racing, he sat down in the chair opposite Sylvia while Ben continued to pace. "But how? We'll need—"

"A tremendous amount of power," Ben finished for

him.

"Well, we *do* have a volcano powering the Geothermal system," Ripley pointed out. "Our power is virtually unlimited."

"Yeah, but we also have a lot of demands on the system already," Ben said. "It's old, and it would require a *lot* of work to modify to get the kind of output we'd need. Not to mention, finding the frequency required is going to call for a lot of short, strong bursts. I'm worried that if we subject the Geothermal system to that kind of strain—"

"We'll destroy more than just the array."

Sylvia shot Ripley a puzzled look. "What do you mean?"

Ripley closed his eyes with a sigh. "Anything we tinker with in Geo is a risk. We demand too much of it and we could end up losing life support, freezing to death, asphyxiating the population, you name it. It's our only power source, and it's old and fragile. It's the heart of the city. If the heart stops beating, we die."

Ben stopped pacing, his face scrunched up hard in concentration. "Then we need a separate power source. Something we can isolate, so that if anything goes wrong, New Sanctuary isn't affected."

"But where are we going to find a power source that can deliver what we need?" Sylvia was wringing her hands. "There's certainly nothing in New Sanctuary that can come close."

"There's got to be a way to funnel what we need safely."

"I might have an idea..." Ben trailed off, eyes flitting around the room absently. "Where's Molly?"

"I'm not sure. What's your idea?"

"It's something I remember learning about but...it might not even be possible."

"Ben?" Sylvia pressed.

"I need to talk to Molly," he insisted.

Ripley was growing irritated with Ben's refusal to give a straight answer. "What on Earth could Molly possibly do to help with this situation?"

"I'll explain it when I get back."

A moment later he had made his way out the door and disappeared. "I really hate when he does that," Ripley muttered as he made to follow, but Sylvia's voice stopped him.

"Ripley, wait. Let him go."

He turned back to find her standing behind him. Her eyes were narrowed as she searched his face. "Whatever Ben's thinking, it needs to work. We have to succeed."

"I know that." Ripley shifted uncomfortably. "If anyone can make it work, he can."

"Lives are at stake."

Does she think I don't understand that? "I knew Fincher was driven, but I didn't think she was so cruel. I'm not sure she'd follow through with it or if it's an empty threat. But I'm not willing to risk the lives of every Halfsie in Geo in hopes that she's bluffing."

"Not just their lives, Ripley." Sylvia moved a little closer, and Ripley backed up again, feeling his tunic brush against the dining table. "Fincher doesn't know anything about you except what you've done and what you look like. You're a threat. She considers you a Halfsie, too. Worse, even, because of the trouble you've caused the Council in the past."

This caught Ripley by surprise. He stopped moving and frowned, considering the irony. The injuries that had caused his current condition had been sustained saving the city. The venting of the D6 condenser had stolen so much from him—apparently, in the eyes of Doris Fincher, it had even stolen his humanity.

"Haven't the Halfsies been through enough? Haven't they proven already that they're cooperative, hardworking people who just want to be allowed to live in peace? They're just people, Sylvia. They're not monsters. *We're* not monsters."

Sylvia looked as though he'd slapped her. "I never thought you were."

Ripley knew that the anger growing inside him was not meant for her. He was angry at the circumstances, the CTC, Doris Fincher, Nero. He felt the pressure of the constant threat building in his chest, the weight of the domes pressing down on him. He scowled at Sylvia.

"There's no point in denying it. You saw me when they dragged me off D6, more dead than alive. You were there through the therapy, the first person I spoke to when I came out of that pod. You saw then what I had become. A hollow shell. No less hideous than the Forlorn. You can't look me in the eye and tell me you didn't see a monster."

"I can't look you in the eye and tell you anything, because you won't even face me!"

She grabbed his face and forced his gaze back to her. Her hands were warm and soft against his flushed cheeks.

"You saved everyone in this city! Physically it may have had a high cost, but it didn't take away what makes you *you*, Ripley."

He tried to turn away, unable to quell the rage, unable to stop himself from taking it out on her, but she held him fast. "My scars are gone, but I'm not who I was. A part of me is...something else. How can I even be sure I'm still the same person?"

Unshed tears fought for release, burning his eyes and blurring Sylvia's face. He couldn't tell. Where those brown eyes full of pity? Did the soft smile hint of sorrow?

"I know because I know you, Ripley. You haven't changed since the day we met. Sure, you look different now, but your heart is the same."

"Sylvia," he said, feeling the anger starting to drain away beneath her calming touch, "you have only ever been kind to me. Because you are a caring, compassionate person. And I think that's clouded your perception. You felt bad for me, wanted to take care of me. But you don't have to do that anymore. I didn't want your pity then, and I certainly don't want it now."

"I never pitied you, Ripley," she whispered. He swallowed hard and the tears he'd fought so hard to hold back spilled over. He blinked rapidly. Her face seemed to be getting closer. "I fell in love with you."

Sylvia was up on her tiptoes. He didn't have time to think before her lips were pressed against his, warmer and softer than her hands, the familiar scent of citrus and honey surrounding. Too stunned to react, he did nothing. He felt nothing. He'd never kissed anyone before. He hadn't even considered it. Somehow, Ripley thought it should feel different than it did.

"Sylvia! Ripley! Molly's back, and I was right, we can—oh."

Sylvia broke away and Ripley turned to the doorway with a sinking, horrid feeling in the pit of his stomach. Ben stood on the threshold, Molly just behind him. Her face was unreadable, but she was quivering, hands clenched tightly at her sides.

Ripley didn't know what to say. He couldn't even think straight. He could still feel the warmth where Sylvia's lips had been a moment before, and now a new warmth that spread through his cheeks. Blood pounded behind his eardrums, his stomach twisted in a knot and his heart racing.

"I uh, think I know how we can get more power," Ben said lamely into the heavy silence.

Molly said nothing, disappearing from the doorway like a whisp of vapor, her footfalls light and quick as she made for the stairwell. Ben grimaced, his eyes apologetic. "We'll, uh...I'll just...hmm. I'm going to go. We'll talk in the morning."

"Ben," Ripley called after him, but the young man had already taken his leave. "Molly!"

"I'm so sorry," Sylvia was saying, backing away from him. "I thought...I don't know what I thought. I should go, too."

"Oh no," Ripley said, turning back to her and ready to physically block her from leaving if necessary. "Not you, too. Stay. Please."

She hesitated, biting her lip, and moved back toward the sitting area. Ripley took a deep, steadying breath before he followed.

Sylvia looked ready to say something, but Ripley held up a hand. "Please, let me start. You have nothing to apologize for, Sylvia. I should be the one apologizing. I've been so caught up in everything that's been going on that I didn't even realize that you might...it even feels strange to have to say it. That you might...have feelings for me. I didn't see it. I considered myself your pet project, a broken, fragile creature in need of compassion. It wasn't until recently that I discovered that something more might have developed between us."

"Discovered..." Sylvia sighed. "Ben told you."

Ripley nodded.

"I wish he wouldn't have done that."

"No, I'm glad he told me. I was stupid. I should have known. I should have said something."

"I just thought...we've been through so much together. I had hoped you felt the same. But when I kissed you, I could tell. I could tell that you felt nothing for me."

"That's not true at all!" Ripley leaned forward and grasped her hand. "Listen, Sylvia. I thought I was going to die on top of D6. And the next thing I knew, I woke up in a world that was alien to me. I was alien to myself. You were my only friend in those days. The only one who didn't cringe when you saw me, or pretend I wasn't there. I will always be grateful for our friendship. I will always care deeply about you. But not in that way."

She squeezed his hand, gave him a weak smile. "It was never pity, you know."

"I do now. And I'm glad. But I'm also so, so sorry."

Sylvia nodded. "Me too."

She stood, and this time Ripley didn't try to stop her. She made her way to the door and then paused, turning. "I want you to be happy, Ripley. You deserve to be happy. If anything good came from tonight, I hope it's that you realize how others feel about you. Not just me."

* * *

"NEW SANCTUARY TO RIPLEY. Stay with us man, this is important stuff."

Ben had chosen, mercifully, not to bring up last night's events. Whether Sylvia had asked him not to or whether he just felt himself above an *I-told-you-so*, Ripley would never know. "I'm paying attention," he insisted. "Go on."

They were in one of Sigil's north wing resource rooms.

After the Elves had made their hasty retreat, Ben's team had been able to unlock access to a great deal of information, all accessible to anyone who needed it from the consoles. It had been this information that had led to many of the advancements they'd made, like Denton's prized gun turret project. But no one had yet let Ripley in on what key information they had dug up to help in their current dilemma. All he knew was that Molly had made herself busy helping Ben with it, getting up earlier than usual to avoid riding the Tube with Ripley. He found himself torn between wanting to talk to her and not knowing what to say. Right now it didn't matter. He needed to focus.

Was he reading into things, or was she standing more formally than usual, as if about to teach a class instead of about to address her friends and peers?

"I've been helping Ben mine some important data from the archives. I knew a bit, of course, since I *do* teach this sort of thing. But I have been able to uncover maps and coordinates that will be crucial on our mission."

"Ain't told us what this mission *is* yet," grumbled Denton, arms folded across his chest as he slouched in a chair not quite meant for someone his size.

Ben cleared his throat. "We're going on a little excursion. To rediscover a piece of history!"

Denton's thick eyebrows raised in mock excitement. "Oh, yay."

"Way before Sanctuary came about, there were several bases here on Antiquity Island." Molly began, not even acknowledging Denton's mocking, "Scott and McMurdo. Though both were incorporated into our city during its construction, they had been around a long time first. McMurdo was the first to attempt to power itself with a modest nuclear reactor, but they ultimately failed. It was, at the time, not something humanity had mastered. However, in the centuries since then, nuclear power using something known as microreactors became a much more reliable and affordable options. There are decommissioned microplants all over the Antarctic, but the closest one to us is here—" Her words seemed dry and rehearsed. Beside her, Ben picked up a crudely drawn map and thrust a finger vaguely at what might have been a smudge. Molly acknowledged the map as she finished. "On Black Island."

"Black *Island?*" remarked Denton incredulously. "And how are we going to get there, you gonna build us a ship?"

"Don't need to," quipped Ben. "We can get there by land, across the ice shelf. Don't worry, big guy. I've got transportation all set!"

Ripley had stood and moved to the front of the room without even realizing he'd done it. Molly took a few paces back, but at least for the present moment, Ripley was able to focus on a new predicament. "I've got some concerns," he told Ben quietly. "Do you have a better map?"

"Yeah, of course." He motioned toward a computer terminal and Ripley took in the old but detailed topographical images.

He scanned the information below the map. "Did you

even read this?"

"What does it say?" Sylvia asked from her seat behind Ripley. He straightened up and turned to the group, focusing on Denton, Edwin, anyone but Sylvia. She, on the other hand, looked straight at Ripley. "It's called Black Island for a *reason*. There's no snow because the wind is too constant and too strong for anything to accumulate. It's constantly scoured down to bare rock."

Edwin raised his hand and Ben rolled his eyes. "You don't have to raise your hand, Edwin. We're not in primary school."

"Right. Sorry. Just wondering why a little wind would be a problem."

Ripley shook his head in irritation. "A little wind might not be a problem. But during storms, we're looking at," he glanced back at the monitor to confirm, "sustained gusts over a hundred and twenty-five miles per hour."

"Then we just won't show up in the middle of a storm," Ben said, sounding as though this seemed perfectly reasonable.

"And what do we do, once we get there?" Edwin asked. "Assuming we make it at all. This, what was it called again? Microreactor? How do we even know it still exists?"

"They were built to last," Molly said, a hint of reassurance creeping into her voice. Perhaps Edwin's pitiful appearance brought back a bit of her warmth.

Or perhaps she'd never lost it, she just had none for Ripley.

"It will still be there. And the cores should still be good. According to our research, it was only in operation for a few years before Sanctuary's Geothermal plant took over."

"So this thing powered Sanctuary when it was being built?" Ripley asked.

"Yeah!" Ben said, his eyes lit with excitement. "So all the cabling, everything like that, it's all still here. All we have to do is, *click,*" he made an upward motion with his finger, "flip on the switch."

"Even if it were as easy as," Ripley raised his eyebrows and mimicked Ben's motion, "flipping the switch, we still don't have a way to get there. I don't even know how long it would take on foot, but we'd probably die from exposure if we attempted it."

"Well, first off, you haven't heard the whole plan, ye of little faith," Ben replied with a smirk. "Come on, time for a field trip. To the Tube!"

When they reached Sigil Station, instead of heading onto the platform, Ben turned left. Ripley stopped short as Ben started to descend the narrow steps down to the Tube tracks. The others followed dutifully, keen to find out what it was that Ben was refusing to tell them, but Ripley was frozen to the spot. His knees trembled and his heart was throbbing in his chest. Images, voices, emotions all swirled through his mind in rapid succession until he squeezed his eyes shut, willing them away.

"We had a good run."

"The best."

"It's time."

He could feel the curvature of the dome beneath his feet, the fierce wind tearing at his makeshift cloak. Ripley was back on top of Dome Six.

Ben had stopped at the bottom of the short stairwell, apparently noticing his reticence to go on. "Ripley? You okay?"

He could see the condenser rising up before him. His hands clenched and they felt icy cold, like the rungs of the ladder.

"Ripley?"

It was Sylvia's voice this time, drawing him back to the present. Ripley stepped back from the ladder and opened his eyes, forcing his grimace into a smile. "Yeah, sorry. I'm coming."

CHAPTER NINE

WHAT BECOMES OF SPIES

L AEVUS RETURNED TO the spot where his human companions were awaiting his findings, once again awed at how oblivious they were to their surroundings. They showed no signs of noticing his presence until he was right on top of them. Nelson nearly jumped out of his skin, but Ponytail simply looked apathetic, rubbing his hands briskly against his upper arms to battle the rising chill.

"Storm's coming," he said, by way of greeting. Ponytail was always less verbose in the mornings, which was why Laevus had come to enjoy rising early during their time together.

Laevus looked up at the clear sky and frowned. "I see no storm clouds."

Ponytail snorted. "Never question a Culeian about the weather. We don't require anything so ostentatious as a cloud to know when a storm is imminent."

"Seems like you've been gone for hours." Nelson stretched his arms high and rolled his head back and forth, cracking his neck.

Laevus felt a sneer curl his lips. He had not been off gallivanting. He'd been scouting out the area, trying to find the safest route into Nero's camp. The number of viable infiltration plans that he'd come up with was dwindling quickly. He was down to his last resort.

"We'll continue toward the tower and find shelter on the way if it proves necessary.

Far in the distance, a rumble of thunder echoed. Ponytail smirked. "Perhaps we'd better make haste. It's a common misconception that because Culeains hail from the depths of the sea we are therefore fond of being wet. This is not the case. Particularly if we aren't allowed to build a fire to dry off."

"You're allowed to do whatever you wish. Start all the fires you like. Just don't expect me to be around to help you when the patrols show up to see where all the smoke is coming from."

They grabbed the supplies, Nelson muttering under his breath about how Laevus, being the strongest, should be carrying more. He didn't dare insist, which was wise. They'd come so far together; Laevus would hate to have to kill him now.

They set off at a brisk pace, and despite his general tendency to lag behind, Laevus could see that Ponytail was making a concerted effort to keep up for once.

The underbrush was thicker here in the interior of the island. It made for slower progress. Nelson continued his stream of uttered complaints, and Laevus continued to ignore him.

"Sweet Evenmire!"

Nelson stopped dead, the exclamation loud enough to make Laevus cringe. "Keep it down. You're like a walking distress signal."

Nelson pointed upward, and Laevus followed his line of sight to a tree just up ahead. A single boot dangled just below the canopy, a plume of red fabric rippling beside it like an oversized cape tangled among the branches.

Shuddering, Nelson drew closer until the unfortunate owner of the boot was almost directly overhead. "What happened to him?"

"Looks like a parachuter," Ponytail replied.

Laevus began moving again. "It is. I believe he was a Pravacordian pilot."

"What?" Nelson perked up, jogging up to Laevus' side, stumbling over a hidden root. "What makes you say that?"

In answer, Laevus gestured toward a place where sunlight poured down through a break in the trees. "Because apparently, none of them are very good at landing their ships."

Before them lay the once-sleek hull of an aircraft, the

fuselage twisted unnaturally where its nose disappeared, buried in the ground. One wing, sheared off to a nub, jutted up at an angle toward the sky.

Ponytail gave a low whistle, moving closer to inspect the wreckage. "Not your run-of-the-mill scouting vessel. Cirrus class, if I'm not mistaken. A sign of how bad things must be, I expect, if the Pravacordians are employing Chronohalks for reconnaissance missions." He ran his hand along the hull, stopping to inspect something more closely. "Must have been taken down by the Therans while attempting a fly-over, poor sap."

"How do you know?" Nelson demanded, stepping up beside Ponytail and squinting, as if he might find the answers written on the downed craft somewhere. "All that stuff about what kind of ship it is?"

"Her Majesty's Navy." Ponytail began walking around, looking for the easiest way in no doubt. "It is the duty and privilege of every Culeian citizen to serve for, at minimum, two years. During my own service I was exposed to a vast array of knowledge concerning the other nations and the assets they employ."

"Oh?" Nelson seemed genuinely interested to learn these bits of trivia. "How long did you serve?"

Ponytail raised an eyebrow. "Two years."

"As interesting as your patriotic escapades may be," said Laevus, striding up to the ship and dipping beneath the remnant of the wing, "I would prefer to *not* discuss it somewhere dry."

"It occurs to me that this is just as good a place as any." Ponytail let out a grunt as he hefted himself inside the downed ship. Intermittent drops of rain had begun their long descent from the clouds, spattering the clearing. "Perhaps you'd be interested to know that Chronohawks feature a canopy that is blown clear of the ship in the event of an ejection. It's fortunate that the angle of impact is such that it should protect us from the worst of the storm, at least."

Both seats had also been ejected, leaving a space just large enough to accommodate the three of them. Laevus briefly considered taking his chances outside as lightning flashed in the west.

Fat drops of water ran through cracks in the twisted frame as the rain began in earnest, the driving wind forcing them into the compartment and creating a little pool near the crumpled nose. Crouched and weary, the three waited, listening to the pounding of the rain on the hull, and the thunder that seemed to shake the earth around them. "Are we safe in here?" Nelson asked after a time. "From the lightning and whatnot?"

Ponytail attempted a shrug in the cramped space, nudging Laevus with his shoulder. "Perhaps you'd rather take your chances outside…"

Another crack of thunder rolled over them, and Nelson shook his head. "No. Just wondering."

"Wonder in silence," Laevus snapped.

"Talking might help pass the time," suggested Ponytail.

You know what else helps pass the time? Being unconscious. Let me know if you require assistance in attaining that state.

"What about the patrols?"

"Won't be an issue."

"They must know they shot it down, though, right? Wouldn't they want to investigate, check for survivors?"

"I'm certain they came and went ages ago," Laevus told him. His intent was not to comfort, but to quell any fledgling conversation topics.

Nelson peered at him in the dim yellow lantern light. "How do you know when it crashed, though? It could have been today. They could be outside right now!"

Laevus frowned. "Trust me. It isn't recent."

"But—"

"That dangling fool has been up in that tree for some time." Laevus had forgotten how dull the senses of the humans were. "The smell of death hung around him like a veil. They came, they saw, they left. They won't bother with this place again."

There was a short, beautiful silence, broken only by the constant drumming of the rain. Then Nelson felt the need to spoil it with more inane chatter.

"We should cut him down. After the storm, I mean. Obviously."

"And why would we want to do that?"

Nelson frowned. "We ought to give him a decent burial."

"And how do you intend to dig the grave," Laevus

asked. "With your bare hands?"

"I don't know, I just thought—"

"Well, stop. Wasting our time will do him no good. I don't think he cares either way, do you?"

The storm came to a crescendo. The humans' desire to talk was drowned out as giant claps of thunder rolled over one another overhead in a constant roar that made Laevus want to claw his eardrums out. He did not like storms. They were unpredictable and impossible to control.

Once the rain had abated, Nelson hesitated. "Should we wait a bit longer, just to be sure?"

"If I don't get out of this coffin *right now*, it may well become your permanent residence," whispered Laevus in a threatening tone.

Time was running short. It was clear that the humans no longer feared him as they had aboard the Culeian transport. They had come to the false conclusion that if he had not harmed them yet, he would not do so at all. That was a trait all humans seemed to share, short-sightedness. Soon they would cease to follow his orders all together, and that would not do at all. Laevus had wanted to be more prepared. He excelled at preparation, enjoyed exercising his skills as if it were a game. But the humans did not wish to play. They were going to force his hand.

The smell of damp earth flooded the clearing, the breeze shaking heavy droplets from tree branches, the gentle pitter patter on the broad leaves of the undergrowth much more agreeable to Laevus than the heavy deluge of the storm.

"Now what?" Nelson demanded, his boots squelching as he tromped around in aimless circles. "It's too dark to go anywhere. I can barely see my hand in front of my face."

"Find the driest patch of ground and get some rest," Laevus told him. "Tomorrow, this will all be over."

*　　*　　*

LAEVUS WOKE HIS TRAVELLING companions with a swift kick to the shins each, causing them both to yelp in quick succession.

"Up! We've no time to waste."

"What?" Nelson asked, rubbing groggy eyes with a dirt-covered hand. "What's going on? What's happening?"

"What's happening is that while we're lazing around, Nero is happily going about the systematic destruction of your world. No more waiting. It's time to act."

Ponytail yawned, stretching. "Good morning to you, too."

Nelson and Terrance dragged themselves up with some difficulty as Laevus practically skipped around the camp-site, tearing through the bags in search of food. He felt refreshed, invigorated. Ready to do what he'd come here to do.

Ready to take Nero down.

"We'll skirt around the edge of the camp and see if we can locate him from a distance," Laevus instructed them as they began the trek back toward the encampment. "Rather,

I'll skirt around the edge. You both are too likely to get us caught."

"You've already seen the camp," argued Nelson. "What else is there to see?"

"I've yet to locate Nero. But that ends today. I can feel it."

Ponytail raised an eyebrow. "I thought you didn't believe in feelings. Sure didn't believe me about that storm."

Laevus offered him a simpering smile. "I believe in feelings. I simply choose not to trust any but my own."

"So then, what will *we* be doing?" Nelson moved toward the underbrush, losing no time in stumbling over something hidden beneath the greenery. "Oof! Stupid rocks. Stupid island!" He kicked the offending stone as if it had purposely caused him pain.

"I share the sentiment," Ponytail empathized. "I would give anything to be back home, with a crate of Nouritas and a hearty meal."

"If Nero has his way, you won't have a place to go home *to*," retorted Laevus. "It's time to stop whining and start taking life seriously. Because this is *deadly* serious. If we fail, Nero will kill all of us. Don't you believe for a second that that monster has a shred of compassion in his body. He has no use for you, or me."

"That doesn't answer the question," Nelson pointed out, stepping gingerly over a fallen log. "What do we do while you're out looking for Nero?"

"I'll show you where you should stay. You'll worry

about remaining out of sight until I find him. Then, on my signal, you'll create a distraction."

"Create a…a distraction?" Nelson said in disbelief. "Sweet Evenmire, man! How are we going to create a distraction *and* manage to evade them?"

"Put your heads together and think of something," Laevus advised. "You've time yet. I'm sure between the two of you, you'll be able to work something out."

Laevus left them in a ditch that shielded them from view of the surrounding forest not far from the crash site. He felt confident that this was as safe a place as could be found on the island. Nero did not have many of his forces combing the interior. He'd focused on the coastline and the area directly surrounding the encampment. Assured that the humans were, for the time being, safe from capture, he set off at a run.

He hadn't even broken a sweat by the time he reached the overlook from which they'd spotted the camp previously. He scanned the troops again, confirming the number of ships and searching the faces for the only one that mattered.

But there was no sign of Nero.

He edged further down the embankment, whispering between the trees, always taking care to stay well away from any passing soldiers. Each time he found a suitable place to stop he would perch like a bird of prey, peering down on the camp and watching, waiting. The rustle of tent flaps would catch his eye, or the opening of a ship hatch. But still no Nero. Laevus was certain that Nero was here somewhere, safe from attack while he shipped off his army to do his bidding. This would be the day…

Laevus felt his heart begin to pound. There, halfway across the clearing, recognizable by the strut alone, he spotted his target. Nero had always thought himself better than everyone else. The very way he walked declared it. Laevus sat quietly, dangling his leg off the edge of the rock cliff where he was seated, as casual as if he were enjoying a day at the seaside. He shifted, removing a troublesome pebble from beneath him and flicking it away without ever taking his eyes of Nero's distant form. He tracked the man all the way back to one of the tents. Nero entered, and did not come out again.

Making note of the placement of Nero's sleeping quarters, Laevus stood and slunk further away. He wondered if the humans would have come up with a suitable plan for a distraction or if he would have to do it himself. Their escape did not concern him; all that mattered was Nero. Of course, he could hardly expect them to agree with this. Humans weren't the brightest species on the planet.

"I've found him," Laevus said brightly, looking down into the ditch where Terrance and Nelson were sitting idly, like rabbits caught in a trap.

"About that," Nelson said, reaching up to grab Laevus' outstretched hand. "We've been talking it over."

"And we're not convinced this is the best course of action," Terrance declared.

Laevus almost dropped Nelson, but just gave him a swift tug instead, causing him to stumble forward. "It is the *only* course of action," he said quietly. "We have discussed it, in painstaking length."

"Indeed we have, but," Terrance said, squinting and scratching the back of his neck. "Well, we just find the odds terribly unfavorable."

"We don't know anything for sure," Nelson explained, unbidden. "We don't know if Culei has shared the existence of this place with the other nations. We don't know what Nero is planning. We don't know if we could get in and make it out alive."

"I *thought* you were better than this," Laevus said, his brow furrowing. "I thought you wanted to be a *hero*. Save the day."

"I *do*," Nelson insisted, not recognizing the open scorn in Laevus' remarks. "And that's exactly why I think...I think we should go to the tower *first*. We ought to warn someone. Anyone. Let them know how many ships we've seen, how many troops...that way if we...if we don't make it out...at least we'll have given them a fighting chance."

"So," Laevus said, turning this over in his mind, "you're saying that *after* we make it to the tower, you're still willing to help me kill Nero?"

"Yes," Nelson said, too quick. "Well, as long as whoever we speak to thinks it's a good idea. I mean, they may have people better trained. More likely to succeed, and all that."

"I see."

227

Laevus pondered the pair for a long while before relenting. "Very well. We'll do it your way."

Both were visibly relieved by the ease with which they had convinced him to see reason. They followed him without argument as he led the way toward the tower, which had been visible on the far side of Nero's camp.

"I recognize this place," Terrance said after a time. "We're headed straight for the camp."

"Your tower is on the other *side* of the camp," Laevus pointed out coolly. "We have to pass it to get there."

"Yeah, but, shouldn't we maybe give it a wide berth?"

Laevus didn't answer as he took several more paces. Then he turned to face his recalcitrant companions. "Why on this accursed planet would we do that?" he asked, his tone one of genuine confusion.

"Uh," said Nelson, mocking, "I don't know. Maybe so there's less chance of us getting caught?"

"Oh, my dear boys," Laevus said, shaking his head sadly. "I hate to tell you this, but there is very little chance that you will avoid being captured."

Both were staring at him, unnerved and confused.

Laevus gave them an apologetic smile before he opened his mouth wide, shouting at the top of his lungs, "*Humans! There are Humans here!*"

"What the hell are you doing?" cried Nelson, looking around with wild eyes.

"I'm creating the distraction you regrettably refused to create," Laevus told him. "I told you my intent. You did not comply. I cannot take the risk that you would refuse to help me after reaching the tower. Therefore," he said, giving a gentle wave of his hand, "I would suggest you start running."

Nelson and Terrance, who had been so uncooperative in his plan, now did precisely as he suggested. Laevus waved goodbye to their backs before turning and sprinting toward the encampment.

Two clones crossed his path, crossbows at the ready. "What's going on?" one demanded.

"Who are you?" asked the other, training his weapon on Laevus.

But Laevus only scowled at them. "Does it *look* like this is a good time for stupid questions?" he snapped. "I've just run all the way from the eastern shore to warn you, and *this* is the thanks I get?"

The clones glanced uncertainly at each other and Laevus let out an exasperated sigh.

"Incompetence!" he stated brusquely. "*You*," he said, poking the one on the left squarely in the chest, with utter disregard for the crossbow, "run back to the camp and inform Nero to disburse the troops. Tell him the humans are closing in. The island is crawling with them!"

When the clone just stared at him with a blank expression, Laevus pointed in the direction Nelson and Terrance had gone. "Go!"

At last the soldier did as he was ordered, turning and sprinting soundlessly back toward the camp.

"And you," Laevus commanded, rounding on the second clone, "come with me. I've just seen two of them not far from here. We'll head them off and take them in for questioning. Find out what they know."

"But I—"

Laevus jabbed a finger in the direction Ponytail and Nelson had run. "If you don't believe me, then use those perfect senses of yours and see for yourself. Can't you *smell* them? They were just here!"

The clone raised his head, closing his eyes as he sniffed the air. "Yes," he agreed, eyes still shut tight. "Yes, I can—"

Laevus had bent down and picked up a large rock in the space of an instant, and put all the force he could muster into a blow to the clone's head. The soldier crumpled to the ground, and Laevus went to work pulling off his uniform and cloak. He would be completely recognizable if Nero were to see him first, but he would blend in much better than he did in his tattered Culeian garb.

He took only a moment to admire the fine comfort of the familiar Theran materials. Then, feeling much better than he had in quite some time, he picked up the fallen crossbow and set off for Nero's camp.

CHAPTER TEN

ONE SMALL STEP FOR SANCTUARY

B EN LED THE WAY down the cool expanse of the main
line. The others followed quietly, having given up on
getting an answer out of him. But Ripley knew where they
were going. He knew long before Ben turned right, long
before they came upon the first of three hatches leading
through the bulkhead.

It was different, now, but not much. The hastily constructed hatch that Felix had pried open that night when
they'd discovered the breach had been replaced by a much
neater door panel with a proper seal along the edges. When
Ben pulled it open, Molly gasped and Sylvia pulled her
arms in against her chest, shivering. "It gets worse," Ben
informed them cheerfully, leading them into the first

bulkhead.

Last time, it had been dark. Someone had added lighting, and a long row of hooks along one wall showcased an assortment of heavy coats, while a tall, nondescript yellow bin held hats and gloves. Ben passed them out and everyone got dressed quickly, thankful for the added layer of warmth.

"You should keep this stuff in the tunnel," Molly suggested as she pulled on a pair of mittens. "Where it's warmer."

"You know how these things are." Ben zipped his jacket right up to his chin. "When you're in charge, people only listen to about half of what you say. I've gotten used to not sweating the small stuff."

There was a sharp pain in Ripley's side and he cast a sidelong glance at Denton, remembering their encounter in the main line. Those injuries had long since healed, but this place brought the pain rushing back.

"Hey, buddy, you doing alright?" Ben murmured softly under the pretense of handing Ripley his jacket.

"What?" Ripley asked, still struggling to focus on his actual surroundings. "Yeah, no, I'm fine."

"You look pale. And you're sweating. You sure you're good?"

"Yeah," Ripley insisted.

"If you want to go back—"

"I said, I'm *fine*." Ripley snapped, a bit harsher than he'd intended. "Let's just get this over with."

A disappointed look fell across Ben's face. He was clearly looking forward to unveiling this surprise, whatever it was. And with all the pressure Ben was under, with the way he was sticking his neck out for the Halfsies, for him, Ripley really should have been a little nicer. But it was all he could do to force himself into the jacket and follow Ben through the next two doorways.

"Come on!" Ben called back to the group, all of whom now shared Ripley's hesitance. Except they were only worried about the cold.

Ripley would have given anything to just be cold right now.

"Come on, you're only dragging it out!"

In, in! You're only making it worse by just standing there!

It was light here, too. Not the familiar cool frosted light of the dome, but a string of lanterns that lit the path ahead with a pale yellow light. Ripley could see where the path forked up ahead. One way headed toward the unfinished Tube station, the other out of sight in the opposite direction.

This mysterious path is the one Ben chose, and Ripley felt himself breathing just a little easier. The familiarity of the place lessened as he picked his way across the thin layer of ice that coated the rocky ground. After a few minutes of walking, Ripley could make out large shadows ahead, looming over the much smaller silhouettes of people moving around. As they drew closer, he realized he was looking at some sort of vehicles.

"What the hell are those?"

Denton's words were accompanied by tiny puffs of white vapor.

"Ladies and gentlemen," Ben declared happily, "May I introduce you to our salvation, the Tucker Sno-Cat 2250."

"The what?" Edwin replied dully, eying the hulking metal beasts with something akin to disdain.

"The Tucker Sno-Cat…2250," Ben repeated, looking crestfallen at the obvious lack of awe from his companions. "They'd been using these for overland Antarctic travel for centuries and centuries. You're looking at the latest model, abandoned here when the D6 disaster took place."

"The latest model," repeated Denton indignantly, "from a hundred and twenty six years ago?"

"Well, yeah," came Ben's defensive reply, "Killian's team is fixing her up. She'll be right as rain by tomorrow! Won't she, Killian?"

Ben's friend had appeared from behind one of the monstrosities, walking toward them as he rubbed his gloves together vigorously. "Sure," Killian replied, his tone unconvincing. "Right as rain."

"Beautiful!"

"Uh-uh. Nope," Denton declared, shaking his head and taking several steps back. "Ain't gettin' on no snow cat, Parker."

"Aw, come on big guy!" Ben said, his eyes pleading. "I call ours *Snow Master*. It's going to be exciting!"

"It's going to be our final resting place," Denton replied, cocking his head dubiously as he studied the vehicle. "Look at it!"

Ripley *was* looking at it. It looked a lot like the inner components of most of Sanctuary. Old, brittle, and unreliable. What may have once been a cheerfully bright orange cabin sat high off the ground. The large rectangular body was suspended over four massive tread-covered feet that looked like triangles whose peaks had been flattened beneath the main bulk of the machine. The whole thing looked defeated and tired. But it also looked, in Ripley's opinion, better than walking.

"I don't know," said Sylvia, "it's not so bad." Her voice sounded less hopeful, and more like she was trying to champion her brother's cause.

"But how will we get it *out*?" Ripley asked, walking slowly around the Sno-Cat, wondering if it would need to be disassembled and carried out through the bulkhead a piece at a time.

"Oh, that's easy," Ben said, brightening up once more. "Same way it came in. You wanna see?"

"What I *want*," Denton said, "is to go back where it's warm."

With some reluctance, Ben took the lead back toward the Tube tracks, walking backward as he spoke. "The dome was still under construction when the disaster hit. So the panels meant to get the vehicles and construction materials in and out were never sealed. The domes are all made up of modular panels, you just can't tell because of how they were fused together. We can drive that beauty right out into the wilderness!"

"And it will get us all the way to Black Island?" asked Molly. Ripley started. He'd been so lost in his own turmoil, and she'd been so quiet, that he hadn't even remembered she was there.

"I didn't realize you were coming," he blurted without thinking. She frowned at him, eyebrows knitted together.

"I am." Was that a hint of regret in her tone? "I'm the one who knows where we're going."

"We have a map," Ripley said. "We can find it."

Molly stopped walking to turn and fully face him. Her face was resolute. "I know more about the microreactors than anyone here. Ben might be the technical wizard, but it may surprise you to learn that, as a teacher, I do know *some* things that could be very helpful along the way. About the terrain and hidden crevasses and—"

Ripley cringed. "I'm sorry. I didn't mean to suggest you weren't needed. I just meant…" he let his voice trail off.

They made it back to the Tube station without further discussion. Once they were back off the track, the group parted ways. Ben instructed everyone except Sylvia, who would not be a part of the mission, to meet back at the Tube station bright and early the next day.

As they made their way back to the Edge, Denton kept casting curious glances back and forth between Ripley and Molly. "You two fighting?"

"No," they said together.

Denton's brow furrowed. "Good. Damned if I gotta listen to drama while I'm all scrunched up in that contraption with you. Gonna be miserable enough as it is."

*   *   *

"EVERYTHING IS TAKEN care of," Ben told them as they climbed into the Sno-Cat the next morning. "We've got plenty of food and supplies, double what we should need for the journey. Tools, tents—"

"Tents?" Denton demanded, sounding alarmed. "What do we need tents for?"

Ben shrugged dismissively. "You want to sleep in this thing? It's pretty crowded."

"*Sleep?* How long is this going to take?"

"At least two days," Molly informed him. "If the weather holds out."

"*Two days?*"

"Relax, Denton. We'll be there and back again before you know it," Ben assured him. Denton looked around as if contemplating jumping out and running away, but heaved himself up and settled in between Ripley and Edwin. Ben sat behind the controls, Molly in the chair beside him.

"Why's the teacher get a front seat to herself?" Denton complained. "She's tiny, she should be back here."

"She's my navigator," Ben replied. "And if anyone has a right to complain, it's Ripley and Edwin. *You're* the one taking up all the space."

"Shoulda let me stay home where I could take up all the space I want without dealing with this abuse."

The Sno-Cat shuddered to life, and Ben flashed a brilliant grin at Molly. Ripley was glad that at least someone was enjoying themselves. All *he* could think about was all the possible ways in which this mission could go horribly wrong. They took off at a snail's pace, the machine creeping along as they headed for the exit, where Killian and his team stood huddled beside the missing panes of the dome, waiting impatiently to put them back and get back to Sigil.

Once outside of the dome it was dark. Ripley fidgeted in his seat, ignoring Denton's indignant grunts, and craned his neck to look out the rear window. There was just enough light to see the tracks they left in the snow.

Edwin, who had barely said two words since setting out, leaned forward. "Is this as fast as it goes?"

"Afraid so," Ben said. "They were built for safety, not speed. Too fast and all the treads in the world won't save us from slipping and sliding across the ice shelf."

Edwin leaned back without argument and they plowed ahead, their slow progress illuminated only by the dual swaths of light slicing through the twilight from the Sno-Cat's headlights. Ben attempted to keep a conversation going, but it was a struggle. Denton groaned, if possible, more than usual. Molly gave quiet answers, and Edwin and Ripley both sat staring out the windows at the endless, barren landscape. The most excitement they had all morning was the interesting transition from the bare rock of

Antiquity Island onto the ice shelf. The Sno-Cat conquered the incline with slow determination, the treads biting into the ice and dragging their mass onward and upward.

When Denton had grunted for something like the hundredth time, Ben twisted around in his chair and gave the back passengers an irritable glare. "If you don't like it, you can get out and walk!"

In response, Denton nodded toward the window. "Might be faster."

The silence grew tense as the hours wore on. At one point Ben offered to stop and let everyone stretch their legs. But outside the wind was lashing the Sno-Cat with an endless stream of snow, forcing Ben to make a vain attempt at using the windshield wipers to stave off the white-out.

"I, uh, think we're good," Edwin said, and even Denton nodded in agreement. "Let's keep going."

Ripley tried not to focus on his increasingly cramped extremities, instead pouring his energy into meditating on the bumps and turns of the vehicle's convoluted trajectory. In the brief respites between wind gusts, he could make out the long, sharp edges of crevasses in the shelf. Many of them stretched far into the darkness, widening as they went. It was clear that their long jaunts off course were to avoid these death pits, though they were adding an annoying amount of time onto an already arduous journey. More than once Ripley gave honest consideration to hopping out and running ahead of the Sno-Cat. With his Theran anatomy, he thought he might be able to keep it up for some time, though perhaps not long enough to make it all the way to Black Island. Still, the idea had popped into his head again just as Ben brought the machine to a full stop.

"I'm hungry," Ben stated flatly. "I'm hungry, I'm cramped up, and I have to pee. We've made good time—" Denton huffed at this, "and I think we ought to stop here for the day."

Edwin grimaced into the darkness. Ripley could tell they were all thinking the same thing; no matter how cramped the Sno-Cat was, it looked practically cozy when faced with the prospect of setting up camp outside.

Another gust of wind gently rocked the cabin. "Do you think it's safe?" Molly asked. "Our tents could be blown away."

"Nah, we have anchors. We'll set them up downwind of the *Snow Master*, she'll act as a breaker for the worst of it." He patted the dash affectionately. "Won't you, girl?"

Ben began donning his snow gear and the others followed suit, twisting and contorting uncomfortably as they struggled into the bulky clothing. Edwin let out a squawk as Denton's sprawling mass forced him against the window, but eventually everyone was more or less situated.

Why did it have to be dark, Ripley thought despairingly as they climbed out into the hostile night air. *At least if it were light we'd have temperatures above zero.* They scrambled like scared animals, all doing their best to mimic Ben as he showed them how to erect the shining silver tents and secure them in the ice with hand powered drills and stakes as long as Ripley's forearm. There were three, squat and low to the ground. Once they were secured in a tight row beside the Sno-Cat, Ben moved from one to the next, pulling a short yellow ripcord on each that caused them to puff up, inflating so that the base and dome became several inches thick. Edwin climbed back into the cabin and tossed down sleeping bags and water bottles wrapped in insulating towels and packs of food, which Molly and Ben quickly distributed among them.

"Lady's choice," Ben said, nodding toward the tents. Molly unzipped the middle one and crawled inside.

"Wanna be bunkmates?" Ben asked Ripley, shouting to be heard over the whistling gusts. Ripley nodded his consent, and just before crawling in after Ben, glanced over to see Edwin giving Denton an unhappy look.

The tent wasn't exactly warm, but Ben had hung a small lantern in the middle that shed a circle of light over the tiny space, and as they arranged themselves in their bags and cracked open their dinner, it began to feel a bit more comfortable.

"These tents aren't bad," Ripley remarked in between bites of his sandwich. He was lying on his stomach, propped up on his elbows. The ceiling was too low to allow them to sit comfortably. "Who designed them?"

"Actually, the team who discovered the Sno-Cat found some just like this when they were cataloguing D6. Only they were too degraded. So we just reverse engineered our own."

Ripley let out a bark of laughter. "At last, something that didn't require a whole lot of thought, eh?"

"Yeah," Ben replied thoughtfully. "Kind of a nice change of pace."

They finished their meal in silence. It wasn't until Ripley turned the lantern off and they had burrowed deep into their sleeping bags that Ben decided to bring up exactly that which Ripley had been hoping to continue avoiding.

"I'm, uh, sorry about the other day," Ben said, keeping his voice low. Ripley doubted that they could be heard in the other tents. The wind was wailing outside. But his reply came out equally quiet all the same.

"You didn't do anything wrong."

"Yeah, but—"

"You warned me, Ben, and I didn't listen." Ripley shifted, rolling onto his side and staring at the wall of the tent, imagining Molly just feet away. What was she thinking right now? How was she feeling? Did she hate him?

"Sylvia told me what happened," Ben continued, undeterred. "And judging by the look on your face when I barged in, I'm pretty sure you'd already made a choice." He was silent for a long while. "She cried a lot," he added thoughtfully.

"Ben, I—"

"Listen, all I'm trying to say is, she gets it. She'll be okay. Sylvia's a tough cookie, just like our mom. But Molly, well…you really need to talk to her. Before the damage is irreparable."

Ripley pondered this until the wind drowned out his thoughts and sleep took him.

Chapter Eleven

Probable Cause

FELIX ENTERED THE meeting hall with a mixture of confidence and trepidation. The Arca plan was the most promising idea he'd heard since the war began, and yet pitching it to a bunch of military leaders and heads of states was still a daunting task. His interactions with the government never seemed to go well. Still, he was representing their best hope here. He had to do well.

As they settled into their assigned seats, Felix spotted Bohai entering with the Culeian contingent, a young girl at his side. He felt a momentary sense of camaraderie with the mysterious girl, so out of place among all these politicians. What was Bohai thinking, bringing a child to a meeting that could well determine the fate of the world?

The girl's eyes swept toward Felix's party, and he offered her an encouraging smile. He wanted her to feel safe, let her know that she was among friends.

But rather than returning it her eyes narrowed, her mouth issuing a sharp intake of breath.

"You," she said, so deadly quiet that Felix might not have heard if not for his Theran senses.

He was tempted to glance back and see if she was perhaps addressing someone else.

But there was nothing but a wall behind him, and her blazing eyes were locked unmistakably on his own. She raised her finger in one sharp motion and jabbed it in his direction.

"Guards!" she commanded, louder now. "Arrest him!"

"What?"

Felix didn't remember standing up but found himself on his feet as Culeian soldiers advanced in his direction. He felt the sudden urge to run, but there was nowhere to go. Too many obstacles in the form of occupied chairs in rows that ran around the entire room, five deep. People in front, behind, and to either side, and Felix trapped in the middle.

His friends moved to form a sort of shield around him, Ambrose in front and Gavin and Tobias on either side. What they hoped to accomplish by doing so, he couldn't be sure, though he appreciated the gesture. Gavin had taken up a defensive stance, and Felix felt him tense, ready to fight.

"Hang on," Felix said, raising his hands in a gesture of surrender, "I think there's been some sort of misunderstanding."

"There is no misunderstanding except for the one you created," the girl said. "You are responsible for the death and destruction that Culei suffered at Antarctica. You and your false promises and lies. You will be held accountable for the suffering of my people."

Where is this coming from? Felix was left speechless in the face of these boggling accusations.

"Your Majesty," Bohai interjected, stooping low to speak into her ear, "If I may—"

Your Majesty. This girl wasn't the child of some diplomat. She was *the* Queen. *That makes a lot more sense,* Felix found himself thinking while he racked his brain for the proper response. How could he possibly vindicate himself without having any clue what she was on about?

"Listen, Your Majesty," he began, struggling to add a bit of respectful reverence to his tone of disbelief, "Far be it from me to suggest that you might be wrong, but…you're wrong. I had nothing to do with what happened to your fleet. I don't even understand how you could…"

His voice trailed off and his gut twisted into a knot as realization came over him. "Oh."

Ambrose glanced back at this, looking confused. "Oh?" Then a look of understanding flashed in his eyes, too. *"Oh."*

"What is the meaning of this?" demanded one of the Nequiem delegates, placing both hands palm down on the table and rising angrily from his seat. "We are about to begin a peaceful meeting of our peoples, and now some among us are accused of treachery? I demand an explanation!"

"I think *I* can explain," Felix said quickly. His heart had begun to race, and his palms were slick with sweat as he wiped them against his pants.

"*Now* he can explain," quipped the child queen, her eyes glinting with triumph. "When a moment ago he had no idea of what I accused him. It would seem your tongue has lost some of its smoothness, hasn't it, Lord Laevus?"

"That's the thing!" Felix said, grasping on the confirmation. "Your Majesty, I'm not who you think I am. I'm not Laevus. My name is Felix."

The Queen dismissed this with a royal shrug. "So even your name was a lie. I find myself unsurprised."

"No, my name wasn't—isn't—a lie. I'm not Laevus! He's my brother."

The Queen scoffed at this outlandish suggestion, but Bohai was nodding vigorously.

"Your Majesty," Bohai said again, dropping his gaze to the floor as she turned her glare in his direction. "I can attest to the validity of this statement. There are two of them, your Grace. I have seen them, simultaneously, with my own eyes."

"That's right," agreed Ambrose, "we've all seen them."

Gavin and Tobias were nodding now, too, and Gavin's attack stance had softened.

"Your Majesty," Felix said, voice humble, "by no fault of your own, I believe that you have been tricked by my brother and mistaken me for him. He is a cunning man, and you are not the first to fall victim to him, nor, I fear, the last. I myself have played right into his hands before. I understand the treachery he's capable of."

"I would beg you not to deal harshly with Felix, your Grace," pleaded Bohai. "I can attest that he is, most assuredly, a brave and upright man of honor."

Felix met Bohai's gaze and offered a curt, but sincere, nod of thanks. Of anyone in the room, Bohai had the least amount of reason to defend him. It meant a lot.

The Queen looked around at the gathering once more, taking in all of the distraught expressions, all eyes locked on her. The tension was palpable. Though none of the nations had been able to accomplish much in defending against Nero's onslaught, they would certainly be all the weaker without Culei's support.

The Alliance had to remain intact.

"Your Majesty," offered Felix, feeling that he might be the only one capable of assuring this, "if my presence here offends you, I will go. I have no desire to do anything that could threaten this Alliance."

"That will not be necessary," she said. The room let out a collective breath of relief. "Ambassador Bohai has proven himself a good and loyal councilor, and I shall take his word on this. However," and here she turned that accusing gaze back on Felix, "should you prove that treachery is in the blood, know this; I may be young, but my people have a long memory. Do not tempt my wrath."

"Wouldn't dream of it, your Majesty," replied Felix, both relieved and unnerved by the exchange.

At least the mystery of Laevus' whereabouts had been solved. But where was he now?

This, Felix decided, was a problem for another time.

Perhaps his tainted view of the ethical standing of the gathered officials swayed his perspective, but listening to the proceedings was just as bad, if not worse, than appearing before the Ministry back in Atmos. Sure, he wasn't on trial for his very right to exist this time…but just listening to a room full of politicians seeking their own best interests and generals softened by an era of peace was enough to make him want to flee. He willed himself to stay strong as he rose and began their well-rehearsed presentation. He only faltered once, and Tobias was quick to whisper a correction in his ear. Despite the sour start to his day, this part, at least, went smoothly. A heated discussion followed.

"If this attempt fails, and they were to become aware of the purpose of the Arca," Margo Benton was saying, "it could put the rest of the Pravacordian Air Force in jeopardy. They may find a way to use it against us."

"The Pravacordian Air Force is *already* in jeopardy," argued General Hall, a refreshing voice of reason. "We lose more good men and women every time we engage. If we cannot stop this enemy, there will soon no longer be an Air Force. Or, for that matter, a Pravacordia."

There was an uproar from the Pravacordian delegates, the few Ministry members who had managed to escape the fateful night that Atmos fell.

Felix's eyes drifted to the Culeian delegation, where the young queen sat flanked by her retinue. Ambassador Bohai was discussing something with her, bent low and whispering. Then he straightened up, hands clasped neatly before his waist as he patiently waited for the voices to settle into a quiet hum before addressing the crowd.

"Honored members of the Alliance," he said, his tone even and forceful, "it is with the deepest and most humble respect that I address you here today. I would like to take this opportunity to point out that the people who have brought this proposal before you have all proven themselves worthy and up to the task. They are strong of mind and will, and if they believe that this plan will succeed, then they have the support of Her Majesty, as well as that of the entire Culeian nation. We stand behind these brave warriors."

Bohai sat back down. Felix had known the good Ambassador agreed with their plan, but the somewhat verbose speech left him feeling taken aback.

Proving, once again, that though he was gullible to a fault, Bohai was made of stronger stuff than Felix had once given him credit for. He may blindly follow the whims and fancies of the Culeian monarch, but ultimately, it seemed, Bohai wanted to do the right thing.

He wanted to save the world.

That was all any of them wanted, really.

"And why should we care about the support of Culei,"

shot Minister Benton, "after the treachery and betrayal we have suffered at the hands of Her Majesty?"

There was a general murmur of assent from the group, and the queen reached out a hand to touch the sleeve of Bohai's uniform. He leaned close as she whispered something in his ear.

"Her Majesty wishes to address the Alliance," he declared formally, before turning back to the queen and bowing low. The Culeians all rose with her, bowing in her direction before sitting back down.

"Good people of this Alliance," she said in an airy voice, "when I agreed to come here, I was under the impression that, faced with a grave threat, the mistakes of our past would not be held against us. In the interest of the greater good."

"That's correct, however—" Margo Benton ceased speaking in response to the collective glare of disbelief that issued from the Culeian delegation at her interruption.

Even Felix could have told her that interrupting a queen was not a good way to foster camaraderie.

But then, when had the Ministry ever listened to Felix?

"If the voice of the Culeian people will be weighed as less than based on past events, whenever doing so is convenient, then I consider this Alliance to be nothing more than an insult and a mockery, and will take my forces and retreat to the safety of Paru, where we shall be quite safe from onslaught from the Theran invaders."

"Your Majesty," pleaded the Nequiem representative,

with whom Felix was not yet acquainted, "I beg you not to make a harsh decision based on the accusations of a single member of this Alliance." He shot a stern look at Minister Benton, who cowed. Felix would be lying if he said he didn't take some pleasure in that. "Please forgive her crass interruption. Why don't we adjourn for a short recess?"

The heads of state left to confer amongst themselves, leaving the lowly to mingle and await their verdict.

"What do you think?" Gavin asked, prodding him with an elbow. "Are we doing this with or without their blessing?"

"Shh," Felix hissed, glancing around. He didn't know all of these people. Many of them were no doubt highly loyal to their superiors, ready to run to them with any suspicion of treachery—precisely what Felix had just assured the Culeian leadership would not be a problem. "Just be patient. You're the one who said there are rules for a reason, don't go vigilante on me now. Not to mention we still need that master code. I don't know how we'll get our hands on that without their cooperation. So let's see what they decide, all right?"

Tobias had gone over to speak with Bohai, and was now crossing the room back toward their group.

"Bohai says that the Queen definitely stands behind our plan."

"And Baba assured me that the Nequiem delegation will agree," Ambrose added. "He knows his people. All they want is peace. They'll do anything to achieve it."

"That just leaves good ol' Margo," said Felix, the name tasting bitter in his mouth. Not so long ago, Margo Benton had been willing to have him and Bohai put to death, just to keep up appearances. "I'm sure we can count on her to put up a fight. She isn't exactly my biggest fan."

"She can't go against the other nations solely based on a personal bias," Ambrose said, sounding less certain than his words suggested. "And General Hall is in there. He'll vouch for us."

When the delegates filed back into the room, Felix held his breath. He knew that his friends were willing to do whatever they had to do to ensure the safety of Earth, but would the heads of state agree? Would Felix once again be asking the people he cared about to don the mantle of traitors for the cause? Who else would need to be dragged into their mess in order to secure the necessary information?

General Hall entered behind a harried-looking Benton, caught Felix's eye, and winked. A wave of relief washed over him. They would be allowed to go through with the plan.

After a dramatic pause, a smattering of applause met the announcement of the Nequiem leader that the Alliance would support the mission to disable Nero's fleet via the Arca solution.

"Finally," breathed Felix. "Finally a reasonable government. I could get used to this."

"Don't," Gavin told him. "It won't last. Never does."

Felix glanced sideways at him, cringing. "Just let me have this one, okay?"

Gavin shrugged, his expression clearly communicating his thoughts. *Don't say I didn't warn you.*

"You will have access to whatever supplies or personnel necessary to achieve our goal," he continued, addressing Felix now. "Good luck to us all. Our hopes go with you."

* * *

ONE WEIGHT WAS LIFTED from Felix's shoulders with the approval of the Alliance. Another replaced it at the thought of having the hopes and future of an entire world resting on him and his team.

It seemed to be his lot in life these days. Constantly trying to crawl out from beneath the crushing weight of responsibility that followed him wherever he went. On occasion he felt himself longing for the mundane but predictable life he'd once had in Sanctuary. Sure, he'd been despised by almost everyone there, but he'd had an amazing wife and the best friend anyone could ever hope for. Things had been simpler.

But the gurgling laugh of his daughter brought him back to the present, and glancing over at the twins, he knew that things could not have been any other way. He could not imagine life without them.

He wouldn't take for granted the sacrifice Ripley had made so that they could have life. He'd continue to honor the ideals he'd shared with Gavin. Felix wouldn't mar his friend's memory by trying to scurry out from under the task at hand, no matter the pressure.

He might not have had the fortitude to deal with the salvation of the world on his own. But he wasn't alone. He had friends, family, people who depended on him to be strong. He wouldn't let them down.

The *Wilks* could have held a larger contingent if necessary, but Felix didn't wish to endanger any more lives. He'd insisted Penelope stay behind this time. She needed more time to recuperate from her injuries and besides, she'd done so much already. She deserved to be with Sebastian.

Tobias, Ambrose, Kestrel, Gavin and Ollie would make up the infiltration team. Baba and Bohai, who had been assigned as representatives of their respective nations, would be listening in from the safety of the Timeless, as General Hall would be heading up the mission to round up Nero's troops if everything went according to plan.

As if that's ever happened before, Felix thought dryly as they sat in the hanger bay, anxiously awaiting news of an attack. His nerves were frayed. Never had he imagined that they'd be sitting around waiting for Nero's ships to come with anything akin to anticipation. Kestrel fidgeted beside him as the minutes dragged by, each feeling longer than the last.

"So what's your story?"

Felix looked up at the query and realized they were alone in the hold. "Who, me?"

Kestrel raised an eyebrow. "You're the only one here. Yeah, of course you. We haven't really gotten the chance to talk much, and I feel like if we're going to be working together, we should get to know each other a little better. What was it like, living in Sanctuary?"

"Oh." Felix leaned back, resting his hands on the cool deck plates as he studied the supply nets that hung overhead. "Well, it was in Antarctica."

Kestrel made an unintelligible noise in the back of her throat. He frowned at her.

"I meant maybe tell me something I *didn't* know," she teased.

"There isn't much to tell. The place was a wreck. We had a Council, too, you know."

"Like on Thera?"

He nodded. "Exactly like on Thera. They just took the idea from there and made a copy in Sanctuary. Nero was in charge, but you probably already knew that."

"Sounds like a bum deal."

Felix chuckled. "Worse than you can imagine. But the funny thing is, it didn't feel that bad, looking back. It's surprising how mundane life was. I guess it's just what we were used to. In Sanctuary, nothing ever really changed. You got up, ate, went to work, maybe ate again, slept. We kept the city running, and the city kept us alive. Not a very thrilling existence, but it had its high points."

Kestrel bit her lip on a laugh that escaped anyway.

"No," Felix insisted. "I'm serious."

"I don't believe it," she told him. "It sounds incredibly dull."

Felix pushed himself back up and leaned toward her, crossing his arms. "All right then, what about you?"

Kestrel's lips pursed and she shrugged casually. "Nothing fancy. High born, rising star in the political scene, swept off my feet by a handsome, daring Envicti recruit and inducted into an underground rebellion." Her eyes flickered toward the cockpit.

It wasn't hard for Felix to put two and two together. "You can't mean—Gavin? You two were involved? He doesn't seem like the romantic type."

Kestrel sighed, biting her lip again. "He's not. But that didn't keep me from being attracted to him. Anyway, that was a *long* time ago."

"Let me get this straight. You joined Tapestry because you had a crush…on Gavin. But…isn't he a little old for you?"

"Nah." She shrugged a shoulder dismissively. "He's not much older than I am. Fifteen, sixteen years? He just looks older because of all that responsibility. He tromps around like he's got the weight of the world on his shoulders. That ages you. Me, I'm more of a youthful spirit. And no, I didn't join Tapestry because of him. I joined because I believed in what they were doing, thank you very much."

Felix considered this. "And what exactly is it that Tapestry does?"

Kestrel's eyes dimmed and her playful smile vanished. "They're in the business of mending a broken system."

Felix shook his head. "I don't know what that means."

"You would, if you were Theran." Kestrel drew her legs up and wrapped her arms around them, resting her chin on her knees. "The Great War destroyed our world. The Humans probably think they had it pretty bad with the Sequencing. But the brevity of their crisis was a blink of the eye compared to the suffering that Thera endured. They had it easy, to be honest. For us, the Forlorn were a plague that lasted nearly a millennium. Almost wiped us out completely. And when it was over, most were too tired to fight anymore. It was easy for a few to seize power—no one else had the will to oppose them. Thera became one giant fiefdom, paying tribute to the few lucky ones at the top of the hierarchy. And just as we started to see the light as a people, just as those at the bottom might have been rallied, that damned Evenmire showed up. It gave the Elder Council the perfect weapon—something to focus the peoples' anger on. A new enemy. A new threat to rally against."

This left Felix speechless. It was the most he'd ever learned about Theran history, and a lot to digest all at once. He'd often wondered about the source of Thera's distrust of humanity but had never had the chance to ask anyone who might actually know.

"They manufactured an enemy so that everyone's eyes would be off of them. *That's* what became of Thera. The people fell victim to a contrived reality. And now, here we are."

Felix nodded slowly. "Here we are."

He looked toward the cockpit. Gavin was leaning

against one of the control panels, nodding at something Ambrose was saying. He wore his customary stoic expression. Felix felt a sense of kinship with the man. He'd come a long way from the easy-going youth he'd been in Sanctuary. Seen and done a lot more than he'd ever expected to. Gavin had been born into such an existence. They shared that same burden. The weight of the world.

The weight of two worlds.

Felix got to his feet and stretched. "Maybe we should head out, no? Get closer?"

"We don't want to head in the wrong direction," Ambrose replied, twisting in his seat to look back at them. "We're pretty central right now to their most recent attacks. If we head south and they go north..."

"Right," Felix muttered. "Just getting a bit antsy, that's all."

They had been stationed just off the Pravacordian coast, near enough to the southern border to be within range of several cities that had not yet suffered an attack but far enough to be out of sight of any incoming enemy ships. The goal was to assess the size of the attack party and then swoop in and disable them. They were not using the Theran ship, which Ambrose had christened *Pluto's Ghost*, but instead were relying on the *Wilks* for the trial run. If anything should go wrong, they could not risk *Pluto's Ghost* being captured or destroyed. They would have no hope of infiltrating Nero's base in anything else.

"Radar has picked up incoming vessels," General Hall's

voice informed them over the cockpit radio. "Make ready."

Ambrose fired up the engine, and in front of them the huge bay door retracted slowly, revealing the coastline. The beach stretched out of sight in either direction, and beyond it the trees had turned brilliant shades of gold and orange. During their last skirmish, everything had still been a lush green. It was as if a strong wind had come in the night and ripped all the green from the leaves, leaving a scene of startling majesty. Felix considered the foliage for a long moment as they awaited confirmation from Hall. Such a marvelous transformation. A bright burst of color just before death. A final, defiant act of beauty before the leaves succumbed to winter's chill.

"Enemy ships confirmed. Count three," said the intercom. "Proceed at will. Good luck."

"We'll need it," Felix muttered. Then, "Take us out, Ambrose."

They'd gone over the plan a dozen times. Baba and Ambrose had made short work of devising a piece of equipment capable of taking control of multiple Arcas at once. For three, even four ships, the power afforded the device by the *Wilks* was plenty. The tower would be necessary to make sure they cast a net wide enough for the whole fleet.

First things first. They needed to make sure they even had a chance.

The *Wilks* banked left out of the bay, shooting straight and smooth toward Weymouth, the nearest city that was still left unbroken by the relentless Theran attacks. The people had long since evacuated, and as they came nearer Felix could make out the tall stacks of factories, all silent and smokeless.

"Where can we set down?" asked Tobias nervously, eyeing the narrow streets and alleys.

"Haven't we flown around in this beauty enough times yet for you to realize she can set down anywhere, Tobias?" Ambrose chastised. "The *Wilks* is—"

"Is Nimbus class, yes, yes, we know," Felix interrupted. "She can do anything. Now get us down there and out of sight before Nero's ships get here and blast us out of the sky."

"Dual-plated armor," Ambrose muttered as their nose dipped, "we could take a few hits."

"I'd prefer we not," Tobias said seriously from the copilot's chair. "How about over there? To the west. That should afford us some nice cover."

"I see it," Ambrose confirmed.

They set down on a long clear stretch of road, coasting to a stop between two buildings that blocked most of the sky from view.

Felix opened the hatch and climbed out as Tobias scurried to the back of the ship and began tinkering with the Arca control device. He listened hard but heard nothing to indicate that the ships had made it to the city yet. A chill of foreboding rushed through his veins. Had they guessed the wrong target?

No. There was a whine in the distance. Felix ducked

back against the body of the *Wilks* instinctively, then forced himself away from the ship, peering around the corner of the building, looking for the white blur of Nero's ships in the sky.

Gunfire erupted and he turned toward it, blocking his ears. The attack had begun. The ships drew long swaths of destruction across their paths, swooping down in neat succession, completely unopposed. Explosions shook the buildings all around them, mortar crumbling and running down the brick facades like streams of raindrops. Debris cascaded over the *Wilks*, and over Felix, as the devastation drew nearer to their position.

They dipped and fired almost lazily as they continued their methodical sweep across the city. They did not bother with ground troops. They knew the city was empty. In their minds, it was already won. They simply wanted to make sure it never rose again.

Felix ducked his head back inside the *Wilks*. "Aren't they close enough yet?"

Tobias grimaced. "Not quite."

Felix waited only a moment as the sounds of the enemy forces grew louder. "Now?"

"Okay. Here we go. Transmitting!" Tobias shouted, voice cracking as the sound of the enemy grew louder. "Jamming signal is…also activate! As soon as they're within range…got them!"

The whine stalled as the ships came to a sudden halt in midair.

Felix walked hesitantly back to where he could get a clear view. All three hovered as if waiting for something. One continued firing.

"What about the guns?" Felix shouted back over his shoulder. "Can you control those, too?"

"No, only the navigation systems."

"Just don't point them this way. Ambrose, call in the *Timeless*. Prisoners are their department."

"What do I make them do?" Tobias asked next, panic-struck. "I'm not a pilot! I'll crash them! I'll—"

"Calm down, Tobias," came Ambrose's calm reply. "We've been over this, no need to lose your head. Step aside and let me handle it from here."

"Oh. All right."

"Don't put them on the ground until backup arrives," Gavin reminded him. "We don't stand a chance in hand-to-hand combat against all those clones."

"Wouldn't dream of it, my friend," Ambrose replied cheerfully.

As the tension of the unknown subsided, Felix felt the thrill of victory overtaking him. It had worked. Their test had been a success. They could take down Nero's fleet.

They just needed their luck to hold out a little longer.

Soon, it would all be over.

CHAPTER TWELVE

BLACK ISLAND

FOR ONCE, IT SEEMED that fortune favored Ripley and the rest of the crew. The wind died out close to morning, and their second day of travel was nothing but smooth sailing. The darkness was pervasive, but the path ahead was clear and the crevasses that had plagued their early journey were few and far between. Ripley took a turn manning the wheel for a while. Molly avoided looking at him by keeping her nose buried in the various maps and charts she'd brought along, speaking only when Ripley veered off course, or when an obstacle caused a detour.

"Not far now," she said at last. "We should be able to see it soon."

After so much ice, the appearance of bare black rock

seemed a very welcome change of scenery. It was rich and deep, soaking up the pooled headlights like a thirsty animal. The subtle cadence of the Sno-Cat's treads changed as they made the transition from the ice shelf onto Black Island, and Ben gave a triumphant cry. "We made it!"

"Yeah," said Ripley, leaning forward and trying to make out a dark, looming shape in the distance. "But there's a storm coming, I can feel it. Whatever we've got to do, we've got to do fast, Ben."

"Oh, look at you. The Weathermaster, now, are we? You worry too much, Ripley. We've got this." Ben leaned forward between the two front seats as the mass up ahead became visible to the others. He pointed at it unnecessarily, squinting his eyes. "What *is* that?"

"Not sure yet," Ripley replied with a frown. "But we're about to find out."

He could just barely make out movement on the right side of the obstacle, and as they drew nearer there was an enormous blast of wind, and a faint glinting caught the motion. Ripley brought the Sno-Cat to a grinding halt.

"What's up?" Ben asked, concern in his voice.

Ripley tweaked the controls, easing forward just enough to redirect the vehicle's headlights. They fell upon an enormous blade, or blades, spinning so fast that they blurred into one. Ben let out a low whistle. "Good thing you saw that," he commented. "A little closer and we would have lost the top of the Sno-Cat…and probably a couple inches of our heads as well."

"It's a wind turbine," Molly said quietly. "They used them to power this island for a long time before the micro-reactors became more popular."

"Seems dangerous," said Denton. "I don't like it."

"Well it's not supposed to be like that, you dolt," Ben retorted. "It must have broken down, fallen over somehow."

"Must have been some storm to tip *that* monster." Edwin's voice came from just beside Ripley's ear, as he'd squeezed himself, with difficulty, up beside Ben to see what was going on.

"Well," reasoned Molly, "it's old. No one's been here to maintain it."

"Let's just hope we don't find the microreactor in similar condition," Edwin said.

Ripley studied the downed turbine. The long body rose fifteen feet from the ground and disappeared out of sight to their right. To the left the blades had slowed but continued to spin, and just beyond that stood a small rectangular building that looked more like a box than anything else. "I think we'd better walk from here," Ripley said. "And I think we ought to make it quick."

"Agreed," replied Ben, slipping on his gloves. "Let's do this!"

They left the Sno-Cat and made their way slowly along the base of the fallen turbine, looking for a space large enough to crawl under. It was difficult to make headway. The wind was inconsistent, the gusting so strong that Ripley had to lean forward into it to brace himself, and would stumble when it passed. The strongest of the group, he took the lead, reaching the end of the turbine several minutes before the others.

He moved his flashlight over the torn and twisted metal as the wind rattled its way into the hollow base, wailing eerily as it echoed like someone blowing over the top of a bottle. But another light caught Ripley's attention, and as he looked down at its source he felt something cold and foreboding twist in his gut.

"Guys?" he hollered. "I think I know what made the turbine fall."

"Uh, this damned wind?" Denton shouted back. "If all of you make it back to the city without being blown away, I'm gonna be awful surprised."

"No," Ripley told them, pointing his flashlight. "Not the wind."

The pulsing violet light was unmistakable. It rose like a serpent from the earth before curving back down again, delicate crystalline tendrils clinging to the ragged edges of the turbine's base, latched to the torn wiring that hung limply in the ruin.

Ben had appeared behind Ripley.

"Sweet Evenmire," he whispered.

"Yeah," replied Ripley grimly. "Exactly."

*　　*　　*

THE GROUP STOOD TRANSFIXED for a long time before

Ripley managed to shake himself free of the mesmerizing sight. "We have to keep going!" he yelled, noticing with dismay how his voice was drowned out by the din.

They pushed on. The wind chill was intense, and Ripley's eyes felt frosty when he blinked despite the goggles Ben had provided. The heavy coats were lined with the same metallic silver material as the tents, but he felt himself starting to weaken and knew that if *he* was impaired, the others were suffering even more. Another of the squat rectangular buildings was just ahead, and Ripley pointed to it wordlessly. The door took some convincing, but finally came free. He waved everyone inside and pulled it shut behind him.

The wind still howled outside, but it was muffled at least, leaving only a fainting ringing in his ears. He turned to the others, who were bouncing up and down, rubbing their hands together. Ben pulled his goggles and scarf off.

"I wouldn't," said Molly. "It might seem warmer in here, but it's still not safe, we shouldn't risk it."

"Even with all this gear, we aren't going to last out there," Edwin said furiously. "It's nearly impossible to stay standing. Everything hurts. At least, everything that still has *feeling*."

Ripley frowned, glancing around the darkened building. "Maybe there's something in here to keep us warm while we wait for the wind to die down."

Five flashlight beams wavered as their owners swung them around, sweeping the room. It looked like some kind

of bunker. Metal beds, their mattresses remarkably pre-
served, stood in one corner.

And where there are beds, there are usually... "Blankets,"
Ripley called out, waving in the direction of his discovery.

"There's some gear here," Molly said excitedly. "I don't
know if it's any good, though."

"Check it out," Ripley said. "Everyone else, keep
looking."

"Anyone up for some dinner?" Edwin asked. "Looks
like someone left in the middle of cooking. We've got some
sort of frozen stew, circa a hundred and twenty-six years
ago, give or take."

"Don't touch it!"

Ben's strangled cry made everyone freeze.

"What? The stew?" Edwin asked with a frown. "Ben, I
wasn't really going to—"

"No. Anything. Don't touch anything."

Ripley moved closer to Ben to try and make sense of
what had spooked him. Ben was backing away from the
bunk beds, his eyes wide with horror.

Ripley followed his gaze and found one of the beds
was not empty. The corpse was partially mummified, its
knees curled up as though it had died in the fetal position,
its eyelids closed and sunken. Clumps of hair still clung
to parchment-like flesh. But it was not the body that had
caused Ben's fear. It was the way the face and exposed neck
were covered in thick, black, wart-like growths. They had
shriveled with the rest, but they were still unmistakable.

He'd seen them many times, in many textbooks.

This was the Sequencing.

*   *   *

"NOBODY PANIC," Ripley said. "Just don't touch anything else."

"It's over," Ben said, his voice cracking as he gave a near hysterical laugh. "It's over. We're all going to die out here."

"We are *not* going to die," Ripley said firmly. "We are going to finish our mission, we are going to return to New Sanctuary, and we're going to destroy Antiquity's Gate."

"We are *literally* standing in a room with a dead body right now, Ripley," said Ben, pointing toward the bunk. "And, in case you didn't notice those disgusting black things all over him, he died from the *Sequencing*."

"Ben, it's going to be all right," Molly said, moving toward him, but Ben scuttled backward, shaking his head furiously.

"No, don't touch me. You might not have been exposed. You still have a chance."

"The Sequencing is spread by bodily fluids, Ben," Edwin told him reasonably. "You know that."

"Yeah? You think those blankets aren't soaked in blood and spit and pus and, ugh, who knows what else!"

Ripley had had enough. He strode forward, grasping an uncooperative Ben by the shoulders and facing off with him. "Now, you listen to me," he said calmly. "I know what you're feeling right now. We spent a lifetime being indoctrinated by the Elves. They wanted us to be afraid of the Sequencing, of the world outside. But it was lies, Ben. So many lies. The virus wouldn't have survived out here for this long, not without a host, not in these conditions."

Ripley wasn't one hundred percent certain of this, but he was confident enough that his words rang true. Ben looked comforted, but only just.

"Ripley's right." Molly stepped up beside him. She had not been so close to him in a long time. His focus flickered from Ben to her and back again.

He looked the young man in the eyes. "I promise you that it's going to be okay. And let's just say, theoretically, that we were somehow exposed. The Sequencing is a virus, right?"

"Yes," Ben admitted slowly.

"A Theran virus?"

"Yes," Ben repeated.

"And can you think of anything in New Sanctuary, anything at all, that can eradicate viruses? Something maybe designed by Therans?"

"The...pods?" Ben asked, ending on a high note that made it more of a question than an answer. Ripley winked at him.

"When we get back, we can all go for a round of P.T."

"But what if we—"

"Expose anyone else?" Ripley finished for him. "If you're really concerned, we can have the pods brought to

D6. You know how to operate them, and there's power there now. Killian can set them up and then clear out, and we can take it from there."

Ben swallowed hard, his Adam's apple bobbing up and down clearly beneath his tightly wrapped scarf. Then he nodded. "Okay," he conceded at last. "But, I don't wanna be in here anymore."

Edwin clapped him on the shoulder. "I don't think any of us do, buddy." Exchanging a glance with Ripley, Edwin nodded toward the door. "Come on. Let's get this over with."

*   *   *

WHETHER THE WIND FELT more powerful because of their brief respite or whether it was really gaining strength, Ripley wasn't certain. His entire focus was on maintaining his balance and making sure everyone stayed together as they forged ahead. There were several more buildings between them and the microreactor, but no one had any desire to enter them. Still, they were a nice windbreak, much as the Sno-Cat had been for their tents.

At last it loomed up out of the darkness. Light grey with a sleek exterior, the building was indeed small. It reached ten feet high before a small stack, like Sanctuary's condensers, jutted up another ten feet. It seemed to be in perfect condition, except for—

"Look," Edwin called unnecessarily. Ripley had already

seen.

A single crystalline tendril whipped back and forth like a striking serpent in the high winds, peeking out from beneath the heavy looking door, its light drawing them like an angler fish. Ripley could sense danger, but they couldn't turn back. They were not going to get another shot like this.

Every second counted in this weather. The others wouldn't be able to hold out too much longer. Ripley thought fast.

"Ben," he shouted, "tell me what I need to do. I'm going in alone. The rest of you, get back to the Sno-Cat."

But Ben seemed to have pulled himself together and shook his head. "No. I'm going in there. It's too complicated to explain and besides, I don't even know for sure what to do. Seeing the schematics isn't the same as actually being there. I need to see it for myself. Might have to improvise."

Ripley's brow furrowed beneath the heavy hood and he looked back and forth between Ben and the plant. "There isn't time to argue. If that wind turbine was any indication, we could be walking into a radiation bath. I might be able to make it back, but you won't stand a chance."

"Nobody said anything about radiation," Denton hollered.

"It's a nuclear reactor, Denton, what did you expect?" Ben snapped. "Anyway, the seal is already broken. If there's a breach in containment, we're already dead. If we hurry, we might make it back fast enough to use the pods. Either way, there's no time to argue. I'm coming with you."

The others hesitated for only a moment before turning and trudging back in the direction of the waiting vehicle. Ripley struggled with the hatch, bracing his feet as he pulled it into the wind, beckoning for Ben to go through. Once they were both inside he released the door and it slammed shut behind them, encasing them in a heavy silence.

"Whoa," Ben said, whistling softly. Ripley turned and found that they were surrounded by the soft glow of several dozen crystal tendrils. They crawled up the walls and over the equipment panels like ivy.

"Is this going to work?" Ripley asked quickly. Ben frowned as he brushed several of the strands away from one of the control systems.

"Not sure yet. The only way to find out is to power this place up and check. Remember how I said that all the cabling and stuff is still intact? Well, we rigged it back up. If all goes as planned, I should be able to get this place up and running by borrowing power from the city's Geothermal system."

"And if you can't?"

Ben shrugged. "I guess we'll need a new plan. I haven't given up on this one yet though—argh!"

Ben jumped back from the panel and Ripley looked around quickly, trying to identify the threat.

"That thing—just moved on its own," Ben said, hand clutched over his heart. Ripley stepped forward and peered at the offending tendril. It was completely still.

"You sure?"

"Of course I'm sure!" snapped Ben. "How can you not find these things creepy? They're freaking me out. I want to go home." He took a deep breath. "What are they, even?"

Ripley shrugged, poking the tendril with the tip of his flashlight. "Honestly? I think they're some kind of root system from the Gate."

"What the hell's it need roots for?"

"We can theorize when we get home, Ben," Ripley urged, moving around the small room. "Let's just do what we need to do and get out of here. Tell me what you need from me."

"Right. Okay. Just give me some space."

Ben moved around the room methodically, sometimes craning his neck as he stood on tiptoes, sometimes squatting down low. Very soon there was a gentle humming. "That's right," cooed Ben softly. "That's right, darling." He stood up straight and moved to another set of controls. Ripley watched silently, knowing the most helpful thing he could do right now would be to stay out of Ben's way.

Light flooded the room and Ben did a little dance that, beneath his thick snow gear, looked as though he was simply wobbling back and forth from one foot to the other.

"We've got power up from New Sanctuary," he informed Ripley. "Now let's see if we're going to be able to give some back, or if we came all this way for nothing."

Flicking his flashlight off, Ripley came up beside Ben and watched over his shoulder as he worked. Ben was mumbling to himself.

"How can I help?" Ripley asked, feeling particularly useless.

"Eh, you can't, really," Ben told him dismissively. "The plant was designed with complete shielding, everything inside the actual reactor is remote. What we're looking for is whether or not there are any cores left that hadn't been initiated before the plant was decommissioned. If they're all spent...okay, pulling up visual now."

A monitor sprang to life, and Ripley watched as Ben maneuvered a camera, much the same way as the Observatory had allowed. It panned across a wide, empty space, settling on a large pool. Ripley did not need Ben to interpret what they saw there. It was full of the crystal roots, thicker than the ones they'd encountered so far, overlapping each other like a tightly woven net, disappearing beneath the surface of the water.

"That's where they would cool the spent fuel rods," Ben remarked, an unasked question lingering in his tone. "They would have programmed the plant to circulate long enough to cool them completely. They're still radioactive, but they aren't hot anymore."

"What about unspent fuel?"

"If there are any, they'll be..." Ben panned to the right. "Here. Jackpot."

A tall cylinder rose out of the ground, its top marked by five round holes, three of which were covered by thick, dark rods.

"That ought to be more than enough," Ben said happily. "They'll have degraded over time, but highly enriched uranium has a long half-life, and we have relatively simple needs. Now it's just a matter of engaging the process."

Ripley thought of the others, wondering if they'd made it safely back to the Sno-Cat.

"How long will that take?"

"Not long. Like I said, everything is automated." Ben moved between the control panels, closing his eyes several times and pointing at nothing, as if orientating himself. "Hey, help me clear this one off," he said, indicating a panel under a particularly heavy-looking tendril.

Ripley strode forward, tucking his flashlight under his arm, and grasped the thing with both hands.

Ripley Prior.

He leapt backward, heart racing. Ben was giving him a queer look. He looked around for the source of the voice, but they were alone. "What's wrong?"

"I thought...nothing. I think the cold is getting to me." He shook himself and tried again.

Ripley Prior.

This time he held fast to the root, dragging it away from the controls with some difficulty. But when he tried to let go, his grip stuck fast.

There was a blinding flash of light, and suddenly a man stood before him. Tall, with dazzlingly white hair and piercing violet eyes that reminded him eerily of Antiquity's Gate.

Ripley tore his gaze away to look for Ben, but he was alone with the stranger.

Alone, and no longer in the reactor. The brilliant light surrounded them both, encasing them in a bubble beyond which Ripley could see nothing.

"Where am I?" he demanded. "Who are you?"

"We don't have much time, Ripley. There are many things I wish to tell you. But for now, know this. It is imperative that you do not activate the reactor."

The words seemed sincere, but the situation was bizarre, and Ripley had no reason to trust this man. "Why shouldn't we?" he asked, more of an accusation than a question.

"Because if you do, the events that follow could be catastrophic."

Ripley squinted at the man. This place, whatever it was, made it difficult to be certain. Were those eyes shining, or was it just an effect of the light? But then the man tilted his head just enough so that the sheet of hair parted to reveal a pointed ear.

"I knew it!" Ripley exclaimed. "How can you ask me to trust you? You're a Theran!"

A gentle smile, a tilting back and forth of the head. The enigmatic figure shrugged. "Yes, in one sense. And no, in another. You and I, we are both creatures of a different sort, Ripley. Two made one. Past and future, Earth and Thera. Curiosities, to be certain."

Ripley felt something. A tugging, as if someone were

pulling him from behind. "I don't understand."

"We are out of time. Do not go through with the plan, Ripley Prior. The consequences will be irreversible."

Ripley hadn't realized his eyes were shut until they snapped open, and he found himself staring into Ben's worried face.

"Oh, man, Ripley, you scared me!" Ben shouted, an expression of relief rippling across his features before a look of seriousness replaced it. "You blacked out or something."

Ripley struggled to his feet, the details of the brief encounter fading fast, like a dream. Had it been a dream? There was a nagging, an insistence, a certainty that the stranger had not been misleading him. "We need to go."

"Yeah, if you're sure you're okay. If you pass out outside, I'm not strong enough to drag you all the way back to the Sno-Cat."

Ripley nodded quickly. "I'm fine. We need to go now. We shouldn't turn on the reactor."

Ben cocked an eyebrow. "What? Why?"

"I just...I have a bad feeling."

This weak reply was met with a noncommittal shrug. "Should have had it before you blacked out, then," Ben told him. "It's done. I've already initiated it. We're good to go."

Ripley groaned.

"I don't know what's come over you, pal, but we did what we came here to do. Now let's get out of here, okay?"

There was nothing for it. Ripley and Ben both had to

throw their weight against the door to get it to open wide enough to squeeze out, and Ripley nearly lost a hand as it snapped shut again. The wind had gotten *much* worse while they'd been inside. There was barely a pause in between gusts so that it came at them in one long, continuous blast. Ben staggered, his forward progress impeded by the way the wind forced him to walk sideways, as if the ground beneath his feet was shifting.

"Take my hand," Ripley hollered. Ben made no argument, and Ripley pulled the young man along behind him, bent low and leaning into the wind as hard as he dared.

It was slow, but eventually they reached the relative calm provided by the hulking buildings. But they were built on stocky supports so that the wind slipped through underneath, whipping against Ripley's legs like incessant waves. He considered riding it out inside one of them, then decided against it. They'd had the chance to warm up inside the microreactor, but the storm was growing stronger if anything. There was no way of knowing how long it would last. They needed to get back to the Sno-Cat and get out of here.

Holding up the flashlight proved impossible, the wind attempting to rip it from his grasp like a desperate thief. He pocketed it and forged on through the darkness, dragging Ben's weight as well as his own. At last they reached the fallen turbine, the sound of its blades of death a constant whine barely detectable above the roaring of the storm. He placed one hand against it and Ben followed directly behind him as they searched for the base. They'd been pushed far off course in their final stretch, and it seemed to take forever before they reached the jagged metal signaling the end of this particular obstacle. They cut across, stepping over the mess of wires, cables, and crystal tendrils.

The Sno-Cat was now visible in the distance, its headlights flooding the ground ahead of it, a beautiful beacon. Three weak flashlight beams scanned the ground just ahead as their companions awaited their arrival. The wind seemed to gasp, taking a deep inhale and then bursting forth once more, and Ripley watched the vehicle rock beneath the onslaught, headlights wavering.

Finally, blissfully, they reached it. Ripley pulled Ben around to the opposite side, and in the tiny eddy sheltered from the wind he pushed him up to where Denton had his arms outstretched, ready to help him inside. Ripley scrambled up behind him, closing the door and breathing in the shockingly warm air.

"Thank goodness!" Molly said, "Oh, thank goodness you're both okay! With the storm, we were so worried."

"I was only worried 'cause none of us three know how to drive this contraption," Denton grumbled. "Now, will one of you *please* get us out of here?"

"For once, I agree with Denton," Edwin said with a relieved smile. "Were you successful? Is it done?"

"Yeah," said Ben, panting. "Give me a minute, will ya?"

"No," Ripley replied, still trying to catch his breath. "We need to go *now*. This is far from over. It's getting worse."

"It *can't* get worse," Ben moaned. But he pulled himself upright, pulling off his gloves and grasping the controls all the same. "All right, all right. We're going."

Looking back, it was probably the sharp turn that did it. The shifting of their center of gravity, the angle of the treads. It didn't really matter, in the end.

The only thing Ripley knew for sure was that suddenly, somehow, the Sno-Cat was tilting. It was tilting, and then it was falling, and then he felt the impact of the cabin hitting the ground, five bodies tumbling over each other like beans in a pot. After that, only darkness.

CHAPTER THIRTEEN

THE BEST DEFENSE

THE RUSE WAS WORKING as well as could be expected. Laevus reached the camp in time to see patrols
assembling and then scattering into the forest in all directions. In tens and twenties they dispersed, fanning out
among the trees. He heard Nero before he saw him and
stopped short, nodding curtly to a passing patrol that barely gave him a second glance.

"I want every last one of them brought here *immediately.*" Nero was growling. "I want every ship grounded, every
crew scouring the island." Laevus had spotted his nemesis.
Cloaked in a lavish purple robe, Nero brandished an orna-
mented scepter as he raved at his officer. "They'll rue the
day they tried to sneak up on me. Who is it? The Culeian

scum? It doesn't matter. Bring them here and we'll execute them one by one until someone leads me to their precious capital. I *will* have my revenge for the slaughter of the Elder Council!"

Laevus smirked. As if Nero truly cared for the deaths of his fellow Council members. Their demise had brought about his rise to power, however short that would soon prove to be. His fingers twitched on the crossbow, but Nero was still heavily guarded, and Laevus had no intention of dying here today. He would be patient. It was a large island. Once the ships were grounded and most of the troops disbursed, *then* he would move in for the kill.

He watched as Nero disappeared into his tent, emerging after a minute without the scepter. He'd belted on his scabbard, the worn handle of his old Envicti blade peeking out from beneath the robe. *Has he ever even drawn it in battle,* Laevus wondered, *or is it worn out from his constant posturing?*

It didn't matter. Nero would never have cause to draw the blade again. By this time tomorrow, he'd be dead and Laevus would have pinned the murder neatly on some non-existent Human patsy, pointing a finger at Nelson and Ponytail as proof. Everything that had been Nero's would be his. Simple.

After that, he would destroy Sanctuary, thus avenging his mother's death and securing his acceptance as the new ruler of Thera.

But he was getting ahead of himself. Still, there was

little else to do but daydream until the opportune moment presented itself. He skirted around the edge of the camp, moving casually but cautiously. No one bothered him. They were all too busy scurrying after the "Human invaders." He allowed himself a chuckle. Those two poor fools had been more help than he could have dreamed. If it were possible, he would have even considered sparing their lives for the favor.

Of course, it would *not* be possible. Executing them for the callous murder of poor Nero would be an unpleasant necessity. He could not let his first act as leader be one of mercy.

People might get the wrong idea about him.

He had circled the camp twice, and had come within earshot of Nero once more. "All ships have been grounded, Emperor Nero," said one of the soldiers. "However, there are three that still have not returned from their mission."

Laevus stifled a derisive laugh. *Emperor,* he thought. *I suppose that is a step up in my inheritance from Most High Elder. Thank you for doing all the hard work for me, dear mentor. You've apparently saved me the trouble of dissolving the Council altogether on my own.*

It was almost time. He could feel it.

"Incoming vessel," said another voice.

Laevus watched Nero turn, just enough so that he caught the ever-present scowl on that smug face before moving a little farther out of view. He looked around. He'd never shot a crossbow before, and he only had one bolt. He had to make sure to do this right. A little copse to his left would be the perfect spot in which to set himself up and take aim.

Laevus' heart thundered in his chest. Not out of fear, but out of a feeling of triumph. This was it. This was what everything had been for. A lifetime was about to culminate in victory.

"Is it Human or Theran?"

"It's one of ours, Emperor."

Nero paused mid stride, tilting his head up. "Only one? Where are the others? Signal them."

"I already have, Emperor. They aren't responding."

Nero uttered a word which Laevus personally felt unbecoming of one who would be called "Emperor."

"It's the one that we lost in Atmos. It's some sort of filthy Human trick!" He unsheathed his sword and thrust it skyward, eyes narrow as he searched for the offending ship. "Take it down. *Take. It. Down!*"

Nero was lost from view as the soldiers who had stayed behind swarmed around him. Suddenly ships were up in the air again, all speeding toward the newcomer which had just come into view in the far distance, heading toward the tower.

Whoever was piloting it had quick reflexes, Laevus had to give them that. The ship pulled into a steep climb, turning. But it was no match for a fleet of its peers. It only took a few of them to disable the infiltrating vessel, and it pulled into a wide arc, falling in a tailspin and crashing loudly somewhere just out of sight.

When Laevus finally tore his eyes away from the spectacle, he found Nero gone. Already headed toward the crash site, and far out of range of Laevus' bow.

Uttering a curse, Laevus got up, brushed his uniform off, and followed.

Chapter Fourteen

On Thin Ice

"IS EVERYONE OKAY?"

Ripley was atop a pile of bodies that squirmed and moaned beneath him. A coil of rope had landed on his face in the fall. He sat up and smacked his head on a compartment that had flipped open, blinded by the tangled mass of rope still covering his face.

"I'm all right," Ben replied, sounding shaken. "Ack! Where's this steam coming from? I can't see anything." There was a loud thump as he smacked the dashboard. "Fixed it," he muttered.

"I'm fine, too," Molly said, using Ben as leverage to right herself. Denton's grunt of affirmation quickly followed, and Ripley was shifted forcefully against the seats as the larger man stood up beside him, teetering ominously. The glass window he stood on let off a high-pitched whine of warning as it strained against the frame.

"Don't stand directly on the glass," Ripley instructed. Denton edged sideways without arguing. Who hadn't answered? "Edwin? You're awfully quiet. You okay?"

"I…don't think I am."

Edwin's voice was strained, a note of pain permeating his words. He let out a sharp whimper, sucking air between his teeth as he attempted to maneuver himself off of the window that now served as the floor, shattered glass scraping beneath him, screeching in protest.

"Watch your hands," Ripley said, reaching down to assist, "You don't want to get cut. Here, let me help you."

"Careful!" Edwin cried warily, shrinking in on himself like a frightened child. "Don't. Please. I think it's broken."

"What's broken?"

"My leg."

A single beam of light peeked out from where Ripley's flashlight had settled beneath a displaced cushion. He rummaged for it and, pointing it at Edwin, confirmed the man's suspicions.

Edwin was leaning against the top of the cabin, his injured leg held fast between fists gripped so tight that the knuckles were white with strain. It was not difficult to diagnose the break. His shin bulged out unnaturally midway between his ankle and his knee. He cringed as, with some difficulty, he braced his good leg against the floor and pressed himself into a more upright position. Molly made a motion as if to touch his pant leg, but Edwin pulled the leg further from her, whimpering in pain as he did so.

"Edwin, that's definitely a break. We're going to need to splint it," Molly said in the soothing-but-serious motherly tone she might use on an injured child. "We need to immobilize it and deal with it properly when we get back to New Sanctuary."

"You mean *if* we get back," grumbled Denton.

"Yeah," said Ben's voice. "Not sure if anyone else noticed, but we're in kind of a bad situation right now."

There was a silence from the others as the full weight of their predicament settled over the group. Ripley looked up, shining his light skyward. A restraining belt swung gently in the beam. The door was still intact.

"Leave me."

Edwin sounded very tired, and the statement was dull, matter-of-fact. "Leave me here and go back to the city."

"Don't talk like that," chastised Molly. "Of course we won't leave you."

"She's right," Ripley agreed. "You're as good as dead if you stay. It's going to take a lot longer on foot. By the time we could get help back, you'd be nothing but a bureaucratic popsicle."

"I'm not asking you to send help," Edwin retorted irritably. "You barely stand a chance as it is, without deadweight. You have to get back. Ben's the only one who knows how to operate the array and destroy the Gate. He's the best chance we have. He *has* to survive. Me? I'm…expendable."

There was a heavy silence. "Man's got a point," Denton remarked after a while. "But I don't think it matters. Ain't no way we're making it back without this wretched machine."

"Denton," Ripley said in a commanding tone, "switch spots with Molly. Ben, help me look for something she can use to splint the leg." Ben nodded in the faint light… Edwin grimaced.

"No offense, Ripley, but I think I'd rather freeze to death."

Ripley ignored him, feeling the blessed relief of pressure as Denton less-than-gracefully swapped places with Molly. He tried to ignore her closeness as he patted everything in sight, looking for something, anything, long and straight. His fingers skimmed along the base of the seats until they made contact with one of the supports. "Denton," he grunted as he tugged at it, "grab that cushion and start tearing the fabric off. The longest strips you can make. There's a knife in my jacket pocket."

"I'm not sticking my hand in your—"

"Just do it! This isn't the time to argue."

"We have the blankets," Ben offered, but Ripley shook his head.

"No, save those. We're going to need everything we have to stay warm."

He reached up with both hands now, leaning back and pulling harder. At first it seemed like it might give way, but it was only bending. He let go, sighing. "No good. We need something else."

"How about the control levers?" Ben suggested.

"Let's see. Push over."

There was more shuffling and grunting as they rearranged themselves again, everyone doing their best not to step on Edwin, who shrank back out of the way as far as he could. Ripley grasped one of the long control arms. He flexed, pulling with everything he had. The whole vehicle shifted beneath them as the treads strained to comply with the controls. There wasn't a lot of room to give himself more leverage, but with a creak of protest the bar came free, the square base with it. Ripley gave it a little shake, and the bolts that had once held it to the floor fell, tinkling as they hit the glass. "That's going to have to do," he said. He passed it to Denton, who took it without a word, then set to work on the next one. This one came away more easily than the first, and Ripley handed it off to Ben, who took it in both hands with an expression of intense mourning.

"Oh, Snow Master, I barely knew you."

"She might save our lives yet," Ripley told him. "As long as the engine keeps running, we'll stay warm. That'll let us ride out the storm."

"I suppose," Ben said wistfully.

Ripley squeezed himself in next to Molly, kneeling, with difficulty, beside Edwin. "You ready?"

"As I'll ever be."

Ripley glanced at Molly, who now held one of the control shafts and a few sad-looking strips of cloth. Then he addressed Edwin.

"This is going to hurt."

Edwin opened his mouth, baring his teeth in a pained smile. "Figured as much. Just get it over with, already."

As delicately as he could, Ripley tore a neat line up the front of Edwin's pant leg, revealing the bulge. He let out a sigh of relief at the sight. He'd half expected, given their luck, to find the bone jutting through Edwin's pale flesh, blood pooling on the cracked glass beneath them. But the wound had not broken the skin. He ran a hand softly under Edwin's calf, feeling for signs of further injury. Catching the man's grimace out of the corner of his eye, he pressed gently around the bulge, trying to figure out how bad it was. Ripley could feel the bones, the way they had cracked and twisted out of place, one sliding back over itself and the other bulging up just under the skin. *It could have been worse*, he supposed. Not that Edwin was likely to agree right now.

"How'd it happen?" Ben asked curiously. "Did Denton land on top of you?"

Something somewhere between a sob and a laugh escaped Edwin. "No. I caught it on something. Chair support, maybe. I fell, the leg didn't come with me."

Ripley grasped Edwin's ankle, feeling entirely unqualified to be doing this. But Molly whispered instructions to him. He gave the foot a calculated yank, feeling at least one bone snap back into its rightful place like a magnet. Edwin

293

gave a piteous wail, his chest heaving as Molly and Ripley worked together to wrap the splint snugly in place. "Please don't make me do that again," Ripley implored him with a reassuring smile. "I might have just done more damage."

"Sure felt that way."

"It would have been better to wait, if we could have gotten him to the hospital right away," Molly said, still using her authoritative teacher voice. "But this will make the journey easier, Edwin. And I'm confident Sylvia's pod therapy can undo any nerve damage we've inadvertently caused. We just have to keep an eye out for infection and internal bleeding."

"Ah," Edwin said, his face pale, "is that all? Good."

"All right," Ripley said, rocking back on his heels to survey their work, "now that that's sorted, we'd better come up with a plan."

"Well," Ben said hesitantly, "Our biggest problem is going to be having enough to eat and drink."

"You said we had twice what we'd need," Denton said gruffly.

"Yeah, with the Sno-Cat in the equation," Ben corrected. "We could have easily gone five more days if she got stuck. But if we're walking, we probably only have enough food for half of that. You need a lot more calories to stay warm out there."

Ripley allowed his eyes to close, trying to block the rest of them out as he considered their options.

"All right," he said at last when he opened them again.

"We're just going to have to make it in three days, then."

"It took us two to get here on this monstrosity," Denton pointed out. "You want us to walk it in three?"

"I'm sure we can use a more direct route. Cross snow bridges that the Sno-Cat couldn't, or jump crevasses. We'll figure it out. We either make it in three days, or we die trying." He looked around at all of them, saw grim determination in their faces. "I'm going to go check the buildings, see what I can find. Everyone else, stay *here*."

If the storm winds did not seem so intent on killing Ripley, getting out of the cramped conditions of the capsized Sno-Cat might have been almost refreshing. It was, at the very least, easier to move without his companions. Being a Halfsie had its advantages.

He rounded the wind turbine and ducked low beneath its blades to reach the door to the first building they'd seen. Inside, he recognized communications equipment. Similar to the Observatory back in Sanctuary but silent and neglected. A quick search yielded nothing that Ripley considered to be of value.

He doubled back, skipping over the building they'd sought respite in earlier. He would rather avoid it if possible. The next long, low unit proved equally fruitless. It was starting to look more and more like Ripley would have to recheck the final resting place of the poor Sequencing victim, and the thought left a bitter taste in his mouth.

But there was one more to check, just shy of the microreactor and on the opposite side of the path they'd been following.

This one proved to be worth the journey. Inside a row of wide lockers lined the length of the wall. Ripley found several lengths of rope which, despite the passage of time, seemed sturdy enough when he tested it with a few solid tugs. Many of the lockers had canvas sacks in them, and Ripley dumped out the contents to take inventory, though most of it was not very helpful. No matter how hungry they got, he doubted anyone wanted to take a chance on centuries old nutrition bars. There was a brittle first aid kit, but the bottle labelled *pain reliever* looked as dubious as the bars. In the end he stuffed three bags into one, along with the rope, some materials to replace Edwin's splint, and a few fierce looking hooks that he thought might come in handy on the long stretch of ice. There were no proper tools, but he managed to jimmy the hinges on two of the lockers with an ice pick. He lashed them together, covering them with a couple of flimsy blankets for padding. The sled wasn't his finest craftsmanship, but it would make transporting Edwin easier.

Slinging the backpack over his shoulders and grabbing a handful of what looked like walking sticks, Ripley headed back to his companions. The trek was slightly less arduous, which suggested that the storm might be breaking. Twice he had to sidestep to avoid being hammered by his own sled when the shifting wind lifted it off the ground and hurled it in his direction. He staked it down well clear of the Sno-Cat then climbed up, dropping his sack to Denton before lowering himself down and pulling the door closed again.

"I've made a sled," he explained as he pulled the medical supplies out and passed them to Ben. "We'll be able to put one of the tents on it and pull Edwin."

"Come again?" Edwin said, wincing as Molly worked on his arm. "I'm going to just lay down and take a nap while you guys battle your way home?"

"The storm is breaking," Ripley told him, "and there's no way you could put pressure on that leg, even in the best of conditions. You can't pull your own weight, here, Edwin. You're going to have to swallow your pride and let me do it for you."

Edwin still didn't look like he liked this plan. Denton was shaking his head and chuckling. "Figures. Once a politician, always a politician. Expecting everyone else to work while you sit on your—"

"Not helping," Ben muttered, elbowing Denton sharply in the ribs.

"Don't worry about it," Ripley assured Edwin. "I can handle it. You just concentrate on healing."

"Yeah, but—"

The engine sputtered alarmingly. Ripley looked to Ben, who shrugged. "It's not really designed to run on its side. I'm kind of surprised it's lasted this long, to be honest."

"You could have mentioned that." Ripley heard the accusation in his tone, but was just as mad at himself for not realizing this himself.

"I didn't feel like it would help group morale to point out all the bad things that could happen," Ben said, raising his empty palms in a gesture of helpless defeat.

Ripley tilted his head toward the upturned door, sighing. He closed his eyes, listening to the wind, wondering if it would be safe enough. The engine sputtered again, and he knew it didn't matter. They could not stay here and waste precious time and energy if they couldn't stay warm.

"All right. Let's get everything into the bags." He hefted himself back up to the door. "Send them out as you fill them."

He landed beside the sled and gestured through the windshield. Ben gave him a thumbs up to indicate he understood. Denton tossed one of the tents out and Ripley set to work inflating it and lashing it down. They tossed down all the rest and Ripley shoved everything that wouldn't fit in the bags into the tent. Once everyone but Edwin was out of the craft, Ripley scrambled back inside and picked up one of the control bars.

The windows had cracked on impact, delicate spider web patterns etched across the glass. Ripley tried just giving it a push, hoping to avoid spraying Edwin with bits of shattered glass, but it was tougher than it appeared.

With a sigh he raised the bar and thrust it forward, piercing the glass like a spear. The sound of the glass breaking was nearly swallowed up as the wind burst into the exposed cabin, shards bouncing off of his goggles. Instinctively, he squeezed his eyes shut. When he opened them again, there was nothing left of the windshield but a few jagged pieces that clung stubbornly to the Sno-Cat's frame.

"You sure about this?" Edwin said, looking between Ripley and the sled. "I mean, after everything I've put you through, now you're going to drag me across Antarctica? Not too late to leave me here. I've heard freezing to death isn't the worst way to go."

Ripley glanced over his shoulder at the man, and hooked a thumb at his own right eye. "I've got super powers now, remember? You can owe me one. Just get in and sit tight. We're going to make it."

He wasn't entirely sure that he believed this, but he had to try. He and Denton lifted Edwin from the carcass of the vehicle and maneuvered him into the tent atop the sled. He was still attempting to situate himself as Ripley zipped up the flap.

"We should tie ourselves together," Ben shouted over the wind. "So we can't get separated."

Denton's mouth twisted into a dubious frown. "And what if you fall in a hole and drag us in after you, eh?"

Ben gave a pitying shake of his head. "No one's dragging you anywhere, Denton." He tried to raise a map to his face, but it collapsed in on itself, hugging his cheeks as he struggled to extricate himself from its grasp. Ben sighed. "Well, maybe I'll leave Edwin in charge of the map. But we're heading in that general direction." He waved vaguely toward the north. "I'll take the lead. Then six feet or so between us, I think."

Ripley moved between the others, doling out the rope. His stomach knotted when he came to Molly. He wrapped the rope around her waist as fast as he could before moving on to Denton, who snatched the end from him with a scowl. "Don't need anyone else to tie a knot for me, Prior. Back off."

Ripley did as Denton requested, moving away and grabbing hold of the ropes he had threaded through the makeshift sled.

Then they were off. Their progress seemed painfully slow, but the wind did seem to ease some as they came over the crest separating Black Island from the ice shelf. Ben had decided that they should save the flashlights, so only Ben's single beam marked the route ahead, bobbing unsteadily as he pressed forward. After a while he called Ripley up from the rear of their caravan.

"There are a lot of potential hazards," he explained. "I could use some help making sure we're not walking straight into trouble."

"I'm not sure how much help I'll be, but sure. What do you want me to do?"

Soon they were moving again, Ripley pulling Edwin's sled alongside Ben, shoving a walking stick into the ground to test for unseen perils ahead. The flashlight didn't offer much in the way of light, but the stick forewarned of deeper areas of snow that Ben said might indicate hidden drainage holes or the beginning of crevasses. On one such occasion, Ripley and Ben both stopped short and looked at each other. Both of their sticks had plunged deep into the ground this time. Ripley leaned carefully on his and found that it continued to sink. They moved cautiously to their right, testing as they went, and found more of the same before the snow bridge ended, revealing a wide chasm that stretched far out of sight.

"Definitely a crevasse," Ripley informed the others. "We're going to have to cross it. We don't have the time or resources to go around."

"Cross it how?" Denton asked indignantly, his gruff voice muffled by his thick face mask.

Ripley put a foot out and smacked the snow hard, once, twice, three times. There was no accompanying sound of snow falling away below, no subtle give to indicate that it would not bear their weight. "It should be safe."

"Should?" Denton persisted.

"I'll go first," Ripley assured him. He fumbled with the heavy gloves he wore as he untied the knots strapping him to Edwin's sled. He wanted to put as much distance between it and him as he could to avoid putting too much stress on the snow bridge.

Stepping out, Ripley let out a breath of relief. He had not plunged downward into the dark depths of the crevasse. That was something.

With long, slow steps he pushed forward, pulling the sled behind him until he was confident he must have reached the other side. He jabbed his stick into the ground again, feeling the resistance of ice just a few inches down.

He continued to pull until the sledge was safely across as well, then waved at the others. "Spread out as much as you can," he called, "and take your time."

Ben took the first step with trepidation, the confidence in his footfalls increasing as he inched slowly across the bridge.

Everyone was tired, freezing, and hungry by the time Ripley decided they'd better call it a day. He knew by their faces that he'd pushed them too hard with too few breaks. Molly looked completely wiped out, and Ben and Denton were both showing signs of exhaustion. Still, the thought of rest seemed to offer a weak but pronounced second wind. They set up camp, forcing Edwin out of the tent while they staked it down, spreading the supplies between them. Ripley made certain to stake the sled a ways off from their camp and downwind, certain none of them had any desire to be sliced in half by the sharp metal contraption should a gust send it hurtling through the row of tents. The shining silver exteriors shook and bobbed much more than they had back when the group had had the benefit of the Sno-Cat as a windbreak, but it would have to do.

Things took a turn for the worse when Ben pointed out that Edwin should probably have his own tent. It wouldn't do to have the likes of Denton jostling him all through the night. Edwin's face looked paler than before, and the sweat pooling in the rims of his goggles was extremely concerning. It seemed likely that he'd been battling a fever. Ripley did not know much about injuries besides what he had gleaned from his time in Sylvia's lab, and Sylvia wasn't a doctor, either. He wondered how big of a concern an infection might be, and how badly it would be exacerbated by the unfriendly environment Edwin was now being subjected to.

"I'll go with Denton," Ripley volunteered quickly, heading off any chance of spending a long, cold night beside Molly in painful silence. He desperately wanted to speak to her about everything that had happened, but this was neither the time nor the place for such heart-to-hearts. It could wait until they got back to the city.

Beside the simple will to live, it was Ripley's driving force throughout the day's journey. They needed to make it back, so he could tell her how he felt. Not under threat of death by exposure, where she might think his motives tainted by fear. He wanted her to know that what he said, he meant. No ifs, ands, buts, or conditions.

Denton was making strange sounds as he devoured his rations like a ravenous beast, slurping furiously on his thermos as if it had been days instead of hours since he'd last had a drink. Ripley's legs were screaming, the small of his back throbbing dully from the extra effort of pulling Edwin. He downed his food without tasting it, uncomfortably aware of the way Denton's bulk was pressing up against his left side as the man bumped and jostled his way through the meal. Ripley's tent mate pulled his glove back on and wiped the corner of his mouth with the back of his hand. When he turned his eyes on Ripley, there was a brief moment where Ripley wondered if Denton intended to snatch up the rest of *his* dinner, too.

But he didn't. Instead, he spoke.

"Never thought I'd miss the Edge so much." Denton's voice was just as gravelly as always, but something was missing. It took Ripley the space of a few heartbeats to work out what exactly that something was.

The rancor. The way his words usually sounded like an attack.

What is it with these tents, Ripley marveled, once again thankful that he'd not been interred for the night with Molly, *that makes people want to talk about all their deep thoughts?*

"Yeah," he agreed at last, nodding slowly. "Kind of makes you appreciate the warmth, huh?"

"Wouldn't even mind hearing the tiny terrors screeching about the place," Denton admitted. "All that's out here is this infernal wind. Grates on the nerves. It's eerie."

"Yeah," Ripley repeated, unsure what response Denton was looking for. Usually the security guard just preferred silence. Ripley had always been happy to oblige.

Denton shot him a familiar glare that, in the soft glow of the lamp, was a much more comforting sight than Ripley would have expected. It proved that Denton had not lost his mind or gone soft from the cold. "Don't tell Watanabe I said that," he growled.

"Wouldn't dream of it," Ripley assured him.

Denton turned, staring at the side of the tent as it

shuddered back and forth. His eyes didn't track the motion, though. He seemed to be staring *through* it, back toward the city.

"You think we're going to make it back?" he asked after a lengthy silence.

Ripley masked his hesitation by raising one hand in a thumbs up. "Sure," he said. "Easy-peasy. We did all right today, didn't we?"

With a shrug, Denton shifted to his side and pulled the sleeping bag up around his neck. "Suppose so."

The worry in Denton's voice haunted Ripley as he turned off the lantern and closed his eyes. And after that, it haunted his dreams, too.

*   *   *

THE SECOND DAY STARTED out much the same as the first. The tents were methodically packed away, the sled prepared, the supplies loaded in with Edwin and each of the others taking a backpack for themselves. Ripley's body seemed to have recovered well overnight, and he was eager to get moving, putting on an excited face for the benefit of the group. If Denton was nervous, the rest of them would be even more so.

"This time tomorrow we'll be doing this for the final time, guys. And tomorrow night we'll be eating dinner at Ben's house!"

"Yeah," Ben said, making a brave but fragile attempt at

mimicking Ripley's enthusiasm. "I'm sure my mom would love that!"

Edwin, propped up against one of the sticks that Ripley had driven into the ground, managed a weak smile, and Ripley looked him over with concern. Molly had checked the leg and found it bruised and swollen, but not terribly so.

He bent down, looking his former nemesis in the eye. If he had ever felt threatened by Edwin, he didn't anymore. The man looked utterly defeated in body and mind. Ripley could see it in his eyes. He viewed the pain as some sort of penance for his past. Ripley knew this, because he'd felt the same, once. The hopelessness in Edwin's soul was familiar to him.

"You don't look so good, my friend," he said. "But we're going to get you back to New Sanctuary, and Sylvia will get you fixed up. Just hang in there."

"Relax, Ripley," Edwin said with mock bravado. "No one dies of a broken leg. We're much more likely to get lost, and starve, or freeze. Like I said before, I hear freezing isn't a bad way to go, really. Peaceful, painless."

"We're not going to freeze," Ripley said, "we're going to make it. You were worried about making someone else pull your weight? Don't make me carry your emotional baggage, too." His words were harsh, Ripley knew, but Edwin was a man who needed harsh words right now. There was no time for coddling and self-pity.

A scream pierced the darkness.

Molly's scream.

Chapter Fifteen

Oh Brother

"WE'LL BE APPROACHING the coordinates short- ly," Gavin said, flicking one of the toggles overhead without taking his eyes off of his screens. "Every- one stay alert."

"Put us down as close to the tower as you can without arousing suspicion," Felix suggested from his now familiar spot, just behind the pilot's chair. "The faster we get in, the faster we get out."

"The tower may be heavily guarded," Gavin warned. "If I were in Nero's shoes, I would consider it an asset worth protecting. It's likely they will have figured out how to use it to intercept communications between Culei and the oth- er nations."

"If you were in Nero's shoes," Felix reminded him, "we would be celebrating a successful Earth-Thera alliance, and not be in this mess in the first place. But don't worry, we didn't bring you along to usurp Nero, you're just the muscle."

"I thought I was the copilot," Gavin said dryly.

"That's right!" Kestrel replied, clapping Felix on the back. "*I'm* the muscle."

Felix looked back at her, silver hair flashing as she tilted her head to one side, her bright smile belonging to someone on their way to a festival, rather than into the belly of the beast. He could see why she and Willow got on so well; both had indomitably cheerful spirits.

"*And* me," added Ollie. The young man reminded Felix forcefully of a Theran version of Tobias. He followed Gavin around like a baby duckling. He talked a lot, seemed very bright, but perhaps a few cogs shy of an airship. Exactly like Toby—except for the eyes, of course. And the ears. And the fact that he was over fifty years old. He looked younger than Felix, or at least younger than Felix felt these days. He'd been quick to volunteer to join the mission, and since they were up against a Theran army, Felix had thought him a better choice than Baba.

"So, Kestrel," said Tobias in an offhand way as he sat on the floor of the ship, surrounded by tools. "Have you given any thought to what you'll do after this is all over?" He picked up a screwdriver, gave it a scrutinizing once-over, and put it back down.

"Yeah," she said, her cheerful demeanor vanishing in a flash. "I'm going to go find the Weaver."

"We're going to go find him," corrected Gavin.

Tobias glanced up, redirecting the frown that he'd been giving his socket wrench on Kestrel. "Perhaps if we knew more about *precisely* what happened, we would be able to come to a clearer deduction as to his whereabouts."

"I already told you *precisely* what happened, Tobias," said Gavin, unlocking his restraint and turning in his chair to face the cargo area. "He was with us when we left Thera. He was gone when we reached Earth."

"But," Tobias said, hesitant, "You don't think he's..."

"No," Gavin said, low and forceful. "He disappeared, and it's a mystery, but he isn't dead. I would know."

"How?" Ambrose inquired, face awash with curiosity.

"Someone like him doesn't just fade into the night with a whisper," Gavin replied. "Something unexplainable happened when we passed through the Evenmire. We're going back for him. But first we need to finish what he started."

Tobias scrambled to his feet, stuffing the last of his tools into a bag and swinging it carefully over his shoulder, cringing as it smacked hard against his back. "We'll help you!"

Gavin glanced back at him briefly before readjusting himself to face forward once more. "It will probably be dangerous. Most things having to do with the Evenmire seem to be."

"That's okay," Tobias replied, giving a fair approximation of a carefree shrug. "We can handle danger. After all this, ending a war and such, I expect we'll have time on our hands. At least," he shot a look at Felix, "I can't speak for all of us, but…"

"Of course we'll help," Felix confirmed. "It's the least we can do. And besides, I'd like to go back to Sanctuary. Maybe my mother is still there. I never thought I'd get another chance to see her."

Gavin only nodded in reply. "We're nearly to the island. Stay sharp, everyone."

It was visible in the distance, clear blue skies over the island that rose and fell in tree-covered mounds. Ambrose leaned forward, squinting.

"Something wrong?" Felix asked.

Ambrose nodded. "Not sure what, though. I don't see a single ship. We shouldn't be the only ones in the sky. At the very least, Nero should have a few scouts watching for incoming vessels, don't you think?"

"You're right," Gavin replied. "That *is* odd."

"They wouldn't have left?" Tobias pondered aloud. "Gone on a mission en masse?"

"No," Gavin replied. "Nero would have kept most of his forces together, protected by their numbers. He wouldn't send out more ships than necessary."

"*Incoming vessel,*" came a harsh voice over the intercom, "*please identify.*"

"I was hoping we'd avoid this," grumbled Gavin, "blend in with the others."

"Should we go back?" Ollie asked.

"No, this is too important. If we run, they'll be on the lookout next time. In other words, there won't *be* a next time."

"*Incoming vessel!*"

Gavin held up a hand for quiet and depressed a small green button. "We are returning from the razing at—"

"*Where are the other ships?*"

"We were separated," Gavin said, depressing the button again. "We believed they had returned already."

"*To whom am I speaking?*"

"Silvan."

The line went silent. It had been the name given by the pilot of one of the captured ships. Felix held his breath, waiting to see if the information was good, or if they'd been duped.

"They would have given us landing instructions by now," Gavin said, turning to Ambrose with a meaningful shake of his head. "It's no good. We need to turn back."

Ambrose nodded in reluctant agreement. "All right. Buckle up, everyone. Time to go."

"But what about the plan?" Felix asked, even as he sat and strapped himself securely into one of the crew seats.

"We can't come up with a new plan if we're all dead," Gavin replied gravely.

"We've got incoming!" Ambrose shouted. He performed a maneuver that left Felix's innards feeling out of place, and Tobias squeezed his eyes tightly shut, clutching the strap of his tool bag in a deathgrip. Felix could feel his feet lifting off the floor as the ship dropped suddenly, then his chest constricted, his body forced against the seat by inertia as the ship rose at a steep angle.

"Damn it, how many are they going to scatter?" Ambrose yelled, his hands grasping tightly on the controls.

"Knowing Nero," Gavin said, "all of them. Double back across the island. Head for open waters. We don't want to lead them back to—"

There was a horribly familiar sound from somewhere near the back of the ship. The moments before Thoris Wilk's death flashed before Felix's eyes. "Everyone down!" he cried, grabbing Kestrel and thrusting her head between her knees. It might not have mattered. The shots could have come from anywhere. But all Felix could remember was the tiny pinpricks in *Pluto's* hull, neatly marching across the ship at chest level.

"We can still make it," Ambrose said bracingly, pulling the ship in a wide arc. "They haven't taken out—"

The engine died with a great shuddering gasp, and the deathly silence left in its wake was a vacuum, sucking Felix's breath away.

Not again!

But it seemed that Ambrose had grown used to horrible things happening to the ships he piloted. As *Pluto's Ghost* went into a spiral, Felix and the others flattened against their spots and racing toward the inevitable impact, Ambrose pulled up at the last second, and they skipped across the ground like a pebble on a lake, each bounce a little less violent than the last. They were jostled back and forth as they rammed into trees, tearing them up by the roots until the ship at last came to a standstill. Everyone gazed at each other for a moment, too shocked to move.

Felix felt the moments passing with excruciating clarity as instinct kicked in. "They'll be on us in a minute," he cried, pulling at his restraints. "We need to get out, *now!*"

No one argued. Sounds of scuffling filled the cabin as they all worked to free themselves from the tangle of restraints. Ambrose unlocked the hatch, but it only made a small, weak popping sound. Tobias jiggled the release handle with a mixture of hope and despair crashing like waves across his panicked face.

"The frame must have been damaged in the crash!"

"Step aside," Gavin growled. He stepped up to the hatch, assessing it, then motioned for all of them to step back. With one well-aimed, powerful kick, the hatch burst outward. Felix cringed as metal scraped on metal, the sound making his teeth clench. The hatch slammed back against the outer hull as a flood of fresh air rushed in, smelling of salt and damp earth.

"Gavin, Ambrose," Felix instructed, "you go that way. Kestrel, Ollie, you'll be the fastest. Try to make some noise, keep them away as long as you can."

Kestrel didn't wait for further instruction. She took Ollie by the hand and raced off into the woods.

"Tobias, you and I are going to make directly for the

tower. We're trapped here now, our only hope is to—"

There was a strangled cry not far off. Ollie. Felix turned that way instinctively, but Gavin grasped his shoulder and whirled him back around. "No. We'll go. You head for the tower."

"But—"

Tobias thrust the bag into Felix's arms. "You're the fastest one who knows how to install this," he said, eyes fearful. "We can buy you time. Pretend they've got us all. Don't argue. *Run.*"

For a fraction of a second Felix was torn between abandoning his friends to an uncertain fate and completing the mission.

Then he gritted his teeth, turned, and ran.

The forest turned into a brown and green blur around him as he raced in the direction of the tower. His eyes never stopped moving, looking for signs of motion among the trees. His head and stomach churned in unison, thinking of the friends he'd left behind. They'd put all their hopes on him. They were counting on him. Could he remember everything Toby had taught him about the Arca device? Could he reach the tower without being seen?

Could he make it in time to save them?

He couldn't think of a scenario in which they all made it out of this alive. Nero might question them, torture them, but ultimately, he would kill them. If Felix failed, he would join them in their fate. If he succeeded, Nero would execute them in a rage over the loss of his fleet.

Either way, someone was going to die on this island.

He replayed Ollie's strangled cry in his mind. Perhaps someone had *already* died.

They hadn't made it anywhere close to the tower at all. They'd been forced to the ground a good distance from the base of the hill where it stood. Felix had to stop, drawing deep breaths into his burning lungs as quietly as he could as he tried to orient himself. *Which way?* He strained his ears for the sound of pursuers.

He heard no footsteps, but there was a faint, and very ominous, *click*.

"That's far enough."

The Theran materialized from between the trees to his right with crossbow raised and pointed at his chest. Felix raised his free hand in surrender, unwilling to lose his grip on the heavy satchel of tools swung across his back.

"Drop the bag," the soldier commanded, very close now.

"I'd rather not," Felix said, "it's a bit fragile."

The guard kept the bow trained on Felix as he approached and began to circle behind him. Felix turned slowly on the spot.

"Stop moving," the Theran commanded.

"Oh. Right. Sorry."

Felix stopped, mind racing through the possibilities. He had no weapon. This was likely one of the clones. He would outmatch Felix in strength and speed, even if he managed to avoid being shot. He just needed a few moments to *think*.

But he did not have a few moments. His captor tore the bag from his shoulder, dumping the contents to the ground and examining them, prodding the tools with his toe. He stopped when he noticed the Arca device, and Felix felt a plummeting sensation much like when the ship had gone into a dive.

"What's this?"

"Well," said Felix, rather hopeless now, "it's a science project. Does science-y type stuff."

The soldier scooped it up and then stood with a scowl, motioning with his bow. "That way. *Slowly*. You can tell the Emperor about it if you won't talk to me."

Felix forced one foot in front of the other, walking as slowly as he dared, waiting for some brilliant idea to come to him.

None did.

"Listen," he said casually over his shoulder, "Nero and I—"

"*Emperor* Nero," corrected the Theran sternly.

"What is it with everybody and their honorifics?" Felix mused. "Everyone's always so hung up on titles. I mean, we're Therans. We've only got one name to begin with, why does everyone feel the need to complicate that beautiful simplicity?"

There was a faint click somewhere off to his right and something whistled past Felix's ear. The soldier guarding him grunted and dropped to the ground. Before Felix could react, someone had grabbed him by the arm, yanking him off the trail and into the thick underbrush. He was thrown to the ground, coughing and sputtering as his face hit the dirt, pebbles scraping across his cheek. He struggled onto his stomach.

A familiar face looked down on him. A *very* familiar face, with a cordial smile and twinkling, mischievous eyes.

"Hello, brother."

Felix stared up at the speaker. Into the painfully familiar face of his long-lost sibling. Laevus.

"Great," said Felix, standing up. *"Just* great. Just who I wanted to see."

Laevus looked pleasantly surprised. "Really?"

"No!" Felix looked around. They seemed to be alone. He walked over to the fallen soldier and snatched up the Arca controller, then began collecting the scattered tools and shoveling them back into the bag. Laevus just watched, his eyes flitting between Felix and the dead clone. A crossbow bolt jutted out of the man's eye socket.

"Not bad, for my first time with a crossbow," Laevus mused. "I rather thought I had a good chance of hitting you by mistake."

"I'm surprised you weren't aiming for me," Felix growled. "Unless you were, and you hit *him*," he jerked his head toward the body, "by mistake."

"Alas, I suppose we may never know for certain." Laevus lifted his shoulders and let them fall, sighing. "Odd way to say thank you. But I forgive you. That's what brothers do, isn't it? Forgive?"

Felix stood up and slung the bag into place once more. He moved close to Laevus, studying those cool, calculating eyes. "Are you asking me to forgive you?" He was trembling all over.

"I'm afraid you've lost me, dear brother," Laevus said. "I have done nothing to you that requires forgiveness."

"You were partial to the plot to destroy Sanctuary," Felix retorted, painfully aware that he was wasting precious time. "You tormented our mother for years. You left us for dead in that Culeian transport. You got all of those people in the fleet killed with whatever little scheme you're playing..." Felix shook his head furiously. "Should I go on?"

Then he glanced down at the body on the forest floor. "Thank you for saving me," he muttered. The words tasted forced and bitter on his tongue. "Now, if you'll excuse me, I have work to do. I would prefer if we could go back to never seeing each other again."

"I don't understand," said Laevus, putting on an air of having been wronged. He stooped down to study the clone for a moment, then placed his foot irreverently over the dead man's face and yanked out the bolt. He eyed it distastefully, wiping it on the soldier's uniform. "I've saved your life. Should it be unreasonable to expect a little gratitude for such a heroic act? Shouldn't you owe me something in return...a life debt, perhaps?"

"You could have just as easily killed me," Felix snapped, anxiety feeding his growing anger. "I have things to do.

319

And I need to do them fast. Lives depend on it."

He began to walk away, Laevus appearing at his side, stepping lightly as though they were enjoying an evening stroll to look at the scenery. "I have plans of my own, you know."

"Good for you," replied Felix with tired resignation.

"I'm going to kill Nero."

"You should go do that, then." A thrill of hope welled in Felix's chest, but he extinguished it quickly.

"Wouldn't you like to join me?"

Felix gave his brother a look of incredulity. "In what reality would I want to help *you* with *anything*?"

"Perhaps the one in which you are all I have left," replied Laevus.

He stopped walking. Against his better judgement Felix stopped too, feeling a sense of foreboding at Laevus' words.

"What do you mean by that, exactly?"

"There is no delicate way to tell you this..." Laevus began.

"Just spit it out."

"Our mother is dead."

Laevus did not deliver this news with his characteristic flourish. There was no drama to his announcement, no coy sparkle in his eyes.

It was this deadpan delivery that allowed Felix, just for a moment, to believe the words he had just heard.

Just for a moment.

"You're lying."

"I'm not."

Felix tilted his head back, scanning the woods. He was completely disoriented now, and he cursed. Dappled sunlight filtered through the treetops, but there was no sign of which direction would lead him to the tower. And time was running out.

"Lost, dear brother?"

Felix snarled. "Stop calling me that!"

Laevus pursed his lips and raised his eyebrows. "But you are. My dear brother, that is."

"Do you know which way the tower is?"

Laevus had turned and was walking in the other direction. Felix wanted to let him go, but he knew that Laevus was the only chance he had right now of reaching his destination with any kind of haste. Laevus nodded wordlessly.

"Well?" Felix demanded, then softened his tone. "Will you *please* point me in the right direction?"

Tapping the bolt thoughtfully against his cheek, leaving a spot of blood, Laevus pondered this. "No," he said at length.

Felix's heart sink.

"But I'll show you. Come along, follow me."

Felix had no other choice. Laevus walked purposefully, marching past him as he cranked his bow and fitted the bolt back into position.

Their pace was painstaking, but with one narrow escape under his belt, Felix thought the caution of stealth outweighed speed at the moment. It would do him no good to reach the tower quickly only to be captured again. He couldn't count on Laevus not to abandon him if he were endangered a second time.

He glared at the back of his brother's head as they moved ever so slowly forward. Why *had* Laevus saved him? The idea that his brother might, for once, be telling the truth, unnerved him. The thought of his mother's death brought bile rising to the back of his throat.

He would have no way of knowing. He's been here on Earth, a voice in his head assured him.

But you don't know where *he's been. He could have gone anywhere.*

Gavin had said that Onyx had not accompanied them because she'd gone ahead to Sanctuary to warn them of Nero's impending arrival. If what Laevus said was true...

"How did she die?" Felix asked, keeping his voice low.

"I'm not entirely sure," Laevus admitted, and hope sparked in Felix's chest for a moment. "She died in Sanctuary, though."

These words sent a shiver up Felix's spine. But still, it didn't *prove* anything.

"We had our differences, mother and I. But rest assured, brother. We will avenge her death. There's nothing more important than *family*, after all."

"And how do you plan to do that?"

"I already told you," replied Laevus in his lazy, matter-of-fact way, "I'm going to kill Nero. Everything that's happened can be traced in a direct line," he took a hand off of his bow and made a motion, slicing his finger through the air ahead, "back to him."

"For once, we agree on something," Felix said, trying not to dwell anymore on whether or not Laevus was lying. That was a problem for another time.

"What are you going to do at the tower?"

"I'm going to take control of Nero's fleet, remotely."

If this surprised Laevus, the parts of him visible to Felix through the thick underbrush showed no signs of it. "And how will you do that?"

Felix was tired. The adrenaline from the crash, the rush to escape, the fear that all of his friends were marching toward their death...it was too heavy a burden to add arguing. He decided to just tell the truth. "I have a device. If I can hook it up to the communications array in the tower, I can broadcast a signal that will remotely access the ships' navigation systems."

"And," Laevus pressed, "what do you plan to do with the ships once you've captured them?"

Felix sighed. "Force Nero and his men to surrender."

This made Laevus snicker. "And you think that he'll do so without a fight?"

"They're trapped on an island with nowhere to run." Felix snapped a branch that had nearly whacked him in the face as Laevus brushed past it. "They have superior strength, but they can't fight off the entire Allied force with just strength and crossbows."

"Perhaps not," Laevus agreed, "but they'll take a fair

few of your *Allied force* down with them. And what if they just kill you all and simply unplug the device, rendering your valiant sacrifice utterly worthless?"

"Once it's activated and connected to the target, it can't be accessed again without a code. And anyway, I don't suppose you have a better idea?"

Laevus turned his head just enough so that Felix was able to make out that unnerving grin. "Yes. Kill Nero and take command of his men. You could rule this whole world with that fleet. It's already crumbling. Let it fall. Show them that they should have given us the respect we deserve when they had the chance."

"*We?*"

"Yes, dear brother. We. Halfsies. Born of two worlds, despised by both. Why shouldn't we have what's due us for our humiliation and suffering?"

Felix couldn't believe what he was hearing. "You have no idea. You grew up on Thera. Under the tutelage of the highest authority on the planet. In luxury. You don't know what it was like, in Sanctuary, with Nero in charge—"

Laevus stopped dead in his tracks and whirled on Felix. His face was pale and fierce, lacking all signs of mockery and pretense now. "I have suffered more deeply than you could ever dream," he said, enunciating each word with painful clarity. Then he seemed to catch himself. He smiled and nodded back over his shoulder. "We're here."

He hadn't led Felix astray. The tower was just ahead. They approached cautiously, but met no resistance. Felix didn't understand. "Why aren't there any guards?"

Laevus only shrugged in reply.

Inside the tower it was quiet. They both listened, but still, there was no sign of Nero's men anywhere.

"I need to get to the center," Felix said, closing his eyes as he tried to draw up every instruction Tobias had given them during their preparation. "There should be…"

"I don't need to know the details," Laevus said, waving him off. "Let's go."

They made their way toward the center, still cautious. It was a good thing, too, because when they reached a sort of balcony overhanging the central mass of the tower, they looked down and spotted someone else already at the controls.

Laevus raised his crossbow, taking aim.

"Wait," whispered Felix, something eerily familiar about the figure below.

"What for?" Laevus replied carelessly. His voice, just a hint too loud, echoed softly through the room. The figure at the controls whirled, looking around wildly. Laevus sighed and lowered his bow.

"Just a scared little rabbit," he said. The man followed the sound of the words up and glared daggers at Laevus.

"*You,*" he said, "*You filthy, rotten…!*"

"Nelson?" Felix asked, taking the railing in one hand and leaping neatly over it, landing softly on the floor ten feet below. "Nelson Boggs?"

Nelson's eyes flickered warily back and forth between

Laevus and Felix. He did not answer. But Felix felt sure of it, nodding.

"Yeah. Nelson Boggs, the little upstart from Core Operations. You were Ripley's friend."

This got Nelson's attention. His scowl deepened. "Yes," he agreed sourly. "I *was*."

"I'm Felix, I met you a couple times, remember?"

"Yes," Nelson snapped. "I remember. And I met your *brother* a couple of times, too. *He* almost got me killed."

Laevus landed like a cat beside Felix, gathering himself to his full height and flashing a charming smile at Nelson. "Ah, but I see your heroic virtue brought you through just fine in the end," he pointed out. "And where is Ponytail?"

Nelson's angry face fell and his voice cracked as he spoke. "They took him. He used himself as a decoy, so that I could get in here...send a message..."

"Listen, Nelson," said Felix in a rush, "I appreciate what you're trying to do, but everyone already knows where Nero is. Now, I have a plan to stop him, but I don't have much time to implement it."

"I'm not helping in any plan that involves *him*," Nelson spat, jabbing an accusing finger at Laevus, who only stared innocently back.

"There isn't any time to argue. They're bound to be sending replacement guards. We need to do this quickly." He pulled the bag off of his shoulder and started emptying the contents onto the floor beside the control panel. "They have my team, too. They were captured trying to buy me time to get here, same as your friend. The point is, if we're going to have any chance of saving them, we've got to act fast. Okay?"

Nelson gave Laevus a long, appraising glare.

"Sure," he agreed at last, kneeling beside Felix. "What do you need me to do?"

"Yes. Explain the plan again, brother," Laevus said.

"We use this," Felix said, holding up the little box shaped device, "to remotely control the ships. There isn't time to explain in more detail, just trust me. Nelson, can you stay by the entrance and let me know if anyone's coming?"

Nelson, stiff lipped and squinting, gave Laevus one last look before nodding. "All right. But be careful. Brother or not, you can't trust this guy."

He disappeared, and his footsteps echoed as he climbed a metal staircase up to ground level.

"And at which point in this 'plan' do we kill Nero?"

"No one is going to be killed in cold blood. If he surrenders quietly, he'll receive a fair trial." Felix blinked, then corrected himself. "As fair as they get on this planet, anyway."

"And what of me?" Laevus continued as Felix busied himself uncovering the inner components of the communications array. *Ah, Ripley. I wish I'd paid more attention to your tinkering back when I had the chance.*

He stared at the nest of wires, panic constricting his chest. "You saved my life. I'll put in a good word for you.

For leniency."

Laevus put a hand to his chest, his eyes widening. "You would do that for *me?*"

Sparing a quick peek over his shoulder, Felix gave him a faint, pained smile. "We are brothers, after all," he said before returning to the task in front of him.

"And how do you think I'll fair," Laevus continued—oblivious, it would seem, to how much concentration and effort this required for a non-technically minded person such as Felix, "in such a trial?"

"Beats me," Felix replied vaguely. "You haven't exactly made any friends on this side of the Evenmire. The Culeian Queen mistook me for you and, believe me, she wasn't exactly pleased to see you. Tried to have me arrested for crimes against humanity."

"I see."

Laevus was quiet for several blessed minutes as Felix worked. He'd found the proper connections, carefully splicing them where necessary to insert the Arca controller. He checked the monitor again to be sure he hadn't somehow fried it in the process. He wasn't as confident in his skills as Tobias gave him credit for.

"Do you know, I don't think I like this plan very much," Laevus decided. "Nero may very well walk away, and I will be left to languish, imprisoned for many long years ahead, my youth extinguished by the musty despair of confinement."

"I'm sorry it isn't more *agreeable* to you," muttered

Felix between teeth clenched over a blue wire as his hands worked furiously to connect two others. *Red to red. White to white. Where is blue? This should be simple, easy peasy. Come on, hurry up!*

Laevus squatted beside him, pulling on two wires whose copper ends were exposed. He flicked them carelessly together and sparks flew.

"Watch it!" Felix chastised, snatching one of them away. "Those are live."

"Yes," Laevus agreed. "I can see that."

Without warning, he pressed the second wire into Felix's neck. Current surged through his body as Laevus held the wire to his bare skin, and though Felix tried to knock it away, he couldn't do anything more than spasm as the shock washed through him. He felt his body hit the floor, heard the metallic clank of the tools as his flailing limbs sent them skittering across the concrete. And he watched, with horror, as Laevus used his free hand to rip the Arca controller from the console, toss it to the ground, and smash it underfoot.

"I really am sorry, brother."

That was when Felix lost consciousness.

CHAPTER SIXTEEN

THE ROOT OF THE PROBLEM

ALL OTHER THOUGHTS drained from Ripley's mind as he shot up, his eyes sweeping the starlit snow. Ben and Denton were nearby, but Molly was nowhere to be seen.

"She fell!" Ben said, pointing. Ripley's eyes fell on a dark hole that must have been hidden beneath a layer of drifted snow. He raced to the edge, heart pounding as he peered into the inky depths.

"Molly!"

There was only silence in reply, and it took every ounce of strength Ripley could muster not to leap into the maw after her.

"Molly! *Molly!*"

"Here!" Denton called, tossing him one of the flashlights. Ripley caught it and shone the light downward.

The drainage hole dropped straight down and curved gently out of sight. Molly was nowhere to be seen.

"I'm going down."

"How?" Denton asked. It was not an argument, only a question.

Ripley jabbed a finger toward the sled. "Ben! The hooks, on the sled. Grab them and start tying them to the longest rope."

Ben dashed off to obey without a word. Ripley raced to his own tent, where the long lead rope that they'd been using to keep the group together was still coiled and waiting. He had looped it around his waist before he was even back to the hole. "*Ben!*"

"I'm trying!" Ben appeared beside him, the younger man's hands shaking as he struggled to thread the rope through the hook's eye hole. Ripley snatched both away from him, making quick work of it and then repeating the motions on the second one. He knelt down and, motioning for the others to step far back, he buried the hook in the ice. He gave it a test pull, listening for the telltale sounds of the ice below him threatening to crack, but nothing happened.

"Stay here," Ripley commanded, unnecessarily. He tucked his flashlight up the arm of his suit and lowered himself over the edge of the hole.

He repelled downward, his feet meeting the smooth,

icy ridges in perfect rhythm with his rapidly beating heart. "Molly!" he called over and over through his descent, though it lasted only seconds. Still no reply.

He hit the curve of the bottom and steadied himself as his feet began to slide down the bank. A small pile of the fallen snow cover was just enough to stop him from tumbling down into the unknown. He took out the light and pointed it deeper into the tube. It continued on an almost gentle downward slope before curving out of sight to his left.

"Do you see her?" Ben called down, his voice echoing down the chute.

Ripley shouted back up. "No. I'm going farther." He drove the second hook into the ice by his feet and fed the rope out a little at a time, slipping, rather than walking, down the natural slide. The flashlight held firmly in one hand threw light wildly in all directions as he struggled to hold it and the rope without falling.

"Molly?" There was no need to shout now. Surrounded on every side by walls that were uncomfortably close together, even Ripley's normal voice shot off into the darkness, rebounding off the icy surfaces and racing back and forth down the tunnel.

"I'm here!" Molly's voice replied from somewhere up ahead. Ripley could not remember having heard a sweeter phrase than those two words. Until the next two. "I'm all right!"

The end of the rope came before the end of the tunnel.

Ripley still couldn't see Molly and he cursed as he looked back at the taut line behind him.

"Are you safe?"

"Yes," Molly said, "I think so."

"I have to go back for a minute. Just stay where you are. I'm coming."

Ripley doubled back, pulling himself along his cable with renewed hope. He reached the bottom of the shaft quickly and shouted up to Ben and the others. "She's okay!" he cried. "But I can't reach her. Toss that hook down."

"But how will you get back out?"

"We'll figure it out, just do it!"

Denton's face disappeared for a few moments, and then the line leading up and out of the hole went slack. He reappeared and began lowering the hook slowly downward.

But Ripley didn't have that kind of patience just now. "Just drop it," he yelled.

"This thing'll go right through your thick skull if I—"

"Just *drop* it!" Ripley called, more insistently. He couldn't make out Denton's expression, but the hook began to free fall, glinting in Ripley's flashlight beam as it spun wildly. He reached up and caught it in the air, then knelt to jimmy the second one free, too. He stood and, more confident this time, began sliding back down the shaft, focusing on remaining upright without the aid of his lead line.

He held the hooks carefully at his side as he slid past the spot where he'd stopped before, ready to jam them into the wall at a moment's notice if he began moving too quickly.

He was starting to get the hang of it now, and if he weren't so worried about finding Molly and getting back up to the surface, it might even have been fun. The kind of thing Felix would have liked.

He felt himself begin to pick up speed and extended his arms outward until he was nearly touching the narrow walls of the shaft. His flashlight slipped and began skittering wildly down the path ahead, occasionally shining back at him so that he had to squint.

Up ahead the tunnel forked. His flashlight continued its journey down the tunnel to his right, but Ripley pulled up short, dragging the hooks along the walls like brakes. "Molly?"

"I'm still here," she replied from somewhere on the left.

"I've lost my light," Ripley told her. "I'm afraid to run into you. Keep talking so I'll know when I'm getting close."

"That won't be a problem," Molly said. "You'll know."

He might have questioned what she meant, if the answer had not become clear moments later. The tunnel ahead was no longer black. The icy walls glowed with brilliant violet light that grew stronger as he slipped further down.

Ripley used the hooks again as he rounded a final corner and Molly came into view. She was standing beside a huge crystalline root. It ran across the middle of the drain hole, piercing through the ice on either side. Everywhere it touched the ice, tiny droplets of water formed, running down the walls in rivulets and refreezing once more.

"Don't touch it!" Ripley warned without thinking. He remembered his encounter in the microreactor. Though he still wasn't entirely sure what had happened, he didn't want Molly to get hurt.

But her face was puzzled. "I already did," she said, reaching out to show him. "It doesn't hurt. I slid right into it. Ripley, it's so *warm*. It really does feel…alive."

He approached with caution, feeling rather than hearing the gentle *thrum* of the root. It was, indeed, growing warmer the closer he came. But he wouldn't take the chance that this one might have the same effect on him.

"It's beautiful," he admitted. "But it's also dangerous. And we need to get out of this place. Here," he said, handing her one of the ropes. "Tie this around your waist."

Coming down had been much easier than going up would be. The gentle incline seemed much steeper now that he was fighting it, rather than using it. He leveraged the hooks for traction, stretching his arms to either side and pulling them both. Molly tried to help, but could do very little besides maintaining her balance on the slippery surface while holding up her light. Once they came around the corner, Ripley frowned up the long, clear stretch. There had to be a better way.

He buried the head of one of the hooks in the wall to his left, twisting back to pull Molly close enough to grab hold. "Here. I'm going to try something. Keep hold of this one so we don't start sliding back again."

She gave a little nod, watching curiously as he eyed the

second hook with trepidation. Then, taking careful aim, he threw it forward as far as he was able, the length of rope uncoiling from his hand as it went.

It took several tries, and Ripley was becoming increasingly self-conscious, but Molly offered only words of encouragement. Having super strength, it turned out, did not equate to having super skills—at least not this skill in particular. When the hook finally caught, he let out a relieved sigh. He'd almost thought he'd have to pull them one arm length at a time all the way back to the surface. Ripley gave the rope a tentative tug to be sure it had set, then pulled the other hook free. Hand over hand, one step at a time, they used the lead to draw themselves farther and farther up the passage.

His arms ached with the strain of it, but despite the pain he found his ability to catch the hook faster improving as they went. It was slow, painstaking work. They moved in silence, one or both of them occasionally letting out a little gasp or grunt as they slipped back and forth.

"Ripley," Molly said as they once again anchored themselves to the wall to throw a new lead, "thank you. For coming for me."

The hook slipped prematurely from his grip, landing lamely several yards away. He hastily wound the rope up, pulling it back for another try. "I would never have left without you," he said, feeling that there were a million more eloquent statements he could have used, if only he could think of one.

Ripley knew it hadn't been the cold that had turned his blood to an icy sludge at the sound of her scream. That the chill wind had not caused his body to tremble uncontrollably as he'd peered into the gaping maw that had swallowed her.

That the thought of losing her had made his heart scream the way he had only done after having experienced the prolonged anguish of coming within an inch of death. When he'd been trapped in an emerald hell where there was no one, nothing, only the endless silence to keep him company for what had felt like an eternity.

"I know," she replied, her voice quiet.

Ripley grimaced, trying the hook again. Success. "I'm...really glad," he said, grunting as he yanked out their anchor, "that you weren't hurt."

"Because you'd have had to carry me up?" she asked with a laugh too light and sweet for this cold, forbidding place.

"Because I can't bear to see you in pain."

He did not turn to look at her. He didn't want to see her reaction. Didn't want to know if she would laugh at him, or be angry because of what had happened with Sylvia, or simply show no emotion at all. He opened his mouth to speak again, but Molly beat him to it.

"Ripley, I don't know what's going on between you and Sylvia, but I wanted to say that—"

"There isn't—"

"I wanted to say that I just want you to be happy."

Ripley swallowed hard, concentrating on keeping his balance. "It's not. Like. That." he managed through gritted teeth as he heaved them up the slope. Was it getting steeper? He was sweating now despite the cold. "I don't have feelings for Sylvia. I mean, I do *care* about her, but…not like *that*."

They reached their next anchor point and he paused to catch his breath and order his thoughts. Molly waited patiently beside him. He turned to look at her. Even hidden beneath the heavy snow gear and goggles, she was beautiful. He'd never really considered that before this moment, how beautiful she was. He'd been attracted to her spirit, her passion, her drive and her empathy. But he'd been so caught up in everything else that he hadn't stopped long enough to realize that *everything* about Molly was beautiful.

The words came rushing out. It felt as though if he didn't say them out loud now he might never have the courage to do so.

"I'm sorry for what happened between me and Sylvia. I'm sorry I let myself get so distracted that I didn't realize how she felt, didn't tell her I didn't feel the same way. I mean, I didn't even know *how* I felt. Not until…I've been an idiot. I just never thought…never considered that anyone could have feelings…for me."

Molly's face shone with such genuine surprise that Ripley hesitated briefly before plowing on.

"After…the incident…I felt so lost. I woke up in the only place I had ever known, but it wasn't the same. *I* wasn't the same. I wandered around in a fog of self-loathing. I felt trapped, isolated. Sylvia was the one who cared for me, and I will always be grateful for that. She's a kind person with a big heart. But she wasn't the one who pulled me out of that fog, Molly. *You* did that. You gave me a reason to live again. And I—"

For the second time in his life, Ripley felt lips press against his. They were cold, but he barely noticed.

Everything else was warm.

And Ripley felt himself kissing her back, felt them begin to slide as Molly let go of the anchor, felt himself reach out to steady them with his eyes closed, consumed with something he had never experienced before, nor had he imagined he ever would.

"Prior!"

The voice echoed down the chute and Ripley broke off, startled. "I didn't realize how close we were," he muttered, glancing at Molly out of the corner of his eye. She didn't say anything, but her face was beaming. He cupped his hand to his mouth and shouted, "We're almost there!"

"Took you long enough!" echoed Denton's reply, though Ripley thought he sensed a hint of relief in the angry voice. Denton really was just a big softy, after all. "You all right, Teach?"

"I'm fine!" Molly hollered. "We'll see you soon!"

They reached the base of the shaft soon after, and Ripley hurtled the hook up to Denton and Ben, who began to pull them up.

"You could have come up one at a time," Denton grunted down at them as he pulled.

Ripley wasn't sure he understood the problem. He felt as light as a feather.

CHAPTER SEVENTEEN

MOMS' DAY OUT

P ENELOPE'S HAND REAPPEARED from beneath the undercarriage of the vehicle. "Socket wrench."

Willow scanned the tools, spread on the floor in a wide arc. Spotting the wrench, she placed it in Penelope's hand and watched it disappear again. It was late, and the workshop was quiet. Baba was on the *Timeless* monitoring the mission and Violet had volunteered to keep an ear out for the slumbering children so that Willow and Penelope could have a little time to themselves. Unfortunately, Penelope's idea of unwinding always seemed to involve airships in some form or another. With no better suggestion to offer, Willow had soon found herself perched on an upturned crate beside the sleek body of the Wilks, learning about tune-ups and parts and tools.

"Okay, now for some *real* fun," Penelope declared as she slid herself deftly out from beneath the craft, rolling on a little dolly that looked rather uncomfortable to Willow. "We took a few hits last time, so I was thinking we could replace the damaged panels. How are you with a riveting hammer?"

Startled, Willow met the other woman's eyes and offered an apologetic smile. "I don't even know what that is."

"Oh, you're going to *love* it. I'll show you."

They worked in companionable silence, the jarring impacts of the riveting hammer and the metallic reverberations of the ship's hull more than making up for the lack of conversation. The work seemed to bring Penelope a sense of pride. She was practically glowing as she stepped back to admire their work. But no matter how she kept herself busy, Willow could only think about one thing.

Felix.

She'd convinced herself that she was used to this new life, where her husband was called from one dangerous errand to the next with the regularity of a clock's pendulum. To an extent, it was true. She had faith not only in Felix's abilities, but in those of his team.

But this time peace with his duties evaded her. This time, he wasn't doing reconnaissance or rescues. He was diving headlong into the midst of an army of Theran clones.

And somewhere at the head of that army was her father.

"Hey."

Willow wasn't sure how long Penelope had been staring at her. Her focus drifted back to the workshop. The ship. The tools. Everything had lost the sense of wonder it had given her when they'd first arrived in Pravacordia. Just now, as her stomach churned with worry, it seemed very cold and unwelcoming. "Sorry," she said, eyes finally coming to rest on her friend. "I was lost in thought. What were you saying?"

"I just said that should do it for now. Are you all right?" Penelope searched her gaze, eyes narrowing suspiciously. "You've been quiet. I mean, you're always quiet, but unusually so."

"I've just got a lot on my mind, that's all."

Penelope nodded, the suspicion wiped from her expression as compassion took its place. "Worried about Felix and the others? Me, too. You want to talk about it? We could take a walk, maybe see some of the sights. Oldetown is a beautiful city, there's lots to do."

Willow glanced at the clock. "It's getting pretty late."

Penelope just waved a dismissive hand. "This city never sleeps. Come on, how often do the two of us have time on our hands? We should take advantage of it, right? It'll take your mind off things."

Willow's reluctance must have been evident on her face, because Penelope frowned. "Not in the mood to be around people, huh?" Then she perked up, her eyebrows rising and her lips forming a small *oh* as a new idea sprang to mind. "Well then, how about we put our hard work to the test?

Let's take the *Wilks* out. Just fly around the countryside for a bit. You can't get much farther away from your troubles than up there." She let her head fall back as she closed her eyes and smiled. "It's been so long since I've been able to just *enjoy* flying. It'd be nice to have someone to share the experience with."

Willow couldn't help but smile in kind. Given her options, this didn't seem like such a bad idea.

Penelope's enthusiasm for the sky was contagious. "Why not?" Willow agreed. Then she looked around curiously. "Only…how do you get it out?"

Grinning, Penelope offered her a thumbs up. "Leave it to me," she said. "I'll show you how it's done."

Once they were in the air, Willow found herself marvelling at the earth below. Everything was so small, each tree and building and road a miniscule detail in the grand scheme of the landscape. "You're right," she said after a while. "I do feel better."

"Works every time!" Penelope declared. "When Sebastian was first born, I swear he couldn't fall asleep except when we were flying. Neal and I must have logged thousands of miles cruising between Ithaca and Atmos those first few months, before…" She stopped, and Willow watched as she busied herself with the controls.

"I'd like to hear about him," Willow told her. "Neal, I mean. I'd like to know more about what he was like."

Penelope let out a sigh, eyes drifting up from the controls toward the barely-discernible horizon. "He was a wonderful guy."

"You must miss him terribly."

Penelope nodded. "I do. It's not so fresh anymore. I don't wake every morning with a crushing weight on my chest, the cold emptiness of his side of the bed washing over me and making it hard to breathe. Back then, the only thing that got me through was Sebastian. He depended on me, more than ever. Every day I fought a battle just to get out of bed, but every day I somehow managed to do it. I got up, life went on, and over time it got a little easier." She paused for a long moment. "But it never went away, not completely. Losing him broke me. I've put myself back together, but there are still pieces missing, and I don't think I'll ever find them."

Losing him broke me. No matter how much faith Willow had in Felix, each time he left, a part of her went with him. The part that wondered if he'd ever come back. If that goodbye kiss would be their last. If she'd be left in a foreign land to raise two children without the love of her life at her side.

She did her best to bury those feelings, for his sake. He had enough to worry about. But it was hard. She looked at Penelope now with a new sense of admiration. "I think you're doing great," she said. "And I think Neal would be proud of who you've become."

Penelope chuckled. "He'd certainly have something to say about my lack of organizational skills. Ever the neat freak, Neal. The house just hasn't been the same without him." Her face went dark. "But then, I'm not sure if the house is even still there anymore. Do you think we'll ever get to just…go home?"

Willow didn't know how to answer that. She wasn't really sure where home was anymore. Her father seemed intent on destroying any chance of them ever having such a thing. The thought brought shame and despair raging to the surface, and her vision blurred as wetness welled up in her eyes. She looked away, not wanting to upset Penelope, but the keen-eyed pilot already wore an expression of deep concern.

"I'm sorry," she said quickly. "I didn't mean—that was a stupid thing to say."

A choked laugh escaped Willow's lips and she shook her head, wiping the tears away with her sleeve. "You didn't say anything wrong. It's just…" She sighed. "It's just that as much as I want to belong somewhere, I can't help but feel like I never will, and I don't deserve to anyway."

The ship dipped as Penelope dropped their elevation slightly. "What do you mean? Of course you deserve a place to call home. Everyone deserves that!"

"My father is the one doing this." Willow's hands trembled, and she clenched them into tight fists, burying them between her thighs to try and stop the involuntary motion. "My father is trying to wipe out everything you hold dear, everything anyone holds dear. He's ravaging cities, killing families, destroying everything in his path. In some ways, I feel responsible. Like he's punishing me for my defiance.

If I had just listened to him…just done what he asked of me…would things have been different?"

Penelope was silent for so long that Willow was convinced the other woman agreed with her. That this…all of this…

Was *her* fault.

"First of all," Penelope said, her tone stern, "as much as I love Pravacordia and miss the shop and the people and the places I grew up exploring, that isn't what made it home. Family makes it home. Friends. Relationships and experiences and…and…a whole bunch of other stuff. So really, when you think about it, I guess home can be anywhere, as long as you're with the ones you love. No matter what happens, Willow, you have a home. With Felix and Ripley and Felicity and me and Sebastian and Toby and papa and everyone else. Don't you ever forget that, you hear me?"

The words triggered a flood of tears that Willow found herself unable to stop. "But my father—"

"Your father is a monster," Penelope declared. Her gaze narrowed and she locked eyes with Willow as she said it. "I won't pretend otherwise. But you, Willow, are *not* your father. You're kind and patient and a wonderful friend. Though I will say you could use a few cooking lessons from Violet."

Tears still streaming down her face, Willow laughed. The laughter and crying devolved into a coughing fit, and when she finally recovered, she was no longer shaking. "Thank you," she whispered.

"Don't thank me," Penelope said with a shake of her head. She pulled at the steering column, bringing them around in a wide, gentle arc high above the treetops. "I should have asked you how you were feeling. I should have known something was wrong. I'm a mom, isn't that what we do? I'm sorry I wasn't a better friend to you, Willow. I'm sorry this has been eating you up inside. But we can't change the past. So from here on out, if you're feeling low, just come talk to me, okay? And whatever you do, don't feel guilty. None of this is on you. It doesn't matter who's leading the enemy. It matters which side you choose. And you chose the right side. That's the important thing." She was nodding to herself. Then her hands gripped the controls tightly, knuckles whitening. "You know what?"

"What?"

"I think...yeah. I think we should do it."

"Do what?"

"Vi won't mind, I'm sure of it. She had a half-dozen kids, after all. Three should be a breeze. We'll need to fuel up, first. And radio, let her know—"

"Maybe you should let *me* know," Willow interrupted. "I have no idea what you're talking about."

"I'm talking about you and me heading out to rendezvous with the *Timeless*," Penelope explained, eyes bright. "When the team succeeds—and they *will* succeed—you'll be right there to celebrate their victory with Felix. That'll be a nice surprise, I think. It would do you good to get a little time out in the field. You never get to come with us.

And it'll give us a chance to talk more!"

The thought of surprising Felix filled Willow with a sudden burst of joy, but it was tainted with uncertainty, too. "Are you sure that the Alliance would be okay with this? Just…showing up at one of their ships in the middle of an important operation like that?"

Penelope just chuckled, flipping another switch before leaning back in the pilot's chair to give Willow a sly grin. "Your kids aren't old enough to have taught you this yet, so let me let you in on a little wisdom Sebastian has already mastered. Sometimes it's better to beg forgiveness than to ask permission."

*   *   *

IT WAS DIFFICULT TO TELL if the journey had taken an hour or a lifetime. The only clues Willow had were the stiffness in her neck, a crick in her back, and the knowledge that Penelope now knew more about her than possibly anyone on the planet besides Felix. Their approach was met with some hostility and confusion, but once Penelope identified herself and demanded an audience with General Hall, the patrolling Chronohawk that had spotted them fell into formation to guide them to their destination.

"There. That wasn't so bad," Penny said, casting a sideways glance at Willow and winking. "I told you they'd let us on."

"Good thing, too," Willow agreed, pointing knowledgeably at the control panel to indicate the fuel gauge. Penny had given her a crash course in the *Wilks'* control systems as they flew, and Willow was eager to show that she'd been paying attention. "I don't think we would have made it all the way back."

"Eh, we would have found a fueling station somewhere. Culei's territory has plenty of them, used to be a decent source of income from little ships like ours making the long haul from Pravacordia to Nequiem."

"You mean Nero's troops haven't found and destroyed them all?"

Penelope just shrugged. "It's a big ocean."

Willow looked out at the turbulent blue sea racing past, stretching out in all directions. "The sea rose up to eat them," she whispered absently, recalling Waldo's odd refrain.

"What was that?"

"The sea rose up to eat them," Willow repeated. "Just something Waldo was reciting to the children once. I didn't hear it all, I think it was a poem."

"Nursery rhyme, actually," Penelope corrected.

Willow raised an eyebrow. "Seems a little grim."

"All the best ones are." Penelope pointed to a growing speck in front of them. "There she is! We'll be there in no time. Anyway, that rhyme's been around a while. It's a cautionary tale."

"About what?"

"Culei, mostly. Just because we were at peace for years

doesn't mean the relationship wasn't rocky. It may not seem like it's been that long since the Sequencing, but for us… that's all there is. That's our entire history. And from our perspective, it's been a long one."

"Just one more thing we have in common, I guess."

Penelope shot her a curious look. "But Therans live for ages, right? I'd think your people would have history books spanning back…well, practically forever."

"Oh, no. Our records don't go back much further than three hundred years or so. The Great War left very little for the Theran people to salvage."

Penelope pursed her lips. "Huh," she said. "I guess I've spent so long seeing Thera as the enemy, I never really thought about them having problems of their own. I'd like to hear more about this 'Great War' sometime. But it'll have to wait!"

The *Timeless* was very close now, and a series of docking instructions issued from the radio as Penelope calmly guided the *Wilks* in. When they disembarked, Willow was surprised to find the General himself waiting to greet them. By the stern expression he wore, she could tell he wasn't pleased. And he made no pretense to feign otherwise.

"Perhaps one of you would like to tell me why my Chronohawk is no longer on its scheduled patrol route?" His eyes moved slowly between the two of them.

"I told him we didn't need an escort—" Penelope began.

"Escorting an incoming, unscheduled vessel is standard

operating procedure," the General replied.

"Well there we are, then," said Penelope. "He was just following procedure."

"I do not have time for games. We are in the midst of a situation that requires my full attention."

Willow's heart leapt into her throat. "What kind of situation?"

"That is not for me to discuss with two civilians who have waltzed onto my ship unannounced."

"It's for you to discuss if it's got to do with our people," Penelope pressed. "What's happened? How can we help?"

"You can stay out of the way," said Hall. Then his eyes softened and he let out a long sigh. "My men will see to your ship, and then I think it's best if you return to Nequiem."

"General, please." Willow could hear the way her voice bordered on desperation. "If this has anything to do with our friends—with Felix—you must tell us."

He hesitated, then nodded toward the bay's exit. "Come with me."

Willow and Penelope exchanged glances, then followed the General. It was still as loud in the ship as Willow remembered from her last visit, but once out of the docking bay it was tolerable. General Hall led them to the first hatch on the left, opened it, and stepped inside. When they joined him, he closed the hatch again before turning to face them.

"We've just received a message from the island," he said. When he offered nothing more, Penelope spoke up.

"Well? What did it say? Who was it from?"

"We aren't sure who sent it. But it indicated that our plan has failed and that most of the team had been captured."

The room spun around Willow as the blood drained from her face. She could hear her pulse, feel the quickening of her heart. She opened her mouth to speak, but no words came out. She didn't know what to say.

Thankfully, Penelope did.

"I take it you're organizing a rescue mission, then? We'll go, too. We won't get in anyone's way, we'll just be support."

"You will do no such thing. There isn't going to be a rescue."

Penelope's freckles faded beneath quickly reddening cheeks. "What?"

"I have my orders. If the mission fails, the *Timeless* is to return immediately to the Alliance headquarters."

"We can't just leave them down there!"

"I don't like this any more than you do. But you're talking about an island upon which sits a massive Theran force. In twos and threes they're a fearsome enough opponent. Against all of them?" He shook his head sadly. "We wouldn't stand a chance."

Penelope stepped forward, her voice coming out in a hiss. "My father is down there. Willow's husband. Our friends. We can't just leave them to be tortured and killed. We have to do *something*."

"There's nothing we *can* do."

353

"Fine," she said, whirling to face Willow, eyes wild and cheeks flushed. "Then we'll do it ourselves."

"I cannot allow—"

"You said it yourself," Penelope snapped. "We're a couple of civilians. We aren't part of the Air Force, General, you can't order us around."

"I can have you detained."

"But you won't."

"And why not?"

"Because you know, deep down, that this is wrong. I know you, General Hall. You don't leave people behind."

The General didn't meet her eyes, gazing at the floor, the wall, anywhere but at Penelope. "Desperate times call for desperate measures..." he muttered.

"That's no excuse, and you know it. General, I know you're loyal to the Alliance. But *you* know that this isn't right. You know what will happen to them if we don't act."

"If I allow you to take your ship and go, I'm as good as signing your death warrants."

"So?" Penelope said, stepping closer once again. The General stood his ground. "Come with us."

"I have my orders."

"To hell with your orders! The plan has failed. We don't have a backup plan, General. This was it. The Therans are going to keep doing what they've been doing until there's nothing left. And if we're all going to die anyway, what does it matter? I'm going to do the right thing. Willow's with me, right Willow?"

"Right," Willow said quickly.

"The only question left to answer then, is what about you, General Hall? Are you going to detain us?"

The General looked between the two women again, not speaking for what seemed like a long time. Then he spun on his heel, opened the hatch, and stormed out.

Willow blinked rapidly, fighting back the growing panic in her gut. After the briefest hesitation, she and Penelope followed wordlessly the way the General had gone.

He burst through the doorway into the docking bay.

"I want every ship in every bay ready in ten minutes," he bellowed. "We're going in."

A spattering of cheers rose from the soldiers and crewmen, and Penelope beamed at Willow. General Hall turned back to face them. "You will stay behind the formation," he began. Penelope made to cut him off but he raised a hand and continued. "You *will* stay behind the formation. You will find a safe place to land and you will not engage. Do I make myself clear?"

Penelope's lips formed a tight line, but she nodded.

"As for me," said the General, looking around at the scrambling men and women that filled the bay, "I'd better suit up."

"Come on, Willow," Penelope said, "We should check our supplies. There are going to be injuries to tend to."

As Willow followed Penelope back toward the *Wilks*, she found that she was not frightened of what was to come. She was only frightened that they may be too late.

No, she told herself firmly. *We're not too late. Hang in there, Felix.*

I'm coming.

CHAPTER EIGHTEEN

THE WEIGHT OF TWO WORLDS

GAVIN RUSHED IN headlong, diving for the nearest enemy. There were at least six of them, one standing over the prone form of Ollie, two others busy trying to pin down a feisty Kestrel, who was doing her best but was still no match for two perfectly conditioned clone warriors. Gavin barely registered Tobias and Ambrose as they rushed in too, both letting out a fearless battle cry that, while unhelpful, was at least brave.

They had no weapons. This was not a matter of winning against the opponent. It was simply a matter of buying Felix time. Gavin toppled the first soldier, slamming the clone's head against an exposed tree root and using the momentum of the blow to push himself back to standing.

He looked around for his next victim, but a second later there was a fierce pain in his arm. A crossbow bolt had lodged itself in his bicep. He pulled it out with a roar that dwarfed the feeble battle cries of his human comrades and charged at the offending party, raising the bolt like a dagger. The enemy dropped the bow that he'd been attempting to reload and both hands shot up like snakes to grab Gavin by the wrists. They grappled, one attempting to stab and the other attempting to avoid being stabbed.

"That will be quite enough," said a voice from behind them. Gavin lost his grip on the bolt as his opponent gave his wrist a sharp squeeze, jerking it downward. He watched it fall to the ground and knew it was over.

He wondered if Felix had gotten far enough away to avoid detection.

The soldier let go of him, and Gavin turned to face the one who stood with a crossbow leveled at his heart. He chanced a glance toward the others. Kestrel was still squirming but had largely given up, having been forced to the ground, the side of her face pressed into the dirt. Tobias and Ambrose stood back to back, Ambrose with his hands raised in surrender and Tobias holding up defiant fists, a large purple bruise blossoming across his cheek. Ollie was motionless.

"Ollie?"

The youth groaned, making a gurgling sound as his sharp intake of breath caused him to spasm in pain. "Still here." The words were distorted by a mouth full of blood.

Gavin wasn't sure how long that would be true. Though Ollie's body was partially obscured by a clump of tall ferns, it looked as though he'd taken a bolt to the chest. He'd be dead already if it had pierced his heart, but by the sound of his breathing, there was a good chance that he had a punctured lung.

"He needs medical attention," Gavin said, knowing what the answer to that would be.

"You'll all need medical attention if you don't shut up and follow my orders," the soldier said coldly. He motioned with the bow. "Hands behind your back."

Gavin did as he was instructed.

"You two," he said, "carry that one."

"Be careful with him!" shouted Kestrel as she was dragged to her feet. "You're going to make it worse!"

Ollie whimpered as the pair hefted him into the air and began carrying him away while the others were tied up. Then they were marched, single file, back toward Nero's base.

Gavin didn't see or hear any sign of Felix, which was a small comfort at least. But it was hard to think of anything else when Ollie's limp hand dangled in front of him, trailing along the tops of ferns. The kid had been a pain, could never shut up, but he'd proven himself brave and loyal.

He did not deserve to die like this.

Felix, you had better get that tower working. Ollie can't die in vain. It isn't right.

There had already been too much bloodshed. He finally understood the deep pain the Weaver had spoken about so many times before. *How many more have to die?*

"Ollie," he called, "you hang in there!"

"Quiet," snapped the clone behind him, giving him a sharp prod between the shoulder blades. Gavin kept walking.

They reached the edge of a valley between the hills. Nero's ships sat quietly, hundreds and hundreds of his men standing at attention in neat rows and columns as the prisoners were frog-marched into their midst.

Nero was waiting for them.

He stood with his hands clasped behind his back, looking as though he'd just received an early Dual Sun Festival treat. His eyes flashed brightly as he scanned the group. "Gavin," he said, his voice as cheerful as Gavin had ever heard it, "it's been too long, old friend."

Nero stepped closer to watch as the two soldiers carrying Ollie lowered him to the ground, his eyes narrowing. "And one of my little experiments," Nero exclaimed with glee. "The one that got away that day you humiliated me in front of my subjects. You and your traitorous leader."

Nero looked them all over a second time, searching for someone he would not find. "Where is he?" Nero hissed quietly, turning his attention back to Gavin. "Where is the Weaver?"

"I don't know," Gavin replied truthfully. Nero let out a huff of disbelief.

"You've been meddling in my plans all along. I should

have known you would always be loyal to our valiant mentor. I should have had you killed sooner."

Gavin raised an eyebrow. "Too bad that pesky *First Order* stood in your way. I would have liked to see you try."

Nero was in front of him an instant later, narrowing the gap between them to mere inches. "There is nothing standing in my way *now*," he rasped, a sneer curling his lip.

Gavin didn't respond.

"Let it be known," Nero announced, stepping back and raising his hands to address the entirety of his army, "that I am not without mercy." He turned back to Gavin. "Tell me what I want to know and I will give you all a swift death."

Gavin glanced over at Ollie. He was pale, but somehow still clinging to life. "I don't know where the Weaver is."

"And who are your companions?" Nero asked, switching his attention to Ambrose and Tobias. "Is Tapestry so far gone that you've had to resort to Human filth to fill your ranks? What a disgrace." He grabbed Toby by the collar and drew him close, causing the man to yelp. "Who are you? Culeian? Pravacordian? Where are the rest of your people?"

"The...rest?" Tobias squeaked.

"The ones infesting this island!" Nero snarled. "I have men searching everywhere. It's only a matter of time. If you wish to die painlessly, tell me where you came from, so I might know who to punish for this transgression. Tell me where your comrades are!"

Gavin could tell Nero was incensed, had lost all sense of reason. There was very little chance that they would make it out of this alive, but if they were to have any shot at all, Gavin would need to keep Nero talking. Give Felix a chance to get the Arca controller functioning. If he got all the ships in the air, it just might be enough of a distraction—

"I said, tell me where they are!"

Tobias drew himself up, staring at Nero with defiance. "Death to the Theran invaders!"

Nero tossed Tobias backward with a motion that looked almost casual. Tobias toppled into Kestrel, who barely managed to keep her footing. Nero stared around at them, ears twitching, nostrils flaring. His eyes fell on Ollie. "Pull it out," he instructed one of the soldiers.

"No!" cried Kestrel and Tobias at once.

Gavin's rage had caused his chest to become an inferno. "It's me you want, Nero, let him be!"

But the soldier had already strode forward, yanking the bolt from Ollie's chest with all the callous disregard that Gavin had come to expect from a follower of Nero. These clones had no compassion, no reasoning of their own. They followed orders. That's what they were created to do.

Ollie screamed, his back arching as the bolt was pulled free. Then he collapsed, silent and still.

"You'll pay for this, Nero!" Kestrel shouted, struggling against the soldier who had taken hold of her arms. "You can't do this! Somebody help him!"

"It doesn't matter, Kestrel," Gavin said, loud enough to stop her struggling. She turned to stare at him in disbelief. "They won't help him. They're only doing what they're expected to do."

"Something *you* should have learned a long time ago!" Nero snapped. "Maybe you wouldn't be in this mess now. Maybe you'd be by my side. We were like brothers, once, you and I." He glared at Gavin, eyes searching, still wild. Always wild. Nero had always been a loose cannon. "What happened to that bond we shared?"

"You broke it," Gavin told him. "You broke it the moment you decided you were better than humanity. Before you started your quest for vengeance when there was no one left who had wronged you."

"I am better than humanity!" Nero cried, his clawed fingers raised high. "How can you not see that? I've taken their world with a handful of ships. They are weak, unworthy, and deserving of this end."

"You haven't taken it *yet,*" Gavin shouted back, his voice rising to match Nero's. "You've always been wrong. You never understood the essence of the First Order. Every life I've taken, I understood it more clearly. Every pair of eyes I watched grow dull cut a little deeper into my soul. The Weaver taught us right from wrong, so how is it that we stand here now, feet away but worlds apart?"

"You don't know," Nero said, his voice a high-pitched whine now. "You don't know what they did to us. Their kind."

"I do know. The Weaver told me everything."

"Then you know they deserve to be punished."

"These aren't Therans!" Gavin cried.

"No! They are Humans! Filth. Weak. So frail that they tortured their own kind to create a better version of themselves. You see? Even *they* knew how weak they were. But did they fall down and worship their creation? Did they even treat them as equals? No! They stomped them down. They were afraid of what they had created." Nero whirled around, spreading his arms wide as if to encompass the camp. "And so now I am simply giving them a reason to be afraid."

"You misunderstand, Nero."

"Emperor!"

"You misunderstand, *Nero*," Gavin spat. "I said they are not *Therans*. Because it was Therans who created us. Therans, Nero, from *our* world, *our* reality. These people, their ancestors, chose a different path. They partook of their own atrocities, suffered their own misfortunes, learned from or disregarded their own mistakes. But none of them, not one, had anything to do with the pain of our people. Or with you."

Nero was breathing heavily now, his chest rising and falling rapidly. "I think because you are so fond of them," Nero said, his voice almost a purr, "I will kill the Humans first. Let you watch. Make them suffer."

Ambrose and Tobias both stood firm, but Gavin caught the faintest hint of a whimper from one of them.

"Gavin?"

The unexpected voice came from the ground, and Gavin and Nero both turned to see Ollie open his eyes.

He blinked several times before pulling himself onto his elbows and looking up at them. It was clear from his expression that he had no more idea what was happening than Gavin did.

"Impossible," whispered Nero.

"Take it easy, kid," Gavin told Ollie, unsure why. None of them were long for this world. Still, the words came of their own accord. "You're going to make it worse."

"But I feel...fine," Ollie said, confusion furrowing his brows, cheeks and chin spattered with dirt and blood. "Sore, but not *dying* sore."

Nero wheeled back several paces as Ollie sat up all the way. Then his eyes went wide as saucers, and a manic grin spread across his face.

"You were a part of the CEDAR experiments," he breathed.

Ollie only stared up at him.

"I've done it!" Nero cried. He swooped down on Ollie, jabbing a finger into the hole in his shirt from the crossbow bolt. Ollie recoiled, but didn't cry out in pain as Gavin would have expected. "I've succeeded! Where generations have failed, I have *succeeded!*"

Nero continued his rant in low, muttered tones, pacing before his captives. Then he looked up at one of the clones. "Ready the ships. We're returning to Thera. We must find out what sets this one apart and begin replication procedures immediately."

No, Gavin thought desperately. *You can't leave, not yet.*

Come on, Felix!

"Succeeded at what?" he blurted out.

"Isn't it obvious?" Nero asked, thrusting his hand toward Ollie. "Don't you see?"

"I see a kid in a lot of pain, that *you* caused."

"No, my old friend. What you see is the culmination of Thera's past and future. I have, through tireless dedication, managed to replicate the very trial which gave the Weaver his immortality. And once I narrow down the variables that brought about this victory, I will bestow it upon all who are loyal to me. Therans will no longer fear the sting of death. We can truly live forever!" He paused, dropping his hands, and looked straight at Gavin. "I am only sorry that you will not be there to see it."

He turned his back and began walking away. "Take the fallen one," he said, to no one in particular. "Kill the—"

The sky filled with the drone of incoming aircraft, and all heads rose as one to search the skies.

"What's this?" Nero shouted. "Those fools would dare...get to the ships! I want the enemy destroyed. Now!"

The world erupted with sound as the approaching vessels opened fire on Nero's grounded fleet, and there were howls of anguish as soldiers making their way to the ships fell beneath the onslaught. Ambrose and the others ducked instinctively, but Gavin watched helplessly as two, three, four of the Theran ships lifted off. In less than a minute more than a dozen were airborne and engaged with the Alliance's force. The attempt was too little, too late. The

Humans had no chance of winning. *Why did they come?* He cursed silently, pulling at his restraints until his wrists screamed in agony.

"Get this one to my ship," Nero was shouting at one of his officers. "I don't care about the rest. You! Retrieve my scepter from the command tent. We must return to Thera at once."

Two soldiers heaved Ollie to his feet, eliciting a cry of pain from the youth. Gavin stepped toward them, but two more moved into his path, swords raised.

"Leave him alone!" Kestrel shouted over the din. But with her arms behind her back and no way to defend herself, it was about all she could offer. Tobias and Ambrose seemed transfixed by the dogfight taking place above their heads.

"Perhaps we should take cover," Tobias suggested as Gavin watched Nero moving away. *He's going to do it again. Slip right through our fingers like the filthy snake that he is, and take Ollie with him.*

There was an explosion overhead, followed closely by the whine of one of the Chronohawks as it careened toward the forest.

"There's no where to take cover, the trees aren't going to protect us." Gavin pulled again at his bound wrists, cursing. "We need to get to Nero!"

The impact as the Chronohawk made contact with the treetops drew the gaze of the soldier on the left. It was only a momentary distraction, but it was all Gavin had.

Kestrel had apparently been looking for the same type of opportunity. She crouched low before launching herself at the guard like a javelin. Together they tumbled to the ground in a heap. The second soldier made a motion and then paused, as if uncertain how best to deal with the tangled pair now grappling on the forest floor.

"Papa!" Penelope was racing toward them from the treeline. The soldier moved to intercept her, but Ambrose lashed out, kicking the clone squarely in the shin with all the force he could muster. Penelope reached the group, wielding a knife that made quick work of Gavin's restraints, and he leapt atop the injured soldier, wrapping an arm around his neck and squeezing as the clone attempted to throw him off. Kestrel cried out and Gavin, having subdued his own opponent, came to her defense. He slipped the unconscious clone's sword from its scabbard and held it to the man's neck where he straddled Kestrel, pinning her to the ground.

"Surrender," Gavin suggested.

The clone did not take his advice. He was on his feet in an instant, still mid-spin to face his opponent as Gavin thrust the sword through his chest.

"Penny, what are you doing here?" Ambrose cried.

"There's no time for that!" Tobias was rubbing his wrists, but stopped to point. "Nero is getting away!"

Gavin had been helping Kestrel to her feet, but now his blood ran cold as his head whipped up, scanning the chaotic scene. "Which way did he go? Toward the tents or the ships?"

"I don't know," Tobias moaned. "I lost track of him in the commotion."

Gavin's heart thundered in his chest, eyes searching desperately for some sign of the would-be Emperor.

But Nero was nowhere to be seen.

Chapter Nineteen

Fools and Folly

THE LAST LEG OF their long journey sped by as they all caught a second wind. Confident that they would make it home now, it had become less a trial and more an adventure. At least, that's how Ripley felt. Edwin's condition remained stable, and when the domes came into view he unzipped his tent to cheer with the rest of them.

Killian and his team ventured out at their approach. "What happened?" he shouted, jogging toward them. "What took you so long? And what did you do with my Sno-Cat?"

Ben clapped Killian heartily on the shoulder. "I'm sorry." His words were grave. "I'm afraid she didn't make it."

Killian groaned.

A medical team met them in the bulkhead, and Ripley watched as they put Edwin on a stretcher. "Enjoy your stay in the pod."

Edwin gave a shaky thumbs up, sweat beading on his forehead, the neck of his shirt soaked through. "At least it'll be warm."

"Not only that," Ben cut in, stepping up beside Ripley, "but by the time you get out, Antiquity's Gate will be a thing of the past! Only sorry you'll miss the show, but I want to get it over with, ya know?"

"Yeah," Edwin called as the medical team began carrying him away. "I'll look forward to hearing all about it!"

Something was nagging at Ripley. "Ben, about the plan—"

"Listen," Ben said, raising a hand to stop him from continuing. "I know I just told Edwin I want to get it over with, but at *least* let me thaw out first. And I'm *famished.* I'm going to go see if mom'll make me something good!"

"*Anything* will taste good," Denton pointed out. "Hurry up, Prior. I'm hungry."

Ripley hesitated, looking at Molly. She smiled at him as she stripped off the last of her gear, tossing it into a pile with the rest. She moved over to where he was waiting and, without a word, slipped her hand into his. Ripley felt a thrill of happiness at her touch and squeezed her hand.

"Come on," she said, nodding toward Denton, who was already walking up the tracks ahead. "Let's go home."

*   *   *

RIPLEY FELT HIMSELF alternating between an emotional high whenever he looked at Molly, and a physical low whenever he registered the sheer exhaustion he was experiencing. He took a longer shower than usual, resetting the timer three times before he felt clean enough. When he emerged he found Denton at the table, stuffing sandwiches in his mouth as if he had never eaten a decent meal in his life. He waved one at Ripley. "Parker's mom just dropped these off," he mumbled through a mouthful of bread. "Teach went downstairs to get cleaned up."

"Clearly not a concern of yours," Ripley replied, taking a bite. It tasted amazing.

"Priorities. Food first."

"As long as you do shower *eventually*."

"I'm not an animal, Prior," Denton snapped, bits of sandwich flying from his mouth with every word. "Maybe if you're so concerned with my hygiene you shouldn't drag me across the whole damn continent on *foot*."

Ripley shrugged. "It's not like you couldn't use the exercise."

Denton stared blankly at him for a moment, then scowled. "You callin' me fat?"

There was a knock at the door, and Ripley's heart leapt into his throat as he jumped up to answer it, his sandwich forgotten.

He opened the door. "Molly, you don't need to

knock—"

But it wasn't Molly. Doris Fincher stood in the doorway, flanked by four stoney-faced security guards. "Welcome home, Mr. Prior," she said smoothly. "On behalf of the people of New Sanctuary, I would like to thank you for your valuable contribution to this assignment. Although I have not yet been briefed, we were becoming worried by the delay, and I was happy to be informed of your triumphant return."

"Thanks," Ripley said, feeling confusion churning in his stomach with the meager remains of his dinner. "Uh, would you like to come in…?"

"Oh, no," said Fincher, shaking her head gravely. "I'm afraid this isn't a social visit. We are here to collect you."

"Collect him?" Denton said, his chair screeching across the tiles as he stood abruptly. "What's all this now?"

"I don't understand," Ripley said, a growing sense of foreboding making him take a step back from the door. "I thought—"

"I am a woman of my word, Mr. Prior. I was willing to grant you a full pardon should this plan succeed. However, Benjamin Parker declined that offer, as I recall. We came to terms in the end, of course. But your permanent release was not necessary to assure success, after all."

"Why you slimy, no good—" growled Denton, taking a menacing step forward. Ripley held up a hand to stop him.

"At least let me see the project through," Ripley asked,

doing his best to remain calm. "I've proven to be helpful, haven't I? I can still be helpful." *I need to talk to Ben. We can't go through with this.* The thought formed suddenly, causing that foreboding feeling to surge. The incident at the microreactor was still vague in his mind, but he knew one thing: destroying the Gate was a bad idea. He wasn't entirely sure why, but he knew it with every fiber of his being.

"I am familiar with your history," Doris stated, eyebrow cocking as her gaze flitted to Ripley's Theran eye. "I make it my business to be knowledgeable about the failings of my predecessor. Knowledge is imperative to ensure that we do not make the same mistakes as we have in the past. And you, I'm afraid, have a remarkable track record for non-compliance."

It was Ripley's turn to raise his eyebrows. "*Non-compliance?*"

"Yes, Mr. Prior. You seem to have a way of causing trouble for this city, and my first duty is to our citizens. That means that keeping you safely out of the way is one of my top priorities."

"I've done everything you asked of me!" Ripley was getting angry now. He could feel himself trembling, feel heat rising to his face. "I've been nothing if not cooperative."

"Indeed you have. Let's end on a high note, shall we?" Fincher jerked her head in Ripley's direction, and the Security officers moved around him and into the apartment. "It would be most agreeable if you were to come quietly."

Denton was watching with a look of disgust upon his bristly face. "Now hang on just a sec."

"It's fine, Denton," Ripley told him, then turned back to Fincher. "I'll do what you want. But just let me talk to Ben first."

She considered this for a moment, then shook her head. "I'm sorry. I'm afraid I can't take the risk that you'll try something."

"*Ripley!*"

Denton's warning rang out too late as Ripley felt something sharp pierce his shoulder. He looked down at it, bewildered for a moment. As his head began to swim, he realized it was some sort of sedative. Denton was shouting now, cursing and yelling at his men to stand down, but they weren't here to take orders from Denton. Ripley swayed, and the guards grasped him by the arms.

Fincher's face was frighteningly close to his. "Don't worry, Mr. Prior. I've taken the liberty of having a viewing station set up in the Geothermal Plant. You will be able to watch the proceedings from the safety of your confinement."

The proceedings. Ripley struggled to make sense of the words. *Ben. Got to tell Ben.* Tell Ben what? *Have to…stop. Stop Ben. The Gate.* Ripley's eyelids felt heavy, his thoughts erratic. *We can't. We can't stop the Gate.*

The darkness was closing in on him. He couldn't fight it any longer.

Can't stop the Gate we can't stop the Gate we can't stop the Gate...

...Molly...

*   *   *

RIPLEY AWOKE IN HIS BUNK in Geo. Between the effect of whatever they'd dosed him with and the exhaustion of their journey across the ice, he'd slept for nearly an entire day. His stomach was tight with hunger, and he still felt woozy as he swung his legs off the bed.

"Take it easy," said a voice from the door of the sleeping quarters. Someone had gone to let Daniel know he was awake. "Glad you made it back okay," Daniel said, striding into the room with a steaming bowl. "But to be honest, I'd hoped to never see you again."

"Gee, thanks," Ripley said, too miserable for jokes right now. His head was throbbing, and he ate the food without tasting it, allowing the hot liquid to burn his tongue and throat.

"I just meant...I thought you were going to be freed," Daniel said in a more serious tone. Ripley let out a derisive laugh.

"None of us are free, Daniel," he said bitterly, tossing his empty bowl carelessly onto the bed beside him. "Not in Geo, and not out in the city. We're all prisoners here." He scowled. "I don't know how I keep letting myself forget that."

Standing, Ripley made for the door.

"Where are you going?"

"I have to talk to the guards. Ask them to send Ben down. I need to talk to him."

"It's not going to happen," Daniel said, following him. "They locked it down after they brought you in. No visits at all until after the Evenmire is destroyed."

Ripley rounded on him. "We need to stop that from happening."

Daniel cocked his head, frowning slightly. "Why?"

"I'm…not sure," Ripley admitted. "I just know something bad is going to happen."

Daniel gave a helpless shrug. "I'm sorry, Ripley, but even if visitors *were* allowed, it would do you no good. Ben's already outside. They've put a screen up with live footage."

Ripley thought his soup might be making a reappearance. "Show me," he said, defeated.

Daniel led the way up toward the exit, where Ripley took stock of the additional guards. For one wild moment he considered taking them out, making a break for it.

But it passed quickly. He would never make it in time. He could see the large screen now, could see Ben's team trailing out of frame on their way back inside. Ben alone stood, staring up at the Gate, as if taking it in for the last time. Saying goodbye to a piece of their history.

Then he turned and disappeared as well.

Ripley closed his eyes, walking the familiar path alongside Ben in his mind. Through the deserted Nursery, into the Rat, down the long Pod Manufacturing department. Left and right and left again through the underground passageways, up the lift, through the lobby. He imagined Ben reaching Core Operations, leading the CTC to the main view screen, asking Fincher why Ripley couldn't be there to watch. Sylvia was there, wringing her hands in tense anticipation. Denton too, snarling openly at the CTC members for their treatment of Ripley. This image brought Ripley the briefest hint of a smile. Never in a million years would he have expected Denton to be the one suffering righteous indignation on Ripley's behalf. But the irony vanished as Ripley opened his eyes, holding his breath as he watched the Gate.

All of Geo seemed to be holding its breath with him.

There was no sound, but the arrays had been left uncovered after the adjustments. Fincher must have been in too great a hurry to see the fruits of their labor. The faintest blinking light on one of resonators let Ripley know that it had been activated. One by one they silently came to life.

That was when the vibrations began. Nearly imperceptible at first, they travelled from the tips of his fingers and up the length of his arm.

As they became more pronounced, Ripley glanced around and saw that the others had noticed it too. All around him the Halfsies had torn their gaze from the screen, searching intently for the source of the disturbance. Ripley, however, had the sickening feeling that the *source* of the disturbance was *on* the screen.

The sound came next. It grew from a faint hum, to an angry buzz, to a dull roar that reverberated in his teeth and seemed to seep into his head to squeeze his brain. Ripley grasped the railing to steady himself. He had to shout to be heard over the grating cacophony. His eyesight blurred, vertigo taking hold as he pounded on the glass guard enclosure to get the attention of the disgruntled men inside.

"*I need to get up there!*" he said, forming the words slowly and clearly with his lips so that they would be able to understand even if they couldn't hear. They looked at each other, down at their equipment, and out into the plant. At last, one of them shrugged at Ripley, shaking his head.

Ripley scowled in frustration. He glanced back over his shoulder. The other prisoners had clustered into groups, frightened and uncertain. All of them were staring at him.

He watched in horror as one of the more precarious catwalks swayed violently, the creaking of its rusty joints masked by the roar. Two people were on it, both caught by surprise at the sudden motion. Ripley felt himself tense, ready to help, but Daniel was faster. He saw the flash of dark blond hair as Daniel leapt from the nearest walkway, grabbing the two occupants of the doomed catwalk by the arms and racing with them onto the safety of the nearest platform. They'd barely cleared the swaying section before it collapsed, falling away and smashing pipes and walkways as it went, clattering against the floor in surreal silence as the rumbling cancelled out everything else.

And then it was over. The sound and motion ceased

abruptly, leaving Ripley's ears ringing in its wake.

He whirled back to face the guard station. "Find out what happened," he demanded, "and tell them we need help down here!" He barely registered the befuddled nod of one of them before he sped off toward the destruction below, anxious to assess the damage.

Daniel and several others shared his concern and beat him to his destination. The two women Daniel had saved were struggling to hold a scrap of metal over a cracked pipe that hissed in protest as Daniel wound metallic tape around it. "We've got this one," Daniel shouted to him. "I sent Lincoln for the welding gear already. Go see how bad it is down below."

Ripley gave a quick nod and peered over the twisted, jagged edge of what used to be a catwalk. The nearest platform would have been an easy jump, but he was hesitant to trust any of the rusted structures down here after such a violent upset. He took the ladder instead.

Small groups of three or four Halfsies had gathered at each afflicted area, and to Ripley's great relief it appeared that most of the damage had been superficial. A few cracks were nothing they couldn't handle, but there were several pipes that had been crushed like tin cans beneath the falling walkway, and the pressure buildup could have serious consequences.

"Forget that one for now, Simon," he instructed a young Halfsie who was hurrying to join a group performing the same stop-gap measures as Daniel on another hissing pipe. "We need to redirect this one here," he pointed to the crushed pipe nearest them, "and those two farther down. Grab some help and follow them to the shut-off valves." The youth nodded and dashed off.

His keen eyes swept over the damage, surveying it for the most critical points. They were lucky—it could have been a lot worse. Thankful that the repaired exhaust system had dissipated the once chronic fog that had plagued the lower half of the Plant, Ripley was able to see clear to the floor. The catwalk lay peacefully where it had landed, unaware of the cascade of turmoil it had left in its wake.

A sound behind Ripley caught his attention. He whipped around in time to see Daniel curse as the scrap metal fell away with an echoing clang. One of the women who had held it was whimpering, clutching her steamburnt hand to her chest. "It's no good," Daniel called, "we're not going to be able to patch a crack this large until we can drain the pressure."

"I'm on it," Ripley replied. He made his way quickly but cautiously to the central mass that formed the heart of the Plant. All pipes, whether incoming or outgoing, inevitably led to this system. He kept his eyes on the damaged length, tracing it back to its origin on the core. Finding the place where it disappeared into a large black tube, he located the wheel that would allow him to adjust the rate of steam. He alternated between lowering the damaged pipe's pressure and checking the gauges associated with that particular system, worried about causing undue stress on the integrity of any other lines that would now be forced to pick up the slack.

"That's enough!" came Daniel's echoing call, causing Ripley to stop. He checked the gauges once more. All was well.

Ripley wondered if the guards had gotten through to anyone yet. Too impatient to wait, he clamored back up to the now deserted guard station. His eyes fell on the screen, and his heart went cold.

Antiquity's Gate was still standing.

It had not been destroyed. Instead, to his horror and confusion, it had...grown. At least double its previous size, the Gate was thicker, taller, throbbing angrily amidst the ruins of Ben's array.

As he watched, transfixed, something came through.

Naked, pale, it took in the icy landscape with wild, gleaming eyes. Then, although there was no sound, Ripley watched as it tilted its head to the sky and opened its mouth. And in his mind he remembered the high, shrill cry of the clones. He knew that was the sound this creature was making now.

Standing taller, the creature spread its arms and let out another howl. Then, baring its teeth, it turned and darted back through the Gate.

Ripley wasn't sure how long Daniel had been standing beside him, but his horrified question suggested that he'd seen enough. His next words seemed to get caught in his throat, escaping as a whisper. "What just happened?"

Ripley shook his head, eyes still locked on the screen. "Something bad."

CHAPTER TWENTY

THE SNOW'S COLD EMBRACE

"WHERE IS IT? It was right here!"

His voice. Just as vehement, just as cruel, as the last time she'd heard it. Back then, Willow had been weak. Powerless. He'd been intent on destroying her home. Her friends. Felix.

It was the same this time. He wanted to take everything from her. He wouldn't rest until he had.

But Willow was no longer powerless. Her grip on the crossbow was steady as she used the tip to push aside the tent flap. They were supposed to find a safe place to land and stay put, but surely the general hadn't actually believed they'd listen? Not with the lives of their loved ones in danger. Penelope had made a beeline for Ambrose and the others, but Felix wasn't with them. While Willow had searched the chaotic scene for some sign of her husband, she'd found a different target. Getting here had been simple. In a sea of running soldiers and bursts of gunfire, no one had even noticed her approach.

"Hello, Father."

Nero whirled from where he'd been frantically overturning his belongings. He gripped the table behind him with both hands, panting, eyes wide and fiery.

"...Willow?"

"That's right," she said, her voice as steady as her aim. "Your daughter. The one you disowned and left for dead."

"But...how?"

"That doesn't matter," she told him, gesturing with the crossbow. "Outside."

"Willow, please," his face contorted into a poor imitation of innocence. "Let's talk about this."

"People are dying out there, and it's your 'talking' that caused it. I think you've said enough."

"Willow." Nero's voice broke halfway through the name, his eyes pleading. "Think about what you're doing. I'm your *father!*"

"Let me tell you something about fathers," she said, taking a step closer but keeping a safe distance between them. "Fathers care about their children. Fathers protect them. Fathers do whatever it takes to keep their family safe. *Felix* is a father. You're nothing but a shell. An empty, heartless tyrant who doesn't know what love even means."

She watched his adam's apple bob up and down as he swallowed, saying nothing.

"Now, you can do as I've asked and step outside and make this stop, or I swear you will die where you stand and I'll drag your body out and demand your followers stop slaughtering innocent people or suffer the same fate."

Nero smiled, shaking his head. Willow couldn't tell if it was pity or mocking on his face this time. Perhaps both. "You're not a killer, Willow. You're too weak. You've always been weak, even though I did my best to teach you better. You couldn't kill anyone, let alone your own family."

"You told me you hoped my children would die."

"Yes," he replied, no trace of guilt or regret in the simple admission. "But you aren't like me."

Willow nodded. The confirmation was both sad and comforting at once. "That's something we agree on."

"Come with me," Nero urged. He stepped forward, and Willow stepped back. "We can still be a family. Your mother's waiting on Thera for our return. I've finally found what I have been searching for all these years. Willow, aboard my ship right now is the key to immortality. Come home. Come home and live forever with your own kind, where you belong."

She leveled the crossbow at his chest. "I have a home," she whispered fiercely. "Last chance. Out."

He straightened, his upper lip twitching as he scowled at her. "You're going to regret this."

"Not as much as you will." She gestured again, and

this time he stomped past, throwing the tent flap aside and emerging into the hectic scene that had overwhelmed the valley.

"I have the Emperor," Willow declared in a loud, clear voice. Those near enough to hear stopped, taking in the odd pair. "I have the Emperor!" she said again. "Call back your ships. Surrender peacefully and no harm will come to you."

"I am warning you," Nero said over his shoulder. "I have let this go so far because you are my daughter. I am willing to forgive your poor judgement. It's that Halfsie's fault, he's corrupted you. But if you continue this charade, I *will* order them to kill you."

"If I die, you're coming with me."

"Willow!"

She didn't let Gavin's voice distract her. Her focus was on one thing, and one thing only. Her father.

"Willow," Gavin said gently as he approached, pushing his way through the confused mass of soldiers who had gathered in a wide semi-circle around them. "You don't have to be the one to do this. Give me the crossbow."

"No," she said. "Spread the word that the Emperor has been captured. Tell them to call back the ships. Look around. They're lost without him. Their only purpose is to serve at his pleasure."

"That's right," Nero agreed. "Perhaps you can be taught, after all. A shame. I shall miss you, my daughter." Then he raised his voice. "Therans! To me! I am ordering you to k–!"

A flash of motion streaked past the heads of the clones who had stopped to witness the scene. Nero never finished his sentence. An eternity passed in an instant as Willow watched his head jolt sideways, a crossbow bolt lodged in the side of his temple.

A moment later his body tumbled to the ground, lips parted by a word that would never be uttered, a look of astonishment frozen on his lifeless face.

Willow was too shocked to move. She stared at Nero, then at the crossbow. It was still loaded. She hadn't pulled the trigger. She'd never intended to pull the trigger. She'd meant to see justice through the right way. *Her* way, not his.

She waited, wondering what it would feel like to die. But no one rushed forward to offer aid to their fallen Emperor, not a single soldier moved to fulfill the order that Nero had so obviously been about to issue. She scanned the crowd, looking for the assassin.

Then the sounds of battle brought her a new clarity. "Call them back!" she repeated for the third time. "Tell your pilots to get those ships on the ground!"

And this time, they listened.

"Willow, look!" said Gavin. He pointed behind her, past the treeline. A glimpse of a white uniform caught her eye.

The back of a curly brown-haired head was just visible before the figure disappeared into the trees, a discharged crossbow hooked casually on a branch behind him.

Felix?

No. It couldn't be.

Her companions gathered around her one by one as they watched the surreal end to an impossible war. The ships landed one by one, their pilots and crews streaming out and forming neat ranks, docile and complacent. The allied forces, too, began to land. General Hall soon stood in the middle of the clearing, looking completely uncertain how so many of them were still alive, interspersed among throngs of clones that had moments ago been intent on killing them all.

"Willow," whispered Penelope. "They're looking to you. You need to say something."

But Willow dropped the bow as if it had scorched her hands and backed away, a fresh wave of adrenaline washing over her. "I can't. I can't."

"It's all right," said Gavin. He put a hand on her shoulder. "Do you want me to take it from here?"

"I...yes. Please."

"Your Emperor has fallen," Gavin informed the masses, shouting the proclamation so that those farthest away might hear. "The war is over. You will surrender, and you will no longer trouble this world."

There was no answer, but as one, the mass of soldiers dropped, each taking a knee. Willow could feel the eyes of her friends upon her, and with difficulty she tore her gaze from the body of her father to take in the scene. "What happens now?" she asked.

"I'm not sure," Gavin told her. "But I think the worst is over."

At the far edge of the encampment, a single white ship roared to life. It rose swiftly into the air, pointed its nose south, and disappeared over the trees.

*　　*　　*

FELIX AND NELSON stumbled into the encampment not long after. Willow ran to her husband, burying her face in his chest. Conflict raged within her as she struggled to breathe between sobs. Her father was dead. It was over. A part of her was sad.

All of her was relieved.

Felix just held her, kissing the crown of her head over and over, whispering that it would be okay. It would be all right. Gradually her sobbing faded, but Felix continued to hold her. It was all she needed. Felix always knew exactly what she needed.

"I can't believe it," Felix said after a time, stroking her hair as together they watched clones gathering in neat lines, awaiting the pronouncement of their fate. "I can't believe that they're just...cooperating."

"They were never inherently evil, Felix," Willow tried to explain as she slowly began to compose herself. "They were more like children than anything, eager to be told what to do and please the ones who were telling them to do it."

Felix made a strange sound in his throat. "*Lethal* children."

"It's not their fault. Not really."

"No," Felix agreed. "I suppose they just had a lousy father figure."

Willow bit her lip. They weren't the only ones.

"Terrance!"

Nelson's joyful cry rang out and Willow and Felix turned toward it, hands entwined in a tight embrace. The young man plowed into his friend, wrapping him in a hug that barely reached around his middle. "Terrance, you're alive!"

"Contain yourself, Peacock!" Terrance replied, wincing. His face was swollen and bloodied, his hair a long, disheveled mess that revealed balding patches atop the crown of his head. "If I could deduce which one of these foul miscreants beat me, I'd pay him back in kind—with interest! But I admit that on the whole, they're damn near indistinguishable."

"Well," Felix said, walking up and sticking his hand out, "they *are* clones."

Terrance shook his hand, but Nelson scowled. "I told you not to trust him, didn't I?" he scolded Felix. "I told you he was no good."

Felix nodded, looking forlorn. "You did. I'm sorry I didn't listen. I just thought...I don't know what I thought, really. I wanted so desperately to believe that he could change. He seemed...different."

"Who?" Willow asked.

Felix's smile was equal parts wistful and sad. "My brother."

Willow said nothing, thinking about the soldier in the woods. The one who had killed her father. The one she'd mistaken for Felix. Before she could say anything, Penelope interjected. "Laevus is *here?* On this island?"

"Not anymore," Felix told her, shoving his free hand into his pocket and gazing up at the sky. "Gavin said one ship escaped, right? I'd bet anything it was him. It's *always* him."

But Gavin shrugged. "Perhaps you were not entirely wrong to hope for change."

Felix looked thunderstruck. "He *electrocuted* me, Gavin! He destroyed the controller and left us all to die."

"I almost made the same mistake." General Hall approached slowly, head lowered and eyes downcast. "If it weren't for Willow and Penelope, I'd have done the same as any of these clones—just followed my orders. Left you behind, like your brother did."

"But you didn't. You came blazing in to save the day."

Hall smiled, nodding toward Willow. "These two saved the day. When we got your message, they were the ones who reminded me why I do what I do. Not to blindly follow orders, but to protect what's important. I hope…I hope you can learn to forgive me."

"There's nothing to forgive, General," replied Felix.

"But your brother—"

"My brother is different. You aren't like him. Not by a long shot."

"True," Gavin said thoughtfully. "But he could have claimed the army for himself. He could have taken the fleet, we were powerless to stop him. That's what you said he wanted to do, isn't it? And yet, he didn't."

"Yeah," Felix replied, looking around at the rapidly emptying encampment. "Why didn't he?"

"Perhaps something you said got through to him."

Felix whirled on Nelson now, who was still bouncing on his heels with excitement over Terrance's escape from the jaws of death. "Nelson, why didn't you tell me about the message?"

Nelson's brow furrowed as he stopped bouncing and came closer. "What message?"

"The one the *Timeless* intercepted. That the plan had failed," offered the General.

But Nelson only shook his head. "I didn't send any message. I didn't even know there *was* a plan until you showed up at the tower, Felix. After your lousy brother overpowered us…we were together the whole time. I couldn't have."

"Then who did?" Tobias asked.

Everyone looked at Terrance. "I was otherwise indisposed," the Culiean said, raising his palms as he shrugged. "On account of being, quite literally, tied up."

Felix's lips were pursed in concentration and Willow watched him as he stared at the ground. "It couldn't be," he muttered. "There's no way."

She waited for him to say more, but instead his head jerked up and he locked eyes with Nelson.

"There's something I need to know," he asked, "Laevus told me…but I didn't want to believe. Onyx…my mother…is she?" He swallowed hard. "Is she…dead?"

Nelson's face contorted into a discomforted expression. "Sweet Evenmire, your mother? I…I didn't know." He gulped. "Yes. It's true. I'm sorry."

Willow's hand shot to her mouth and Gavin rocked backward as if about to topple. The high of their victory seemed to drain out of the group, and Willow felt Felix's grip tighten in hers.

"Dead?" Gavin demanded. "Onyx is *dead*? How?" He was advancing on the shorter man so fast that Nelson shrank back against Terrance for protection. "Are you certain? What happened?"

"I, uh—yes. Yes, I'm certain. I saw her myself. After…after it happened."

Willow had never seen Gavin like this before. The normally cool visage of the older man had been replaced, an agony etched on his face so fierce that she feared might kill him.

"How did she die?" he asked in a low growl. Felix let go of Willow and placed a hand on Gavin's arm, but the Theran didn't even seem to notice. He was beyond comforting. *He loved her,* Willow realized. She looked at Felix, saw pain there too. The two of them had both lost something, something unique to each of them. She thought of

Penelope's words when they'd been travelling. *He loved her, and losing her will break him.*

"They didn't like the idea that we were going to use the clones we grew in New Sanctuary," Nelson said, his voice cracking nervously under Gavin's intense stare. "There was something wrong with ours. They weren't like these, they were…completely uncontrollable. Wild. So they destroyed them. Only I guess something went wrong. She was killed. By one of the clones."

Felix exchanged a glance with Willow. Sorrow radiated from him, but there was something else there. A question.

"It should have been me," Gavin was murmuring. He pushed past Nelson, nearly knocking him over. "I never should have sent her. If I'd thought—if I'd known…"

Kestrel made a motion to follow, but Ollie stopped her. "I'll go," he said, his words mournful.

Felix hardly seemed to notice they were gone. "Who's 'they'?"

"Sorry?" said Nelson, glancing around at the others, clearly unsure if Felix was still addressing him.

"You said 'they' didn't like the idea. You said 'they' destroyed the clones. Who did you mean?"

"It doesn't matter," Nelson told him. "It might seem that you have allies in New Sanctuary, but you don't. The Halfsies…they've all been sent to Geo, Felix. You should stay well clear of that place if you don't want to end up down there, too. That city has nothing to offer you."

Nelson's eyes darted back and forth between Felix and

Willow as he fidgeted.

But Felix pressed. "Who helped my mother destroy the clones?"

Nelson swallowed hard. Willow saw guilt in the young man's eyes before he spoke. "I just wanted to protect the city," he whispered, more to himself than to Felix. His hands were balled into fists at his side, lip trembling. "I just wanted to do what was best for New Sanctuary. He shouldn't have interfered. It wasn't his place."

"I only want to know who helped my mother, Nelson. I only want to thank them someday. Ask them…about her last moments."

Sighing deeply, Nelson uttered a name that Willow had never expected to hear. She almost couldn't believe that she'd heard correctly, but the way Felix's body tensed confirmed that she had.

"Ripley Prior."

EPILOGUE

WIPING MATTED HAIR from his dripping forehead, Ripley worried about his friends on the surface. Where was Molly? Probably with the children. The whole city would've been watching what Fincher had intended to be her crowning moment.

As the hours wore on, Ripley's anxiety gnawed at him, worst-case scenario images flashing through his mind. Why hadn't they sent news?

He tried to focus on the crushed machinery right in front of him, a central intake for the coolant system. The secondary and tertiary lines couldn't keep up with demand, and Ripley had to reroute water from the nearby recla-mation pipelines to aid in cooling. The people up above wouldn't be pleased about the temporary shortage, but that was their own fault. He might have avoided it, or at least warned them, if they'd bothered to send someone down to help.

Legs aching from exhaustion, Ripley made his way up to the guard station once they were out of immediate danger.

"Has there been any news?" He tried to keep the edge from his tone, but it came out an accusation all the same.

"Nothing," apologized one of the guards. "Just orders to stay at our post. They'll send help as soon as possible."

Ripley's heart thumped a little harder. "Is everyone up there all right?"

The guard lifted his shoulders, let them drop again. "Minimal damage. That's all I know."

Ripley felt a mixture of relief and a strong desire to roll his eyes. How ridiculous that he'd spent so much time convincing Edwin of the precarious situation down here, only to have Edwin ousted and replaced by some pompous know-it-all who understood but didn't seem to care.

Sleep evaded him. He'd barely managed to drift off when he was being shaken awake again.

"What is it?" he asked, rubbing his eyes.

"Sorry, Ripley." Daniel's face slowly came into focus. "But we have a new problem."

"Of course we do," Ripley groaned, sitting up and stretching, more sore than he had been since he'd undergone his Theran transformation. "What's up?"

"Something's off with the heat exchange," Daniel said, leading the way out of the sleeping quarters. "We must have missed something. I have people looking, but you're honestly the most likely to solve the mystery for us."

"No problem," Ripley replied. They made their way to the Geothermal core, where concrete tubes peeked out of the ground like sea serpents cresting the surface of the ocean. Long and slender, these ran in parallel along the floor and into the massive exchange that drew heat from the water into the system that powered the turbines. Reaching the base of the mammoth system, Ripley climbed a small ladder to the platform where the system vitals were monitored. He felt a flash of remembrance from his days in Core Operations, logging these numbers dutifully each day. He frowned, leaning in close to re-read the monitor as Daniel climbed up beside him.

"You see?" Daniel said. "The numbers are off."

"A bit low," Ripley agreed, more than familiar with the normal variance. "It could be we overcompensated on the coolant system before. We could try to speed up repairs on the crushed intake, and back off on the backup. I'm sure they're cursing us up there by now over that anyway."

But Daniel shook his head. "We already *did* dial it down. I thought that might be the problem too."

"Huh." Ripley chewed the inside of his lip as his mind churned through the possibilities. "What about the outflow? Maybe someone left a valve wide open and now that they're all repaired, it's running too quick?"

Daniel shrugged apologetically, his brows furrowed. "Checked those, too."

"Well, if it's not the outflow, and it's not the coolant, I'm not sure what it could be. Maybe the gauge is faulty." His voice sounded doubtful in his own ears. "The underground system is a constant. There's no way that could have been affected. The quaking wasn't severe enough. If there was damage, we'd be dealing with flooding or collapses right now."

Daniel sighed, running a hand through his hair and glancing over Ripley's shoulder at the control panel. "You're right. You should get back to sleep. Sorry for waking you."

"It's got to be connected," Ripley muttered, squinting at the numbers without really seeing them.

Daniel offered a quizzical look. "What does?"

"The Gate growing, and the problem down here."

It hit him like a gut punch. It all made sense. How had he not seen it?

He forgot Daniel, racing to the guard station and pounding the glass so hard that it reverberated beneath his fist, causing the startled guards to jump.

"You *need* to get through to Ben," he told them. This time it was not a request.

"But they said—"

"I don't care what they said. This is urgent."

"Ripley?" Daniel had appeared at his side. "What's going on?"

"There's only one explanation for those readings," Ripley said, gesturing back in the direction of the control panel. "In the few minutes we were watching them, they dropped again. Maybe not significantly, *yet.*" He clenched his fist, still resting against the glass. "It's the *Gate*, Daniel. The Gate has a root system. It was seeking out more power and we gave it just what it needed. I should have figured it out sooner. I should have fought harder."

He looked at the screen. They hadn't bothered to switch off the feed. If not for the wreckage of the array, it might have been peaceful.

"The damn thing is alive." Ripley stared at the Gate as it throbbed with a violent, brilliant light. "And we just pissed it off."

ABOUT THE AUTHOR

In the amount of time it takes you to read this, R.F. Hurteau will have finished yet another cup of coffee. At this point, she's more caffeine than human. Harnessing the powers of this magical bean juice, R.F. creates stories that explore worlds unknown through the lens of the age old curiosity that drives all creatives: the human condition. She lives in New England with her husband, five kids, and an impressive array of animal friends. Her ultimate mission is to craft light, character-driven science fiction that is accessible to all, and by doing so slowly turn everyone into nerds. It looks like she's got you hooked, so it's time to start reeling you in.

The Adventure Continues...

Antiquity's Gate:
A Soliloquy of Souls

S OMETHING wasn't right.

Eli paused, frowning at his bedroom door. For some reason he'd expected it to open on its own.

Trodding into the hall, he peered over the railing beside the stairs. Shadowy figures moved in the room below, overlapping and shifting. A few moments ago he'd been eager to join them; now he felt unsure.

As quickly as the ill feeling had come, it melted away into a sort of fuzzy contentment. Eli took the stairs two at a time, landing at the bottom with a soft thud. Mabel was leaning against the kitchen counter, batting Shane's hand away from the tired-looking picnic basket waiting there. "I told you, we can eat when we get to the park."

"But I'm hungry now!" Shane scrunched up his face into an exaggerated look of longing, blue eyes pleading. "Just a bite."

"You can have as much as you want…when we get to the park." Mabel leaned farther across the counter and offered the boy a quick peck on the cheek. Then she turned on her brother. "Let's go Eli, we're burning daylight."

Eli was already searching for his sneakers. The words slipped from his mouth without thought. "Relax. Wagner Park is only a few blocks away."

Was it? That didn't seem right.

"Well we're supposed to be there already, and you know how Linus gets when he's hungry."

"Oh, sure," whined Shane. "You care about Linus' wellbeing."

"I want to be captain this time." Eli sat at the base of the stairs, lacing up his shoe. "You always let Reggie be captain, and he always picks me, and we always lose."

Mabel snorted. "Well, first off, Reggie is nine, Eli."

"Just because he's the youngest—"

"And second, maybe Reggie isn't the reason your team keeps losing," she finished, raising a knowing eyebrow.

Shane chortled.

"All right, all right, I'm ready. Let's get this over with."

Eli's words meant little. The others knew he was just as excited to spend a carefree day at the park as any of them. They were tired. They deserved it.

Did they? Why?

His mind went fuzzy again. It had been happening a lot lately, but never lasted long enough to cause concern. He'd be trying to focus, trying to dredge up a memory, and suddenly it would slip out of reach.

Eli was the first to reach the door, but just before he opened it there was a knock. Eli paused, his head tilting to one side as he glanced at Mabel. "Are we so late they'd have come to look for us?"

She shrugged. "I doubt it. Only one way to find out, though!"

She shoved him playfully out of the way and opened the door before Eli could put words to the sickening dread that had risen up in his gut. He expected the fuzzy contentedness to kick in at any moment, whisking away the bad feeling, but it didn't.

"Hello." The voice was hesitant, unfamiliar. "I'm sorry…I don't know how I got here. I was looking for…my friend."

Mabel gave the stranger a pitying look. "You poor thing. You look shaken. Here, come in and have a seat. Can I get you a drink? Don't worry, we'll help you find your friend. Do you live here in Gables?"

"Gables?" repeated the stranger, "no. I don't know what that is. I don't know how I got here."

"Mabel," Shane whispered, "the others are waiting for us."

"They'll be fine. He's disoriented. Give him a minute." She had taken the stranger by the elbow, leading him to the couch. He sat, appearing distraught as he took in his surroundings. Mabel gestured toward the picnic basket. "Hand me one of the sandwiches and take the rest on ahead, I'll be there soon."

"I'm not leaving you alone with a stranger."

"Eli will stay, won't you, Eli?"

Walking around the couch, Eli nodded as he took in the new arrival, wondering what about him had triggered such lasting fear. "Sure. Go on ahead, Shane."

The man's clothes were a bit odd, but that didn't mean much. The city of Gables was known for its obsession with cutting-edge, even ludicrous, fashion. He had a kind face, even now when it was full of confusion. Nothing about him seemed to warrant such a reaction from Eli. Nothing set off any warning bells. In fact, everything about him appeared perfectly mundane, down to the unthreatening tone of his voice when he spoke.

Except the eyes. Those were intriguing, even eerie.

One was a pale blue; the other, a shimmering violet.

A Note from the Author

Whisper of Echoes was the most difficult book to write yet. A lot of pieces are just starting to come together. But at long last Felix knows the truth. Ripley is out there. Will they be reunited, or will fate keep them just out of each other's reach?

A Soliloquy of Souls holds the answer. So I suggest you get your hands on it if you're eager to find out!

We are nearer to the end of the series than the beginning now. Only three books to go. How will it all end? No one knows for sure. (Just kidding. I totally know.)

If you enjoyed this book, I would greatly appreciate if you would take a few moments to leave a review. Indie authors depend on the honest reviews of readers like you to help spread awareness of their works! It would mean a lot to me.

I *love* hearing from my readers! Feel free to contact me directly at r.hurteau@outlook.com or connect with me on Twitter, Instagram or Facebook, where I'm @rfhurteau.

Sincerely,

R.F.

MORE BOOKS BY
R.F. HURTEAU

There's plenty more to discover in the Antiquity's Gate series!

Antiquity's Gate: Three Days Till Dawn

History would not remember Ripley Prior.

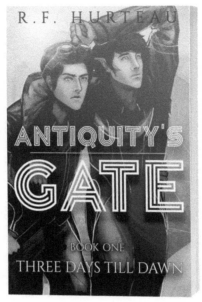

Antiquity's Gate forced two realities to collide—what followed tore one of them apart.

An Antarctic city of domes is the last safe haven for survivors, held together by a tenuous peace between the remnants of humanity and the Therans who rule over them.

A mid-level systems operator, Ripley does his best to stay out of trouble. His best friend Felix, an irreverent half-breed shunned by society, can't seem to do the same. When Felix's family is targeted by an unjust law, there's nowhere to run.

In a desperate bid to escape, Ripley and Felix uncover a conspiracy that will mean the end for the city. But tangling with fate has a heavy price.

The people of Sanctuary have never seen a sunrise.

If Ripley and Felix aren't prepared to make the ultimate sacrifice, none of them ever will.

Antiquity's Gate:
Through a Mirror, Darkly

Some seem doomed to repeat history…others are determined to.

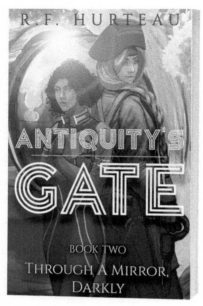

Chaos reigns in the vacuum left after the Therans' retreat. While Sylvia and Edwin work to pick up the pieces of a broken city, they find that Sanctuary is now the first line of defense in a war no one realized was still being fought. In dire need of supplies and allies, they seek out alliances while factions within the city itself threaten its fledgling freedom.

Meanwhile, Felix discovers that no matter where he goes, he can't outrun who he is. The Pravacordian government dangles his amnesty like a carrot on a stick. Under pressure, he agrees to a mission that will take him into unknown territory: the other side of Antiquity's Gate. If he succeeds, his family will be safe. If he fails, he'll never see them again.

The fate of two worlds lies in the hands of a desperate few. Some of them seem doomed to repeat history… others are determined to.

ANTIQUITY'S GATE:
STRANDS OF FATE

Even as the world is dying, there are those who would seek to live forever.

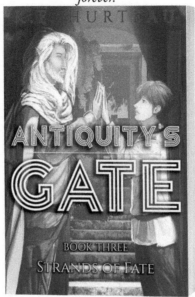

Corporate orphans—children whose parents are forced to abandon them just to make ends meet—have become commonplace. Twins Eli and Mabel Harper are two such kids, trapped beneath the heel of an establishment that seems content to burn the world's future in exchange for today's convenience.

In this world, compliance is key to survival. When Eli loses his temper protecting Mabel, he's prepared to shoulder the weight of the consequences alone—even if the cost is his death.

If only that was all they wanted from him...

Someone has put a price on the very things that make us human. Someone willing to pay it with the suffering of kids like Eli. Genetic engineering can only get so far without human subjects, after all.

The strands of fate are tightening, the tapestry which binds Earth and Thera slowly coming into focus. Neither time nor space can rend the bonds of destiny.

A destiny that is coming for Eli Harper.

Antiquity's Gate:
Memoirs of the Forgotten

Even the sky has boundaries.

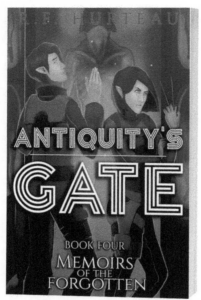

Teetering on the brink of destruction, Sanctuary finds hope in tech-savvy Ben Parker, a young rising star in Sigil's new order. They laud him as a hero for his newest project...one that may be the key to their salvation.

But the instability and danger of his experiment raises heavy questions. While Edwin and the rest of the Council are troubled by the moral implications of using such unpredictable power, those more willing to do whatever it takes demand he step aside.

Right and wrong no longer hold any meaning... friend and foe have become indistinguishable... And those meant to protect society are more concerned about protecting themselves. Whoever manages to rise to the top will wield not only the authority to decide the fate of the city, but of all life on Earth.

It is no longer a question of defending themselves. It has come down to one simple choice—who lives...

and who dies.

Antiquity's Gate:
A Soliloquy of Souls

Worlds collide as past and present join forces to safeguard the future.

Coming July 2020

Sign up at for updates at rfhurteau.com.

Lightning Source UK Ltd.
Milton Keynes UK
UKHW041845020720
365951UK00003B/110/J